Sex Dole

Steven C. Harvey

ISBN: 979 8 6743 4104 8

FOR VASSILIKI

PROLOGUE

London, 1998.

He was brought awake by the slow, sensual rocking of his own hips as the weak, milky light of the London dawn spread across the empty sheets around him. He lifted his vaguely attractive, shaggy head from the pillow, unable to recollect the dream, though left with the pelvic undulations of his physical reaction to it. His body had the better memory, it seemed. He smiled sourly to himself; he knew of course that it was his body that had prompted the dream, had sent it bubbling up like so much sugared froth to keep his brain sweet while the lower organs pursued their furtive, primeval business. Well, his brain wasn't sweet, it was fucked off. It was only 6.30. Fuck's sake, he'd only got five hours sleep again. He punched the pillow, turned it over and landed on it hard with his forehead, before attempting to doze off, pleading for another two-hour hit of unconsciousness. He lay a while, nurturing his exhaustion, emptying his mind in an effort to coax oblivion.

As his thoughts began to die away, his sinking consciousness became slowly engulfed in a vast, suffocating weight of perfumed blond hair. Holding back the flaxen waves with one hand, picking scented golden strands from his mouth with the other, he awoke again to the empty room.

Christ almighty! He rammed the duvet with a single virile thrust of his body. His fucking body: oblivious to its own fatigue, contemptuous of that of his knackered spirit. He flung himself onto his side, kicking a fold of duvet away from him. Throwing his arm over the pillow, he let his head fall heavily onto his shoulder, and listened in desolation to the distant joyful twittering of some early rising bird. He pictured it perched on a mobile phone mast somewhere. Getting cancer from the texts and calls of half a million desperate Londoners. What in the world did it have to be so happy about? He twisted his face in a hollow smile. Birds and bees. Perhaps it had just met a nice bee and later after wine and a select choice of nibbles it was going to take it back to its place and fuck its furry little black and yellow arse off. He stared at the pillow. This particular pillow-case: untouched by so much as a hair from a girl's head. How long had he had this fucking striped pillow-case? A year and a half? Two? Just don't think about it. Don't even think about it.

He brushed a thick lock of dark hair away from his eye to gain a better view of the crook of his elbow, the better to take refuge in a visual delusion with which he had been calming himself since the age of fifteen. It was a little strange, he knew, but from this angle he could always make a gentle, mellow labial fold from the vertical crease of skin between his forearm and his biceps, which in turn became thighs, a little uneven perhaps, though slim and almost shapely in their way. At least, his hips needed no further convincing. And this time, too tired to fight, he went with them.

ONE

Roger Williams winced as he carried his plastic cup of boiling, flavourless coffee back to his desk in the ground floor reception area of the Kentish Town Sex Benefit Centre. Taking his place at the furthest of the four signing-on desks ranged across one end of the large open-plan space, he sipped his coffee and made a face, screwing his thin lips and narrow eyes into a grimace of distaste. As if the rotten coffee weren't bad enough, the steam from the cup had misted over his spectacles. He let out a heavy sigh as he took them off, and ran a hand through his thinning sandy hair.

Across from him stretched the empty plastic seats of the waiting area. For a moment he fixed his blurred vision on this dull furniture, wondering what kind of social driftwood was going to wash up and beach itself there today. He put his glasses back on and focused beyond the seating to the dark stains running up the cream-painted walls from the heating units. It made him think of Briony and the whole weekend they had just wasted arguing over that bloody bathroom. He took a deep breath and let it out again slowly, before punching the on-switch of his desk-top monitor. He glanced over at the aisles of personal ad boards. Waste of time, those things: most of the claimants never bothered looking at them, and those that did never followed anything up. He picked up his coffee, then put it down again, and instead cast his eyes around the room, checking that everything was ready and in order for the day. Oh, for Christ's sake. None of the junior staff had bothered yet to open the large packet from the stationery office, which was still lying on the floor near the reception desk. He'd told them to do it Friday lunch-time and now here it was Monday morning, with the first claimants due in shortly.

'Morning, Roger,' called Peter Mills, one of the junior claimant advisors, as he entered from the street, making his way to the staff office.

'Peter, I thought I told you on Friday to get that packet open.'

Mills stared at Williams, amazed that he hadn't returned his greeting. 'Well, I'll do it this morning. What's the rush anyway? What is it?'

'I told you on Friday. The new SB 31s.'

'Which are they again?'

'The new Charter leaflets. I told you on Friday. Now I want them on the stands for when the claimants arrive, which is in about fifteen minutes' time so you'd better get on with it.'

'Oh come on Roger, I want a coffee. Look, they're just the same as the old ones. The legislation hasn't changed. It's a lick-of-paint job. Bung some agency a hundred grand to fiddle about a bit with the colour of the leaflet.'

'There are reasons for design overhauls, you know. Look, I'm not going to argue with you Peter, just get the stuff on the stands, will you?' said Williams with sudden exasperation.

Mills picked up the packet and stormed off to the staff office.

'Thanks, Peter,' Williams called after him belatedly, 'Won't take you a minute, then you can get a coffee.'

There was no reply from Mills as he pushed open the door.

'Though I don't know why you're in such a rush to drink this filthy stuff!' joked Williams weakly as the door swung back into place.

He turned back to his desk and began checking that his two pens were still working. Noticing the security guard, Geoff, taking his place at the public staircase leading to the first floor, he heard the office door swing open again and became aware of Harper taking his seat at the signing-on desk next to his own. Harper, middle-aged and of Jamaican descent, sat back and slowly moved from side to side in his swivel chair, quietly tapping his pen on his desk.

'So, Roger', he said, smiling broadly, 'You have a good weekend?'

'Not really. Look, Alex , I thought I told everybody on Friday I wanted that parcel of SB31s dealt with. It was still lying around here when I came in. Peter's doing it now.'

'Ah, yes ... I saw.'

'I don't want this place looking like a tip first thing on Monday morning!' exclaimed Williams throwing an arm in the air.

'Hey, Roger,' smiled Harper, flashing his eyes, 'It's a beautiful day.'

'No, it isn't,' laughed Williams mirthlessly, looking down at his desk, yet indicating the rain-washed, traffic-choked street just discernible through the streaming windows.

Harper tapped himself over the heart and laughed good-naturedly, saying, 'But we can *make* it beautiful *here*!'

In an effort to escape any further exchange with Harper, Williams bent down to the drawer to his left, making a pretence of looking for a document. He stared at the pile of claim forms in the drawer, but without seeing them. Saw instead Briony, pushing him out of the bathroom and slamming the door.

He rammed the drawer shut and looked up as Lucinda and Toby, two of the facilitators, entered from the street, chatting. Williams watched as Toby shook the rain from his coat, laughing at Lucinda's remark about whatever codswallop it was they'd both seen on television the night before. Williams contemplated Toby's somewhat rough yet regular features. He didn't envy him having to get it up for some of the more desperate middle-aged women that came in here, and he fought an involuntary mental image of Toby's smooth young skin rubbing against theirs. But on the other hand, there were the lookers, and the young ones too, even the occasional teenager. Williams pictured Toby's big hands gliding over all the smooth young female flesh that must have gone through his cubicle over the years.

'All right, Alex, Roger?' called Toby, as he made his way with Lucinda to the staff staircase leading to the cubicle facility on the first floor.

'Hi,' came Lucinda's greeting, with a brief smile for them both.

'Aaall right, people!' beamed Harper.

'Morning,' said Williams, happy to get a smile from Lucinda. He allowed himself a lingering observation of her dark Latin profile as she strutted past. And he kept watching as Lucinda's attractive behind jiggled its way up the stairs. She was not what you might call *stunningly* beautiful - as of course a sex benefit worker ought not to be - but he wouldn't kick her out of his bed. He glanced at her black tights and thought about the inadequates that would soon be sampling the delights within. He couldn't work out what annoyed him more: having to send really repulsive claimants to her, or having to send those reprobates who were clearly not doing enough to find their own encounters. Neither category deserved to despoil her body in his view. In fact, he decided now that she was a bit too attractive for this work. Sex benefit was only meant to be a basic handout, for Christ's sake. But that was Henshaw's department. The centre manager did all the hiring and firing of the facilitators.

He waited until Lucinda's trim ankles disappeared from view, before turning back to his desk. But as he turned, he found himself looking directly into Harper's face, from which all trace of the customary smile had vanished. Harper held him for a moment with bright fierce eyes, before swivelling slowly in his chair to watch as Mills emerged from the office.

Christ, Harper, thought Williams to himself as he stared at the back of the black man's head. Just watch it, boy. Nevertheless, he could feel his cheeks burning. In an unconscious compensatory action, he took a sip of coffee, and immediately decided to get rid of the whole cup. He got up from his desk and brushed past Mills who was now at one of the revolving information stands, adding the new leaflets to the sheaves of pamphlets offering advice on everything from meeting new people to appealing a sex benefit adjudication.

Williams entered the office, making for the tiny sink next to the coffee machine. He glanced at a plain-looking woman in her fifties reading a paper. 'Chop, chop, Sandra,' he said, pouring his coffee down the sink, and flinging his cup in the bin. Mildly irritated, Sandra tilted her grey-bobbed head to one side, folded up her paper and made her way outside, closely followed by Williams.

'Where's Moira?' he asked, as the door closed behind them.

'In the loo.'

Williams made a tutting sound and sighed, looking pointedly toward the reception desk.

Sandra stared at him for a moment before speaking. 'Surely the desk can look after itself for a few minutes. She won't be long.'

Williams made no answer, other than to emit a loud huffing sound, and stormed over to the desk. 'Jesus Christ' mumbled Sandra under her breath, and took her seat at the signing-on desk next to Harper.

'He's in a bloody funny mood today,' she said, letting the air out through her teeth.

'He's aalways bloody funny,' replied Harper in his Caribbean drawl.

Williams sat down heavily at the reception desk. The street door swung open, admitting the sound of the traffic and the rain. Looking up, he heard the flat 'Hi, everyone' of Pamela, one of the plainer facilitators.

'Morning, Pamela,' he grated.

He reminded himself of her dumpy figure, and felt a flush of satisfaction. If, as a claimant, you were going to come in here and burden the state by becoming a sex benefit statistic, if you wanted to be a sad case and come in here, then you should expect to receive sad flesh. And Pamela had that in abundance. Williams was so pleased with this formulation that he even gave Pamela a quick smile as she passed him. She smiled in return, a simple warm smile. He felt a pang of guilt at his inhuman reduction of the poor woman to a piece of unappetizing meat, and took off his glasses to rub the bridge of his nose.

A babble of voices came in from the street, first Elaine, then John and Veronica. They were followed by two others, sex workers from the regional pool of facilitators whom he didn't know so well. That made a full complement then, together with the early arrivals. Why the hell couldn't they all come in early? The first claimants would be here in a matter of minutes. If it were up to him, he'd give this lot here a bollocking, but the last time he'd done that he'd got into trouble with Henshaw for doing Hopley's job. As facilitator supervisor, it was her responsibility, but she was always stuck up in her office on the third floor, and never seemed to give two hoots what problems might be caused for the smooth running of the reception area by the tardiness of some of the sex workers. He watched them shake out their umbrellas and give a general greeting to the office, to which he made no response, allowing the dutiful salutations of the others to cover his silence. He watched them with irritation as they headed for the staff staircase. Nevertheless, he allowed his gaze to linger on Veronica. Not a great looker, that one, but he had always liked the cut of her body. As he watched the backs of her knees ascend the stairs, it occurred to him that Harper might be watching him again. For a second he almost didn't wish to know, and then he quickly glanced in the direction of the Jamaican. But Harper was engrossed with his monitor, pushing his mouse around the slate-grey surface of his desk.

He became aware of someone at his shoulder. Moira, the receptionist.

'Sorry, Roger.'

'About time.'

'Look, it's-'

'Just take the desk, will you?' said Williams brusquely, rising quickly and marching off to take his own post.

However, halfway to his desk, he changed his mind and went into the office for a cup of water. Christ, that coffee. He had to rinse the taste out of his mouth. Crossing to the sink, he filled a plastic cup and leaned over the basin, sipping and spitting into the swirling water, watching the brown strands of saliva distort and stretch themselves away down the plug-hole. He was reminded of loose lengths of Briony's auburn hair spinning down the shining plug-hole of their bath, back in the days when such sights had been a part of his life. That bath. Perfectly good bath. Good for another twenty years, thirty. But of course she had to have a new one because of one slight abrasion in the enamel from when he'd dropped the hammer in the ruddy thing while trying to improve the flow from the shower faucet. From that moment he had forfeited all rights in that bathroom, because she had told him beforehand not to mess with the shower, that she'd call Trevor in the morning. Good God, the look on her face when she'd shouted, 'Look what you've *done!*' And then she'd decided she wanted a whole new suite, not just the bath. He'd had no say in that, of course, having 'destroyed' the old suite. So he had relented. But now the whole thing had blown up again because he was standing his ground over the amount of tiling they could afford for the rear wall.

He realised that he was staring at the sink, holding the half-full plastic cup before his chest. He turned quickly, flinging the cup in the bin, and exited the office.

As he strode to his desk he saw that the first claimants had begun to drift in, one of whom was already on his way over to Harper. There were three individuals ranged over the plastic seating in the waiting area across from him. A fading woman in her forties, probably beautiful once; some sort of yob with a black ponytail; a red-faced middle-aged guy in a donkey jacket reading *The Daily Mirror*. Reading the paper when he should be looking at the personal contact boards! Williams sat down, and sighed. Here we go then. He leaned forward and pressed the button to cue on the ceiling-mounted LED counter which regulated the flow of the claimants through the numbered ticketing system. The donkey jacket glanced up at the counter then folded his paper, got up and headed toward him.

The man sat down heavily in the chair opposite Williams, his tired, pouchy eyes cast down as he pulled a crumpled document from his pocket and placed it softly on the table. Williams waited a moment to see if the guy was going to utter anything by way of a greeting. Apparently not. The characters that came in here!

'Good morning,' said Williams pointedly, taking the claimant's grubby SB40 between his thumb and index finger. He got up and crossed to the filing cabinet, carrying the claimant's signing-on document like a discarded piece of banana peel. He pulled open a grey metal drawer, glanced at the man's SB40 and began rifling through the ranks of manila envelopes for the claimant's file, before finally selecting a folder, ramming the drawer shut and marching back to his desk. The guy was sat hunched over, staring at the edge of the table through heavy-lidded eyes, absently tracing a finger back and forth across the deep lines rippling up his forehead.

Williams sat down and removed the claim sheet from the claimant's file. He glanced over at the man, who had still not acknowledged his presence other than to submit his SB40. Williams sighed, took his pen and wrote the date and time on the claim sheet before asking the question, the question his job required that he ask forty times a day. He delivered it in a monotone shaped and sculpted by years of empty repetition, directing it to some point on the grimy wall beyond the claimant's shoulder.

'Have you had a sexual encounter at any time in the last two weeks?'

The claimant lifted his head and looked at Williams directly for the first time, peering at him through eyes shot through with defeat, his perhaps once handsome face well on its way to dissipating completely in a mess of age and alcohol.

'Leave it out, mate,' he said softly, smiling faintly, half-closing his eyes.

Williams had been tempted to haul him over the coals and ask him what efforts he'd made to secure a liaison of his own, but he knew there'd be no point. The guy was obviously suffering enough, let's just leave it at that. He took the claim sheet and turned it around for the guy to sign, pushing the pen toward him. Williams watched him bend over to write, stared at the man's scalp, at the dying roots of his wire-wool hair. For a moment he imagined the guy thirty years ago, the fingers of some slip of a girl running across this same patch of skull. He dismissed the thought, and turned to his monitor as the claimant looked up and pushed the claim sheet back across the table.

The screen before Williams showed which cubicles were occupied by which facilitators according to the day's shift pattern and which were currently free. As it was first thing in the morning he could take his choice from the column of green lights running down the screen. He ran the cursor down the names listed next to their respective cubicle numbers: Elaine in 1, John in 2, Veronica in 3, Tina in 4, Lucinda in 5. Lucinda! There was no way he was sending this guy to Lucinda if he could help it. Kevin in 6. He didn't know him, must be one of the regional workers. But here was what he was looking for: dumpy little Pamela in 17. He clicked on her box, which immediately turned red, as it would on the other three monitors, indicating to the other three claimant advisors that Pamela was now occupied. It would stay red until Pamela finished with the guy and pressed her 'clear' button which was wired to the centre's internal net.

Williams returned his attention to the claimant, at the same time running off a timed and dated ticket from the dispenser to his right.

'Number 7', then, said Williams, handing the man the ticket.

With the ticket in one hand, and retrieving his SB40 with the other, the claimant stood up slowly, emitting a barely audible 'Thanks, mate,' before turning and heading for the stairs. Williams watched him cross slowly to the stairwell. My pleasure, chum. The guy showed his ticket to the security guard who nodded disinterestedly and waved him through the double doors giving on to the stairs.

Williams' eye was caught by a sudden change on his screen. Lucinda's box had turned red. He glanced over at the claimant rising from Harper's desk. Lad with a baseball cap on back to front. Strong enough looking lad. Probably just couldn't be bothered to look for it himself. And Harper had sent him up to Lucinda. Probably without asking him anything either, if he knew Harper. Had probably just smiled and sent him up to Lucinda just like that. Williams shook his head as he watched the lad cross the floor to the stairs. He stole a glance at Harper, scrutinised the side of his head for a second. You had to wonder about the guy's attitude sometimes.

He turned his attention to the waiting area. The fading woman and the yob with the ponytail had vacated their seats and were now being dealt with by Sandra and Mills. However, two more claimants had arrived, and a third was just entering, bringing with them the sound of a council refuse vehicle effecting a clunking gear change in the rain, which was cut short as the door swung back into place. The newcomer, a woman in her thirties, professional by the look of her, closed up her umbrella and took her place with the others on the plastic seating, crossing her legs and pulling her skirt over her knees. Good-looking woman. He could never quite get the hang of the fact that these lookers felt the need to come in here. Still, you got them occasionally, more so in recent years. He regarded the others for a moment: an old duffer in a fraying brown suit, and a bland-looking girl in black leggings and trainers, probably from one of the estates.

He hit the button to cue on the LED display, then picked up the previous claimant's folder and rose to return it to the filing cabinet. Gaining the cabinet, he pulled open the drawer, dropped in the file, rammed the drawer shut and walked briskly back to his desk as the plain girl in the leggings approached from the other side.

As they sat down together, he took in her heavy chin and her botched pony-tail, noting the untidy dark hanks of hair falling over her temple and sticking out over her left ear. She glanced into his eyes, smiled quickly, fearfully almost, and uttered a nervous 'Hello.'

Williams simulated a faint smile in response, adding a hollow 'Good morning,' which he addressed to his monitor.

'Oh,' exclaimed the girl, frowning and bowing her head to unzip her damp fleece jacket. She reached inside and pulled out her SB40, holding it out to him, the trace of an embarrassed smile at the corner of her mouth. Williams made no effort to take it from her, merely sat with his arms folded on the table, noting her forlorn expression.

'I noticed you didn't bother to take much interest in the boards.'

'Eh?' She lowered the signing-on document to the table.

'The personal contact boards. You didn't have much of a look at them, did you?'

'Well, I was in last week, yeah? To look at them, yeah? Didn't fink you would've changed 'em yet?'

'When did you come in?'

'Eh?' There was a look of genuine consternation on her face.

Williams looked off to his left, sighed heavily and looked back at her.

'When did you come in to look at the boards? The personal contact boards!' he said, looking at the table, then back up into her eyes. There was fear in them.

'... Fursday ...' she said quietly.

Williams could almost smell her confusion and alarm. He held her look for a moment before covering her SB40 with his palm and drawing it slowly across the desk toward him. He rose from the table and watched her face flood with relief as he turned and headed to the filing cabinet. Never does any harm to keep them on their toes. Never does any harm.

He opened the drawer, drew out the claimant's file, shoved the drawer shut and strode back to the desk, passing Mills, who was on his way to the filing cabinet. Williams attempted to catch his eye, feeling the need for reconciliation with the junior claimant advisor after the slight contretemps over the leaflets earlier. However, Mills quite deliberately averted his eyes as they passed each other. Williams felt the slight keenly. Funny chap, that. Bears you a grudge the rest of your life just because you tell him to do his job. Well, sod him. Sod him, then.

As he took his seat once more, he noticed the centre was beginning to fill up: Moira had a queue at reception; there was a regular assortment of claimants grouped together on the drab seating of the waiting area; there was even a guy wandering up and down the aisles of contact boards, Chinese by the look of him, or some such.

He removed the claim sheet from the folder, took up his ballpoint and wrote the time and date in the relevant columns, before looking up at the girl and once more rolling out the question, dressing it as ever in the same time-blasted monotone.

'Have you had a sexual encounter at any time in the last two weeks?'

She shook her head, an earnest expression on her young dull face.

'Nah, I ain't. Nah.'

He turned the claim sheet for the girl to sign her name, and watched as she took the pen, leaned forward and began to fill the box with

Meanwhile, the small bearded man had sat down before him and was now proffering his SB40. For a second, Williams stared at the guy's beard, imagined it pressing into Lucinda's flesh as perhaps it already had several times in the past. Williams took the document from him, muttering a terse salutation in response to the overly cheerful 'Hello' of the claimant. For a moment he considered giving the guy a bit of a grilling about what strategies for sex-procurement he was employing out in the real world, but he just felt too tired, and his head was still killing him from the blow from the drawer. Instead, he merely got up, walked to the filing cabinet, found the corresponding file, returned to the desk, picked up his pen, wrote out the date and time on the claim sheet, asked the question, and without even waiting for the answer, swivelled the paper round for the claimant to make his mark, before snapping the pen down beside it.

TWO

Lucinda Delgado stepped into her plain white briefs, pulling them quickly up her smooth, olive skin thighs, before reaching for her robe. Drawing the soft flannel around her shoulders, she observed the claimant through well-defined Latin eyes, the dark beauty of which was somewhat undermined by the disharmonious arrangement of her prominent nose and overlarge lips with their permanent, faint sneer. She watched the guy pull on his sock. He was probably a builder or a bin man or something like that. He didn't seem too clever, but he had a young, well-toned body, the kind that could actually make a Monday morning trot along quite pleasantly. Still, he was taking his time getting dressed, and she was due a break. She shifted her weight to her other foot, folded her arms, and cocked her head, eyeing the guy critically. He caught her look.

'Sorry, darlin', I won't be a minute,' he said, pulling on a boot.

But she had decided she wasn't going to wait any longer. 'Look, I'm going for my break now. Just make sure you leave the room the way you found it, please,' she said, tossing her voluminous, shiny black hair over her shoulder and making for the door.

'OK, yeah, but look ... thanks, yeah?'

She turned and met his earnest, honest look. She gave him a half-smile and shrugged her shoulders slightly. 'Don't thank *me.* All in the line of duty', she said, peering at the ceiling.

He nodded, but uncomprehendingly, the fervour fading from his eyes. As she turned again to the door, he brightened suddenly and called out to her.

'Well, bye, yeah?'

She stopped, faintly irritated, and shot him a look over her shoulder.

'Yes. Goodbye,' she said firmly, looking at the floor for emphasis, before whirling her head round in a sudden gale of thick black hair and disappearing from the cubicle.

She emerged into a long corridor, lit by harsh overhead strips, the furthest of which was affected by a slight flicker. Along one side ran rows of cubicles, while the other was largely blank, punctuated here and there by doors to the public toilets, first-floor security, a linen room. It always amused her that the centre manager, Henshaw, had attempted to alleviate the cream-painted functionality of the long blank wall by hanging two mis-matched art prints at two random, vastly separated, points along its length: a Modigliani nude, and a photograph of a rippling male torso by Robert Mapplethorpe. At the far end of the corridor was a single potted palm, while halfway down stood the cigarette bin with its tarnished chrome rim, redundant now since the building-wide ban on smoking, though still present due to some perpetual oversight on the part of the management.

She strode briskly past the row of cubicles running down the corridor, going over the day's jobs so far. It hadn't been a bad morning: the young guy in the baseball cap, reasonable enough; the older guy, okay; the fat slob - well, she could have done without that, if she was honest, though yes, okay it was a crucial part of the job, providing sex-support for the total no-hopers blah blah; and then there was this last guy, with his nice wiry body - a bit dim, but what did she care about that?

Coming to the end of the corridor, she pushed open the double doors giving on to a small vestibule from which she could take either the staff staircase or another set of double doors leading to the facilitators' suite. She took the doors to the suite, the complex of rooms running behind the long blank wall of the corridor. Entering the relaxation area, she walked over to the kitchenette, passing Toby and Pamela who were sat on a sofa each, drinking coffee, dressed in flannel robes. Toby was busy expounding the merits of the film he had seen the night before to an unconvinced-looking Pamela. He looked up as Lucinda passed.

'All right, Lucinda?'

'Yeah, you?'

'Yeah, ta. The kettle's hot, by the way.'

'Hi,' said Pamela flatly, her plain face somewhat disconsolate.

'Hi, Pamela,' replied Lucinda, disappearing into the kitchenette.

Toby resumed his thread. 'Come on, Pamela, how can you say it was crap if you switched it off halfway through? It's like - you missed the whole point of the film!'

Pamela sighed, 'I just didn't think it made much sense, everybody just turning into vampires half-way through.'

'But that was the whole point of the film! And anyway, it wasn't *everybody* turned into a vampire, only all those biker freaks in the bar. All right, Tarantino *did* turn into a vampire but only cos he got bitten by one.'

'I don't know, it just looked like two different films joined together,' sighed Pamela, wearying of the debate.

'*Genres*. Two different genres joined together,' corrected Lucinda, emerging from the kitchenette with her coffee, 'and that *was* the whole point of the film, Pamela.'

'*Thank* you, Lucinda,' smiled Toby with satisfaction.

'All right, all right. Look, I don't really care. I just thought it was crap, that's all,' said Pamela, letting her hand fall on her big round knee, and taking a sip of coffee.

'I tell you what *was* crap last night,' said Lucinda, looking at Pamela and taking a place next to her on the sofa. 'That bloody dinosaur crap.'

'Yes, you're right,' replied Pamela, contemplating her coffee, 'That was shit too.'

'What's shit?' asked the rangy figure of Derek, entering the room and making for the kitchenette.

'Oh, just something on the telly, last night,' replied Lucinda for Pamela non-committally, not wanting to get into a critical debate with Derek, whom she took to be a boor.

'Oh, right,' said Derek disinterestedly, loping into the kitchenette, running his hand back over his number one haircut.

Toby attempted to restart his preferred topic. 'I mean, granted, it's not the best film ever made ....' he said, looking over at the two women. However, they were not to be tempted. Pamela returned his look, but said nothing, and took another sip of her coffee, while

Lucinda appeared to have withdrawn into a moment of private contemplation. Toby gave up and reached for the copy of *Time Out* lying on the small coffee table. He leafed through it for a moment, then stopped, his attention caught by something. He glanced across at Lucinda as she took a sip from her mug. 'Hey, Lucinda, you're into salsa, aren't you?'

'Well, I'm looking for a good venue, yeah. Why?'

'You should have a look at this. A whole feature on salsa in London. The best places and that.' He threw the magazine across to her, its pages fanning out before the slightly alarmed face of Pamela. Lucinda snatched it from the air, flashing a powerful dental smile.

'Cheers, babes,' she said, becoming immediately engrossed in the article.

Derek emerged from the kitchenette with his coffee and dropped his young, sinewy body into Toby's sofa, planting his feet wide apart, his pinched hooligan's face moving rapidly from side to side as he tried to gauge the mood of the room.

'All right, Derek?' asked Toby.

'Yeah, cool, cheers,' replied Derek, nodding his head vigorously. 'See the footie last night? Criminal, criminal,' he said, now shaking his head.

Toby took a sip of coffee, and laughed. 'How many times have I told you, man? I bloody hate football.'

'Oh, yeah, right.'

Pamela leaned forward. 'I saw it, Derek. Well, the highlights, anyway, and you're right. It was.'

'It was, wasn't it? Bloody criminal.'

Pamela laughed to herself. 'Yes. It was.'

To Toby's relief, this exchange was broken by the arrival of Elaine, who came skipping into the room, laughing and shaking her head.

'Guys, I've got to tell you this!' she announced, standing before them, her long, thin blond hair flying around her face as she went on shaking her head, giggling loudly.

Lucinda put down the magazine and regarded her eagerly. However, Elaine's laughter showed no immediate signs of abating.

'Tell us what, for Christ's sake?' chuckled Toby.

Elaine finally looked up at them, revealing her somewhat baggy hazel eyes and slightly protruding teeth, before taking a deep breath to fully rein in her giggles.

'My last guy ...' she managed, before breaking down again.

'Come on, Elaine,' coaxed Lucinda.

Elaine pulled herself together. 'Ok, my last guy came in, right? No, I actually said this to him, right? This guy comes in, gets his kit off, yeah?' She erupted in laughter again.

'Said what?' asked Pamela.

Elaine collected herself. 'Sorry,' she said, fighting for breath. 'Ok, the guy gets it out, I take one look, yeah, and go - I don't know what made me say it - I go, "do I *look* like a female elephant?...the zoo's down the road darling!"' She burst into another paroxysm of laughter, as Toby and Derek threw in their own guffaws, delighted with the story.

'God, Elaine, must you?' said Lucinda with disgust. 'I'm trying to drink my coffee, for God's sake!'

'Whaaaat?' said Elaine, drawing out the syllable in a tone of falsely accused innocence. 'The boys thought it was funny.'

'They *would.*'

'You actually said that to him, yeah?' asked Derek, as Elaine padded off to the kitchenette.

'Yeah!' she giggled back over her shoulder.

'Wicked!' laughed Derek, looking at Toby who was shaking his head in admiration.

Pamela was looking as forlorn as ever. 'You might get into trouble if you talk to them like that.'

Elaine's voice sounded from the kitchen, suddenly annoyed. 'Come on, Pamela, the guy didn't give a shit.'

'The zoo's down the road !' repeated Derek, looking at his knees and shaking his head. 'Fuckin' brilliant!'

Lucinda eyed Derek for a second before returning to her magazine.

Toby was about to speak, when the door swung open to admit a tall woman in a sweater and black slacks carrying a manila folder.

'Hi, everyone! Everything okay?' cooed Jenny Hopley, the sex facilitator supervisor.

She was greeted by a general positive murmur from the company.

'Good, now I've got your monitoring forms here, which I want you all to fill in as usual, so we can see you're all coping okay. If there's anything not covered in there, anything that's concerning you at all, don't hesitate to come and see me in my office. That's what I'm there for.'

She leaned over the coffee table, distributing the forms around the sofas, Lucinda taking hers without looking up from her magazine. Derek was disgruntled. 'Oh, do we have to?' he wailed, reluctantly taking the form.

'Yes, you do Derek. Come on, it's for your benefit.'

'But it's daft! The questions are daft. And they're always the same ones.'

Pamela leaned forward. 'They're not daft, they're actually quite pertinent.'

'No, they're daft,' laughed Derek, shaking his head, 'I mean, look at this one, yeah? "Have you experienced any unwanted... emotional side-effects?" I mean - what? It's just a shag, yeah? It's just a *shag!*' He hit the form with the back of his hand, laughing and shaking his head in disbelief.

Lucinda shot him a look of contempt. 'God, are you really such an animal?'

'Well, I dunno ... I shag like one so maybe I am.'

Toby chuckled.

'God!' said Lucinda with feeling, shaking her head once and looking down at her magazine.

Jenny the supervisor had been looking on anxiously, and now spoke up. 'Just answer "no" if you don't feel it's relevant to you, Derek, but please fill it in for me.'

'Derek's got a point, though,' said Toby. 'Some of these questions go on as if it's trench warfare we're involved in here.'

'It can be sometimes,' laughed Pamela humourlessly.

'You tell him,' said Elaine, emerging from the kitchenette.

'Come off it,' countered Toby, 'Look, we only work a few hours a day. We get half the week off ... I don't know, you may think it weird, but I actually enjoy my work.'

Derek laughed and said, indicating the women, 'They don't even *do* any work! They just lie on their backs, yeah? We're the ones who have to put some effort in, yeah?'

'Do you *mind*?' snarled Lucinda, leading the chorus of protest from Pamela and Elaine.

Jenny took charge. 'I'd thank you not to be so crude, please Derek.' She turned to Pamela, '*Are* you having problems, love?'

'No ... nothing I haven't learned to manage. All I'm saying is the job's not always easy ...' She smiled for a moment. 'But then what job is? I mean it's okay most of the time.'

'Well, if anything comes up that you can't handle or you're having difficulty with, then make sure you come and see me, okay?'

Toby smiled at this unintended double entendre.

Pamela nodded, 'Thanks, Jenny, but it's okay. Really.'

Derek had meanwhile begun a furtive conversation with Elaine, who was now sat beside him on the sofa. 'So, Elaine, this elephant geezer. Really big, yeah?'

'Absolutely ridiculous, Derek, yeah. I mean really *way* too big! And let's be honest, yeah, the guy was no oil painting either... which also made for difficulties, shall we say!'

'What did you do?'

She shrugged her shoulders and smiled, 'Oh, I just let him play around with me for a bit, yeah? And then -'

Jenny had now finished her exchange with Pamela and broke in on Elaine. 'You're not really meant to be discussing the claimants, you know. Breach of confidentiality. Not very professional,' she said with a pained expression; she never liked to wield the rod with her charges.

Elaine threw herself back in the sofa and folded her arms. Lucinda stared at Jenny's back but said nothing.

Jenny turned to address them generally. 'Okay, now, if you can get these forms returned to me by the end of the week, that'd be great. Oh, Elaine, sorry, I haven't given you one yet, have I? There you go.' She handed Elaine a form. 'If you see any of the others you can tell them I'll see them in their break tomorrow. Have to dash now. Meeting in Graham's office. Oh, yes, I almost forgot. The shift rota for next week. I'll bring it down tomorrow. I wanted to give it to you today, but the regional agency hasn't been able to find me anybody for the end of the week. Anyway, I'll sort them out this afternoon and get it to you tomorrow.' She gave them a parting smile, turned and headed for the door.

When she had gone from the room, Lucinda stared after her. 'She must be mad if she imagines we don't talk about that lot,' she said, indicating the doors leading off to the cubicles.

'But we shouldn't, you know,' ventured Pamela.

'I don't see why not!' said Elaine, rising from the sofa, throwing an arm in the air and crossing the floor to flop down next to Lucinda. 'I mean, they should all be grateful, yeah? Why should we do them any favours? Why should we, Lucinda?'

'They should all get down on their bended knees and thank us for doing this job,' replied Lucinda.

'Some of them do,' laughed Pamela without humour. 'I've seen them.'

'All right,' said Lucinda, 'some of them do show a bit of appreciation - I had a guy this morning - but still, it's only natural that we'll talk about them -'

'As a means of release for one thing,' broke in Toby.

'Absolutely. Look, to ask us not to ... not to vent our ... never to talk about what goes on with that lot in those cubicles - *unless* we make a special appointment with Jenny - that's a pretty big demand, yeah? They should all be grateful for what they get, I'd say. They're not in any position to make any demands!'

'But it's not them. It's not them making the demands,' countered Pamela. 'It's the regulations. The Charter.'

'Yeah, no, you're right, okay, it's the dear old *Shag-Seeker's* Charter that's got the balance wrong. Anyway ... fuck the Charter and fuck the regulations. Eh, Toby?'

'Yeah, fuck 'em', laughed Toby.

'But Lucinda, the Charter is there to protect *us* too. Without it, we might as well be working the streets, and I've *done* that. It's - '

Elaine leaned round Lucinda to frown at Pamela, saying, 'Oh, lighten up, will you, Pamela, for God's sake! We're just having a little knock at the system, yeah? Just a little knock!'

Pamela looked down at her lap, saying quietly, 'And Lucinda, I wish you'd stop using that name when you talk about the Charter.'

'Oh, for crying out loud, Pamela! Why?'

'For dignity's sake, that's why!'

A peal of low laughter emanated from Derek, and he slapped his thigh, shaking his close-shaven head. 'I don't know what you're all on about. I really don't, yeah? I really don't!' He was looking over at the three women, shaking his head, his eyes wide with incredulity.

Lucinda regarded him with a dead expression.

Derek continued. 'I don't understand you, yeah? Best job in the world, this. Best job in the *world*! Bar *none*!' he said, screwing up his eyes, and leaning back in the sofa. He stared at the ceiling for a moment, then began giggling, bringing himself upright again. 'I mean, look!' He glanced down at his lap. 'I mean, I'm ready to go again already, and I don't even know what I'm gettin' yet!' A slightly throbbing hill had formed in the flannel contour of his robed lap.

'Jesus Christ, that is disgusting,' said Lucinda evenly, instantly averting her head.

'For fuck's sake, Derek, this is our *break,* you bastard!' yelled Elaine, throwing a cushion at him.

Toby, for his part, on seeing the cause of the girls' outrage, shoved his colleague sideways with such force as to jolt him bodily off the end of the settee, saying, 'Yeah, leave it out, man! Show a bit of respect to the ladies, yeah?'

'All right, all right, I'm sorry, yeah?' said Derek, regaining his place on the sofa.

'That's sexual harassment, that is,' hissed Lucinda.

'Oh, bollocks is it!' said Derek, screwing up his eyes and throwing his head back.

'A tribunal might construe it as such,' cautioned Pamela, smiling.

'Get real, yeah? Look -'

'Just drop it, Derek, yeah? You were well out of order there, mate,' admonished Toby.

Derek was about to respond but was silenced by a look from his colleague. He fell back into the sofa and stared at the coffee table, an ironic expression on his face, the contour of his lap once more innocuosly flat.

Lucinda glared at him for several seconds before looking down at her magazine, while Elaine eyed him over the rim of her cup as she sipped her coffee.

'Morning, everyone,' called Ricky, entering the room and making for the kitchenette. The group acknowledged his arrival with a brief hubbub of salutation.

'They keeping you busy, Ricky?' asked Elaine.

'Well, not really, actually, since you ask,' replied Ricky from the kitchenette. 'In fact, it's getting a bit bloody boring, to be honest with you.'

'Not picking up then?' enquired Lucinda, peering up from her magazine to catch sight of Ricky's arm through the doorway taking a carton of orange juice from the refrigerator.

'No, Lucinda, no. I mean, I had a grand total of two guys in on Friday and so far nothing at all today. Not a sausage.'

Derek laughed. 'So everyone's well satisfied in gay-land, yeah,

Ricky?'

'Well, either that, Derek,' said Ricky, emerging from the kitchenette, a glass of juice in his hand, 'or someone has spread a nasty - and entirely *unsupportable* - calumny around town that I'm something of a lame fuck. I incline to the former view, personally.'

Lucinda's voice rose above the good-natured laughter of the others. 'Poor Ricky!'

'I don't know, Ricky,' said Pamela, 'I'd be glad if I were you. To have a bit of a let-up.'

'You're joking, aren't you, Pamela? I'm beginning to get a bit lonely sitting in that cubicle by myself for hours at a time with nothing to do but read the bloody paper. I could do with a bit of company! It's ironic, but I feel like *I'm* the sad bastard who isn't getting any! I mean, I've volunteered my noble, charitable cock for a tour of duty and - no takers! It's all very *undermining,* you know! Quite apart from which there is the sense of lack of fulfilment in one's work! The unfulfilled potential. So no, Pamela, I'm not glad of the let-up, and quite frankly if I don't get at least one bout of good hard rogering done today, I think I'm going to go out of my mind with boredom.'

Elaine and Lucinda were now doubled up in laughter.

'They might make you redundant, man,' laughed Toby.

'You know, at this rate, it's not impossible, Toby,' said Ricky plaintively.

Elaine brought her hysterics sufficiently under control to ask, 'How's June doing?'

'Oh, June's all right,' replied Ricky, waving his hand dismissively. 'There's been a veritable pilgrimage of the sisters to her cubicle all morning. Queues of sad-eyed, elfin prick-haters lining the corridors ... heaps of matronly dick-avoiders camped out for a mile down Kentish Town Road....'

Derek slapped his thigh, shaking with laughter.

'You're terrible, Ricky,' said Pamela.

'I know, but seriously, there has been a steady flow, so to speak,' said Ricky, and then, suddenly serious, 'There's no shortage of desperation in *lesbian*-land.'

Lucinda was struck by an idea. 'So do you think maybe gay men have the least fucked-up sexual marketplace, then - you know, like, for some reason intrinsic to gay men their scene actually functions ?'

Ricky was despondent. 'No, Lucinda. Maybe there's more action – and then only here in London – but ... it's as screwed up as any other. Believe me,' he said, looking at the carpet, before taking a sip of his orange juice.

There was a general silence for a moment, before Toby half-grimaced, half-smiled and rose from his place on the sofa, saying, 'Well, I'd better be getting back. You coming, Pamela?'

'I suppose so,' said Pamela quietly. She wrapped her robe closer around her podgy legs and got to her feet as Toby returned his empty mug to the kitchenette. Pamela picked up her mug and wearily followed him through. There came the sound of two quick bursts from a high-pressure tap as the mugs were given a perfunctory rinse. Lucinda turned a page of her magazine as Toby and Pamela emerged from the kitchenette and headed for the double doors, Pamela lagging behind.

'See you later,' called Toby, leaning into the swing doors, as Pamela smiled wanly over her shoulders at the others, riding the slipstream of Toby's farewell. The group murmured an appropriate response, Lucinda flashing Toby another dental smile. 'See you later, babes!'

Returning to the salsa article, Lucinda was aware of a breath on her cheek; Elaine had begun reading over her shoulder.

'So anyway, Ricky,' began Derek on the other sofa, chuckling in a sufficiently coarse manner to raise a look from Lucinda, 'Elaine was tellin' us, yeah, about this geezer she had this mornin', with this huge cock, yeah?'

Lucinda raised her head in annoyance, and let her hand fall heavily onto the magazine.

'I see...' said Ricky, somewhat bemused, waiting for the point.

'Wasn't you, Elaine?' said Derek.

'What? Oh, yeah,' said Elaine glancing up, but now too engrossed in the salsa article to bother repeating the story. Derek stared at her for a moment before suddenly turning back to Ricky. 'Well, anyway, yeah, the geezer was way too big, yeah, and she couldn't handle it, yeah?' Derek broke off and resumed chuckling.

'Christ,' breathed Lucinda through clenched teeth, staring at the ceiling.

'Right....' said Ricky slowly, urging Derek on with his eyes.

'Well, I was wonderin', yeah, if you've ever had the same thing, yeah? Like how you'd handle that, yeah?'

'Ah, I see, Derek, yes. Well, I'm afraid I would have to class that as something of a trade secret.'

'Trade secret ... right ... or .... a *tradesman's* secret! Ha, ha, you know, like in tradesman's entrance! Do you get it? Tradesman's secret!' He burst into laughter.

Lucinda threw the magazine to the floor and jumped furiously to her feet. 'I've just about fucking had enough of you today, you crude arsehole!' She pinned Derek to the sofa with her ferocious dark glare, fixing him with a certain primal something raging behind her eyes. He saw it, and was cowed. He looked away, swallowing hard. She stood over him a few seconds more before slowly turning, snatching the copy of *Time Out* up from the floor, and strutting across the room to the swing doors, knocking them out of her path with a single blow from the flat of her palm.

'For fuck's sake!' spat Derek after her when she was gone from the room. Elaine shrugged and fell back into her sofa, while Ricky stared ahead and took another sip of orange juice.

By the time Lucinda regained the familiar, strangely almost comforting, white walls of her small sound-proofed cubicle, she had begun to calm down. At least the claimants mostly kept their mouths shut. Closing the door softly behind her, she briefly surveyed the room, her world for the next two hours: the small single bed, with its sheet that was never drawn back - changed by the linen woman every couple of hours, but never drawn back; the small bedside cabinet with its two drawers containing a few changes of underwear, a bottle of aspirin, a jar of lubricant, a large packet of tissues and box upon box of low-sensitivity condoms; a chair, used only as a place to put the claimant's clothes and her robe. The only other object in the room was a small pedal bin, the final resting place for the condoms from the drawer, or rather, a holding zone before their journey from the industrial bins at the back of the building to the council incineration unit. She smirked darkly at the thought of all that unwanted human seed going up the chimneys. The pedal bin, along with everything else in the room, was white, but not quite brilliant white, as if the entire room were somehow slightly underlit. There was in fact a dimmer switch for the light, but she preferred to keep it up at all times, there being a clinical quality to the room which she saw no reason to interfere with. Alongside the dimmer control was a small panel fitted with an alarm button running to the security guard's station along the corridor, and another control, which she pressed now, to notify the ground floor staff that she was ready to receive the next claimant.

She tossed the copy of *Time Out* onto the chair, took a tissue from the drawer and blew her nose silently, dropping the tissue in the pedal bin, before sitting down on the edge of the bed. She picked up the magazine and read for a moment. Then, deciding to make herself more comfortable, she swung her legs up onto the clean white sheet and lay full length on her side. Dressed still in her robe and underwear, she began turning the pages of the magazine with her free hand, supporting her head with the other, the thick black waves of her hair coursing through her fingers down to the sheet. Her dark brow was hard with concentration as she carefully scanned the TV schedules for the coming week. While she read, she took her free hand from the page and absently ran her fingers up and down her calf, only half-consciously enjoying the self-bestowed caress. Reaching the end of the next day's TV schedule, she quickly brought her hand up to turn the page and left it there.

She was just ploughing through a dispiriting column of daytime chat and life-style shows, when she heard the familiar muffled knock from the other side of the door. 'Yeah, come in,' she responded loudly enough to be heard through the sound-proofing of the cubicle, but without looking up from her magazine. She went on reading, aware, on the periphery of her vision, just beyond the foot of the bed, of a figure entering the room. She heard the kicking off of a pair of shoes, followed by the unfastening of a jacket. Then came the metallic jangle of loose change and keys as a pair of trousers made their way to the floor. Reading all the while, her attention absorbed by a synopsis of some mid-week drama, she slowly opened her robe with her free hand, hooked a thumb under the waistband of her white briefs and began pulling them slowly down her legs, the apparent languor actually an effect of her mind being entirely elsewhere.

THREE

It was all he could do to lean forward through the grey-green, lukewarm water and reach for the hot tap. As the steaming jet once more churned the water around Lawrence's feet, he sat hunched over in the bath, the dark locks of his unruly hair hanging in front of his face. Only when the water had attained a scalding heat did he spin the faucet shut, and lie back, carefully positioning his passably good-looking head on the striped pillow balanced precariously on the rim of the bath. He peered down at his foreshortened water-distorted body, at the flecks of soap-born scum drifting across its lithe, tense form. In the past he had despised his slight frame, but had since recognised a kind of classical elegance in it from certain angles. He knew there was something to admire there, but also that the admiring was up to him: no one else was fucking interested.

There was an island of diminishing foam hovering over his crotch. It drifted slowly on, revealing his dick, which the handful of girls in his past had found not without charm. However, as he stared at it, there was no tender look of self-love in his eyes, and as a source of academic aesthetic interest it was entirely without value to him. Let a *girl* find her way to it; let *her* look at it. He closed his eyes and smiled sardonically to himself. Let her *deal* with it. He was tired of having to provide for it. Sick of it, even.

He adjusted his head on the pillow, and went on wallowing in the steaming water, thinking back to his small collection of ex-girlfriends. He pictured them all gathered together, queuing up to present this strictly average dick of his with little nick-nacks, small tokens of their appreciation they'd picked up in flea-markets. He imagined his uncouth knob poring dumbly over the Celtic pendants and small leather-bound volumes of poetry and so on, while the small circle of good, trusted, transient females looked on happily. He focused on the face of Laura, who had been the last girl to see his cock alive before it had disappeared from the sight of womankind into the vast stretches of sexual wasteland through which it and he currently wandered.

This bout of half-amused fatalism gave way to the realisation that he had begun absently stroking his arm. Whenever he had a bath, he would always begin stroking his right arm at some point. Quite when that point was he never knew; he only became conscious of it after the gentle caressing of his slender biceps was well underway. For a moment, he balked at the effeminacy of the action and thought of withdrawing his gentle left hand, but decided to go on, luxuriating in its tenderness, because fuck it, who else was going to stroke his arm if he didn't? And besides, he knew the pleasant stimulus was thrilling his nervous system and firing off a healthy seratonin detonation in his brain. His convalescing brain. He mused on the capacity for pleasure stored in this one group of nerve-endings on the upper surface of his arm, thought of the billions of such nerve-endings all over his body, and of how they went untouched day after day, year after year, and not only by him, but of course by all the girls in the world. He thought of the tenderness in his fingers, and of how that in turn went untasted every single day by every single girl on earth. And yet there was probably some young woman somewhere at that very moment putting up with a cold, mechanical shag from some selfish slob, some young lady who would appreciate perhaps a brief interlude with this exquisite feathering touch of his hand.

He smirked to himself, but without amusement. He felt suddenly crushed by the sense of life wasted, but then immediately resented it. Did the mere fact that his body was not currently being caressed, kissed, pampered and fucked - demonstrably absurd actions in any case - invalidate his whole existence, in particular all that *work,* the mainspring of his *life?* In an access of anger, he launched himself forward through the water and ripped the plug out of the plug-hole. Bollocks to it! He could hack it! He was man enough to take the

even complimented him once on his charm and his intelligence, but maddeningly never had time to meet him; proposed rendezvous would be postponed time after time until they were forgotten, to be replaced a month later by a new proposal which would also fall by the wayside. He would give up on the idea of meeting her altogether and then out of the blue she'd say something about going for a coffee, thus resurrecting the agony of hope, and so it would go on. However, she would in the meantime be very much in touch on her mobile, and the passing weeks would be littered with endless circular phone conversations about God.

He drew his knees up to his chest and dialled the number. He sucked on his Marlboro life-support and listened to the ringing tone, imagining some overused classical tune being digitally massacred at the other end, an irritating cavalcade of notes emanating perhaps from a chic Gucci bag sliding back and forth across Martina's smooth round hip as she sashayed down the King's Road. From experience he knew she was either going to answer after the next tone or not at all. Miniature sound effects of a London street broke over his ear as she took the call.

'Hello?'

'Hi, Martina, it's Lawrence.'

'Oh, *hi!* How are you?'

'Bloody awful. All my sugar was stolen in the night. No sugar on my cereal this morning.'

She was laughing.

'Who stole it?'

'Some sad old men from the flats near where I live.' Lawrence winced. Maybe this was a bit too surreal for her.

'Some *what*?'

'Never mind. Anyway, how are you?'

'I'm as well bloody awful. I have work, so much work you would not believe! Two essays for the end of this week.'

'But your sugar's safe though...?' Lawrence felt a brief thrill of delight at the peal of laughter coming down the phone.

'Yes, my sugar's safe!'

There was a tempting innuendo to be made here. Something along the lines of 'yes, I bet it is.' But it was too crude. He thought fast. No, forget it.

'How are you?' she laughed. 'How's your sculpture going?'

'Oh, you don't want to know about that...'

'Of course I do.'

'Well, it's practically finished.' He took a drag on his cigarette, and smiled. 'I've just got to breathe some life into it now. You know, just pinch its clay nostrils and give it a bit of mouth-to-mouth. Give it the breath of life. Like *your* mate did with Adam. What's the bloke's name again? Guh ... Guh ... begins with G anyway.'

She laughed. 'You are very bad, you know, Lawrence. You shouldn't talk about God like that.'

'But *you* do all the time!'

'No, I do not!'

'Yes, you do! You're always bringing God down to our level, calling him your friend and all that. Which ... seems to me to deny his best attributes. You know, the vast terrifying omnipotence and that. The awesome, rather bizarre office he holds as Lord of the Universe. The sheer, well, *enigma* of the guy. It's funny, really. I think I actually have more respect for God than you do. And I don't even believe in him.'

He listened to her speechless exasperation come down the phone, imagining the sweet smell of her breath as she held her mouth open, momentarily struggling to find the right words in English.

'Sometimes you are really crazy! God can create the universe and of course still be our friend. Why shouldn't he? We... you know, we are not so small as you think. Your body is the size of a universe compared to the ... ah, I don't know the word in English ... very small things -'

'What, you mean atoms... molecules, particles?'

'Yes, exactly.'

'Yeah, but I think that if God exists then he probably has as much interest in friendship as he does in other base human activities... like hanging wallpaper or going to the toilet. I mean, look, human values only exist in one infinitesimal corner of the universe. Quite probably they grew and developed like a bacteria culture in a Petri dish, and with as much meaning. Why should God regulate himself to fit them?'

'But you don't understand! God gave us these values to begin with!'

'What? God gave us this contradictory mess of conflicting cultural codes and morals and ethics? And this mess is supposed to be the law of the universe? Come on...'

He heard her sigh down the phone. Shit, maybe he was overdoing it.

'Well, I'm at the supermarket now, so I have to go, but I don't want to leave the argument here - with you thinking you have won! With this rubbish you speak. Although it *is* very *clever* rubbish!' she said in a sing-song voice.

'Then meet me. And we can sort out the whole God thing once and for all, and then hold a conference and present our findings to humanity.'

Again, he luxuriated in the laughter coming down the phone.

'Yes, we should meet soon. But I am really busy. There is an assessment coming up. And I have to work on my thesis. But maybe we can meet in a couple of weeks.'

A couple of weeks. Always the fucking same! He felt disappointment to the verge of anger, but then immediately felt ashamed of himself: he should simply be grateful for the friendship of this lovely girl and never mind getting angry that he never got to discharge his base organ in her - an activity in any case as mindless as the blind multiplication of the bacteria in his heretical Petri dish.

'Yeah, sure,' he said. 'Okay. I'll be counting the seconds.'

More laughter. 'Okay, I have to go now. Big kiss, Lawrence!'

What big kiss? If she wanted to give him a big kiss, she would come round and *give* him a big kiss. He realised the childish petulance of this thought but wallowed in it all the same.

'Yes and the same to you. Bye,' he tried to say cheerfully.

'Bye!'

The phone went dead in his hand. He sucked hard on the remains of his Marlboro. Nothing else to suck on. Not for him the luxury of, say, a nipple. And where other men sucked on the compelling absurdity of, say, an engorged clitoris, he had to make do with this stained brown filter - although there *was* a pleasant sponginess to it. And even a degree of warmth, as the polluting smoke was drawn through. So in fact, all in all, it wasn't such a bad replacement after all. And indeed, when viewed from the dizzying heights of the swirling universe, a clitoris and a cigarette butt were all much of a muchness at the end of the day. They both were just pointless conglomerations of molecules and what-not. What Martina had charmingly termed 'very small things'.

As though to prove to himself that he didn't really believe this, he crushed the cigarette out and dialled another number. Zoe. Zoe the dancer-cum-graphic designer. Zoe who always did whatever she wanted. He wasn't given to judging people, but he did feel that her humanity was limited; often he considered her to be downright rude. But that of course counted for fuck-all when set beside her sexual charisma. Anyway, she wasn't answering. Almost certainly be a waste of time even if she did. Although he had never declared his sexual interest in her, he always got the feeling he wasn't her type. No, it was definitely a waste of time. He'd called her five times since they'd met at the party on the river. They'd met a few times for a coffee, and since then she'd never called.

The ringing tone in his ear suddenly gave way to a pre-recorded female voice. He'd been hanging on the phone too long and gone over into the voicemail message. Fuck that shit! He quickly put the receiver down - and picked his fags up. He put one in his mouth and took it out again, but without putting it back in the packet, laying it instead by his side on the carpet. He'd be smoking it soon enough, no worries.

The phone burst into life, ringing away between his knees. Holy Christ!

'Hello?'

'Hello, I just got a call from this number?' Fucking hell, she didn't even remember his number. No, it was worse than that: she must have erased his number from her phone.

'Oh, yeah, hi, Zoe, it's Lawrence.'

'Hey, Lawrence, how are you? I lost your number - I mean, there was like some problem in my phone, in the phonebook.' Right, well, he would never know if that was a true statement or not.

'Oh, right, well, I just thought I'd see if you had a free night this week.'

'No, I can't. I'm flying out to Brazil on Thursday. But I've got your number now. I'll call you when I get back.'

'When do you get back?' Lawrence made the question deliberately repetitious and stilted.

'June.'

For fuck's sake. He retrieved the cigarette from the carpet and lit it, inhaling mightily.

'You're going for six *months*?'

'Yep!'

'And what are you going to do there? Go water-skiing up the Amazon or something?' he joked glumly into the carpet.

'No, I'm gonna do some design work for an agency in Rio? The money's *fabulous*!'

She hadn't even laughed at his water-skiing joke, or even registered it as a jest. Fuck her.

'Well, that's *fabulous!* I hope you have a good time, and that it all goes exceptionally swimmingly for you,' he replied, maintaining a civil tone.

'Yeah, look, I've got to go now. I'm with people, yeah? Call you when I get back. Ciao!'

'Yes. "Ciao,"' he said into the humming receiver, before dropping it back into place.

There was no countenancing them sometimes. There was just no countenancing them. Why did he put himself through this shit? And for a moment he rebelled: he wouldn't bother calling Anna or Jane. But as he pulled on his cigarette, the earlier association he had made between the thing in his mouth and fleshy female nodules filled his head with such a torrent of sexual whimsy that he was immediately consumed with a desperation to keep trying. He dialled Anna's number, and sat on the carpet waiting, the cigarette burning down in his face. The ringing tone outlasted any plausible hope of her answering, and he wearily crashed the handset back into its cradle.

He rocked his head back onto the wall and took the cigarette from his lips, letting out a long slow exhaust. Without taking his head from the wall, he picked up the notebook and held it open with one hand, turning the pages slowly with his thumb until he came to the place where Jane had scrawled her number for him in a hand so slovenly and broken it looked like the work of a retard or an autistic child. He stared blankly at the wild, crazy figures. Well, she had been absolutely pissed out of her head the night he had met her at Phil's place. The number had worked though. He'd got through to her on it a couple of times. She'd even invited him to a party once, and talked to him all night, but the only thing she had said that he could remember was that she was tired of men and sex, and didn't want either one in her life. He had actually thought he was about to reach port until she had come out with that gem. And the only reason he was trying her now was because he was tempted by the weak and silly notion that she may have changed her mind. And because there was absolutely no girl else left to call. Apathetically, with his head still tilted back to the wall, he started dialling. He spent the time it took for the ringing tone to hit the pre-recorded voicemail announcement staring at the peeling cornice between the wall opposite and the ceiling. Then he calmly placed the receiver back in its cradle, and sat quietly for a moment. Because it never paid to get excited, and it never paid to get upset.

'*Fucksake!*' he shouted, springing to his feet and kicking the cigarette packet into the skirting-board. And then he spiralled back down to the phone and began dialling. He was left with option five - the option that was always open - but he didn't want to go out there alone if he could help it.

'Neil!' he said brightly into the phone. 'How's it?.....Yeah, fine. Listen, are you doing anything tonight?....... Oh, okay.... Christ, don't they ever let you out of that place!.... Right..........Yeah, no, yeah, that sounds great, we could - .....Well, yeah, if you get out of it call me at the weekend....Yeah, cheers. Bye.'

Martin, then. He dialled again and stared at the carpet. A BT "call-minder" announcement kicked in, and he clattered the receiver back into place.

Well, that was it for his wingmen. He was on his own. A fucking grim prospect if ever there was one: to go out into the night on a low ebb and trawl through Camden Town on a weekday - a Monday, for fuck's sake - and expect to secure sexual rescue from some delightful stranger. But nature demanded it of him, that he entertain the hope. His balls expected it of him that he carry them out into the night and somehow magic up some pliant female rump for them to slap against. It wasn't even his *idea*, but he was expected to do all the thinking and work the miracle of providing some nice girl for his bollocks to flood with semen. But actually not to flood with semen at all - the only thing to be flooded in this delightful, impossibly unlikely scenario would be the condom; nature, whose idea the whole pantomime was, would in any case be cheated, so what was the fucking point of it? Christ, the absurdity of it! The dizzying absurdity of the whole stinking mess.

He got slowly to his feet, made his way to the bathroom and threw on the rest of his clothes, the sight of the mirror reminding him of his earlier resolve to work that evening. He looked away quickly, ashamed, depressed by the wasted inspiration. In fact he longed to make the drawing he had planned, but there was no way he could summon the necessary discipline now, not now he had been picked up by the scruff of the neck and ordered out on a girl-hunt - even so futile a girl-hunt as this one would inevitably prove to be. For Christ's sake, had he ever been on any other kind? And it was too much to say he hunted them as such - he just hung around forlornly in places where they gathered.

He bent over the sink and rinsed his mouth out with a mixture of toothpaste and water, feeling that this act alone, preparing his mouth to encounter another, was enough to guarantee that it would never happen. He had the same totally irrational response to the idea of going out pre-armed with johnnies: it practically guaranteed they wouldn't be needed. And not only that, but the weary slog home at the end of the fruitless campaign would be made all the worse by the presence of the pristine, cellophane-wrapped packet nestling in his inside coat pocket, held close over his heart. A hidden badge of failure. He smirked to himself. TV cops carried warrant badges in their inside pockets to identify themselves to villains and little old ladies. All anyone needed to know about *him* was contained in the little red line running round the unbroken seal on that square packet. That little red seal - a kind of packaging hymen! So, fuck that, he wasn't taking his faithful packet out with him – that particular packet that seemed destined to walk through life with him, or at least sit, resented, at the back of the top drawer in the chest by his bed. If, by the grace of God, some miracle *should* occur, then he'd improvise and pick some up at a petrol station or a 24-hour shop or some other such delight of the sleepless London night.

He went out into the hall and pulled on his long camelhair coat, feeling a moment's respite, a brief flicker of well-being as his body adjusted to the familiar protective weight of the material. He loved this coat. It made him look a bit spaghetti western, having as it did something of the cut of the dusters worn by the gang of killers in *Once Upon a Time in the West*. Maybe that was the problem. Maybe the girls didn't like the coat. Well, fuck *them!* His coat was his ally against the world, and he wouldn't give it up for any mere *woman*, though she be the last shag on earth. He laughed at the luxurious extravagance of the sentiment, and also the fury of it. As if anyone had asked him to forsake his precious coat, as if anyone gave two *shits* about it! Jesus, he was really losing it!

He opened the door and left the flat, slamming the door behind him and plunging into the freezing night.

Marching at a breakneck pace down Fortiss Road, his shoulders drawn up against the cold, Lawrence brooded on the fact that his route to Camden Town would take him past the sex dole on Kentish Town Road - the scene of his embarrassing lapse earlier that day. He couldn't believe he had actually gone in there that morning. What the fuck had he been playing at? And he'd just stood in the entrance like some witless twat. Christ Jesus. All right, he was having a run of bad luck, a stretch in the wilderness, a hike through the Gobi desert, but that was no reason to just go to pieces and sign on, for Christ's sake!

As he made the turn into Kentish Town Road, he unconsciously turned the collar of his coat up, mentally bracing himself for the sight of the sex benefit centre. There it was, coming up immediately on the left just past the garage, a dull, glass-and-panel-fronted three storey block. He'd been passing it for years on his walks into Camden, but had only really noticed it about a year back. A spill of orange light from the street lamp fell some way into the darkened building, illuminating edges of desks, chairs, a potted palm.

As he passed by, he quickened his pace, but nevertheless cast a sideways glance at the facade, at the posters in the windows, the faded pollution-streaked panels and concrete support pillars fouled by relentless traffic exhaust. The posters were incredible: absurd displays of beaming faces - a grinning young guy, a middle-aged woman - presumably meant to represent ordinary punters who had been "helped back to satisfaction" through government sex-support schemes.

The shittest poster of the lot was for the "Contact-Seeker's Charter". So astonishingly shit was it that he stopped in his tracks and stared at it for a moment, contemptuously running his eyes over the graphic of two figures - male and female - approaching each other on stilts across white sand, backed by the inevitable ultramarine sky. Quite apart from the crap concept, the figures had been executed in a sort of cod-Matisse line which the design team presumably thought was stylish and expressive, but which was in fact fussy and irritatingly indecisive. It was the same image as on the leaflet that had so nauseated him in the morning. With the same patronising tag line: "Helping you back to satisfaction". An irredeemable, pathetic piece of shit. But maybe he should be grateful to whatever morons came up with it for getting him the hell out of there....

As he was about to move on, he noticed a bit of graffiti sprayed over a panel below one of the posters.

WELFARE FOR WANKERS

He resumed his hectic march down the street. Welfare for wankers. Absolutely fucking correct. To have taken a form and signed on would have been to change his self-image forever to that of a total bloody failure. He was furious with himself for having been tempted. Furious with his cock for having taken him to the edge of such ... self-destruction.

And it wouldn't have been the first time. Flaxen waves of heavy blond hair rolled briefly across his mind. All that ... fucking Bibi nonsense....

Sex dole, though ... would it be more honest to go to a prostitute? Less sanitised perhaps, but he'd never do that either - couldn't afford it for one thing, and again it amounted to complete personal failure. And presumably you'd never know to what extent the poor soul you were shagging were being worked as a slave by some lethal criminal gang. Actually, he didn't know if many women still worked outside. From stuff he'd seen on telly it seemed a lot of them preferred to come in from the cold and get jobs as sex dole workers, rather than take shit from the criminal arseholes and drug-pushers who controlled them on the street. If it kept women out of the clutches of those bastards then that was probably a good thing....

But it wasn't for him. It couldn't possibly be for him.

For one thing it was charity, and he was instinctively averse to taking charity - he'd be embarrassed to impose himself on the women who worked there. He never liked to impose.

And yet....

He unconsciously slowed his pace as he remembered the attractive young woman sat in the waiting area that morning when he had stood in the doorway scowling at the room and everyone in it. It seemed incredible to think that she had gone there for "sex-support", that she would have soon been going up those stairs for some sort of state-sponsored bonk handout. An involuntary image crept into his mind of her undressing in some bland functional room in front some sort of government fuck-worker. And as the blood rushed inevitably down to his knob, he felt his attitude shift from contempt to something more ambivalent. If it were all right for her to do it, then ... then it might be all right for him too. But no, fuck it, whatever her reasons were for being there, they couldn't possibly be the same as his. She may have been there because she got a kick out of it, had a taste for it, *preferred* it. If he went, it would be because he had no fucking choice. A woman like that surely had a choice.

But even if she didn't - fuck it, there had been something - fuck, there had been something to do with the light in the place, the damp smell of social security ... the stink of patronising government 'initiatives'. Take some of those leaflets, for instance. What in fuck was a "LiaisonSearch Workshop" for heaven's sake? And that other one, "Take a Fresh Look at Yourself" featuring yet another pathetic graphic, this time of some kind of repellent cartoon bear looking at itself in a mirror.

But apart from all this, there was something else: the palpable air of defeat hanging in the room, even on the faces of some of the people behind the desks - and there were one or two pretty sour-looking bastards in that number. Did he really want to have to deal with *them* on a regular basis? But above all, it was the other punters. Never mind the attractive young woman. She was an anomaly. What about the blokes? They were there because they sure as Christ had nowhere else to go. Did he really want to join the poor defeated fuckers huddled together on those seats? He smiled darkly to himself. Did he really want to join the ranks of unemployed cocks? *Acknowledge* to the world that he had an *unemployed cock*?

For the love of heaven, there were thousands of beautiful women from all over the world in this town. One or two of them, for all he knew, might be destined to know the taste of him before the month was out. He just had to keep his nerve and keep chipping away at the opportunities.

Coming to the end of Kentish Town Road, he found himself stepping round the familiar detritus of discarded fast-food packaging, band flyers, beer cans and filth which always surrounded Camden Town tube station on any day of the week. He imagined it viewed from above, a thin halo of crud ringing the terminus, speaking to the stars overhead of another little concentration of humanity seeking to divert itself, distract itself.

He halted at the junction in front of the station. So, here he was in Camden then. And what the hell was he going to do now? Stand at a bar and nurse a dreary pint in silence? But of course. And then balk at the expense of a second pint and piss off, his 'sad' credentials thoroughly endorsed. Well, let's get on with it then.

He crossed the mouth of Camden Road, heading for the big, cavernous pub on the corner, The World's End.

Christ, there weren't many people about. Apart from the huddle of noisy derelicts camped around the cash machine in the station wall, there was only a handful of people in sight. What in Christ's holy name had he hoped to achieve by coming out here tonight?

He pushed open the door of the pub, swapping the sound of a breaking bottle in the distance for the animated hubbub coming from the surprisingly crowded bar. He stepped through and halted just beyond the threshold, uncertain what to do with himself next, wondering which part of the bar to approach.

The decision was made as his eyes fell on the back of a long pair of legs entwined provocatively around one another, clad in black tights. Conscious of not wishing to stare, he moved his gaze quickly up the girl's body to her bob of coal-black hair, but in taking his glance even as fleetingly as he did over her bottom, he exposed himself to a sudden implosion in his heart, a kind of clutching seizure filling him with a flushing hot wave. For a second, the only thing in the world he wanted to do was bury his face in her behind. My God, he hadn't even seen the front of her head, yet - hadn't even *begun* to form a sense of her as a human being. Whatever her disposition might be, whatever her nature, her interests, her state of mind, whatever her sensibilities, whatever spiritual heights her soul was capable of touching, whatever depths her soul had already plumbed, whatever her opinions, her hopes, her disappointments, her aspirations - it didn't matter; whatever. He was already consumed with the fantasy of nuzzling her derrière.

Christ, it was pathetic. The total inability to rise above it. Women who saw men as little better than animals were absolutely fucking right: a shallower herd of pigs never walked the Earth. He focused on the back of the girl's head as he drifted toward a space next to her at the bar. Leaning on the counter, waiting to be served, he turned his head cautiously to the left, hoping to discover her face, but she was holding it away from him, engaged in rapid energetic conversation with a slim Asian girl leaning on the bar beside her. He could hear the foreign accent of the girl next to him, but over the noise of the pub he couldn't place it, as she talked excitedly about some development or other in her career. He imagined the enormity of breaking in on their conversation, pictured their blank faces trained on him as his voice struggled to carry and fill the void where previously had flowed the music of their own inter-action. No way in fuck would he try that.

The friend was pretty, and he allowed himself to watch her for a moment, drinking in the mesmerising darkness of her eyes as they followed the movements and gestures of her companion. He tried to imagine how he would feel if she were to suddenly swing them on him and smile. But he knew the fabric of the universe would creak and groan under the strain of such an aberration. It could take earthquakes and supernovae and all that crap in its stride, but it couldn't take the weight of this girl flashing him a smile. Fuck, it'd rip apart, wouldn't it? The whole of fucking creation would be rent asunder at her smile for him, at the positive charge of her smiling look colliding with the dark anti-matter of his spirit. Christ, he might as well *be* a piece of anti-matter as hope for a girl to notice him in this bar.

Well, he'd better get a pint in, for God's sake. The bar stool to his right became free, and he shifted himself onto it, taking care to spread the wide-cut hem of his long coat across the seat.

Turning to the bar, he caught the attention of the attractive young blond woman serving. She approached him smiling. But smiling in context and in place, of course - in keeping with the cosmic order. Nevertheless, he still felt a sudden overwhelming warmth, as of coming home, but which faded in the time it took for her to take his order and move down the bar to the pump. He was annoyed with himself for having felt it - because it was an illusion, a mirage. The Gobi desert had them like any other.

She returned with his pint of piss - since he'd been small he'd always thought beer looked as though it had already been drunk once before.

'Two-eighty, please,' she said in an accent he guessed was Slavic.

'Thanks,' he said, placing three pound coins in her soft open palm.

FOUR

Williams ran his eyes across the final responses on the application form, noting the atrocious spelling, a consistent feature of the claim. The handwriting itself was barely any better. He glanced at the signature and the date, before bringing his eyes once more to bear on the claimant, a fair-haired youth of eighteen dressed in baggy, brand-emblazoned casualwear. The lad had made himself comfortable, leaning back in the chair, his fingers laced together in his lap, a cap with a ridiculous white tick on it stuck on top of his head - inevitably back to front.

'And do you have your medical form?' asked Williams shortly, closing the document in front of him.

'Yeah ... er, hang on.'

Williams watched as the lad pulled a rolled-up paper from inside his jacket and handed it to him.

Williams placed it on the desk and began pointedly to flatten it out with his palm, keeping his eyes on the claimant for a moment, before proceeding to examine the document closely, taking his time. He turned the pages slowly, scrutinising the columns of boxes running alongside the lists of venereal ailments and other conditions, looking for any ticks under the 'yes' heading. Coming to the final page, he peered closely at the doctor's signature and the stamp of the surgery practice. Then he went back through the form, looking for any signs of tampering, such as correcting fluid or an inconsistent stroke of the pen. It seemed ridiculous to him that the medical forms were now entrusted to the claimants to bring in. Much better to have them posted on by the doctors' surgeries, as they used to be, before Finance had deemed it an unnecessary expense. However, he was satisfied that the document before him was in order, and he placed it in the manila envelope to his left.

'And your ActionPlan, please.'

'What?'

Williams sighed and looked off to his left. 'Your ActionPlan. At your first interview you were told to bring an outline of what you intend to do to relieve your current position.'

The youth was squinting at him quizzically.

'What you intend to do to find your own sexual encounters, so you can sign off as quickly as possible,' grated Williams, not bothering to conceal his impatience.

'Oh, right ... I forgot. Sorry, yeah, I forgot about that. Erm ...' He leaned forward in the chair, trying to look amenable.

Williams was tempted to tell him to go away and come back when he had written out a plan. Still, he was required to help new claimants, not hinder them. Yet he also knew that the little twerp didn't deserve help. That seemed pretty clear from the fact that he'd come in here the minute he was eligible. He was probably here to lose his virginity as quickly as possible - which was not what the system had been set up for. Williams felt in his bones that this was the case, but couldn't prove it, and so had no choice but to allow the claim.

'Look, you can write one out for me now,' muttered Williams, taking a blank sheet of paper from the drawer and pushing it across the desk. He handed the youth the pen, and watched as he leaned over the paper, the peak of his cap sticking in the air. The lad remained like this for a moment before looking up at Williams for help.

'Er ... what -'

'Write down what you intend to do each week to find encounters.'

'Like talking to girls and that, you mean?'

'Yes, where are you going to meet them?'

There was a pause as the youth thought.

'Well ... dahn the pub?' he frowned, a dubious look on his face.

'Write it down, then.' Williams watched him write. 'How often are you going to go?'

'How often I'm gonna go dahn the pub, you mean?'

'Yes, how often?' said Williams tersely, looking down at the desk.

'I'm always dahn there!' laughed the youth.

'Write it down then. And how many girls are you going to try to talk to while you're there?'

'Eh? I dunno, do I!'

'What do you think would be a reasonable number?'

'Er ...'

'Two a night? Three a night?'

'Er... yeah, three a night, I suppose. But ... it'd depend on who was in there. You know, whether they were fit or not. I mean if they were all dogs -'

'But you're not in any position to be choosy, are you? Otherwise presumably you wouldn't have come in here. Perhaps you'd like to think again about your decision to claim.'

The youth leaned forward quickly. 'Nah, it's okay, you're right, you're right.'

'It's not a question of whether I'm right or not, is it?'

'Nah, but I'll check them all out, dogs as well, yeah?'

Williams regarded him, chose to keep him suspended for a moment before replying.

'And you'll endeavour to approach three girls a night, yes?

'Yeah, three a night, yeah.'

'Write it down, then.' Williams watched the inelegant movement of the pen. 'What else are you going to do?'

The youth looked up at the ceiling, and then back down at Williams. 'Erm...'

Williams held his look and rapped on the side of his monitor. The lad looked at him in confusion. Williams tapped his monitor a second time. The youth opened his eyes wide, trying to grasp Williams' meaning.

'The internet,' said Williams. 'People have been known to meet over the internet sometimes.'

'Right, yeah,' said the claimant. 'Yeah, I'm gonna look on the internet,' he said, looking oddly at Williams, who was glancing down at the desk.

'Write that down as well, then. What else?'

'Er ... can't really think of naffing else.'

'What about work?'

The youth laughed. 'You must be joking, mate.'

'And why must I be joking?'

'Well, there's no birds where I work. Don't get too many girls working as exhaust-fitters.'

'What about the customers? I imagine you must get quite a few female customers.'

The youth appeared slightly taken aback. 'Well, yeah, but I'd get the sack pretty sharpish if I was to spend all my time chattin' up the lady customers.'

'I never suggested you should spend all your time chatting them up - just that you ... endeavour to capitalise on any opportunities.'

'Oh, right ...'

'So, write it down then.'

The claimant looked down at the piece of paper, but then shook his head, raising his eyes to Williams and chuckling slightly with embarrassment. 'Sorry, I, er, don't know how to ... don't know exactly what to write for that...'

Williams glanced heavenward, then back at the claimant, before quickly reaching for the paper.

'Well, I'll write it for you, and then you can sign it,' said Williams, drawing the piece of paper across the desk. 'The pen, please.'

'Sorry, mate,' replied the youth, handing the pen to Williams.

Williams looked down at the paper, at the handful of words scrawled across it: 'pub', 'always', '3 girls a nite', 'intenet'.

He sighed. 'Well, as it stands it doesn't read too well, does it?'

The youth shrugged his shoulders. Williams resisted the urge to begin hectoring him. After all, it wasn't his job to teach these yobs how to write. Instead, he quickly set about constructing declarations of intent around the raw material in front of him, correcting the spelling, and rounding off with, "I intend fully to capitalise on any opportunities that may arise in my place of work."

'Now,' he said, spinning the paper round, 'Read it through and make sure you agree with what I've put.'

The youth pored slowly over the revisions.

'Yeah, that's okay.'

'And you agree to put these measures in action every week?'

'Yeah,' said the lad, nodding his head.

Williams handed him the pen. 'Sign it, then.'

The peak of the cap tilted up once more as the claimant bent forward to write. As he sat back again, putting the pen down, Williams took the piece of paper, rose from the desk and crossed to the photocopier in the corner of the small interview room and ran off a copy of the youth's plan. Returning to the desk, he placed the original in the manila envelope, and handed the copy to the claimant.

'For your reference. Now, you understand that if you have any success with any of these strategies you must inform us immediately. You must inform us immediately if you meet with any sexual engagement of any kind involving another party.'

The youth was squinting doubtfully at Williams. He shook his head and leaned forward.

'Er ... I don't understand ... You mean I've got to tell you if I get engaged...?'

Williams couldn't believe this. 'No, I mean "engagement" as in "contact" or "inter-action". If you have sexual contact of any kind.'

'With girls, yeah?'

'Girls, boys, anyone,' snapped Williams.

'Hang on, mate, I'm not a poof!' laughed the youth, glancing quickly to his side and back to Williams.

'Fine. But you get the point, yes?'

'Yeah, sure,' said the lad defensively.

'Because if you don't, if you don't tell us, and you go on claiming, you will be in very serious trouble. You will be making a false claim and there are serious consequences for falsely claiming sex benefit, do you understand? Anything up to ten years in prison.'

'All right, fair enough ...' said the youth, shifting uncomfortably in his seat.

'And you will also be in serious trouble if we think you are not doing enough to get yourself out of your current position. Is that also clear?'

'Yeah,' said the youth morosely.

Williams kept his eyes on him for a moment and then pulled open a drawer to his left and brought out a narrow booklet-sized document sheathed in a clear plastic wallet. Tossing it on the table, he rammed the drawer shut and took up the pen. He removed the plastic wallet, and in a box on the front of the document he wrote a reference number, copying it down from the monitor. Next he wrote quickly in a box in the centre of the cover: "David Pickford."

As Pickford left the interview room and closed the door behind him, a wide smile broke out across his face, his rosy cheeks growing even redder. He half-ran along the corridor to the stairwell. Fackin' *yes!* He was in. He was fackin' *in*!! He gripped the handrail and leapt down the stairs, taking the steps five or six at a time. As he came to the first floor, he suddenly halted and peered at the double doors leading off the landing. Tomorrow, then. He'd be going in there tomorrow. Before Turner. He'd beat Turner by a whole fackin' week! He'd bagged it, he'd fackin' bagged it! He thought of the others waiting for him outside and resumed his mad flight down the stairs, almost colliding with a middle-aged man on his way up.

Coming to the ground floor, he forced himself to slow his pace as he entered the reception area, but could not keep the skip out of his step as he crossed the room, passing the signing-on desks and waiting claimants. As he neared the street door his pace quickened again and he pushed his way out onto the street, where he looked quickly about him. Where *were* the useless barstards? There they were, hanging around outside the newsagents. Loz had seen him.

A diminutive kid of fifteen dressed in baggy sportswear was pointing him out to the others. They turned their heads and broke into a run towards him. He likewise launched himself in their direction, taking the SB40 from his pocket and holding it aloft like a trophy, causing a tumult of cheers to break out ahead of him. And then they were on him, around him, shouting and laughing, jostling for a chance to hold the signing document, but he went on holding it over their heads, teasing them with it until finally he lowered it to his face and pressed it to his lips.

The group of teenagers made its raucous way down the street with Pickford ringed by his acolytes like some all-conquering king. Loz was holding the precious booty of the SB40 up to his face, trying to make out every line of the social security jargon printed on the front.

'Fuckin' wicked, Dave...' he said.

Pickford glanced down at him, snatched the document from his hand and stuffed it back inside his jacket. 'The geezer was a miserable barstard, though, yeah? Layin' down the law all over the fackin' place. Still, it'll be worth it tomorrow when I'm on the fackin' job!'

He put his fists out before him and made an exaggerated thrust of his hips, emitting a loud whoop.

'What time do you go in then, Dave?' queried a hooded sixteen-year-old dancing along in front of Pickford.

'2:15. Let's go round to Turner's place, yeah? I can't wait to rub that barstard's face in it!' he shouted, breaking into a fit of giggling.

'It's gonna kill him that you're gonna be the first one to fuck a girl!' laughed Loz.

Pickford stopped and gave Loz a hostile look.

'The first to what?

'Fuck a girl,' said Loz uncertainly.

Pickford clouted him across the head. 'I'm not a virgin, you cheeky little twat!'

'Well, what's all this *about,* then?' said Loz, rubbing his head.

'I can't believe I'm fackin' 'earin' this! You're gonna get a kick in the bollocks in a minute. Look ... it's about ... gettin' as much fackin' as you can, right? And ... girls, yeah? girls can be a right pain in the arse wanting this, wanting that. But the girls you fack on sex dole don't have no right to say naffing to you, yeah? But I'm still gonna be fackin' other birds as well, though.'

The group continued its progress down the street.

'But you're not meant to, yeah?' asked the hooded youth.

'What?'

'Fuck other birds.'

'Nah, you're not *meant* to, but they're never gonna fackin' know, are they?'

'*What* other birds, anyway, Pickford?' asked a thin sallow youth, lagging a little behind.

'*Birds*, right?' snapped Pickford, whirling his head round aggressively.

'What fuckin' birds? You haven't fucked *no*-one. You haven't fucked no-one in your *life*!' sneered the thin youth.

'Don't be fackin' darft.'

'You haven't, have you, though? That's why you're so excited about this sex dole shit.'

'Right, you're fackin' dead, Kinton.'

'Yeah, like I'm really fuckin' bothered!'

Pickford gave Kinton a violent shove, causing him to trip on the kerb and fall into the path of a middle-aged man with a beard approaching from the other direction. Pickford and the others burst into laughter, with Pickford's giggles touching a high child-like pitch as Kinton threw his arms around the man's legs in an effort to break his fall. It wasn't enough, and the teenager's face hit the pavement as the man stumbled over him. The man halted, appeared about to say something but continued on his way, as Pickford stood giggling over the prone figure of Kinton.

'Fackin' fancy that old geezer, do you, Kinton?'

He squealed with laughter. 'Oi, mate, this shithead fancies ya!' he called to the figure hurrying away up the street, before turning and half-skipping away down the road with his entourage.

Bill Masters peered over his shoulder at the gang of youths as they continued down the street. The lout that had crashed into him was up again and had caught up with the others. They went on down the road, filling the air with foul language, the two antagonists trading weak blows, pushes and shoves, all of them made strangely shapeless by their clothes and by the white sky.

'Delinquent bastards....' muttered Masters into his beard, adjusting his glasses, which had become slightly dislodged during the collision. He was feeling the stress of the encounter keenly, taking him back as it did to those terrible ten years teaching in the comprehensive. It was exactly types like that lot that had driven him to early retirement, and the consequent penury.

With his face tucked into the grey fuzz of his beard, his hands thrust deep in the pockets of his anorak, he covered the remaining distance to the sex benefit centre, and with the usual flush of shame pushed open the door.

Glancing around hesitantly, he crossed to the ticket dispenser and took a number, ripping the white triangle of paper from the slot. He moved over to the seats in the waiting area with the odd feeling that he were being drawn toward them, as though under the influence of some unseen physical law. Which in a roundabout way he supposed he was. Though whatever the nature of that law, it was a most regrettable one.

He took his place with the others and waited his turn. He raised his eyes nervously to the woman working over on one of the desks, glanced across to the black chap to her left. Masters always thought him a good fellow. A good humane fellow. To be dealt with by him always took some of the pain out of the situation.

But in a different sense it made it worse. It made it worse for the simple reason that Masters was technically abusing the system, and he didn't like to deceive people, especially good sorts like that chap. Sometimes he wanted to come clean with him, but there was a subtlety to his personal situation which he believed the indelicate machinery of the state would be powerless to accommodate, and that if he told them the truth the most likely result would be the cessation of his benefit. And that would be - and it shamed him to admit it - intolerable. Because, unsatisfactory as it was, it was all he had. These days there really wasn't much else.

He peered up at the LED display, saw that his number had been called and that he'd been summoned to the desk of the somewhat dour middle-aged woman. He crossed the room and sat down slowly, drawing the SB40 from his anorak and placing it softly on the desk.

'Good morning,' he smiled weakly.

'Morning,' replied the woman blankly, taking the SB40, and rising from the desk.

As he waited, Masters sat with his head bowed, staring down at his coat zipper, his hands in his pockets.

The woman returned with his file and sat down, pulling his claim sheet from the envelope. He watched her write the date down, took his eyes from the paper to the crown of her bobbed grey head, and was struck by a sudden poignant ache. Good Lord. Her hair from this angle... This woman ... *this* woman would suit him better ... better than the ones upstairs ... but on the other hand the experience might be too close to....

She looked up and the chimera vanished as he was confronted with her wrong ... alien ... face.

'Have you had a sexual encounter at any time in the last two weeks?' she said, already turning the claim sheet round for him to sign.

'No, I haven't. No.' he said quietly into his beard.

He was unable to meet the woman's eyes, afraid that she might read in his that he had deliberately made no effort in that quarter. That he never did.

He took the pen and signed, then exchanged the claim sheet for his SB40 and ticket.

'Number 5, then,' said the woman, staring impassively into her monitor.

'Thank you,' replied Masters, addressing the edge of the desk, and rising from his seat.

The two white neck-toggles of Masters' anorak swung in tandem from side to side as he made his way up the last few stairs to the first floor. Gaining the landing, he paused for a moment before pushing open the double doors and proceeding along the cream-painted corridor, with its row of numbered white doors running down the right-hand wall. The doors were white but somehow never appeared quite as white as they had presumably been painted, despite the harsh overhead strip-lighting. Passing the open door of the security-guard's station, he glanced inside, catching a glimpse of a large chap in a brown cap and uniform munching on a sandwich and peering up at a TV set aglow with daytime chat. He glanced at the Modigliani nude as he passed it on the left, and felt again the strange consolation the image always gave him, despite the disturbing black slits of the model's eyes - or perhaps because of them.

He came to number 5, and paused, as he always did at this point, battling with the guilt, trying to bed his conscience down with the coming encounter. He lifted his face out of his beard and knocked. A muffled 'yeah, come in,' sounded from inside and he pushed open the door.

He was somewhat disappointed to see the dark-eyed Mediterranean-looking girl, lying on her side absorbed in a paperback. He didn't mind the fact that she was paying him no attention at all. That was all to the good, in fact. The problem was she was too young ... much too young. However, he was only partly dismayed; the part of him that was not stirred to life in his faded washed-out underwear.

He had been hoping for one of the older ones he'd encountered in the past. But the sex facilitators always seemed to get moved around by their employers, perhaps to prevent the formation of attachments. Which was understandable. One could understand that.

Although the girl was still reading, her lips curled back in a faint sneer, she had opened her robe and begun tugging her pants absently down her legs. Unzipping his anorak, Masters watched, his conflicting emotions and impulses mixing into a messy amalgam of guilt, pain and mind-spinning delight, as the dark pubic region of the girl was exposed to the bright electric light of the cubicle. She pulled the knickers free from her ankle and flung them over the chair, without once looking away from her book.

He threw off his coat and quickly stripped to the waist, his sagging pot belly and deflated pectorals mercilessly expressed by the harsh light. Bending down to remove his shoes, he glanced up at the girl and saw that she was still reading, idly rocking her leg back and forth. Taking off his shoes, he was embarrassed to see that his socks were a little damp. He took them off and stuffed them as far as he could into his shoes, and placed his clothes on top, hoping to mask off any odour. Stupid fool! He had meant to change his insoles this morning.

As he stood up, the girl gave him a quick look, as if to check on his progress rather than to make any dutiful show of a greeting. However, he still felt as though he should say something himself, though he would rather not. But she returned her attention to her book, and with her free hand pulled open a drawer in the cabinet by the bed. After rummaging for a moment, the hand lifted out a small round jar. Lubricant. Well, thought Masters, the poor thing couldn't be expected to get too excited about a tired old wreck like him. He watched, humiliated yet excited, as she took a gob of jelly from the jar, and taking her fingers between her legs slowly worked them up into herself, glancing occasionally at her book, which she still held open with one hand.

He pulled down his trousers, noting the bloated form of his staid old penis under the cotton of his underwear. The girl was still reading and lubricating, which gave him a useful opportunity ... while she wasn't looking ... should he dare? His heart fluttered as he made his decision. He stepped back to his pile of clothes, knelt down, pulled out his jacket and withdrew a small round object from the inside pocket. Bending over the jacket to prevent the girl from seeing, he closed his eyes and brought the object slowly to his chest, held it there for a moment, as if in prayer, then kissed it, smothering it with the grey nest of his beard, before quickly replacing it. He stood up, experiencing by turns both guilt, and its opposite, in the form of an almost mystical - and therefore probably delusional, he told himself - sense of approbation, even forgiveness.

Standing in his pants, holding his head low on his chest, he turned to the girl, who had momentarily abandoned her book in order to wipe her hands on a tissue. Letting the tissue fall to the floor, she reached in the drawer and flung a box of condoms to the foot of the bed, and turned back to her book. Masters stepped out of his underpants and approached the bed, his wrinkled semi-erection leading the way.

He took a foil packet from the box, and tore it open. Extracting the oily ring of rubber, he held it for a moment, musing, as he always did at this point, on its diameter, how it oddly corresponded with that of the item in his jacket pocket. Then, using all his concentration, and stimulating himself with the view between the girl's legs, he carefully rolled the latex down.

As he climbed on to the bed, the girl finally put her book down, and rolled onto her back to receive him. Masters was struck by the intensity of her eyes, and knew that he didn't want them on him, knew that he didn't want such direct engagement with her.

'Er ... you can go on reading if you like,' he mumbled through his beard, staring at her pubic hair, feeling the blood pounding in his neck.

'All right, I will,' said Lucinda. 'So, I'm going on my front, okay?' she said with a fierce look.

'Fine,' said Masters quietly, as she rolled over, taking the book from the cabinet and making herself comfortable. As he shuffled forwards between her legs, coming to a kneeling position behind her bottom, Masters noticed something. A mole to the left of the girl's coccyx. It wasn't much, but Good Lord, it was *something* he could use to bring the experience an infinitesimal tad closer to the impossible satisfaction he sought. The mole really was situated in exactly the same place, and actually now he thought about it, the whole of this girl's bottom was in many ways similar... to hers, years ago, in the days of her youth of course, in those long-vanished days...

Taking the coincidence of the mole as another mystical licence to pursue his pleasure, and surveying the wide sweep of the miraculous resurrected posterior, Masters eased his aged penis inside, causing Lucinda to bite her lip slightly as she turned another page.

Closing the door of the cubicle behind him, Masters turned and walked slowly down the cream-painted corridor, his hands in the pockets of his anorak, his head bowed. The similarity had not been so great after all. That had become clear as soon as he had finished, and, as usual, found himself naked and abased with some poor naked girl. How could he have imagined that the shape of her rump had somehow made the business in some small way more acceptable? He felt a thump of shame in his chest, and an impulse to sob, which he barely managed to stifle. Stopping in the middle of the empty corridor, he reached inside his jacket pocket and pulled out a small round object.

He turned the locket around in his palm, before gently undoing the clasp. An oval portrait of a bland-looking woman in her late fifties faced a lock of grey hair sellotaped to the inside of the brass lid. Removing his glasses, he brought the locket close to his face, blinking at the image with wet eyes. Through the grey cloud of his beard came a single word, as quiet as a breath, as light as heaven.

'Julia.'

FIVE

The long dark sheen of Carla's auburn hair flowed back over the soft fur collar of her burgundy Afghan coat as she peered down with intelligent clear eyes at the patterns on her mittens. Her hands were held together in her lap, her jeans forming a sky-blue backdrop to the little woollen rabbits gambolling round her wrists. Her delicate, serious face was characterised by a strong beauty which only she was capable of denying, over-conscious as she was of the faint asymmetry of her nose. She was as over-critical of her nose as she was unaware of the full range of her good looks, as the window of the bus carried the reflection of her beguiling profile past the second storey of a dull parade of North London shops.

She began playing with the thumb of her mitten, pulling it up, and wiggling her thumb back in. She repeated this several times. For some reason, it made her think of childhood games, and an old nursery rhyme popped into her head. She began moving her head from side to side in time with the rhythm, before she caught herself, and stopped. What was she doing? How could she still be so childish at 24? And why was she gripping her legs together so tightly? All at once she was aware of the tight feeling below her stomach, and in a quick, impetuous movement whirled round in her seat to stare out of the side window of the bus.

Why couldn't she relax? She'd been coming to the place now for nearly three months. Her clear brow creased into a frown. Maybe she should stop. But she got into such *moods* if she went without. And it was safer to come here. Holly had been right about that. But it was so *empty*. She turned again in her seat, and sighed. Well, so it was empty. So what? She let her head fall against the window, and stared at the passing trees. So what if it was empty, mechanical, sterile? So were most of the guys she had known! The one-night stands *and* the boyfriends. And unlike them at least it wasn't dangerous, abusive. 'Frontals' Holly called them. Carla agreed: the clubs were infested with frontal lobe jobs. She moved a long strand of hair away from her eye, and peered out at the passing parade of shops. The problem with this, though, was that you never knew what you were going to get. She realised this was probably why she got nervous. She wished she could be assigned one guy who she would see every time, but they weren't stupid at that sex dole office. They didn't want people getting too attached to their fortnightly sex-crutch! They didn't want it to be too easy, that was for sure. They didn't want people to actually be *happy*! No, of course not. She became suddenly angry, and pulling off her mitten, she began nibbling the nail of her ring-finger, furrowing her brow and glaring out of the window at a passing ramshackle electrical goods outlet.

But it was silly to think it would really be any better if she did get the same guy every time. For a start there hadn't been one yet that she was particularly bothered about having again. She looked down again at her mitten. The men in there.... They were just there to fill a hole. Emptily. Emptily filling the holes of all the sad ladies of London ... all the sad ladies of London.... That was quite *good*, a nice rhythm.... No, there was no one she'd really want to see again.... So she might as well go on sampling the stock ... the stable. Oh, no, that sounded awful, as though she desired an unending stream of men. But she didn't! Well of course she didn't. It was just the way the system worked. And anyway, she'd only just now been wishing she could have just *one* guy there! She shook her head, disturbed by the slight confusion in her thinking. It was as though she couldn't quite work out exactly what it was she *did* want from the sex dole. But then she didn't know what she wanted at *all*. A good man, maybe, like in the Janis Joplin song. Well, obviously, but that seemed... that just seemed impossible. And it was silly to hope ... to hope for that. Look at her relationships. *This*, sex dole, was probably better than any *relationship* she'd been in. At least after the sex there were no temper tantrums, no rages, no *insanity.* No shaking in the dark listening to them trying to kick the front door down. And no living out of a tin of beans for two whole days because you were too scared to go out of the house. And unlike with them, you *knew* from the *beginning* that your sex dole 'lover' would be shagging other women, so you didn't have to care about that, you *couldn't* care. You were free of all that. Blissfully free of all that.

But despite this, and despite Holly's enthusiasm for it, there was obviously something pretty desolate about satisfying your needs in a sex benefit cubicle.

The first time she had gone in one of those cubicles, she had nearly turned and run out, but the guy had stopped her at the door and she had stayed. She had been so completely mixed up that day. A few weeks prior she'd finally decided that she wanted to try it, she'd talked to Holly, and thought it all through and finally brought in her forms and had her interview. And she'd thought she'd got it settled in her mind, but the first time she went for the actual sex, she was all over the place emotionally. It was so weird; downstairs, while waiting, after a lot of worrying about whether she'd find the guy attractive enough, she had actually begun to feel pretty horny and excited by the idea of getting some sex again after so long, but also upset that she was resorting to signing on for it. Still, she had told herself that it never bothered Holly to come 'down the sex dole,' and also that she always found the guys 'inspiring' enough. But when she had gone in that cubicle for the first time, that blank white room, the whole thing had seemed suddenly ridiculous, so ridiculous! The guy had been sat on the bed, already naked, with his prick already going up before she'd had time to shut the door behind her. The crazy thing was that despite the really weird situation of finding herself standing in front of this bloke, a warm pang had spread immediately through her tummy and the next thing she knew, the wetness was starting! It had started so quickly it had shocked her, especially as she had been beginning to get cold feet just moments before, as she had stood outside the door, forcing herself to get on with it and knock. So she had stood there in front of this guy - and that was another thing, she'd actually felt embarrassed because of her moist pants! And that was the whole reason for being there in the first place! *She*'d felt embarrassed by her *secret* arousal while *he* was sitting there naked with his *dick* shooting up. Well ... looking back on it now she could see it was obviously because he was a stranger. You didn't normally meet new people by shaking their dicks and wetting your pants.... But for her to become aroused so quickly like that just showed how much she'd been needing it. Well, that had been obvious from the way she hadn't been able to concentrate on anything for weeks. She'd gone a long time without. She must have done, because the guy hadn't been anything special. And she hadn't liked his eyes at *all*, though his body had been okay. It was looking in his eyes that had made her want to leave. It was odd but there had been nothing specific about them, although, you could say ... yes, he had the eyes of a football manager or something. She had turned, then, but he had got up, smiling and come toward her, his level dick moving from side to side as he approached. He hadn't said anything - none of them ever said anything much - had just come up to her, put his hand on the door and stroked her hair. Just once, impersonally. She had still wanted to leave, and then she had glanced down at his dick, and sort of tried to convince herself that she wanted it, that she should take it because she'd come this far and she'd regret it if she chickened out. Thinking back on it, she realised she had been confused because she hadn't gotten the hang of how to stop relating to the guy as a person. It had been so weird that first time. But then he'd put her hand on his dick, though, and that was it, she'd decided to stay, even though at the same time it felt as if he were abusing her by doing that, putting it in her hand. But she had kept hold of it. And it was so strange because even though she had begun touching the end of it hesitantly with her finger, she had felt outraged when he'd put his hand on her bum. He'd seemed to her then like some pervert on the tube, and she had moved instinctively one pace backwards to the door. His hand had remained in place, though, impersonally, and had already gone squirming down between her legs feeling her through her jeans. She had felt furious for a moment but still let him go on, realising that he was basically trying to help her, to help her make the best use of her limited time. And when his fingers had touched her most sensitive spot, even through her jeans, she had felt such a liquefying in her knickers that she had made a silly little squeaking sound, and without knowing what she was doing, had started vigorously rubbing his dick. 'Okay?' he had said, then. 'You're going to stay, then?' Yet at the sound of his voice, it had all seemed ridiculous again, and she had felt once again like leaving, but nevertheless nodded her head and went with him to the bed holding onto his dick like some lost little girl holding her father's hand. And the crazy contradictory feelings had kept coming; as she had walked with him over to the bed, she'd felt that since she'd put so many people to so much trouble for this she had better get on and do it, but also that she *did* want it very *much*, the growing wet hunger in her pants was telling her that. She didn't fancy the guy much, but she was already learning to look at it differently: his body was good and the idea was that she should use it for the next twenty minutes to satisfy her own. And then she could just forget about him afterwards. A living, throwaway vibrator. How suddenly excited she had been by that thought at the time. The novelty of that had certainly worn off since. But it had been that thought that had gotten her to take her coat off. As she had undressed, though, he had gone over to the small cabinet and begun sorting out the condom, entirely absorbed in himself, which had made her feel curiously abandoned by him, left to undress herself in the middle of the room. In fact, as she had bent down to unzip her boots, she had glanced up to see him cracking his knuckles and staring at his sheathed erection. That had made her want to leave again, but she'd told herself that sex benefit was always going to be a pretty basic affair and that she'd better adjust to it or go home, and so she had gone on unzipping her jeans, determined to go through with it. But she had still been troubled by his boring conventional face. So then she had decided that when they were on the bed she would close her eyes and simply feel him, and think of someone else. She would fantasise, as she had as a young girl, imagine she was doing it with one of her old idols. And after flirting with the idea of Sean Connery, with whom she'd been painfully in love from the ages of 11 to 13, she had finally chosen Nick Cave - to Holly's great amusement when she'd told her about it afterwards ('Oh, *Carla!* You're so silly and sweet!' she had laughed.) Then, when she had fully undressed, he had patted the bed, and she had obediently crossed over and sat down beside him, expecting some further preliminaries, but he had simply taken her shoulders and pushed her backwards down onto the sheet. And now that she thought about it, that had been the last time he had touched her with his hands, because when she was on her back he had simply planted his palms on either side of her body and positioned his hips to enter her. She'd remembered her strategy and closed her eyes and thought of Nick Cave as planned, imagining how the gaunt singer might kiss her, one hand perhaps cupping her mouth, the other gently stroking the side of her head. It had worked that first time, because when she'd felt the guy make his way inside she'd felt herself clenching around him immediately. It had gone in cleanly, efficiently, and it *had* felt pretty good to have one in there again. And it had made her feel happy, not *really* happy, but a kind of imitation happiness - soya-happiness! - which was at least ... something. Those first ten minutes had actually been pretty good, and she had even thought she was going to come at one point, but the reality of the guy had broken in on her, and she began to detach from the experience. It had been the smell of his aftershave, partly. It was the same as that used by a horrible driving instructor she'd taken lessons from last year. So she'd hung on for the next ten minutes until he'd finished. And that was another weird thing: he didn't finish by coming. That was really weird, he had just glanced over at a small clock on the wall, and withdrawn from her as cleanly, efficiently, as passionlessly as he had gone in. And that had been that. It was so strange, she had felt like *she* was the one being used as a commodity, and had to remind herself that it was *him*, as she watched him peel off the condom and throw it in the bin. 'Okay?' he had asked. 'Yes. Thanks....' she had replied, feeling ridiculous and sitting up quickly to retrieve her clothes. And so then she had dressed in silence, while he sat naked with his wilting prick, examining a mole on his chest. But then, unbelievably, as she was stepping into her jeans, he'd begun speaking and made some comment about some football match he'd seen on the telly the night before. She had simply said, 'Oh,' and continued dressing, realising *one* good thing about being on sex benefit: she'd had her ten minutes of fun and could now dispense with the guy and not listen to hours of rubbish about football. But then she'd suddenly felt sorry for him, for her rough attitude toward him. After all, this had all been for *her* benefit, hadn't it? There was no getting away from it, she had gone there for help, and he had given it. And so, at the door, she had stopped and thanked him, but when he had said that with girls like her it was a pleasure, she had felt like something had been taken from *her,* had felt violated - which was silly, she knew. It had all been just so confusing, she hadn't known *what* to think, and had simply said 'Okay, well, bye' and left the room. But then, going down the corridor, she had felt the emptiness really hit home, and by the time she got to the street, she'd decided never to go back.

And now here she was coming in for more. As she always did, because despite the emptiness afterwards, it always faded or became submerged in the general dreariness of everything else, and by the time the two weeks were up she was always feeling horny again and ready at least to chase the *chance* of a little satisfaction at the sex dole. And on the whole ... on the whole, it *was* better than nothing.

She stepped lightly off the juddering platform of the bus, and began walking up Kentish Town Road, as unconscious of the beguiling rhythm of her gait as she was of the swaying of the little red bobble on the point of her fur-lined hat.

As she approached the sex benefit office she thought back to her description of that first guy's eyes as being like those of a football manager, and began vaguely trying to tease a lyric out of it. 'You have the eyes of a football manager ... but the legs of a player'. No, that was stupid. But maybe drop 'football'. 'You have the eyes of a manager, but the legs of a player.' That was better, but cold as it was, it still sounded too warm to be about that guy. But maybe she could use the line in an abstract way or something in a song about something else. But no, Joni would have put a big red line through a line like that! And anyway, it was more interesting with the word 'football' in it. It was a more interesting insult that way. Forget the 'legs of a player' bit, and just leave it as an insult. 'You have the eyes of a football manager.' It was a great put-down! Maybe she could try to write a Carly Simon-type thing using that as a starting-point. Yeah, right.

Passing the hair salon two shops before the benefit centre, she glanced in at her reflection, and stopped for a moment to adjust her hair. Oh, no, her nose just looked awful, and she stamped her foot in an unconscious hold-over from her childhood repertoire of actions and gestures. She thought again about getting her nose pierced, but as usual, was completely undecided as to whether it would improve the situation or just make it worse. She threw her head on one side and grimaced, before walking on.

For the final approach to the benefit centre, she stared at the pavement, her eyes fixed on the black smudges of dried chewing gum passing beneath her feet, trying not to feel ashamed - why should she? - but feeling it all the same, raising her head only to push open the door.

Stepping over to the ticket dispenser, she felt the slightly stale atmosphere of the place close around her, had an odd impression of the filing cabinets and the silly potted palm somehow brushing her body from afar, leaving small grazes, while ahead of her, came the low, flat voices of the people at the desks. She took the white triangle of paper from the dispenser, trying first with her mittens on, failing, and then removing them, before finally taking the ticket and shaking her head, irritated with herself.

She glanced over at the desks, checking to see who was on duty. Checking to see if *he* was there. The guy with the glasses. No, he wasn't, thank God. But *she* was, though. The awful sniffy woman with the grey bob. The other three were the two harmless young guys and that old Caribbean guy who at least always had a smile for you.

Instead of sitting down, she drifted over to the personal ad boards, and walked slowly up and down between them, her head pointed at the small white cards, but reading nothing. She always did this when she came in, pretended to look at the contacts, because she'd been present once when the guy with the glasses had threatened to cut some bloke's benefit because he hadn't looked at the boards - which had seemed pretty mean to her. And that old cow looked easily capable of making the same threat.

The reason she didn't read them was because she wasn't interested in empty sexual contact with the outside world; she could get that herself easily enough if she wanted. What she needed was the safety, the *boundaries*, that came with being on the sex dole. Looking at these awful white cards always brought that home to her. She picked one at random and read it through, just to remind herself of how dreadful they were.

> Man (31) seeks woman (16-50) for casual sex. People say I'm good-looking. You must be slim and attractive. Croydon area. Tel: 07928376159. Or contact me at fatdog7@hotmail.com

God ... it made the sex dole cubicle seem warm in comparison, and she found herself thinking of it almost as a place of shelter as she crossed to the waiting area and sat down. There were about seven or eight other people waiting, all sat apart from each other, separated by at least one seat.

The guy nearest her looked a bit like that Adrian bastard, but it wasn't him, thank God! What a nightmare that had been. She'd taken him home after they'd snogged a bit at Trash only to get hit in the face for refusing to put her mouth round his filthy, unwashed prick. She'd locked herself in the loo and called her brother on her mobile, who'd told her to call the police and that he was on his way round. She hadn't called the police but had told the bastard animal on the other side of the door that she had and he'd gone quickly enough, then. But how she'd flown down the stairs when she'd heard Andrew at the door, how she had sobbed and sobbed on his chest.... Andy Pandy baby brother, what's Canada got that you can't get here? Some pretty trees and some pretty mountains, but it hasn't got *me*... And then there was the one-night stand who'd *insisted* on coming in, and who then got a call from his girlfriend while they were *doing* it, and had simply reached over to his mobile and taken the call while he was still *inside* her. At least he'd had the grace to stop thrusting, the foul, foul pig! She could still remember what he'd said into the phone: 'Babe, I'm so glad you said that....... I was wrong to do it, though... ...Well, do you want to meet, then?....... Okay, I can be there in ... 30 minutes - no, make it 45. Okay... I love you. Bye.' She had been too stunned to react at first, but when he'd finished the call and looked down at her, saying, 'I'm sorry, I have to go, but ... we can finish, if you like, it's up to you,' she began pushing him off her. She remembered actually pushing him out of the bed, and then covering herself completely in the duvet and rolling up into a ball, any thought of ever looking at him or speaking to him again gone, as though he had mutated into some alien creature that wouldn't have understood human speech anyway.

That little episode had put her off going out for weeks. Looking back, she should have taken Holly's advice and started signing then. Then she would never have had the pleasure of that other rotten pig, Julian. The morning after *his* noble turn, she had woken up to nothing but a puddle of vomit where he had lain. As though he'd simply been reduced to a pool of puke during the night. The only other sign that he had ever been there at all was a small strip of purple paper on the floor, torn from the top of the condom packet, a sad little relic of a sad little shag.

She placed her empty mittens together on her lap, making all the woollen rabbits run together in a line. What was the *matter* with them all? What *was the matter* with them?

But thinking about that stuff wasn't doing her any good at all. Yesterday she had been desperate to get in here and do it, and now she was putting herself well and truly out of the mood, and if she blew it now, she'd only go home and within hours just be all ratty and frustrated again. She told herself to get on top of it, and try to think herself back into the horniness that had practically been consuming her the day before. This was one of the annoying things about the sex dole, actually - keeping yourself in the right mood for your appointment. Ironically, the only way she could work her way back into the mood now was to drift back to those trysts of quiet *self*-love to which she would treat herself alone in her room with a bottle of red wine and her Tindersticks CDs. She tried to imagine herself sat on the edge of her bed with her jeans round her knees, a spliff in one hand, herself in the other, lost in that strange crooning of Stuart Staples. It was helping, and she began squeezing her thighs together, imagining her own delicate touch, as the warmth began slowly swirling around below her tummy. So intense and lovely could those moments be, that for a second she found herself questioning whether she really needed anything else, but she knew that as exquisite as her own carefully calibrated caresses were, they were never enough. She opened her eyes, unaware that she had closed them.

The LED counter flicked on another digit, announcing her number. Which was unfortunate, because the only free desk had that woman sitting behind it. That was just typical of her luck. As with her men, so with her 'claimant advisors.' She rose from her chair, anxiously distorting her lips, and crossed to the woman's desk, unaware of the bemused looks from the assortment of men left on the seating behind her.

As she approached the desk and took her seat, Carla peered at the woman from under her well-formed brow, the smooth dome of her forehead only accentuating the wariness lurking in her eyes.

'Hello,' said Carla, as blankly as she could; she never knew exactly what note to strike when signing on. It probably didn't pay to sound too chirpy, to look too happy to be here.

'Good morning', replied Sandra.

Carla stiffened at the accusing tone already present in the woman's voice. So, it was starting already, was it? She took out her SB40 and placed it on the table, and kept her eyes on it, away from the woman, who was scrutinising her with her head tilted slightly to one side, slowly drawing the signing document toward her. But then Carla felt a sudden anger and lifted her eyes to the woman, who held her look for a second, before rising from the desk, taking the SB40 with her.

With the girl's SB40 in her hand, Sandra made her way to the filing cabinet. What could a girl like that be doing here? It was hard not to conclude that some of these girls must be milking the system, though God alone knew what for! She pulled open the drawer, rummaged briefly for the girl's file, slowly closed the drawer, and crossed back to the desk.

Taking the claim sheet from the file, she peered closely at the date alongside the girl's first signature at the top of the document. Three months. She's been coming for three months. Time to ask a few questions, then.

Carla watched as the woman went on staring for far too long at the sheet of paper. She would normally have been signing her name on it by now. Come on, what's the problem? Carla moved her anxious glance quickly from the document to the woman's face.

Sandra caught the girl's eye and began speaking, placing the signing sheet on the desk, but without sliding it across.

'As you've been coming to us now for three months, I'm going to ask you a few questions. So we can see what you've been doing to change your situation.'

Oh, *no*! You *cow*! thought Carla, though she nodded her head and tried to wipe the hostility from her face, clearing her brow, and making her eyes shine amenably, though at the woman's first questions the mask soon gave way to the former unhappy frown.

'Can you give me an outline please of what strategies you've been employing?' said the woman, looking at Carla's file and removing another document from inside.

'Well, I've been ... going to a lot of clubs...' Carla lied, gripping her mittens tightly with one small, white hand.

'What else?' said the woman, her attention fixed on the paper she now held in her hand.

What *was* that she was looking at? Oh, God it was the stupid action plan thing she'd had to write when she applied! What had she written? How could she remember, when she'd had no intention of doing any of it anyway? And the cow was testing her against what she'd put! The *bitch,* the *bitch!!* But think, think, it would only have been all the obvious stuff.

'Well, I've been ... going to a lot of pubs too - you can't go to a club every night, it's too expensive. And ... I do look on the internet as much as I can ... but....'

'But ...?'

'But ... well I think, you can never know who's who on the internet.' She tossed her head to one side, trying to throw a strand of hair away from her face, but finally having to do the job with her fingers.

The woman eyed her for a moment.

'And have you had any approaches...?'

'What? On the internet, you mean?'

'No, generally.'

'Well ... no, no....' Carla lied again.

The woman gave her a bemused look, and paused before responding. 'I'm surprised, actually. I would have thought an attractive girl like you wouldn't have had too much trouble....'

Carla was momentarily panicked. Of course she'd had offers. She floundered for something to say.

'Well, I don't know....' she ran her eyes across the ceiling, 'My nose is pretty awful, maybe that's it,' she said, shrugging her shoulders and bringing her eyes down to her lap, suddenly hating the woman with a new intensity.

Sandra scrutinised the girl sat before her. She decided not to accuse her outright of lying, because it was possible she was telling the truth. But she would keep prodding. There were ways of discouraging a claimant, even if the evidence were insufficient to stop the claim outright.

'I hardly think your nose is the problem. And what happens when you approach *them*?'

Carla was silent, but brought her eyes from her lap to the desk.

'I take it you do *make* approaches?'

'I – I ... try to ... I suppose I find it hard ... I don't know....'

'You would say you're very shy, then?'

'Well, yes, I suppose so.'

'But not too shy to come here.'

Carla frowned up at her. Why are you *doing* this, you horrible bitch?

'Well, no ... it's different to come here.... Easier,' she said, sighing, making a concessionary movement of her eyebrows, while looking off to her side. 'But I *am* trying to *find* something!' she added suddenly, leaning forward.

'I hope you're not finding it too comfortable to just come in here and -'

'NO! No, I don't, believe me! I want something else and I'm *trying* .... But I'm having difficulty -' She suddenly became angry. 'That's what this place is *for, isn't it? For people in difficulty?*' She flashed her eyes in a sudden transport of pleading and anger, raising her voice well above the noise level of the room.

A few heads turned, but it was the silence falling around the room which forced Carla to begin struggling with an impulse to cry. She fixed her eyes on the edge of the desk, and spoke quietly, 'I'm sorry ... but honestly ... I'm trying, it's just ...' She trailed off.

Sandra read the emotion on the girl's trembling face and gave her colleagues an assuring glance, indicating that she had the situation under control. She cast her eyes over the girl's lowered head, saw the pain in the lovely wrinkled brow. Perhaps she did have a problem after all.

'Okay, all right. It seems to me, though, that you lack self-confidence.'

'Maybe....'

'So, I'd like you to consider doing something for me,' said Sandra, reaching in her drawer and pulling out a leaflet. Carla looked up and received the leaflet dubiously.

'I'd like you to consider taking a confidence-building course.'

Carla looked down in dismay at the leaflet handed to her. On the cover was a stupid drawing of a crocodile or alligator or something walking proudly down a street on two legs sticking its chest out and grinning idiotically.

'Just have a read through that, and have a think about it,' said Sandra, taking the signing sheet and writing out the date.

Carla looked up from the illustration, nodding silently, and put the leaflet in her bag, relieved the cow was finally going to let her go. She took the pen and signed her name, adding another signature to the growing column of her previous signings. As she passed the paper over, it looked to her like a bizarre petition collected from a town populated only by clones of herself.

'Number 7, then,' the woman was saying, proffering her a ticket and her SB40. Carla took her eyes from the list of her own signatures, took the ticket and SB40, and began rising from her chair.

'Thank you,' she said quietly, turning from the desk.

Sandra watched the back of the girl's head as she walked off, then quickly looked down at her desk and replaced the girl's claim sheet in her file.

Carla crossed the room and showed her ticket to the security guard at the doors to the staircase, glancing nervously into his face when she wasn't looking at the floor. As she started up the stairs, she knew she wouldn't be able to do it now, she wouldn't go in the cubicle; that woman had simply upset her too much. But she kept going up the stairs anyway, if for no other reason than to prolong the gap between her outburst at the desk and her exit from the building, imagining that would make her look less stupid. As she reached the first landing, she was passed by a woman in her forties, sporting an unmistakable flush on her cheeks. The woman glanced at her almost conspiratorially, causing Carla to gaze after her for a moment. Carla watched her go on descending, and then swung her gaze up the stairs. Well, why *should* she let that bitch downstairs ruin it all for her? She found herself running up the remaining stairs to the first floor landing, the red bobble on her hat swinging madly from side to side. But when she reached the landing, she slowed her pace, and then stopped altogether several steps before the double doors. She slowly raised her shoulders - the preliminary to a gigantic sigh, which she let out with a simultaneous collapse of her face into despair and loss. She bit her lip, turned and ran down the stairs.

Out on the street, she stopped by a waste bin and rummaged in her bag until she drew out the leaflet. With her mittens on, she was unable to tear the paper, so she crumpled it as best she could and stuffed it into the top of the overflowing receptacle, leaving the distorted graphic of the reptile's face - now more insane and grotesque than ever - staring proudly up into the blank, white sky.

SIX

Porn, then - since there was no wonderful life-enhancing life-partner immediately forthcoming. Porn, then - since the lovely long-term girlfriend was nowhere to be seen. Porn, then - since a nice casual affair was not in the offing. Porn, then - since there was no hope soon of even a brief romp with some random little darling. Since there was no hope - porn. In the absence of women - porn. His knob craved porn, and porn it would get, served up fresh from a crisp brown paper bag, hand-picked and bussed-in from the choice, rain-washed fields of Soho.

Like feeding a dog, thought Lawrence, as he tipped the video out onto the coffee table, deliberately letting it fall from such a height that it bounced and clattered several times before coming to rest on the edge of the table. He stood over the box, allowing the harsh, lurid cover to insult and affront his sensibilities. He stared down at the mob of naked, unerotic, desensitised, balloon-breasted, snake-dicked, shaven-pussied clowns on the cover and suddenly had faint hope of finding anything inside that might accord with his own personal psycho-sexual soft spots.

He read again the inane title and tag line. The tag line particularly was a stream of cretinous, barely literate piss. Cretinous was the word for it, all right. The best word to describe modern porn. He thought of the seventies porn mags he'd found in a hedge as a twelve-year-old, and which he'd kept for many years afterwards. In those days the women had generally been shown as aloof, unattainable beings of promise and mystery, and the accompanying texts, though still written by tossers, were at least languid, atmospheric, always somehow just about mindful of the respect due to the women as individuals. Whereas, today, the punters were simply exhorted to 'pump' their 'fat cocks' in the girls' 'sopping twats', while the poor girls themselves were photographed starkly and flatly holding open their everything with both hands for the world to see. The difference between these two eras of porn, it occurred to Lawrence, despite gains in equality for women in other areas, was that in the old days, the inference had been that beautiful women were something to look up to, out-of-reach treasures to aspire to attain, whereas now they were to be looked down upon, used and walked over, and sold by increasingly barbaric morons to an increasingly barbaric and moronic audience. An audience he was part of. Well, so be it. The cock was a two-edged sword. In the company of a willing woman, it could be a shining lance (if he remembered correctly), Rabelais' 'valiant champion', but without ... it was nothing but a maleficent slug to drag you kicking and screaming through degenerate hinterlands ... You could try fighting it ... but you can't fight the life-force... and without the hole – ah, the fucking crudeness of it all – without the hole there was only, *only* misdirection. And often the result would be the trading in of a couple of tenners for exactly the kind of piece of hideous shit which now graced the corner of his coffee table.

He went into the kitchen and put the kettle on. Waiting for the water to boil, he leaned against the fridge and stared at the photo of himself and Jason pinned to the door, the pair of them gurning out from a ring of band flyers and postcards. The fucker should've stayed here. What use was he to him stuck over in Seattle? And if he *had* to fuck off to the States, why couldn't he have moved out properly, instead of continuing to rent his old room for storage? Rather than a roomful of boxes and dismantled motorbikes, there might have been a pretty student installed in there by now, receiving house-calls from a coterie of delightful visitors. But no, the selfish bastard wanted to keep his 'base in London', bless him.

Lawrence impatiently flicked off the kettle switch and poured not-quite-boiling water over the teabag in the chipped mug before him. Dropping a teaspoon in the mug, he picked it up and crossed to the cupboard, taking out a large plate which he then carried out to the living room. Placing his tea and the plate on the coffee table, he felt for the lighter in his pocket, brought it out and reached for the lurid black box on the edge of the table. The cover on that fucking video had to *go*.

He sipped his tea, watching as the flames ate the straining studs and whores, converting them into a heap of curling black shreds piling up on the white plate. He held one corner of the glossy wraparound cover in one hand, idly turning the miniature fall of the damned as small slow flames of hell lapped at cock and vulva alike.

The phone rang. Unusual behaviour for the bastard; it was generally such a taciturn fucker. With his free hand he reached for the receiver.

'Hello', said Lawrence, still twisting the burning paper over the plate.

'Hi, Lawrence? Eet's Sophia.'

He felt a thrill of delight, not caring that she was one of his declared platonics; it was just good to hear a friendly female voice. And the husky Italian accent was not exactly unwelcome either.

'My God, Sophia! How are you?'

'I'm fine, but why 'aven't you called me? You 'aven't called me for ages!'

That was true, but how could he tell her that she made him feel ... unmasculine because of her failure to respond to the pass he had made at her once when she was between boyfriends, and that, as his stretch in the wilderness dragged on, that feeling only became worse.

'No, I know, I'm sorry ... I've just been burying myself in work,' he said, staring at the burning porn falling into the plate.

'Look, I'm up in Tufnell Park right now, and eef you're not doing anything, I thought maybe I could drop een on you on my way 'ome - I mean, I'd really like to see what you been up to. I mean, it's been months since I seen your work!'

Fuck, it would be good to see her. And if he did feel like a eunuch in her presence, well ... he'd just put up with it, the hell with it. And you never knew ... something might have changed with her.

'Definitely! That would be completely marvellous!'

'Okay, I'll be there about 8.'

'Great!' he smiled, 'See you at eight, then. That'll give me an hour to brush some of the tumbleweed out of the living room!'

'Okay!' she laughed, hanging up.

He replaced the receiver and let the final fragment of paper fall from his fingers, watching impassively as the baby-smooth pudenda of the final blond porn star turned to carbon in the plate.

Lawrence brushed Sophia's left cheek with his lips and brought them around to her right, his mouth passing an inch above hers as she turned her head to receive the second half of a double-kiss continental greeting. His senses swimming in the scent of her perfume, he closed the door behind her as she stepped into the hall, shaking out her dark shoulder-length hair.

'You're looking good,' she said, flashing him a smile as they walked down the hall. Lawrence felt good too, but he told himself that she always said stuff like that; it didn't mean anything. Still, it seemed appropriate to say something charming back, and anyway he wanted to.

'And your own appearance is ... as devastating as ever....' he said, showing her into the living room, with a grandiloquent gesture of his arm. 'So what were you doing in Tufnell Park ?' he asked as she sat down.

'Looking at some property ... Anyway, that's boring. Boring stuff.' She took out a packet of Gauloise and lit up. 'It's so good to *see* you, Lawrence! Why 'ave you been 'iding away? I've missed you, you know...'

'Now, don't talk nonsense, my dear,' said Lawrence, filling his voice with a mock suavity.

'No, I 'ave,' she said, looking down, and then intently up into his eyes. 'You know how to make a person laugh. That's important. *Important.*'

'Well, it's extremely fucking sweet of you to say so. Thank you,' he smiled, inclining his head in a show of exaggerated courtesy. He sat down opposite her and lit a cigarette.

She laughed, and hit her thigh. 'You're perfect, Lawrence! *Perfect*!'

Sometimes her amusement seemed more than his little witticisms warranted, and he had to remind himself that people from the continent, especially the south, often found his particular style of undermining convention startlingly delightful, because they'd never encountered anything like it back home. But he wasn't complaining:

to bring forth such a peal of laughter from a good-looking girl always worked a power of good for one's mental health. Still, the flow of compliments was already beginning to do his head in, because tantalisingly sweet as they were, he mourned their lack of sexual motive. And he was bitterly annoyed that it bothered him, because it clouded his reception of Sophia's genuine affection for him. In short, his sexual ego rebelled against the friendship. His sexual ego: what a piece of shit!

'Look, do you want some wine? I've got some red open,' he said, making for the kitchen.

'Ah, I can't stay long ... so -'

'Sophia. Drink a glass of wine with me,' called Lawrence firmly from the kitchen.

'Oh, so you are ordering me, are you?'

'You bet your sweet Mediterranean *ass*, toots!' called Lawrence in a voice granite with pseudo-Hollywood macho, as a cupboard door swung open in the kitchen.

'Well, okay, then,' she laughed, and drew on her cigarette.

There was a muffled thud from the kitchen.

'*Fuck!*'

'Are you all right?' cried Sophia, jumping up from the sofa and running through, to find a wincing Lawrence rubbing his head.

'Yeah, yeah, I just thought I'd smash my head on the cupboard door. Part of my daily routine, actually. Force of habit. I've been thinking of giving it up but -'

'Shh, stop, stop,' she said, laughing, reaching up her hand to his head.

He saw her fingers rise quickly through his vision and felt them make contact with his forehead. He almost closed his eyes at their touch, so profoundly and instantly was he transported by the feel of them to some better, more worthwhile plane of being. It was an ersatz higher plane of being, he knew, because she didn't want him. Still, he wished he could drift forever under her touch, become simply a forehead under her fingertips. But the blood was already flowing mercilessly into his cock. And he was under friendship orders. He inched away from her, and as her fingers fell away, he smiled at her and filled her wine-glass.

As he handed it to her, she was still frowning up at his forehead. 'You might get a bruise. That would be a *shame.*'

'You think so? The condition of my forehead is hardly of much ... consequence to anyone, is it?'

'Come on,' she said, suddenly annoyed, staring at him with big, accusing eyes. She moved her gaze back to his brow and smiled. 'You know, you 'ave a nice forehead. What you can see of eet under those long curls! But they're nice too,' she laughed, quickly ruffling the dark unruly locks hanging in front of his eyes, before returning to the living room.

What was she doing? Well, nothing, probably. Don't for Christ's sake become seduced by the idea she means anything by it. He followed her through to the lounge.

'So when you goin' to show me your new *scultura?* It better be good seence you been 'iding away from me to do eet.'

'Well, we can go and have a look now, if you like.'

'*Bene!* Yes, Yes!'

Lawrence unlocked the patio door as Sophia crossed to his side and took his arm. As they stepped out into the cold dark garden, Lawrence surrendered himself to the welcome proximity of the girl's side, to the safe, enclosing pressure of her small hand in the crook of his arm, and again began fighting the impression there was something in the air.

'Mind out for all this crap out here. There's a ton of wood debris and stuff that I use for raw materials sometimes.'

'Okay, I'll step where you step.'

They reached the long work-shed at the bottom of the garden. Sophia drew her coat around her as Lawrence opened the padlock and ushered her inside. As he closed the door behind them, they found themselves in freezing darkness, breathing in the earthy smell of clay and mortar. Facing them, silhouetted against the dim brown light of the sky beyond the windows, reared up a large black shape, roughly analogous with a human figure.

'Oh, my world....' breathed Sophia.

'Hang on, I'll get the light,' said Lawrence feeling for the switch.

The small workshop flooded with light, revealing a life-size tortured figure. Sophia just had time to make out what looked like the hideous snarling head of a dog growing from its loins, just made out the dog-thing's jaws tearing viciously at the figure's right hand, before the bulb exploded, showering the clay with glass and plunging the room back into darkness.

'*Madonna mia!*' shrieked Sophia, instinctively pressing her body to Lawrence's for protection, the image of the dog's hollow black eyes dancing on her retinas.

'Christ, I'm sorry, are you okay? It's the bloody light circuit in here....'

'I'm fine, don't worry...'

'I think there's a torch in here somewhere....' He rummaged about for a while, before giving up. 'No, it's hopeless ... I suppose we'd ...' He trailed off as he turned once more to the agonised black figure.

There was a pause.

Sophia spoke, gripping his arm. 'Anyway, Lawrence, Lawrence, eet's wonderful ... *wonderful!* But so *dark.*'

Lawrence was silent.

Sophia peered up at his silhouetted tousled head as it stared across at the other tousled head opposite, also black against the brown night. The icy air of the shed seemed to hit a deeper register.

'Lawrence ... you are very sad eenside ... aren't you?' she said softly. The head turned and peered down at her. It seemed to look down at the floor, and then back to its dark clay counterpart.

She reached up her hand and began gently stroking his hair.

With the soft mesmerising touch of her fingertips he felt once more consoled beyond all belief, felt his spine shudder with pleasure, and the longer it went on, the less possible it seemed that she could mean it as anything other than a sexual overture.

He looked down at the floor of the shed, and shut his eyes, relishing the feel of her fingers in his hair but readying himself to bring it to an end. He took a breath, and spoke. 'What are you doing?'

'Touching you.'

'Why are you touching me?'

'Because I love you.'

'As a friend.'

'As a friend.'

'Then don't touch me.' He gently removed her hand from his head.

'Why?'

'Well ... ahem, decorum won't permit me to say ...'

'What? I don' understand ...'

'All right, look. I'm sick.'

'How?'

'Because you're my friend and I want to, er ... do the old *it* with you. Or rather, *I* don't, but the dog does. Look, you stroked my hair so sweetly that I have ... well, I have ... forgive me but I have an, AHEM, an erection now. And you don't want to give me one of those, do you?'

'Well, no, I don' look at you een a sexual way.'

'There you *are*, then.'

'I'm sorry if I upset you. I wanted to 'elp you. Because I care about you!' she said, suddenly angry.

'I know, I know Sophia, and it means more to me than I can say, but –'

'Sex isn't everything, you know.

'Sure, but unfortunately it's still fucking *some*thing. And around girls like you I have to act like my balls have been cut off - I mean, that's what you *require* of me - it's a job of work, I can tell you, and you know - that's actually why I haven't fucking called you -'

'That's why you 'aven't called me?'

'Yep!'

'Oh, Lawrence...'

'And the worst part is ... it's not like I have a particular thing for you or anything.... If it weren't you in here, if it were some other girl, I'd want to knob her just as much. It's just meaningless! A terrifying, meaningless fucking *hunger*.'

There was another silence. Despite what he had said about touching him, she couldn't help but put her hand on his arm.

'You shouldn't feel so bad about eet. Eet's just natural -'

'Yeah? Then that makes it even worse! I have a problem with fucking *nature*! I've got a big fight on my hands!'

'You just need to meet a nice girl, that's all.'

The sentence suddenly made Sophia seem very far away.

'Well, Christ knows, I'm trying.' He looked down at the pitch black floor, heard the crunch of tiny glass fragments beneath his shifting feet. 'Anyway ... we've stood here long enough talking about my shit ... let's go inside.'

'Okay, but, Lawrence, let me tell you something. There is a ... there is a real beauty about you, you know, a beautiful look in your eye - and a girl will respond to eet one day. I might have, if I 'ad first met you in a different situation, but ... I was with someone then, and so you and me grew together only as friends.'

Lawrence knew that he should have felt a lot better on hearing this, but in fact he felt worse, and was alarmed to realise he didn't know why. It was as if his mood had simply come adrift from the story-line. He began to panic. Fucking hell, get on top of it, get on top of it.

'Thanks ... thanks, Sophia, but you don't have to -'

'Look, I mean eet, you fucking asshole genius!'

He gazed at the silhouetted oval of her face, an abstract blank mask in the darkness. He thought of a nun's habit with nothing but a black hole for a face, some terrifying shit from some crap he'd seen on TV as a kid, almost felt himself go, but forced himself to keep in with the track of the conversation.

'I'm not a genius.'

'An asshole, though. Look, don't worry, the girls will come, the girls will come.'

'Bless you, Sophia,' he said quietly, and began leading her out of the shed and into the garden, trying to ride out the wave of panic in his chest.

The anxiety had eased a little once they'd regained the warmth and light of the flat and chatted about other things. And he'd enjoyed listening to her stories about the two arseholes in her office. She'd liked the sculpture, that was for sure, going on about it again at the front door, and he was glad he'd gone back and fished out the pencil study to thank her for putting up with all the horse shit in the shed. He thought again of the way she had held it like a piece of precious parchment in her hands, and how she had looked up disbelievingly when he'd told her it was hers if she wanted it. And after she'd protested that she couldn't take such a treasure from him, and he'd told her she wasn't leaving without it, they'd gone back into the flat to look for something to put it in for the journey. And then finally at the front door she had given him the hug she should never have given him because later it was the memory of that hug that made him abandon the vague plan they'd made to meet again soon, because he was so fucked-up he wanted a hug like that to go on forever, he wanted all or nothing, and since all was obviously not a goer, then nothing it would be, and nothing was what he now held in his hand as he leaned toward the VCR, nothing, in the form of a dismal, black cassette full of porn.

In the absence of Sophia's sexual interest - porn.

Porn, then - in the presence of Sophia's platonic love.

SEVEN

The group of teenagers stood in a loose circle in front of the newsagents, a sullen mass of baggy sportswear and stooped shoulders. Exhaled cigarette and cannabis smoke mixed together and drifted up into the sky, fresh from a combined assault on soft young lungs.

Loz, smaller than the others, passed the spliff up to Pickford, whose cheeks were redder than usual in the cold mid-day air. As Pickford snatched it from him, Loz peered up at him quizzically, his face announcing the imminent formation of a question.

Pickford inhaled heavily, looking at Loz with unfriendly eyes. 'What?'

'Davie ... I was thinkin'... how *fit* are the birds gonna be down that sex dole?'

'Well, they're gonna be *well* fit, aren't they.'

'How do *you* fuckin' know?' laughed a tall, callow youth, casting his eyes round the others.

'Stands to fackin' reason, Kinton.'

'No, it doesn't.'

'Course it fackin' does. Look, they're there to do a job, yeah?'

'So?'

'And that job is to fack, right?'

'Yeah, so?'

'So it stands to reason they're only gonna let fit birds work there, yeah? Fit birds that people are gonna want to fack.'

'Like fuck. The fuckin' sex dole is for sad twats, right? And sad twats'll fuck anythin.' So you can fuckin' forget about the birds being "well fit", Pickford. What? You think you're just gonna walk in there an' shag fuckin' Jordan or somethin'?'

'Yeah, Davie,' said Loz, 'Pezza's brother said his mate went and just got some fat old slag.'

'What does Pezza's brother fackin' know about anythin'?' snapped Pickford, giving Loz a hard sideways shove.

A rangy hooded youth spoke up. 'Hang about though, yeah? My cousin's on the sex dole down Putney. Says the birds can be quite tasty.'

'See, Kinton?' sneered Pickford.

'Yeah, well, you're not in fuckin' Putney, you're 'ere - with Pezza's brother's mate's fat old slags!'

'You'd better fackin' shut up or your head's goin on the pavement again. Remember the last time, y'barstard!'

'Yeah, man,' said the hooded youth, 'It's his first time down the sex dole and you just wanna ruin it for 'im, man!'

'It's his first fuckin' time, *period.*' muttered Kinton, turning his head to the street.

Pickford pretended not to hear, loath to draw the group's attention to the insult. Instead, he slapped Loz's face, and snapped his fingers.

'Come on, give us a fag, then, you little tit! It's time I headed up.'

Loz put his hand to his stinging cheek, and proffered his cigarette packet to Pickford.

Lighting up, Pickford smiled at the others. 'One last cigarette for the condemned man,' he said, exhaling through his nostrils, to a cheer from one or two of the group, Loz's cheer sounding more dutiful than enthusiastic.

'What *are* you talkin' about, Pickford?' sneered Kinton, screwing his eyes shut and shaking his head.

'Kinton, when *you* go dahn the sex dole, we all know which cubicle you'll be fackin' goin' in... don't we, lads?' giggled Pickford.

'The fuckin' poof's one!' chortled Loz, as the group's laughter fell away to leave his voice hanging in the air. His face fell.

Kinton regarded him evenly. 'I'll remember that for the next time you, me and a baseball bat find ourselves alone in a dark alley, you stupid fuckin' little twat.'

Loz looked to Pickford for support, but Pickford avoided his gaze, glad to have Kinton off his back.

'Awright, I'm away, then, lads,' grinned Pickford as he walked off, the odd hand clapping him on the back.

'Give 'er one from me, Dave!' called the hooded youth above cries of 'Fackin' give it to 'er!' and 'Get stuck in, man!' Kinton's remark was lost in the shouting. Loz screamed, *'Fuck 'er brains out, Davie!!'*

Pickford walked off, jabbing the air with his little finger and thrusting his hips in mock-copulation.

'I see this is your first time, Mr ... Pickford,' said Sandra, her grey-bobbed head facing the monitor.

'Yeah....' said Pickford, sitting back in his chair and lacing his fingers together. She turned her eyes on him.

'I suppose you were told at your first interview what to expect -'

'Yeah, I was, yeah,' interrupted Pickford, impatient to be on his way up the stairs.

Sandra eyed him sternly and continued.

'- but I will just go over one or two points with you again before you go up. Firstly, you must do everything your facilitator asks of you, is that understood?'

'Yeah,' said Pickford, shifting in his seat. He wanted to go up the stairs. He'd just about sat through enough fackin' lectures from these barstards.

'Secondly, there is to be no oral contact whatsoever between you and your facilitator. Is that also understood?'

'Yeah,' said Pickford, glancing around the room.

'Are you listening?'

'Yeah, course,' said Pickford, turning to her.

'Thirdly, you are required to wear the protection provided by the facilitator. You are not to use your own protection. Is that clear?'

'Yeah.' Fackinell, turn it up, you fackin' old trout.

'Finally, there is a strict time limit, as you know. You're allotted twenty minutes alone with the facilitator, after which time you must quit the cubicle. I must stress that this time includes the time it takes you to get dressed and undressed.'

'Yeah, sure.'

She took a timed and dated ticket from the dispenser and handed it to him, saying, 'Very well, then. Show this to the guard at the door, make your way to the first floor, go through the double doors, and you'll come out onto a long corridor. Go to cubicle 6.'

'Right,' said Pickford, taking his SB40 and rising from the desk. As he crossed the room he caught the eye of a guy with a tie and glasses standing behind one of the desks. It was that miserable preachy barstard from the interview. What was he fackin' lookin' at? What are you fackin' lookin' at, you barstard?

Williams looked away and headed into the staff office as Pickford showed his ticket to the guard and pushed his way through the double doors. Feeling the oppressive atmosphere of the signing area fall away as he came into the stairwell, he peered up the stairs with a racing heart, gripped the handrail and launched himself up the steps, taking three at a time.

But what if Kinton was right? What if it *was* just full of old slappers? He slowed his pace. But Fennel's mate in Putney had said the birds were pretty fit. A sudden montage of all the girls from his favourite porn magazines cascaded before his eyes, and he increased his speed, gaining the landing in seconds, despite the awkward swelling in his trousers.

Right, then. Through the double doors we *go.*

He found himself in a long, silent corridor. It seemed hard to believe that people were actually facking on the other side of them doors. But here we go, here's number 6.

He stood for a moment before the door, adjusting his baseball cap and straightening his sleeves. He knocked on the door. It fackin' better not be some fat old slapper in there.

A faint 'Come in' sounded from within the cubicle, and he opened the door. Stepping inside and closing the door behind him, it was with some relief that he regarded the woman standing in the middle of the room. Well, she wasn't fat, anyway. Blond. He liked that. Bit old maybe. But nah, she was okay. Probably younger than Madonna. Teeth stuck out a bit. And her eyes were a bit baggy. Thin, though, with a nice arse, and fackinell, her tits were well wicked. You could already see one tit completely naked where her robe was open. Nah, she'd do, he'd be all right here. Kinton could fack off.

'Hiya,' she smiled, undoing her robe, and throwing it over the back of the chair.

'Awright?' he mumbled, lowering his head, suddenly losing his confidence at the sound of her voice, thrown by its revelation of her as a person. The abrupt exposure of her naked body also threw him unexpectedly off-track; somewhere inside him, though he'd never admit it, he was totally unprepared for the three-dimensional reality of the naked female form. But the hesitation only lasted a moment, and when she held her hand out to him he crossed toward her with a bow-legged swagger, throwing his head back and flinging his baseball cap onto the bed.

Elaine watched the youth approach. Probably the boy's first time at a centre. Oh, well, here we go. As he came up to her, she circled his waist with her arms and rested her cheek against his in a welcoming preliminary. In putting her cheek to his like this she was aware she was going beyond the recommended guidelines on head contact, but found it a useful, harmless substitute for kissing.

But Pickford was in any case practically oblivious to the blond head pressed to his as he stared hungrily down at the woman's body, his jaw hanging stupidly open. This was it then! The moment of fackin' truth! He put his hand to her breast, feeling its shape for a moment before squeezing it hard. Fackin' yes! This was it! His first fackin' tit. He began mauling it relentlessly, feeling his dick expand with each squash and squish. He brought up his other hand, pressing her other breast hard into her rib-cage, ignoring her discomfort. He was feeling a bit dizzy and it was fackin' wicked! Oh, yeah, let's feel her arse, now for her fackin' arse! Oh, yeah, yeah, yeah, that's fackin' *sweet -'*

'Ow!'

Elaine prised his hand off her bottom and pulled away.

'Not so rough!' she said, scowling, and turned to the cabinet by the bed, opening the drawer. 'Come on, get undressed. You haven't got all day, you know,' she said, clearly annoyed, slapping the condom packet into his palm.

'All right, all right, don't lose your temper.'

'Don't get cheeky with me or I'll have you thrown out.'

Pickford reddened and looked at the floor, swallowing. But as she turned to the bed and bent over to straighten the sheet, one glance at her behind was enough to send a big surly grin spreading across his face. Fackin' look at *that!* For a moment, he almost wished the others were here to see it with him, to see what he'd be gettin'. But nah, he didn't want those twats in here. This was all for fackin' *him*. He bent down quickly and began unlacing his brand trainers with trembling fingers.

With a frantic, broken rhythm, Pickford pounded into the woman lying disinterestedly beneath him, trying to put out of his mind the look on her face when she'd had to put the johnny on for him. She'd made him feel a right twat, made him feel like he was back in fackin' school, looking at him like that. And now it just felt like he was shagging that Miss Preed slag. And it shouldn't be like this.

Still, he'd only just got inside her, and the feeling of her round his cock *was* pretty fackin' sweet, so maybe if he concentrated on some really fit bird, and just looked at her tits he'd forget about that fackin' maths teacher slag.

He looked down at her breasts, and tried to think of the girl on the cover of that month's *FHM.* However, the visual stimulus of Elaine's large dark nipple was suddenly too much, and with the mental image of Miss Preed throwing a blackboard rubber at his head, he felt the onset of orgasm.

Aw, fackin' no way, no way.

He squirted once, twice, three times. He heard himself emit a single embarrassing high-pitched squeak, and dropped his head slowly to the pillow, his body wracked by the dying shudders of his premature ejaculation. He rested his full weight on the woman beneath him, and stared at the wall, fighting his embarrassment.

It was this slag's fault, this old cow lying underneath him!

And then he felt her hand on his back. She was caressing him. What ... what was she fackin' doing that for? He blinked in confusion, keeping his cheek pressed to the pillow.

Elaine suspected that it was not only the boy's first session at a sex-benefit centre, it was probably his first session anywhere, and she felt sorry for him now he had revealed his ineptitude in virtually every aspect of the sexual act.

'Come on, you've got time yet.... You can have another one,' she said, ruffling his short blond hair.

This time he felt better. He'd been bangin' into this bitch now for well over ten minutes, and she was screwing her eyes up and gritting her fackin' teeth which was a good sign. Had to be. It meant she knew she had a fackin' dick in her! And that was what it was all *about*! All right, you're gonna feel it some *more*, darlin'! I'm gonna go as hard as I fackin' *can!*

'Can you just ... shift your weight off my leg, please.... You're digging into me with your hip, yeah?'

'Oh, right, yeah....' Pickford eased up his irregular, but frantic thrusting, moved his weight around slightly, but not enough for Elaine's liking, and continued bucking away. Elaine decided to just ride it out; a glance at the clock on the wall told her that his time was up any minute anyway.

'Try to finish now, yeah? Time's almost up.'

Pickford made no response, other than to keep slamming into her as violently as he could. He had trapped her leg again with his hip, but she managed to change her position slightly and ease the discomfort. She glanced at the clock.

'Okay, that's it,' she said, giving his back a tap.

But he ignored her and kept up his vigorous, awkward ramming, burying his face in the pillow.

'I said, that's *it!* Now will you stop please?' she shouted, slapping his back hard with the flat of her hand. He kept going. She swivelled her eyes to the big pink ear vibrating at the side of her head. The fucking little *bastard!*

'Hey!' she shouted, making a fist and jabbing him in the ribs, '*Hey!*'

But he kept on.

Right, she was getting Brian in. That's what he was there for. To do the fighting.

She reached her arm over her head to the small panel over the headboard and stabbed the large red alarm button with her finger. Then she spoke low and rapidly into Pickford's ear.

'All right, you little sod, the security guard's on his way.'

But even this wasn't enough, and Pickford's clumsy hard thrusts continued unabated. Elaine hung on, delivering the occasional jab to his side. Come on Brian, for fuck's sake!

Pickford continued to pound into Elaine for all he was worth.

The door flew open and a large figure in a brown uniform came running into the room.

'All right, OFF!' shouted the guard, grabbing Pickford by the shoulders. Pickford lifted his straining red face from the pillow, 'Hang on, mate, just give me a minute, yeah?'

'Get off her now, you little bastard!' replied the guard, gripping Pickford round the waist with one hand, holding him under the shoulder with the other, and pulling him backwards, up, off, and out of Elaine. As Pickford's jerking body was lifted from her, Elaine saw his penis disengage and then pulse suddenly, turning the end of the sheath an opaque white as the guard lifted him round, his legs kicking the air, and dumped him groaning on the floor. Landing painfully on his trainers, Pickford underwent the dying spasm of his orgasm under the outraged gaze of Elaine and the guard, clenching his teeth and screwing up his eyes as his pelvis jolted out one final convulsion, before huddling himself to the wall, one quivering hand hovering over his spent loins, the other pressed to his back. He hung his head, breathing loudly through his nose.

'Are you all right?' asked the guard of Elaine.

'Yeah, yeah, I'm fine, Brian ... thanks. But you'd better get somebody up here. Get Sandra.'

'You wanna watch it, mate!' moaned Pickford in a high, breaking voice, his face bitterly contorted.

'Shut up and get dressed. And get that contraceptive in the bin now! And don't spill anything. What was he doing to you, Elaine?'

'He just wouldn't stop, yeah? I mean he wasn't trying to hurt me or anything. Anyway, look, you'd better get Sandra up here.'

Keeping his eyes on Pickford as the shaking red-faced youth struggled to remove the clouded condom from his shrinking glans, Brian punched a combination into his walkie-talkie and waited.

'Yeah, Sandra. Can you come up to 6? We've got an incident. Okay, see you in a sec.'

Elaine pulled on her robe and stared at Pickford as he stepped shakily to the pedal-bin and dropped the fouled latex inside.

'Come on, get dressed,' demanded Brian. 'The advisor is coming up.'

Pickford bent down and reached for his underpants, watched by Elaine as she sat down on the edge of the bed and folded her arms. She sighed and looked up at the guard.

'Anything good on the telly this afternoon, Brian?'

'Nah, not really. I've got the racing on,' said Brian, his eyes on Pickford as the youth picked up his trousers.

The door opened, admitting a grey middle-aged woman. Sandra took two steps into the room and surveyed the scene before her, glancing from Elaine to Brian. Then she ran her eyes over the youth pulling on his trousers, instantly removing her gaze from the lad's white underwear, repelled by the graphic reminder of the reality of what went on on the first floor. She hated coming up here. Downstairs she could pretend to herself none of this filth actually happened. She fixed her eyes on Elaine.

'What happened then, Elaine?'

'He wouldn't stop, Sandra. He went over time and he wouldn't stop, so I had to get Brian in.'

'I had to pull him off her,' threw in Brian.

Sandra turned her gaze on Pickford.

'Is that true?'

His face twisting in agitation, Pickford looked off to his side, and shifted from foot to foot, his T-shirt in his hand.

'I said, is that *true*?'

'Yes!' spat Pickford at the floor, thrusting his head forward violently.

'Perhaps you can tell us why you didn't stop when you were told?'

'I dunno ... I just couldn't, right?' said Pickford, in his agitation snorting like an animal, his eyes boring into the floor.

'Couldn't...? Or wouldn't?'

'No. I *couldn't!*'

'Well, the point is academic, in any case. Your entitlement to benefit will cease forthwith. Now put on the rest of your clothes, please -'

'What?! Now 'ang about -' cried Pickford, wildly flinging his head round to face Sandra.

'I SAID put on the rest of your clothes. As soon as he's finished dressing, Brian, escort him from the building,' said Sandra, turning to the door, where she halted for a moment and addressed Pickford one last time.

'You should have paid attention to what I said downstairs,' she said and exited the room, as the guard took a step toward Pickford.

Close to tears, Pickford threw his T-shirt on the floor, shouting, 'Fackin' no *way*, yeah?'

As the guard picked up the T-shirt and stuffed it in Pickford's arms, the tears came.

Elaine jumped up from the bed and walked quickly to the door. Exiting to the corridor, she soon caught up with Sandra. The older woman stopped and turned.

'Sandra, can I have a word...?'

'What is it?'

'Was this the boy's first session?'

'Yes, as a matter of fact.'

'Thought so.'

'Why?'

'Listen, I think maybe we're being a bit harsh, yeah?'

Sandra sighed. 'Come on Elaine, his behaviour was totally unacceptable.'

'Look, he's crying his guts out in there. Give him another chance, yeah?'

Sandra stared at her. '*You* pushed the button.'

'He's just inexperienced, that's all. Please, Sandra. Do it for *me*.'

Pickford, now fully dressed, sat on the edge of the bed wiping his nose with the back of his hand, the guard standing over him, as Sandra and Elaine re-entered the cubicle.

'All right, Brian, you can go now, thank you,' said Sandra.

The guard gave Pickford a bemused look and headed for the door.

'Well,' said Sandra, looking hard at Pickford, 'It's been decided to give you a second chance in view of this being your first session here, and your being new to the ... system. We'll let this incident pass, but any repeat of this behaviour or any other disruptive conduct will result in immediate suspension of your benefit, do you understand?'

Pickford nodded his head sulkily.

'And I think you owe Elaine here an apology.'

Pickford raised his flushed head. 'Yeah, I'm sorry, yeah?'

'Just make sure you do as you're told next time,' said Elaine.

Pickford nodded, his eyes drifting from Elaine to the floor.

'Now, come on. Out,' ordered Sandra, glaring at Pickford, 'You've taken up far too much time as it is with this palaver.'

Coming to the end of the corridor, Pickford pushed through the double doors. Barstards. And he wasn't fackin' sorry, neither. Why should he be fackin' *sorry*? It was only fackin' natural to keep goin' to the end, and if the sex dole stopped you before you were ready then the way he saw it, it was the fackin' sex dole's fault, not his. Or the fault of the bird for not being fit enough. Yeah, it was that bird's fault and *he'd* had to fackin' say sorry to *her*.

Still, he'd had his first fack, though, and despite all the ... bother, he was *deffo* up for a return match, so he'd better play it their fackin' way in future. And anyway, at the end of the day, naffin' in life was perfect, was it?

He leaned into the double doors on the ground floor and crossed through the signing area, glancing over at the signing desks. The fackin' old bag was back at her desk, givin' verbal to some other punter. Pickford's gaze drifted on until he found himself looking directly into a pair of spectacles trained on him. That fackin' tight arsehole from the interview was looking at him again! Barstard, fackin' *barstard!* Pickford switched his eyes to the carpet, and crossed quickly to the street door.

Outside, Pickford looked down the street in the direction of the newsagents, but where the others were supposed to be waiting for him there now stood only a pair of schoolgirls. Where the fack *were* the useless twats? Maybe they were waiting inside. They'd fackin' *better* be waiting inside.

As he set off at a pace down the street, he was assailed from behind by a loud 'OI!' He resisted the impulse to turn around. The barstard couldn't be talkin' to *him*. The barstard better *not* be talkin' to him.

'OI, PICKFORD, you *sad, sad fackin' wankaah!*'

Pickford whirled round to find himself facing a crowd of laughing youths. At the centre stood Kinton, bent double with laughter, and next to him, the source of the shouted insult: Turner. Around Turner's neck clung a beautiful girl Pickford had never seen before. The insults rained down, pouring from jeering, snarling mouths, but the real pain came from the sight of the girl's fresh, young, laughing face, her blond hair flying back in the wind.

EIGHT

Lawrence's back lay exposed to the gloom of the bedroom as he slept, the duvet having been thrown partly off during the rigours of a fitful sleep. His head was twisted to one side, his face calm as he breathed quietly. One arm projected out of the side of the bed, affected by an occasional tic of dream-movement. Though he dreamed, he dreamed with all his intelligence, and so exhaustingly he might as well have been awake.

On a bus, moving slowly through the London rain, he sits facing perpendicular to the direction of travel, leaning forward, his elbows on his knees, casting his eyes around the vehicle. The usual London mix, a multicultural haul of mothers, students and suited professionals. A beautiful girl sits toward the rear. He watches her, unable to take his eyes off her, trying to work out the secret geometry of her face - she catches him, looking him severely in the eye. He looks away. Then waits a moment, pretending to read a safety notice on the wall, before cautiously looking round at her again. He's safe; she's looking out of the window - but almost instantly she turns, catching him a second time. She looks away immediately, disgusted. He looks away too, ashamed, and the bus trundles on to the sound of the heavy rain hammering the roof and the electric whine of the windscreen-wipers. Despite his shame, he is unable to keep his eyes away from the girl and looks round again, only to see that she has got up and is moving down the aisle toward him, head up, looking ahead. She'll be getting off at the next stop, then, but at least she'll pass him. However, when she reaches him, she stops, and in one continuous, flowing movement, turns round, bends over, pulls down her jeans and, with one swing of her bottom, brushes Lawrence's face with her white pants, plunging him for a second into a soft, white vortex of delicious contour infused with a cocktail of heady scents, machine-washed and musty, before following the movement through so as to place herself facing the direction she has come, at the same time pulling up her jeans once more, and then making her way back along the aisle to her seat at the back of the bus. She flops down, her hands in her lap, and lets her head fall against the window, resuming her impassive gaze out at the street. Lawrence is aware his breathing is coming in short, broken gasps. The rain has turned into a thunderous barrage of hail and the bus is stationary, stranded between stops. Three or four of the other passengers are staring at him as though it were *he* that had committed some outrage. The woman next to him, a mother, is particularly nervous of him. He looks to the girl in her seat at the rear of the bus. A lock of her lovely hair has fallen across her face. She sighs heavily, brushes it back with her hand and goes on staring out of the window at the hail. It's coming down even harder now, striking up a deafening clatter on the roof. Lawrence looks from the girl straight into the hostile face of the man opposite him. There is a sudden loud crack and tinkle of glass as a piece of hail the size of a tennis ball smashes through the window above Lawrence's head and comes to rest in the lap of the woman with the push-chair next to him. The passengers watch in shock as the huge hailstone dissolves, not into water, but a thick, sticky puddle of semen, which immediately starts sinking into the woman's dress. She starts shrieking, and tries to wipe the mess with a bit of old newspaper. The man opposite Lawrence gets up and moves toward him, snarling, 'Look what you've done, you fucking freak! I'm gonna rip your head off!' Lawrence tries to escape through the smashed window, tearing his fingers on the glass. His head is half out of the window, but he's taking a battering now from the hail. Suddenly the rest of the window gives way under his weight and he falls out of the bus as it gets underway once more. He just gets a glimpse of the girl, who is now happily talking on her mobile, before he swims his sickening way back to consciousness.

'Jesus Christ,' he said aloud, weakly thumping the pillow.

NINE

'Oh, Holly, what am I going to *do?*' sighed Carla into her mobile, as the A4 pad of chaotic jottings and crossings-out stared up at her from the carpet. As she listened to Holly's urgent, insistent advice come blasting down the phone, she gazed down blankly at the hem of her nightie, at her smooth knees, musing on the softness of her skin, but wondering frankly about the point of it. What was the point of it, this so-called beauty everyone was always telling her she had so much of? But she was drifting from what Holly was saying, which was terrible of her, because she was trying to help. She forced herself to concentrate, blinking and frowning at the floor. Concentrate, concentrate! She peered up at the Radiohead poster over her bed.

'But Holly, Mike says he just doesn't want to do these songs any more, so that's it.......Yeah, no, yeah ... okay.... I'll put an ad in Loot ...... NME?! You must be joking - Look, NME is for people who are actually going somewhere? I'm just stuck in my bedroom!.......All right, all right, I'll try........ Oh, don't even talk about *that!*........ No, I had that miserable cow......Yeah, yeah, the "dried-up old bitch"..... She just kept asking all these *questions*, and then practically accused me of - .....Yeah, and by the time I went up the stairs, I just knew I wouldn't be able to do it, she'd done such a good job of putting me off....... Well, I just walked out......... W*hy* was it stupid?....... Oh God, you're kidding! They won't, will they?.... Why?........... Well, what was I sup*posed* to do, Holly?..........Well, what am I going to *do?*............Well, of *course* I want to carry on with it, what's the alternative, right? For *now*, anyway, I mean I'm not ready yet to go back to trawling the clubs - ....and you think that'll do the trick, if I just phone them?...... What if I get *her...?*'

She picked up her pen and started filling the rest of the A4 page with red figures-of-eight.

'......Well, I suppose I'll have to...... But -.......... Oh, okay, then, but thanks Holly, thanks so much. I'll see you on Wednesday, then...... ....Yes, I *will!*.....I *know,* I *know*.....Bye, lovely.'

She placed the phone by her side on the carpet, steeling herself against the silence as it cruelly rolled in, taking the place of Holly's rapid, energised voice. It felt as though the conversation had never taken place at all, so completely had Holly now been taken from her, along with all her advice and all her care and love. It was crazy, she knew, but the sensation was real enough.

She jumped up off the floor and hit the play button on the CD player, summoning Joni and her hissing summer lawns for the third time that morning. Returning to her place on the carpet, she leaned over the A4 pad, put the nail of her ring finger between her teeth and read through what she'd come up with so far, her long dark hair falling forward and down to the page, imprisoning her with the scribbled and crossed out verse ideas.

Well, it was mostly crap, as usual, apart from a verse of the 'insult song', which wasn't great but it was *some*thing. There was a nastiness in it which was unusual for her. And she liked it.

You got the heart of a nightclub scavenger
You got the eyes of a football manager
And with the hands of a coke-head bachelor
You get the soul of a men's mag calendar

It needed some fine-tuning, although... did it? Was it okay? Was it okay, or not? She didn't know. She couldn't concentrate - and she knew why. She sighed and sat up, pushing the pad away from her. Well, she'd better do something about it. She'd better make the call. But she hated making official phone-calls. And what if that sniffy bitch answered? Holly said that was unlikely because the call would go through to the reception desk. She forced herself to remove her finger from her mouth, got up and went over to the table and rummaged through some papers, looking for some correspondence from the sex benefit centre which might give the phone number of the office. What had she done with that letter from them? But it would be on the SB40, wouldn't it? She fished around in the handbag on the back of the chair and pulled out the signing document.

Taking the mobile phone from the floor, she speed-dialled the number with her thumb, and waited, a fingernail once more going up to her mouth as she began circling the off-white polyester rug in the middle of the room.

'Yes, hello. I came in two days ago and -........Carla Moore. Oh... er....' She frowned at the front of the SB40 document. '5298398.... Qell, I came in two days ago - to sign on, and I was a little upset so I left without ... going upstairs, and, and so I wanted to make sure that that wouldn't affect my claim?.......Oh, is that, is that really necessary?..........All right I'll come down this afternoon, then...... ....Thank you...Bye.'

Damn them! She threw the phone at the bed and then rushed to catch it as it bounced off and headed to the floor, where it landed with a thud. She put her hands to her head and sank back to the carpet. Why did they need to see her in *per*son?

Carla watched the back of the guy's head as he rose from the reception desk, noting the dandruff on his collar as she passed him and took the freshly vacated seat.

'Hello, can I help you?' said the woman behind the desk, her attention on the stack of information leaflets she was shuffling with both hands.

'Hi, I phoned earlier about something, and was told I had to come down in person to get it sorted out. Where should I -'

'What did you call about?'

'Maybe you took the call -?'

'No, I've only just come on,' smiled the woman flatly, 'What was it about?'

'Well, I came in two days ago, to sign on, and well I got a little upset, and I felt that....' She lowered her eyes, 'I felt that I couldn't go up the stairs, and so I left straight away. And a friend told me it might affect my claim, so I thought I'd better sort it out. So I phoned this morning and was told that I'd have to come down in person.'

'I see. Well, you'll have to see a claimant advisor for that.'

'Oh ... where do I -?'

'Just here,' said the woman, indicating the signing-on desks. 'Where you normally sign on.'

Carla peered round at the desks, noticing with dismay the presence of the guy with the glasses. The woman was speaking again.

'Just take a ticket and wait to see one of the advisors. They'll sort you out.'

'Okay ... thanks,' said Carla, rising. She crossed to the ticket dispenser. Great. Just great. Here she was about to get the third degree for the second time in three days, and for *what?* At least there didn't seem to be long to wait, although it looked like there was a good chance of landing up in front of that little Hitler with the glasses.

She sat down and stared at Williams as he dealt with an elegant-looking middle-aged woman. My Little Hitler. Sandy-haired fascist. *Fair*-haired fascist - let's put a bit of alliteration into it! But she felt suddenly guilty for these insults. Who was he anyway? What did she really know about him? But hang on, she was being too soft as usual. Holly was right, she was always, *always* being too soft. So, that My Little Hitler bastard over there could *keep* his new name.

Carla watched as the woman rose and left the desk. The lady really was very refined-looking, almost like ... an Egyptian Queen or something. Wasn't there an amazing ancient sculpture of some beautiful Egyptian Queen? Nefer-something -

She was distracted by the ticking over of the LED counter, which had just announced her number. *Shit!* So not only was she going to have to reel out the embarrassing story for a third time, but she was going to have to do it in front of *him* of all people! She picked up her mittens and crossed to the empty seat, throwing a strand of hair away from her eye, hating the guy behind the desk all the more for having been called to him.

Tucking the fur-lined hem of her coat beneath her as she sat down, Carla met Williams' dead-eyed gaze.

'Good afternoon,' he said, staring at her neck.

'Hello, I -'

'Your SB40, please.'

'Actually, I'm not here to sign on today....'

'Well, whatever you're here for, if you've been referred to a claimant advisor, I'm going to need to see your SB40,' said Williams testily. 'Do you have it?'

'Yes ... hold on.... Here.' God! What *was* this guy's *problem*?

'So, what can we do for you?' said Williams, his eyes drifting slightly to the shining dark hair piled on her shoulder.

'Well, I - the thing is, I came in two days ago - to sign on ... and I became a little upset,' Carla noticed him raise his eyebrow at the word. 'And so I left without, without -,' she hesitated, sighing heavily, '- without going upstairs, and I wanted to make sure it wouldn't affect my claim.'

Williams regarded her blankly. 'Well, we'll have to see about that. I'll have to get your file.' As he rose from his chair, her SB40 in his hand, and left the desk, Carla glared at his receding back. Why do you have to look at my *file*, you bastard?

She shifted quickly in her seat, slapped her mittens against her jeans, and looked about the room.

Williams returned with a manila file and sat down. Carla turned to face him, carelessly leaving the angry contortion of her brow unsoftened. She watched him take out the signing sheet with its list of her signatures, and realised with shock that there was a handwritten note attached. Williams glanced up at her.

'It seems the claimant advisor you saw had something to say about the incident.'

As he lowered his narrow eyes once more to the note, there came a loud bang from the direction of the stairwell. He looked up to see a large woman come storming through the wildly swinging double-doors, past the guard, and toward Harper's desk, where she sat down heavily and slammed the table, shouting furiously in an American accent, 'I wanna see someone in charge here!'

Williams looked over to the Jamaican, whose eyes were wide almost with amusement as he struggled for a moment to deal with the situation. As the woman went on shouting, Williams rose quickly from his chair. He wasn't leaving this to Harper.

'All right, Alex, I'll deal with this. Take over from me, would you?'

Harper shifted over to Williams' desk, from where both he and Carla continued to follow the woman's outburst, ignoring the papers on the desk before them.

'What seems to be the trouble?' asked Williams once he had sat down, his face set, barely concealing his hostility.

'All right, goddamnit, I've filled in all your fucking forms -'

'I'd be grateful if you moderated your language please.'

'I've filled in all your goddamn forms, I've filled in all your goddamn medical questionnaires, I've answered all your goddamn fucking questions, I've attended all your fucking programs, I've followed all your fucking courses, and sat for days on end in all your fucking mickey mouse workshops, now I want you to fulfil *your* side of the goddamn contract! I know my rights, goddamnit! And I'm *entitled!* I've got all the right credentials: I'm fucking fat and I'm fucking ugly and I demand some goddamn fucking satis*faction* out of you people!!'

'As I said before, what appears to be the problem?' said Williams evenly.

'What's the *problem?* You sent me up to a goddamn faggot up there who can't get it *up!! That's* the *problem!* And this is the second time for Chrissakes! What's the matter with you people? I mean, for crying out loud!' She turned in her seat and appealed to the rest of the room. 'Am I right or am I right? Who does the hiring around here?'

Carla looked on, amazed. Go for it, girl!

Williams looked at his monitor. Jesus Christ. Who had he sent this bloody lunatic to? Toby. What the bloody hell was the guy playing at?

'All right, madam, I'll look into it.'

'I wanna see your fucking superior.'

'I said I'll look into it.'

'You expect me to be satisfied with that shit?'

The security guard put his hand on the woman's shoulder. 'If you don't calm down, madam, I'll be forced to remove you from the building.'

'Butt out pal!' she said, shaking his hand off her shoulder, before again addressing Williams. 'Listen, you're -'

'Look, I'll send you up to someone else.'

'Not good enough! I'm too fucking *upset* now. But I'm telling you, I ain't leaving until you promise me a replacement session plus one extra. You've fucked up my goddamn rhythm, do you understand? And I expect to be compensated!'

'I don't know about that.'

'What do you mean, you don't know about it?' She got up and kicked the chair. The guard stepped forward and grabbed her arm as Williams got to his feet.

'Get your fucking hands off me! I've lived in this rinky-dink little country for twenty-two years, I've paid all my damn taxes -'

Carla watched as the guard tightened his grip on the woman's arm. Before Carla realised what she was doing, she was on her feet, shouting, 'Leave her alone!'

Williams shot Carla a dismissive look, shaking his head, 'Now I wouldn't advise you to get involved in this. Sit down, please!' Surprising herself, Carla remained where she stood, and Williams returned his attention to the struggling woman before him, attempting to raise his voice above her shouts.

'I think you'd better calm down before you damage any more government property.'

'All right I won't kick any more chairs but tell this gorilla to let go of me now, damnit!'

A tall figure with a neat beard and brown jacket emerged from the staff staircase and came up briskly behind Williams.

'What appears to be the situation, Roger?'

Williams turned to the newcomer. Henshaw! What the hell was he doing down here? Williams was about to speak, when the woman broke in.

'The situation is you people sent me up to a *limp-dick*, goddamnit, and for the second time in two *months!* And this guy is refusing to do anything about it!'

Henshaw turned to Williams, who responded to the woman. 'No, I'm not. I told you you could go up to someone else.'

Gesturing wildly at Williams' face, the woman appealed to Henshaw. 'What's the *matter* with this guy?' She turned to Williams, 'I already told you I'm too fucking *upset,* didn't I?'

Henshaw raised his hands, 'All right, look why don't you just step through to the office here, and we'll sort it out.'

'*Thank* you,' said the woman, scowling round at the guard as he released his grip. As she made her way round the desks and through to the staff office, Henshaw made to follow, but stopped and turned, fixing Williams with a disapproving look, before finally turning and entering the office, closing the door behind him.

Williams cast his glance at Carla, who immediately looked away and sat down in her seat. He was tempted to get back on her case, see what that note was all about, but no, it was Toby he wanted. He sighed once, and impetuously marched off to the staff staircase, running his hand through his thinning hair.

Harper gave Carla a smile, 'Well, it's aall happenin' in here today!'

She laughed a little into her lap.

'Well, let's see what we got here, then,' said the Jamaican, peering down at the note attached to Carla's signing sheet, recognizing Sandra's handwriting. He read to himself:

> After a somewhat unsatisfactory interview, the claimant left the building without making use of the facility, which indicates the claimant may not be a genuinely deserving case. Recommend issuing a SB13.

Harper looked up at Carla, a friendly expression on his face.

'Do you want to tell me what it's aall about?'

After Carla explained the story one more time, Harper leaned back in his seat, peering down at the note for a moment. Then, leaning forward again, he removed the note from the signing sheet and screwed it up, saying in his friendly drawl, 'Well, that aall seems to be aall right, then. Don't worry any more about it. Just come in again at your usual signing time, aall right?'

'Yes, okay... Thank you very much.'

'Aall right, no problem,' beamed Harper, slowly placing the document back in Carla's file, as she rose from the desk, smiling.

Finding herself once more out on the street, Carla basked in relief. Thank God for that old Caribbean guy. And thank God for that amazing woman! The way she had lain into My Little Hitler! She'd probably saved her bacon by charging up to that desk when she did. And at least she, Carla, had stood shoulder to shoulder with her for a moment in return. A moment of solidarity: 'claimants' versus 'advisors'. But God, what spirit the woman had! What fighting spirit. If only *she* could act more like that. Like she used to ... Instead of just mousing around all the time. Well, maybe she could. And she would start by putting that ad in *NME* like Holly had suggested. As she reached the bus-stop, she realised she felt happier than she had done for weeks.

Williams marched briskly down the cream-painted corridor on the first floor. Christ, what an afternoon. That woman. What a bloody abomination. But he'd been on top of it until bloody Henshaw had turned up and stuck his nose in. Where the hell had he sprung from anyway? The bloke was never about when you actually needed him. And what the hell was Toby's story? He'd better have a bloody good reason for unleashing that woman on him.

Williams found the cubicle he was looking for and entered without knocking, closing the door behind him. A naked well-built figure was sat on the edge of the bed, head in hand. Toby peered up at Williams but said nothing, turned instead and reached for his robe. As Toby stood up and pulled the flannel about him, Williams couldn't help but glance down at the facilitator's hefty penis. Not a lot of use if you can't get it up, though, chum, is it? He felt his anger increase.

'All right, Toby, what's the story?'

Toby looked away, with a dismissive gesture of his hand, 'I'm not going to get into this with you, Roger. Jenny's on her way down; I'll answer to her. She's the supervisor up here, not you, man. Your business is downstairs.'

'That's right, and just now we had a right bloody *scene* downstairs, because *you* don't know how to do your job!'

'As I said, Roger, I'm not going to talk about this with you.'

'Well, you're going to have to!' shouted Williams. 'For one thing, you'd better tell me if I can send any more claimants up to you this afternoon! Is this just a temporary hitch or what? Will normal service be resumed soon?'

'I think you're a bit out of order there, Roger, talking to me like that.'

Williams was about to respond when there was a knock on the door.

'Come in,' called Toby.

A tall woman in slacks entered the room, glancing at Williams. 'Hello, Roger,' said Jenny. 'What's the trouble, Toby?'

'Touch of the droop, I'm afraid, Jenny.'

'Ah, well, it happens, I suppose.'

'Yes,' snapped Williams, 'and downstairs *we* have to deal with the bloody consequences!'

Jenny whirled on Williams. 'Well, that *is* your *job*, Roger.'

Williams pursed his lips and stared at the wall, before turning again to face Jenny.

'Ask him at least if we can send any more claimants up to him today.'

Toby spoke, addressing Jenny. 'Actually, I think I'd better leave it today.'

'Okay, take the rest of the day off -'

'Fine!' broke in Williams, throwing his arms in the air. 'Take the rest of the day off and leave us to deal with the backlog.' He turned to the door, 'You know, Toby, if you're not up to the job, you shouldn't have taken it on.'

'Oh, for God's sake, Roger, he's only human!' snapped Jenny.

'Oh,' said Williams, letting his eyes rest for a moment on Toby's groin, his expression taking on a new bitterness. 'I thought he was meant to be *super*human.' His eyes dropped to the floor, and he left the cubicle, slamming the door behind him, but it failed to latch properly and fell slowly open again, as his brisk footsteps receded down the corridor.

'What an *arse*hole....' said Toby slowly, while Jenny merely stared at the open door, shaking her head.

Williams marched back down the corridor. At least he'd told him a thing or two. And he'd have told him something else if bloody Hopley hadn't barged in. Well, anyway, better get back and see what Harper's done with that interfering little bitch.

Passing through the double doors leading to the staff staircase, he caught sight of a robed figure moving beyond the glass panels of the doors to the facilitator's suite. He halted and watched as a dark mane of thick, shiny hair was thrown back over a shoulder and the woman sat down, magazine and mug in hand, crossing her naked knees. Lucinda. She was alone in the room. He observed the slightly feral downturn of her mouth as she flicked quickly through the magazine. His eyes drifted across her rapid page-turning hand, along her lap and down, taking in the shadows in the soft depressions around her kneecap, before sliding along the smooth air-brushed curve of her calf and coming to rest on the tiny, startling, red-painted toe-nails.

That lot downstairs didn't deserve to be getting any of that, that was for bloody sure. He turned and headed down the stairs, each step jarring to life a nagging pain in his back, until on the landing he was struck by a sudden excruciating twinge. He stopped and bent forward, putting a hand to his back. He'd told her. He'd bloody told her that sofa-bed was no good for his sciatica. Closing his eyes, he waited for the pain to ease.

Pushing through the double doors on the ground floor, he immediately scanned the signing desks, saw that Harper was now back in his own seat, the girl nowhere in sight. What did you do with her, Harper, and what was on that note? He crossed to the filing cabinet, and quickly brought out the girl's file, removing the girl's signing sheet. What did you do with the note, Harper? Placing the file back in the cabinet, he turned and glanced over at the Jamaican. He waited until Harper had finished dealing with the chubby derelict on the other side of his desk, and then went over.

He leaned over Harper, planting one hand on the edge of the desk, and began speaking slowly, alternating his glance between Harper's face and the wall behind him.

'I've just looked in the girl's file, Alex. What happened to that note?'

Harper gazed up at Williams, his eyes bright. 'I acted on it, Roger.'

'What do you mean you acted on it? What did you do?'

'The girl explained the situation to my satisfaction, and so ... I threw the note away.' He made a small wave of his arm.

'I see. And what did it say?'

'I used my discretion, Roger.'

Williams glanced impatiently at the ceiling, then back at Harper.

'What did it say, Alex?'

Harper stared out across the room. 'It caalled for an SB13, but on questioning the claimant further ...' He swung his bright gaze back to Williams. '... I deemed it unjustified.'

'You deemed it unjustified.'

Harper held Williams' sour look. 'You handed her to me, Roger. Now, you either have confidence in me or you *don't.*'

Both men held the eyes of the other, until Williams dropped his gaze to Harper's chest, gave a single grudging nod of his head and returned to his own desk.

Well, after all, it brightened the bloody place up a bit to have lookers like that little heartbreaker come in. Let Harper have it his way, then. Williams allowed himself the luxury of bringing to mind once again the girl in the long fur-edged coat, but was suddenly irked by the idea that Toby had probably been there. Or if he hadn't, he'd probably be up it soon enough. As he took his seat and pressed the button to cue on the LED counter, he nevertheless pictured the girl as she'd sat there in front of him, the luxuriant hair flowing out from under that bobble-hat. However, as the next claimant approached, the mental image of the girl's long auburn locks metamorphosed into a shining black cascade: the darker, thicker mane of Lucinda. And he could almost see, transposed over the face of the plain middle-aged woman approaching him, a pair of faintly sneering lips, full and thick and red.

Furiously rinsing out her mug as she stood over the sink in the kitchenette, Lucinda glowered at the plughole. Behind her retinas still danced the absurd, pinched, bespectacled head gawping at her knees from the other side of the double doors. She banged the mug down hard on the drainer. Didn't that stupid wanker downstairs realise that their breaks were *sacred? Absolutely bloody sacred?*

She stormed out across the empty lounge, banged the doors out of her way and strode back down the corridor to her cubicle.

TEN

For the third night running, the bearded porn star was being put through his paces, casting a low orange glow into the darkened living room. Lawrence lay slumped in the sofa, almost stupefied by the relentless, empty boffing taking place on the screen. The girl was out of shot again, and he reached out his leg to the VCR to cue on the tape with his big toe, watching blankly as the guy's shafting accelerated to fast-forward absurdity. The camera suddenly pulled back to reveal a girl on all fours - the bearded arsehole's port-of-call - and Lawrence removed his foot from the console, as the girl's buttocks once more filled the frame. Taking his eyes from the screen, he peered down at the vague, dark shape which lay twitching hesitantly back to life between the open folds of his unzipped jeans. Happy now, you dismal bastard? He glanced up at the screen, and let his eyes feed on the girl's naked hindquarters, feeling the surly weight lift clear of his abdomen. He reached for a cigarette and stuck it in his mouth, the igniting flame momentarily illuminating the blind, rearing thing below. As the flame closed, the phantom was once more swallowed by gloom. Dropping the lighter, he gave grudging licence for his right hand - that noble instrument - to go down and start stroking the fucker.

His cock was now having a grand time of it. But *he* fucking wasn't. He wasn't interested in these bastards on the screen. He was in fact only making use of a select few elements of the girl, her shoulder, her behind, her occasional moans, to reconstruct some fleeting idea of a real-life sexual encounter. All the rest, he was trying to blank out, unsuccessfully.

Although there was no doubting the basic sexual charms of the girl, there was something hopelessly bovine about her face, and she was saying 'yeah' too much. And in a fucking irritating American whine to boot. Also, she was wreathed here and there in ugly black leather shit. And the shape of her heavy breasts had been destroyed by a typically insensitive implant job, the upper concave curve of the natural sweep down to the nipple having disappeared completely in a hideously abrupt convex swelling.

And this specimen doing the ramming - he wasn't so much a porn *star*, as a sort of porn *character actor*. Or extra, even. He looked like a fucking caveman, grunting and snarling away - if cavemen had worn sweaty red bandannas round their heads. A fucking caveman out of *One Million Years BC* or something. A pity the girl didn't look like she'd stepped out of the same film; this was no Raquel we were looking at here. But even if it were, we wouldn't want to see her being buffeted by this hairy fuck-up in this tacky over-lit plastic MTV dungeon set-up.

The thought of Raquel Welch suddenly crystallised again for Lawrence everything wrong with the tape. It was utterly devoid of anything remotely approaching class, and where there was no class there could be no sensuality, and Welch had so much of it the mere flow of her hair was enough to merit instant and complete arousal. Beyond the bodies on the screen, he saw her in a lime green bikini perched on the back of a speeding motorboat, racing across the waves, bathed in sixties sunlight - a scene from some daft spy movie he'd seen her in, and he felt a strange pang, as of the resurgence of a long-forgotten loss.

What the fuck was he doing debasing himself in front of this moronic garbage?

In a sudden fury, he launched himself from the sofa, and stabbed the eject button on the video. Then, stuffing his complaining dick back into his trousers, he loped awkwardly into the kitchen. A drawer opened and slammed shut, and he re-entered the living room, storming over to the video-player, a hammer in his hand.

He pulled the cassette out of the slot and began smashing it to pieces, reducing it quickly to a heap of black splinters and unspooling tape. He stared down at the debris, breathing hard. Dropping the hammer on the pile of broken plastic, he went over to the wall of shelving that housed his books and tapes. What he needed was a fucking mainline injection of *class*. Running his eyes across the spines of the cassettes, he read the titles, mentally calling up the stars within: Deneuve, Hepburn, Fonda....

But somehow, right now, the sight of these profoundly elegant women would be too painful, because contrary to the popular view, they were actually too fucking real, the problem being that they existed - or had existed somewhere in the world, somewhere in time - without his ever having stood a hope in hell of finding his way to them. And other men had, such as that criminally jammy glamourpuss-seller Vadim. Whenever he saw a photo of Catherine Deneuve or Brigitte Bardot or Jane Fonda, he felt an excruciating hatred for the serial icon-fucker. He continued to scan the tapes. What he needed was a woman with poise, but who wouldn't fill him with a crushing sense of hopelessness at the thought of never getting to lie down with her. Ah. He smiled at the cassette. Here we are. Just the ticket.

He went over to the VCR and shoved the tape inside, hit the play button and collapsed back onto the sofa. The playback started at some point halfway through an episode, and the head of the blond puppet filled the screen, instantly washing his visual palate clean. Whoever sculpted that head was a fucking genius. As she spoke into the secret microphone in her compact mirror, her huge eyes black with mascara moving slowly from side to side, the head tilting charmingly, but impossibly, on its single fulcrum, he watched, transported by an unfathomable, un*action*able erotic whimsy. His cock could go fuck itself: this was beyond its mean terms of reference. There was something in the essence of Lady Penelope's features and her luxurious great whorl of sugary blond hair which surpassed reality, and yet there was nothing you could do with it. You couldn't sexually engage with a piece of fucking fibre-glass; you were instead left pleasantly suspended, floating in a kind of innocent sexual limbo, and yet at the same time, to look at that head was to encounter a level of sensuality not even a*pproached* by a single frame of the mangled tape on the carpet.

Fucking hell, but it was hardly a solution to the greater problem, was it? Sitting alone in the dark watching fucking *Thunderbirds*. He leaned forward and put his head in his hands.

Staring at the floor, he listened to the sound of the action on the screen, the action that had so thrilled him as a kid with its promise of a blue-sky super-plane future. And now here that future was. He shut his eyes tightly, let his head hang for a moment, swung it violently to his left. What, was he going to start fucking crying now? He threw himself back in the sofa, lit a cigarette, and opened his eyes wide, blinking hard to dispel the moisture. He stared at the futuristic jet from the past soaring across the screen, trying to calm himself with measured inhalations of the cigarette.

If he wanted ... he could go down that place tomorrow ... and feel it ... feel a woman enclose him again.

His eyes drifted to the wall, the moist, dark irises reflecting TV-light. Should he do it...? The cigarette came up to his mouth, seemingly before he had given the command. He filled his lungs and exhaled at the TV screen.

... no. Not yet. He wasn't done yet. He had *some* fucking spine. He wasn't giving up yet. Not till the point came. The point when he just couldn't stand it any more.

ELEVEN

He was trying to work. In truth, that was all he wanted: to be left in peace to work. He wanted to sculpt, not procreate, so why the hell did he have to spend half his creative energy lamenting the lack of the warm soft funnel? As he dragged the shaping tool across the clay neck of the large, straining figure, he smirked sourly; there was actually something rather effeminate, baby-like, in the need to be coddled by the soft warm flesh of another, to snuggle and shelter from the cold, dark, universal night. Well, he didn't need it, fuck it; he could stand up to the night like a man, work *through* the fucking night, because work was the most important thing. It was more masculine, nobler, surely, to face the night with all one's soul, than to take craven refuge from it in some pleasant female cave.

He laughed aloud at the perverse compensatory systems of thought he was capable of erecting in order to sustain himself. And yet, there was something in it… but he couldn't really get behind it. Or could he? He shook his head in an effort to drop the line of thought, brushed the hair back from his face and made a determined effort to concentrate. But even as he sheared a large sliver of clay from the gnarled, pitted shoulder of the figure, he was assailed yet again by the memory of an innocent flash of white underwear glimpsed accidentally in the pub the night before. Oh, for *heaven's sake*. He flung the shaping tool at the floor, and stared at the snarling dog's head growing from the figure's groin, the figure's right hand clamped between its jaws. You rotten fucker. He let his eyes rove to the dog's eye-sockets, black pits under the ruthless overhead light from the single naked bulb. But still the girl's knickers would not leave his imagination, and still the blood refused to be taken up by the gentler, more decorous arteries and veins. The fucking dog bastard was going to yank him back up to the flat for another walk round the fucking park. An impromptu late afternoon wank was one of the many dubious perks of the self-employed - but this was the third fucking time today. He wanted to work, for fuck's sake, but he knew that when the sensation had reached this pitch, the quickest solution was to just do it and get it over with. But to drag himself back up to the flat.... He looked about him. He could do it here... No, he wasn't going to sit wanking in a shed, for Christ's sake!

He turned wearily, booted open the door, and trudged through the grass back up to the house, picking his way through the broken planks and bricks. Gaining the flat, he pushed open the door with a blow of his palm, and stormed off to the bedroom, stopping off at the bathroom to spin a long ream of white tissue from the paint-flecked chrome toilet paper holder.

He entered the bedroom, and sank to his knees, furiously tearing open his black jeans.

The phone rang. Some small fragment of real life was beckoning.

He pulled up his trousers and staggered down the hall to the living room, where he collapsed to the floor and lifted the receiver.

'Hello?'

'Lawrence, hi, it's Martina.' He quickly zipped up his fly.

'Well, hello! How are you?' he said, smiling broadly at the wall, warmed by the prospect of, if nothing else, at least another pleasant sparring match over the Almighty.

'Not good. I'm not good, Lawrence.'

'Why, what's up?'

He had never heard her like this before. But he had heard the same low, almost catatonic, delivery from other girls in the past. He felt a weakness in his legs, instinctively afraid for her. The more so, because she hadn't answered yet.

'Hey ... what's up?' he said softly.

'I almost can't explain ... it's all black, and there is no *reason....'* He could hear her fighting her emotion, and she lost the fight in the next sentence, which came broken up by sobs and tears: 'It is like ... it is like ... I don't exist ... I don't exist any more ... I'm not me any more ... and no one can understand...'

'Hey ...' he soothed. Oh, fuck, Martina, not you. Don't go there, babe. He wanted to call her "babe" down the phone, just because it seemed the warmest thing *to* say ... and *only* for that reason, but he didn't say it, afraid of being misconstrued.

'I'm sorry, Lawrence, but I don't know who to talk to...'

'Hey, don't worry about it! I'm fucking happy if I can be of even the smallest help to you. Now, look, what the hell's happened?' He sat forward, trying to gauge the level of her desperation, and wracking his brains for remedies.

'I don't know....'

'Well, did this feeling come on suddenly?'

'... over the last week ...'

'And ... you say it feels like you don't exist. What do you *mean* by that? *Exactly.*' He made himself a little more comfortable on the floor and lit a cigarette.

'... it's difficult ... I look at my hands and it is like they are on a cinema ... and my thoughts are separated - separated from me ... so if I am not in my thoughts, where am I? Where can I be? You probably think I am mad - I can't say this good in English -'

A fresh volley of sobs came down the phone.

'Listen, Martina, hey ... sshhh....'

She was calming down slightly.

'Listen. Martina. I've been through something like that myself. You're not going mad ... but it does sound like a kind of depression... I mean I'm not a psychiatrist, but it sounds like depersonalisation or something....'

Her sobs had calmed to a low sniffing. 'But it is so frightening, Lawrence....'

'I know. It's fucking shit. But look, what you've got to do is see a doctor, okay? And remember that these sensations are - even though they seem so real to you - just try to remember that these sensations are actually - illusions. Because they *are*.' He realised he was gesturing urgently with his cigarette hand. 'If you cling to that it will help. But promise me you'll see a doctor, okay?'

'... yes ...'

'Hey, that didn't sound very convincing. Come on, I want to hear you promise.'

'I promise,' she said, evidently trying to sound stronger.

'Good girl. And don't drink too much while you're feeling like this, and for God's sake don't take any fucking drugs, okay?'

'No ... I won't ... Lawrence, thank you....'

'Forget it, look, I was in a similar space once.' There was a pause. He looked about the room. 'It's a bastard, innit?'

'Yes .... it's a bastard.'

He heard her try to laugh. Come on, that's it, babe. He suddenly found himself swallowing back his own emotion.

'You see, you laughed. I know it was hard - I could hear the effort - ' he heard her laugh again, a little easier this time, 'but, you know it shows you're gonna be okay.'

'It's the first time I have laughed in six whole days.'

'Well, try to do more of it. It's good therapy.'

'... Lawrence....'

'Yeah?'

'It's so good to talk to you....'

'Well, what are friends for, and all that shit.'

'You are the only person I have spoken to who... seems... real.'

He stared at the floor and swallowed, before flinging his glance at the ceiling. 'Well, that's probably just because I can empathise - I kind of understand what you're talking about. You know, your other friends have probably had no experience of this crap.'

'... perhaps ... but you are a kind person.....'

'Well, I think that's overdoing it a *little.'*

'Oh - I - I have to go. I am at work.'

'Okay, but listen, remember everything I said -'

'I will -'

'And call me any time of the day *or* night, if you want to talk. I mean it.'

'I will. Thank you, Lawrence... you saved my life. Big kiss.'

'Hey. Just keep laughing.'

'I'll try.'

'No. Don't try, do!'

'All right, I will,' she laughed uncertainly, 'Bye.'

'Bye, Martina, take care.'

After Martina's call, he had gone on sitting for a while, smoking on the floor, and then gone back to work, the earlier indomitable urge having apparently receded in the face of Martina's pain and the overwhelming need to help her. In fact, as soon as he had heard the fear in her voice, from that moment, the sex shit had played no part in his motives, having been swept away by a pure, chaste need to comfort her, just comfort her. It had been a long time since he'd been called on to care about anyone. And if he did say so himself, he hadn't done a bad job of it. And he had to admit it: he was fucking proud that he seemed to have been of some help. And relieved he was still capable of rising above his own crap when the need came.

Nevertheless, he was seriously worried about her, and after his solitary meal of Marmite on toast with some mashed potato next to it, he had called her to check up on her, but she hadn't answered. He hoped she was okay. He was tempted to try again now, but it was late; he didn't want to wake her if she was asleep. Sleep was crucial when you were going through some shit like that.

Throwing the battered *TinTin* album to the floor, he reached round and switched off the bedside light, drawing himself instantly into a foetal position as the darkness closed in. It was fucking freezing in here, but he was knackered and could already feel warm sleep tugging at him.

His thoughts drifted and crashed lazily into the coming half-formed dream images of incipient unconsciousness. He was on a bus again somewhere, fighting heavy leaden waves of scented blond hair pouring in through all the windows. He got off, picking strands of yellow hair from his teeth. The scene changed. He was in a cafe with Martina, they were smiling at each other across a table. On the table lay a hammer and her mobile phone smashed to pieces. And now she was standing before him, while he sat. Her mouth was moving. 'My hero. My hero.' She had pulled her skirt up and was slowly running her finger up and down the soft groove in her panties.

He started awake, stared at the ceiling for a second, then flung back the duvet. He peered down at his body, at the dumb throbbing head protruding from the waistband of his briefs. The thing was having the fucking piss out of him! He continued to glare at it, his hair falling round his eyes, his face slowly contorted by a sneering contempt, until finally, thrusting his head forward furiously, he spat two heartfelt words in its direction.

'You *cunt*.'

TWELVE

He rolled over and pressed his head into the pillow.

That his knob was indeed a cunt, and a blind and stupid one at that, had of course already been satisfactorily proven to him during his ridiculous and completely fruitless pursuit of –

But he didn't want to go there tonight....

… fuck, don't let her in ... but she was coming in any way, wasn't she? She was on her way in, pouring in like her own hair coming through the windows of the bus in the dream. He couldn't keep her out any more ... he was fucking tired and he couldn't keep her out... so come on then ... come in if you're coming … come on, then, you crazy, long-legged, married dancer from L.A ... come on, then and bring those sick waves of blond hair with you....

Come on ... *Bibi....*

Bibi of the flashing brown eyes and almost Jim Morrison-strength jaw-line, supermodel-tall, and reckless...

... for whom - for a *mere chance of lying down* with whom – he'd very nearly trashed his mind and invalidated his soul...

... but it wasn't her fault ... it was the *dog bastard* that had let him swallow her cruel life-sapping party-drug ... it was the dog bastard that had sent his hands crawling over her behind that time while her husband and little daughter slept in Chelsea - she hadn't let him kiss her and the behind had been clad in jeans but it had been out of *fucking order* all the same...

... but it wasn't her fault ... so let her in, then ... let her come crashing in once more ... like she did the first time ... during the small party he had been giving in the flat two years ago.

There had been a knock on the door and in she had stumbled on those long, incredible, supermodel legs, laughing, all blond hair, baby-blue skirt and teetering high-heels. She and her husband had just kind of fallen through the door together when he had opened it for them; had just gushed in like some dammed up body of water it would have been useless to try to keep out. He and his friends had held them at bay for a moment in the hall, questioning them like border control guards at a crossing point between frontiers of sanity and madness, before finally letting them in, and with them the infection: within twenty minutes she had dragged him to his bedroom, actually pulling him by his shirt, and had begun weaving her cocoon around his head, that cocoon made of a million scented strands of heavy yellow hair. And although they had just sat there on the bed, leaning their heads together, he trying to follow her Valley Girl babble about American literature, the near-constant view she had given him of her knickers had so thrilled the rebel in his own underwear that he was already more than half lost.

Still, in the weeks that followed, he had made an effort to hold aloof from her obvious and declared interest in him, to resist the huge brown eyes, high cheekbones and California tan, but in the end his cock had held sway, setting its little dog-heart forever on a tenancy in whatever dark pink flop-house it was that she kept behind that white nylon mesh, that insane white triangle that she was always somehow exposing, at parties, at clubs, on sofas, on the backseats of taxis as they clawed their way back from some drunken vodka-fuelled night of near-adultery. Talking about Faulkner and showing her pants.

She'd known the power of those white flashes. She knew she could illuminate the gloom of an entire dank throbbing basement club with the reflected halogen light from that wedge of white fabric, as she had done one night with him, sprawling on the low sofa of a West End club, a teasing arm round his neck, filling his ear with a constant stream of deep-register coke-driven gabble, while letting her long smooth legs fall ever further apart for the delectation of the other ravers. If he remembered correctly, she had actually been saying something about her daughter. 'Isn't it like totally *funny* to think of her popping out of that little thing down there? I mean, it kinda makes me *freak* sometimes? I mean can you even imagine like just a *head* coming out of there?' And she had raised a brown super-sleek thigh to expose herself all the more to the two guys staring up her tiny blue skirt from the sofa opposite, all the while holding her flashing, drug-struck eyes before his face. 'You see how they want it?' And she had given him one of those spasmodic smiles of hers, shutting her eyes and jerking her head slightly to the left. 'See how they want my little thing, honey?' And a provocative undulation had run through her body setting up a slow rocking motion in her pelvis. 'They *so* want my thing, don't they? But like what *is* it, my thing, my '*pussy*'? Well, I'll *tell* you what it is. It's *nothing!* That's right! Nothing but a simple little fold of skin!' she had sing-songed, and she had actually glanced down at herself, stolen a quick glance at her own panties, before flinging her face back to his own, smiling with her eyes shut and shaking out her thick cloud of blond hair. And then she'd opened her eyes startlingly wide, pulled her legs together, and addressed him again, her voice low and even. '*Absolutely goddamn nothing at all.*'

And she had been right, it *was* nothing - at least from the perspective of the existential ache they had discovered they shared, but try telling his cock that: his cock had made him see that far from being nothing, her 'thing' was everything, everything in the world, absolutely everything in the entire world, and if only one day he could possess it, if only for a few minutes, one day in some shining husbandless future, then his whole existence would finally sort itself out and come right. Such was the nature of the beautiful promise made to him by his cock.

Silly sausage. Silly fucking sausage. Or rather, silly non-fucking, fuckless, fuckwitted pole of dog-meat, because a year later by the time she finally decided to stay with her husband, the fucking thing hadn't even been touched by her hand or seen by her eyes, let alone been buried to the hilt in her faithless vulva.

His cock: witless fucking shaft. But in total command, it seemed. Ordering him in on a married woman. Having nothing else to fuck, it had fucked his soul. Yet it wasn't that that had initially put the fear of Christ into him; he wouldn't be needing his soul-spirit-thing anyway, at least not until later, and only then if this 'life' stuff went on after the grave. No, it was the drug-smashed vale of tears into which his blind knob had thrown the delicate balance of his sanity that had made him so terrified and later so furious. A child couldn't have been so stupid, but that was the point: a child didn't go about with an insistent purple-headed imbecile polluting his thinking at every step.

It had only taken a single ecstasy pill to do it, and she had administered it to him one sunny and bitter midwinter morning, as they wandered the residential streets around her Chelsea home. 'What are you up to today?' she had said in a rich, low voice down the phone to him earlier, interrupting his efforts to rig up an armature for a new sculpture. 'Hey, nothing!' he had smiled, oblivious to the fact that he was standing on the threshold of a new life, that in just five short hours' time everything was going to be ripped up and replaced with a species of mental agony he never imagined possible. The coming event would leave no visible mark, and all the world would appear exactly as it had before, but a disaster would have cracked his mind, separating him in a second from his old life forever. In short, something big was headed toward him.

'Well', she had continued with barely controlled excitement down the phone. 'I have a free day today and I'd like to do something *awesome* with it. With you. I so need to just like totally break out today? And so ... like, will you come with me on a little trip?' She had murmured the last line softly, her voice dripping with so much honey that his cock was growing before he had even fully apprehended the question. He knew she was talking about class A drugs, specifically her beloved pills, and he knew she was trying to assail his hard drug virginity, though she would insist she was not, that it was always his choice. In the past he had never had any difficulty preserving his chastity in this department, perceiving heroin, cocaine, LSD and ecstasy as being obviously dangerous. Besides, he liked his faculties, and saw no point in endangering them for the sake of some dubious fleeting pleasure or equally dubious fleeting insight. His mind may have been a little depressive at times, but it was sharp, he knew, and he wanted to keep it that way, needed to keep it that way for the sake of his work. And anyway, for him, work was the midwife to the products of his innate imagination; he didn't need drugs to access visions. So when Bibi would beg him to join her chemical lifestyle, and he refused, as he had done in the past, it amused him to repeat to her Dali's maxim: 'I am the drug!' And he had enjoyed her bemused dismay as he had pushed her little pill back across the table, she looking for all the world as though it were she herself that had been rejected, shrugging her shoulders and pulling out her purse, returning the demon for now to its little cave in Hades.

But then, over the next weeks, she had begun talking about the history of her beloved wonder-drug, or its main component MDMA, and its initial invention and use in therapy as an unblocker of unwanted psychological barriers. 'Fine. I don't need it then. I don't need any psychological blockages unblocking at the moment, thanks,' he had laughed, brushing a weight of her blond hair from his face. 'So please save your precious fucking brain laxative for someone who needs it! ' 'Okay, well, Jesus, I'm *sorry*. But I really think you're just making a goddamn fuss over nothing!' 'Maybe, but I just don't want it,' and he had watched her once more put the drug back into the purse she was holding between her knees, letting his eyes linger there long after the purse had been returned to her bag.

And so he had held his ground. But when she had started telling him about the California love-drug phase of MDMA's illustrious history, his lonely aberrant knob had begun forcing him to listen. And he had listened. Listened to stories of couples accessing a higher level of empathetic connection between themselves through the drug. Ecstasy the love-facilitator. And she had wanted to do it with him. The claims she was making for this noxious substance sounded like a heap of bollocks to him of course, and anyway what kind of love was it that needed chemical enhancement? But that wasn't the point: she believed in it and she wanted to do it with him. She wanted to get closer. This deeply sexy woman - it didn't matter that she was married and more than half-cracked - this deeply sexy woman wanted to get closer to him. And from then on, whenever she had brought the subject up, his cock had risen too, sensing a home at last after the barren sexual wilderness through which he had been wandering before she and her husband had come staggering, almost frighteningly, into his hall.

And so the day had come, that day which had started so fucking blissfully with her call, but which was to become the godawful midwinter Saturday that he'd never forget. Arm in arm under the cold sun, they'd wandered the streets of Chelsea, she urging him to join her in her 'trip', he fighting her off, but hoping for their first kiss, until finally she had stopped on a corner and faced him. And he had looked into the leaping sexual spark in her huge, cajoling brown eyes, and all at once the blood had sunk into the fucking dog bastard in his pants so quickly and with such draining power that he felt sick and weak, but at the same time possessed of a cock stronger than he had ever known. The thing had taken his strength. And it had taken charge. She was holding in her tiny hand two pills.

And he heard himself say, 'All right.'

'Way to go!' she had smiled. 'Okay, now we're gonna have a *real* cool time together now, okay? Now ... one for *me....*' She put one in her mouth, lowering her lashes at him, '...and one...' she raised the pill to his mouth, '... one for *you.*'

He'd felt her fingers brush his parted lips as she dropped the drug onto his tongue. And she'd smiled at his mouth as he'd closed it. As it had dissolved in his saliva, he'd said, 'You'd better fucking look after me if I start freaking out.' And she had just laughed, crazily flinging her arm through the air. 'Don't *worry!* You know, you can be like so totally not *hip* sometimes, it's not true, do you know that? Nothing's going to *happen.*'

And then they'd found the bar, the bar that was to provide the setting for his departure from himself, from her and from everything else and from all of reality. Slumped together in a low sofa, his senses smothered by the nearness of her crashing waves of perfumed yellow hair, he had begun to get high, but probably as much from the fact that her hand had taken his and slipped it under her top, pressing his palm to the small of her back, putting him for the first time in contact with the naked flesh of her body. And then her head had come in close, a looming dangerous weight, like some great blond wrecking ball swinging in on a chain. She was going to kiss him. She moved her head in to within an inch of his and waited, looking into his eyes. Aware of the strange closeness of her breath, he stared at the brown irises, observing the tiny flecks and radial patterns of fibrous tissue, then peered deeper, into the black pupils, where he discovered the simple, astonishing fact that he didn't give a shit about her.

Or about the beautiful bank of cloud just visible through the window behind her head.

Or about his work.

Or his friends or his family.

Or about himself.

As he went on looking into her eyes, his knees actually shaking, the blackness rolled on down through his spirit, switching everything off as it went. It quickly seeped into his memories; he no longer gave a damn about his favourite childhood cat - instantly reduced to a meaningless scrap of animated fur; or the long-cherished summer Saturday mornings with Karen in the fields - we had joy, we had fun, we had seasons in the sun, but now he could see that the fun had merely been the automatic activity of larval organisms unfurling beneath an indifferent star. The blackness had come down and instantly spread outwards to contaminate everything that he had ever known, everything that he had ever loved. Even the curves of Bibi's body, the curves of every girl in the bar. What were they but abstract geometry? And so the world had fallen away from him.

And he hadn't kissed her. He'd leaned forward instead, reaching for his drink, listened in panic to another twenty minutes of her honey-talk, while he went on falling down his black hole, and then made his excuses and left, his stupid, fucking thwarted cock pressed somehow still half-erect to the top of his leg.

And of course she had been no fucking use or help in the weeks and months that had followed, had just gone on partying, while he had gone to pieces, depersonalising, derealising, his misfiring brain shattering every scrap of social and natural programming that had informed his cohesion as a functioning human being.

All except one.

The irreducible urge to fuck. Incredibly, it remained, unfulfilled as usual, though weathering every assault of his self-destructing psyche. Ironically, it was probably the concrete floor of his accursed sex drive that had helped him gradually claw his way back to some semblance of sanity, by distracting his deranged intelligence from the path of self-immolation. But he could never forgive it. He would never forgive it for dragging him into that fucking blackness. How could he? When he knew, he *knew* it was about to drag him into more.

THIRTEEN

He let his head drop heavily back to the pillow and pulled the duvet up over his shoulder. As his thoughts finally began to wander and distort, perverted once more by the approaching loss of consciousness, he found himself in the body of his childhood, blinking against a warm and immense sunlight ...

... Karen is running at his side, racing with him across the meadow. They are both about eight years old. Karen is his friend. Her soft fair hair is streaming back from her exquisite little smiling face as they gambol across the stunning emerald grass. A small rabbit-shaped bag is slung over her shoulder, bouncing lightly around her back as she runs.

Suddenly, she throws herself to the ground, calling out to him, 'Come on, let's read our books for a bit! I'm *tired!*'

Lawrence brings himself to a halt and doubles back to her. She watches him silently, smiling at his approach. Then, serene with the first blossoming of her intellect, she takes a small illustrated book from the little rabbit-shaped bag. He flops down on the grass beside her as she brings out another little book.

'Which one do you want?' she asks.

'The dinosaur one!' he replies. She gives him the book, laughing.

'I *knew* you'd want that one!' She places the remaining book in her lap, and is soon absorbed by the parade of mediaeval castles passing between the turning pages under her little fingers.

He watches her for a moment, and seeing a buttercup growing nearby, he plucks it and leans over to offer it to her. She lets out a giggle of delight, and takes it from him, holding it under her chin. Obligingly, she turns her face for him, her gentle spirit proclaimed by the calm smile bathed in the honey-glow of the buttercup. Then she holds it under his chin for a moment, and he watches her blue eyes stare in smiling delight at the lower part of his face. She draws back with a sigh of satisfaction and places the stem of the buttercup between the leaves of her book.

'Hey,' says Lawrence. 'Have you got anything to eat in that bag? I'm *hungry*!'

Karen's eyes light up and she turns again to the bag. Whirling back round to face him, she presents Lawrence with something wrapped in a napkin.

'Flapjacks!' she cries. 'My mum gave them to me, before I came out.'

'Brilliant, thanks! Your mom's brilliant!'

'I know,' says Karen, leaning round to take a flapjack from the bag for herself. They sit a while, silently munching, occasionally glancing around the meadow, or at each other, or up at the clean blue sky. Karen is the first to finish. She wipes the crumbs from her lips, smiles at him briefly, and turns again to her book. He brushes the crumbs from his own mouth, and gets back to his dinosaurs. After a while, he is distracted from his prehistoric monsters by Karen's voice.

'Wow, this is a long word ... contemporary ... ayne- ous, contemporaneous.'

Lawrence replies, 'If you like long words you should like dinosaurs. Listen to this one: para ... cephela ... paracephelasaurus.'

'Gosh! How do you spell *that*?'

Lawrence peers down at the page and begins to call out the letters. However, as he does so, he is momentarily confused by the shifting pattern of sunlight across the page. Over the illustration of the oddly named creature, shadows are forming where they should not. He breaks off spelling and raises his eyes from the page to see the same thing happening across the whole meadow. All the shadows are lengthening. He looks over at Karen. He is shocked to see that she is staring open-mouthed at some point high above the ground. He looks up.

The sun is coming down from the sky.

Gliding down from its place in the rich blue firmament, the sun descends toward them until it comes to hover six feet above the grass before them. Karen rises to her feet, staring in rapt wonder at this shrunken, hovering sun. Not knowing what to do or think, he does the same. Compressed to the size of a man's head, the sun nevertheless burns on, flaming with nuclear heat. The sun feels as warm as before, as pleasant as before, but it's going to do something to them. Lawrence feels it intuitively the instant before the changes begin.

Under the influence of the small sun, the bodies of Karen and Lawrence mature in a moment, breasts and genitals quickly unfurling beneath their changing clothes like swelling fungi from a time-lapse nature documentary, until they stand there as fully grown adults, though bewildered as children.

The sun has grown a body too. He has two titanic arms. They possess the sullen gravitas of a Michelangelo sculpture, yet they are alive, tanned and pitted with scars. By contrast the sun's legless torso is a shapeless white barrel, and there is no sex. Naturally, the sun has no face, just the usual billions of radiating cosmic rays, as it hovers there between Lawrence and Karen. The sun raises its arms slightly and lifts its index fingers, pointing one at Karen and one at Lawrence. At this gesture, Karen is thrown down to her hands and knees by an invisible force, and lets out a cry, as her skirt takes on the impossible action of slowly rolling itself up her legs and over her knickers. Lawrence is likewise thrown down, but only to his knees, yet he too moans in shock as his trousers unfasten and fall to the ground. He can't move. He is looking along Karen's back, all the way down to her bottom which is tilted up before him. He can't see her face but he can hear her whimpering. He tries to call to her but all that escapes his own lips is a panicky, unintelligible moan. And then he feels a violent spasmodic tingle in his pants. Thoroughly unnerved, he looks down to see something huge bucking inside the fabric, as if trying to burst out. He is terrified. He notices that his underwear has become blinding white. He glances at Karen's. Her pants too are suffused with a blinding radiance. He can feel tears of panic well up in his eyes, and he takes his glance from Karen's wide grown-up bottom to the back of her now grown-up head and her shaking shoulders. She gives out a terrified cry and Lawrence looks on, bewildered, as her searing white behind starts up a strange gyrating motion. The sun is standing in a beatific posture, its commanding arms held symmetrically a little way out from the sides of its body, with Lawrence positioned before one, Karen, the other. They are set a foot apart, fixed to their respective positions on the grass. Sobbing with fear now, his hips having taken on an involuntary, disturbing bucking action, Lawrence tries to keep Karen's head as the focus of his vision. He doesn't want to look at her bottom pointing up like that, making those strange round and round movements. She wouldn't like it. Oh, Karen! He can hear her crying, in her new grown-up voice. If only he could pull her dress back down for her, but he can't move his arms more than a few inches from the sides of his body. If only she could turn her head! And then, from the blinding blank disk of the sun's fusion-wracked face comes a sudden piercing shriek, quickly followed by a low rumbling, so deep and sonorous as to set up a vibration in the ground, and with it comes a new and even more horrifying development: as if obeying a signal, Karen's knickers begin slowly rolling themselves down. She begins to wail pitifully. He tries to look away, but can't, and several seconds pass before he realises his own pants are likewise slowly rolling down his body. As their underwear inches on down, accompanied by the growing apocalyptic rumble, blades of grass detach from the ground around their legs and are sucked up into the sky, so violent is the shaking in the earth. Amid all the noise of the growing bass roar, and his and Karen's hysterical sobbing, all he can think as his underwear descends is: no one wants to go to the toilet, so why is this happening? Feeling as though he will die of shame and fear, he stares down in disbelief as the big, bucking thing in his pants is revealed, springing up, unsheathed by the receding fabric. Its base is rooted in the obscene dark hair of his father, displayed to him every Sunday morning in the changing rooms at the swimming baths. He feels sick: where is his pale little winky? He wants it back: he can't look at this new thing, he can't return its fearsome blunt stare. But that's not all; it's hurting him. There is an ache in it, a kind of straining pain like when you pull your finger back too far. He winces and the tears run down his cheek. He is grateful now that Karen can't turn her head, that she can't turn and see him in this rude, awful, humiliating state. The scream of the sun has reached the pitch of a jet engine, yet it cannot obscure Karen's baleful cries as her pants go on impossibly pulling themselves down, now sliding past the darkest recess of her bottom. In his confusion and panic, Lawrence has forgotten his resolve to keep his eyes on the back of Karen's head and is now gaping in shocked fascination at what is being revealed. But only for a moment. It becomes too much for him; he never imagined that the things girls had between their legs would look like this from this angle, that they could even be seen from this angle, nor that growing up could change what he imagined to be such a simple clean shape into this frightening tangle of dark hair and complicated flesh. He can barely even relate it to the rest of her body, and he can't connect it at all to the sight of the back of her head with its soft fair hair flowing past her fragile ear. And then she lets out a moan of such heartbreaking distress, that his eyes fill again with stinging tears at the memory of her calm, now-vanished little girl face, her chin made honey-yellow by light from a gentle more immense sun, reflected there by the buttercup in her hands. And all the while, the mad involuntary bucking motion of his pelvis goes on, as if in conversation with the strange undulations and rotations of Karen's upturned behind. Yet beyond her poor shaking shoulders he can make out two objects lying in the grass: their reading books. He concentrates on the glad drawings of the jacket illustrations, striving to hold on to them, and with their colours erect a buttress in his mind against the bedlam of panic and noise threatening to engulf him, and from the way Karen is now holding her head, tilted slightly toward the two books, he imagines she is trying to do the same. But the books become smothered in green, engulfed in a vertical fleet of levitating blades of grass, before disappearing forever. Karen's sobbing head sinks below her shoulders, lost in defeat, mirroring his own despair. The searing, blasphemous screeching of the head-sized sun continues for a few moments more, long enough for both their descending pants to come to a final stop around their knees, and then suddenly ceases, leaving nothing but Lawrence's whimpers and Karen's sobs to hang in the air over the green meadow.

Lawrence struggles again to move his arms from his sides, but in vain. In glancing down at his still grotesquely bucking hips, he notices that his underwear has lost its brilliance, has become an infinitely pale grey. He steals a glance at Karen's rolled-down pants and sure enough notices the same infinitely pale grey stretching across the void between her legs. Once again his sight is affronted by the strange flesh hiding in the mist of dark hair growing seemingly from inside her still moving, still circling bottom. Again, he is tortured by the desire to help her, to pull her pants up for her, to comfort her, but his voice is capable still of nothing but cries and grunts, and his arms as useless to help her as they are to wipe the stinging salty tracks of tears from his face.

But not everybody's arms are so helpless. His eyes are caught by a movement to his left. Sullen musculature is slowly raising the arms of the sun. Its small head blazes silently, a mummified cosmic inferno, as its arms slowly reach out in perfect symmetry to Lawrence and Karen. The symmetry of this new, intensified beatific gesture is maintained into the gradual unfurling of the hands. Lawrence watches, rigid, as the huge, solid fingers slowly curl back from the scarred palms, the furthest hand seemingly reaching for Karen's waist. Realising that the other is reaching for him, and not for his waist but for the straining bucking thing between his legs, Lawrence struggles once more, but his only visible movement remains the ongoing involuntary thrusting of his pelvis. Each of the sun's hands is morose as stone as they move into position. The hand approaching Karen has opened and enlarged as though to grip her around the middle, but she is oblivious to it, unable as she is to turn her head. Lawrence is frantic, desperate to warn her, but his attempts are as futile as ever. Meanwhile, around the obscene jerking column of partially skinned meat that was once his willy, now hovers the sun's other hand, its sinews and veins shot through with a battered gravitas. Lawrence, terrified, glances in dumb appeal at the blank head of the sun. There is a moment of suspense, as even Karen's sobs fall to a whimper, and then silence. A small brown leaf caught on the light breeze drifts into the sun's face, and disappears with a slight crackle. Lawrence quickly glances back and forth from the tiny blinding sun to the hands, and then without any further warning, and in the manner of a merciless pouncing predator, each hand locks into place around its target. Lawrence hears a low gasp from Karen as the breath is knocked out of her by the impact of the colossal hand gripping her midriff, the massive fingers closing round her slim waist. He is surprised and oddly dismayed that she does not cry out or sob. In the same instant he feels the fingers close around the shameful thing pointing up at his face, and he bawls out his humiliation and fear, as the sun bends it almost horizontal, pointing it at the weirdness slung beneath Karen's still rotating bottom. The sun begins squeezing its hands one after the other, establishing a bizarre hypnotic rhythm, a slight pulsing in the shape of Karen's behind answered by a throbbing from Lawrence's appendage. He is alarmed to see the back of Karen's head moving calmly from side to side as if she were now in some sort of harmony with this horrible, horrible nightmare! Oh, if only he could talk to her! The painful ache in Lawrence's thing reaches a new intensity, and there is a new flavour to it, a kind of yearning. But he is suddenly distracted from his own sensations by a movement from Karen. She is turning her head. It appears she has been granted that freedom. Beyond her gyrating, upturned bottom, she is slowly turning her lovely head, changed and grown up now like the rest of her, to face him. He feels a wave of relief as her noble profile once more comes into view. At least if they can look at each other they can be of some comfort to one another! Preparing to welcome her with a supportive look into her eyes, he is shocked to see that, as her head comes to rest on her shoulder, she is not peering round at *him* at all, but at the disgusting throbbing thing between his legs. She is smiling at it. He feels his legs go weak with fear, and tries to call to her, but she ignores the resultant grunt. She goes on staring at his thing, no longer smiling but moving her lips strangely. Was she mad? Oh, Karen, Karen! Her eyes are almost closed but he can see she's still looking at it. The ache he feels in it is almost more than he can bear. There must be some way of easing it. All he can think of is to go to the toilet, but how can he do that with this going on, and anyway he doesn't even want to go! Why doesn't Karen *look* at him? It's rude to look down there, to look at him down there with his pants and trousers down. Why is she *doing* it?! Why does she want to look at that horrible thing? He tries again to get her attention, but she turns away, at the same time lowering her shoulders to the ground, pressing her cheek to the grass, and tilting her bottom up even further, giving him the clearest, coarsest view yet of everything to be found there. A devastating hot flush breaks out in his chest, twisting his heart and churning his stomach, making it difficult for him to think. At the same time, he is aware of an excruciating series of tingling, fizzing sensations in his bloated mutated winky, especially in the end of it. He half-wishes the hand would touch it for him, so desperate is he to respond to the maddening itch. But the hand of the sun remains firmly in place around the shaft, entirely motionless, having now ceased its squeezing, as has the hand holding Karen. Lawrence is amazed to find that the absence of the pulsing pressure from the hand has left him in a kind of agonised limbo, and he squirms in frustration, desperate above all else for something, *anything* to provide some relieving contact and ease the maddening tingling. Meanwhile, before him, Karen's bottom appears almost to be splitting apart, so wide apart are her legs, so high in the air is she pushing it. The view is frightening and dirty beyond anything he can imagine, and yet it's somehow turning his heart inside out, the way the smooth pale skin meets and becomes the obscene dark gash of rippling, split flesh and hair. He takes his gaze a little higher and looks on, mesmerised and aghast, noting, with a curious sense of detachment, how her bottom, in being opened up like this, has lost the usual crease running down between the two cheeks, to leave only a shallow valley, blank but for the outrageous punctuation mark of the twitching brown pit in the centre. And all the while, the barrage of sensations in his own body continues. There is a churning feeling in his 'tinned tomatoes', the two things under his willy, and the end of the thing itself is screaming now to be touched, held, *contained.* He peers down and notices a tiny bead of white moisture emerging from the gruesome slit – like the mouth of a fish - in the end of it. He notices that the deeper, longer, more complex slit between Karen's legs has produced a tiny ball of whiteness too, a mesmerising pearl of moisture nestling in a little nook where the folds of skin are coming apart slightly to reveal an alarming, black, alien void. And suddenly he knows what he has to do. Everything points to it. No matter how dirty and bad it is to think it, it seems the things between their legs were made to fit each other. And that's why Karen had been looking at his winky like that! She was probably feeling the same kind of terrible itch and hunger in her thing as he was in his! Well, okay, he'll try it; there doesn't seem to be any other way to deal with the onslaught of sensations between his legs. But will the sun allow it? Well, why not? After all the, sun initiated the whole business, and the plan he has in mind seems to be the logical continuation of it. And so, making the first deliberate use of his pelvis since the sun came down from the sky, he thrusts his hips forward as far as they will go. He hasn't noticed that Karen is again hungrily looking over her shoulder at his willy; he is concentrating solely on the dark, hypnotic core of her thing as she backs it toward him as far as she can. The two pearls of moisture, his and hers, glistening with local sunlight, approach each other over the few inches of grass separating them, but stop short of meeting, destined never to mix their fluid, as the rigid arms of the sun remain implacably in place, barring any further movement of the pair toward one another. The iron grip of the two hands is now apparently intended to prevent them from doing what all the universe is screaming at them to do! Lawrence strains wildly, panicking, struggling to touch her thing with his, but meets with nothing but the two inches of empty air between them. He glances into the impassive, burning face of the sun, only half-aware of Karen's frustrated moans as she goes on vainly thrusting her bottom toward him. Again he makes the attempt, fixing his whole attention on the coarse, shocking aperture before him. Again, he is thwarted by the treacherous immobility of the hand. Oblivious now to Karen's hungry moans, he succumbs to an overwhelming tide of panic, and embarks on a mad frenzy of bucking and thrusting.

As the minutes pass, and become hours, he finally realises, with a sickening terror, that the grotesque performance is trapped in an infinite stasis; the sun will go on holding them this way forever, affording them no hope of either satisfying their need, or of ever again rising from their knees to cover their shame and leave the meadow.

He started awake with a low grunt, consumed by a lurching nausea. His breath was coming in short, shaking bursts, as the room around him slowly identified itself, taking over from the dream.

Fuckinghellfire!... sick fucking joke of a nightmare ... He brushed a lock of damp hair away from his face. Christ, his whole head was wet with sweat. He raised himself up on his elbows, now aware of an intense discomfort between his legs, a piercing ache centred on his groin.

And he was afraid. Fucking sick and afraid.

He lifted the duvet, the physical effort increasing the nausea, and stared down at his erection, stared at the glans as though for the first time; a morose, purple lump twitching in the darkness, craning up to reach him, as though it were him it wanted, as though it were him it wanted all along.

It jolted. A white bolt of fluid shot toward him, hitting him right in the centre of his forehead. There was a sensation of stunning white heat at the point of impact and he threw his hands to his face as his forehead slowly caved in, the seed sinking into his brain.

He sat up, shaking violently, frantically feeling his head, gasping with relief at finding it still in one piece. Another dream – shit and fuck. The old cliche! *Christ.* He was panting hard. Christ, his breathing was running away from him. Controlling his breaths, he felt the panic ease a little as he wiped his forehead and let his head fall back against the wall. From the corner of his eye, he glanced down at the duvet, overcome by an irrational urge to lift it, just to prove to himself that the nightmare was over. He lifted his head from the wall and quickly raised the cover.

But the sullen monstrous head was still there, appearing exactly as it had in the dream, craning toward him, a blind, bloated, twitching worm, throbbing slowly in the darkness.

FOURTEEN

He stared tiredly down at the bowl of Cocoa Pops, a weak grip on his spoon.

He'd fucking had enough. God knows he'd tried. He'd tried to satisfy the fucker, and failed; he'd tried to fight it, and failed. One thing was now certain: he had to take the edge off the bastard somehow or he was going to go off the fucking tracks completely. So never mind the stench of compromised principles; it was time to succumb to the inevitable.

To recognise that the sex dole was made for him.

And he for it. A match made in heaven. The stars in the sky were probably crying out for their union, had been since time immemorial. He could see that now. It was silly to deny it any longer, to waste any more time, to go on resisting when the joyous embrace of the sex benefit centre beckoned. It was time to grasp his *destiny*. He'd go down there this afternoon, chat the place up a bit, buy it a few drinks, run his fingers across the smooth silken upholstery of its swivel chairs, and with his lingering touch feel the yielding satin surface of its application forms ...

Christ....

He plunged the spoon into the bowl of cereal, and felt himself lulled by the familiar comfort food, so good it served well for lunch too, as was the case today. Good thing he hadn't got anything else in, like beans or soup or any of that crap, which was just a fucking chore to cook *and* eat; he had to enjoy his lunch if he were to be properly set up for the delightful rendezvous this afternoon, and Cocoa Pops were the chaps to do it.

He lifted the bowl to his face and gulped down the remaining brown milk, unconsciously closing his eyes beneath a forehead stricken with sweat and plastered-down hair. A drop of brown fluid ran down from the corner of his mouth before losing its way among the bristles of his unshaven chin.

He slowly lowered the bowl to the table, and stared at it, sitting calmly, savouring the numbness that had accompanied his decision to sign on, the strange peace that came with surrender. And only now did he raise his hand and brush away the brown droplet from his jaw.

Marching down Kentish Town Road, he stepped off the pavement and into the gutter, making way for a triple-seat push-chair, breathing deeply and deliberately the life-shortening exhaust of the bus juddering along in front of him. He was now caught in the road, separated from the pavement by a stretch of black safety railing. He ploughed on, hemmed in by the almost stationary traffic until, finally regaining the pavement, he peered up at the dull three-storey building beyond the garage, flat and anonymous under the low white sky.

This fucking ugly piece of sixties concrete: his new girl, his special lady - his blushing *bride,* probably, to have and to hold forever. Still, he had to win its tender heart yet, which would presumably entail the filling in of a load of fucking forms and sitting through a tedious interview.

The interview.

Christ, what a delightful little number that's going to be: 'So, you claim to be a sad wanker.' 'Yes, that's right.' 'Can you prove it?' 'Well, I've walked in here, haven't I?' 'That's fine. Sign here, then, please....'

As the grime-streaked facade of the building came up on his left, and he passed again the posters in the windows, the big beaming faces advertising the various sex benefit schemes laughed at him, revelling in their victory over him. He pushed open the door, watching the reflection of his unkempt head swing back and give way to the strip-lit interior of the benefit centre. He noted the cluster of oppressed punters sat in the waiting area, and the flat murmur of voices coming from the four signing desks. Despite his pathetic and reduced status as a soon-to-be claimant of sex support, he was determined at least to act decisively and with whatever dignity he could muster now that the decision to claim had been made. Accordingly, he crossed straight to the reception desk, and took his place in the small queue.

He folded his arms and waited, keeping his eyes on the back of the man in front of him, a guy in his fifties. He felt acutely self-conscious - and fucking ashamed and embarrassed. But then he told himself that it was a way of life for all the poor fuckers in here, and that for the staff too it was just the daily grind, and that now that he had joined this queue he had probably already begun to blend in with the surroundings, and he could relax a little.

He glanced around the room, running his eyes over the group of claimants. He smiled sourly to himself; well, his suspicion that the attractive young career woman he'd seen in here the other week was something of an anomaly was so far proving correct. Apart from one unhealthy-looking middle-aged woman caked in foundation, sitting with white high heels crossed, and a heavy-set girl mucking about with a mobile phone, the rest of the place looked like Ladbroke's on a Saturday afternoon. What kind of sex workers did they employ to service these people? He realised he hadn't given much thought to this, but just as quickly realised that was because he didn't really care. His expectations were not high. He was here simply to discharge his biological function in someone, and then fuck off.

His eyes drifted away from the claimants to the Contact-Seeker's Charter poster over the radiator on the back wall. He felt the bitter sting of defeat as he stared once more at the loathsome graphic that had so enraged him the other day, but the feeling soon gave way to numb acceptance. Still, as he read again the tag line "Helping you back to Satisfaction" he found himself rebelling: "Helping you... exorcise your demon seed."

The bloke in front had now sat down at the reception desk, and Lawrence went on surveying the room, his gaze now taking in the aisles of vertical boards displaying their little white cards. What in fuck was that all in aid of? He squinted at the board nearest to him. Oh, right, of course. Personal contact ads - presumably the satisfaction they were helping you back to, while the on-site knobbing was just the reluctant hand-out to keep you ticking over.

Fucking hell.

And over in the corner, the fucking potted palm. Christ.... He let his eyes coast down its length, noting the flat plates of the leaves, the green turning grey under the screen of accumulating dust. Trailing his glance across the worn carpet, he became aware for the first time of a random scattering of tiny white triangles strewn across the grey expanse of floor, concentrated most heavily in the space between the waiting area and the signing desks. For a second he was at a loss as to what they were, but then he got it: discarded tickets from the dispenser in the centre of the room.

A stooped figure crossed immediately in front of him: the chap who'd been in front of him in the queue. Lawrence turned to the reception desk, saw the woman peering up at him, and, smiling involuntarily from embarrassment, took a seat, moving the hair away from his eyes.

'Hello, and what can we do for you?' said the woman.

She reminded him of his favourite primary school teacher, and he felt a sudden insane impulse to win her over, to win her approval, to demonstrate his charm and show that he wasn't like all the other sad fucks that came in here. But that would be a lie. He swept the impulse aside, and leaned forward slightly.

'Er ... yeah, I'd like to make a claim.'

He was surprised to see her face remain unchanged at this open declaration of his sexual wretchedness, but of course she heard such declarations every day.

'Right, okay, first thing is to make an appointment for an interview with a claimant advisor.' She turned to her monitor and began moving her mouse about. 'Can you come in next week? Say, Wednesday at 10:30?'

Next week? Now that he had taken the plunge he wanted to just get on with it, and now the place was playing hard to get.

'Er ... yeah, yeah. Yes, that's fine.'

'Right, you'll need to fill in a claim form....' She pulled open a drawer, and peered inside, frowning. 'Ah, I'll have to go and get you one. Can you wait a moment please?'

'Yes, of course.' Resting his elbow on the arm of the chair, he held his chin in his hand, and watched her rise from the desk. He began unconsciously stroking his stubble, and looked about him, focusing on the signing desks. You could almost see the weird psychology of the place condensing on the walls and ceiling around the four 'claimant advisors', obliged by the state to help the poor fuckers sat across from them, yet at the same time obliged by the same state to thwart them wherever possible. The guy with the thinning hair and the glasses seemed to be exuding this paradox through his very pores; the punter sat before him was being moved through the process efficiently enough, but if the poor bastard took the trouble to search the eyes of the official dealing with him he would see that he was being told quite clearly to piss off and never come back. Lawrence watched the narrow eyes of the advisor for a moment, before returning his attention to the receptionist, now lowering herself back into the seat across from him.

Williams watched as his claimant, a gaunt middle-aged man with a moustache, took his ticket and rose from the chair. As the guy moved off, Williams let his gaze wander across the waiting claimants to the reception desk, where his glance came to rest on the unshaven young man sitting back with his chin in his hand as Moira sat down to deal with him. Sitting back for all the world as if expecting to be waited on hand and foot. And then Williams smiled in recognition. Oh, so you're back already are you, chum? Didn't take long, did it? He watched as Moira began going through the forms, and had to tear his eyes away at the approach of his next claimant.

Lawrence regarded the thick forms with dismay as the reception woman landed them on the desk.

'Sorry about the wait. Right. Here's your claim form, then, which you should complete and bring to your appointment. And your medical form which should be completed by your GP and also brought to the appointment if possible, though we know it can be difficult to arrange doctor's appointments at short notice.'

A medical form? Well, of course. They weren't going to let you near their fuck-workers if you'd caught the plague. Well, he was all right; it wasn't as though he'd had the opportunity. Ah, the irony.

'What happens if I can't get the medical form sorted out by next Wednesday?'

'Well, your first session will simply be put back until we can get a look at it. Now, here is a leaflet which outlines our obligations to you, and yours to us under the Contact-Seeker's Charter. It generally explains everything about how the system works and I suggest you have a careful read-through of it before you come for your interview.

Okay? That's everything, then.'

But he had stopped listening and was staring down blankly at the information leaflet, running a slender finger across the cover, tracing the outline of the hated graphic of the couple on the idiotic stilts approaching each other over the impossible white sand of the impossible white beach.

The receptionist regarded his long down-turned eyelashes, and leaned forward slightly. 'Okay, that's it, then. That's everything.'

He glanced up.

'Oh. Yeah. Thanks very much.'

He smiled faintly, gathering the documents together, and then, with his claim form, his medical form and his information leaflet held firmly in his right hand, he stood up and headed for the door.

FIFTEEN

Colin Carlton emptied another cardboard pallet of mushrooms into the large plastic trough. A customer was already half-pushing him out of the way to get at them. He heard her tutting and cursing under her breath, so he shuffled back to let her get past. He stood, watching her from behind as she rummaged through the mushrooms, the cardboard pallet hanging from his pudgy fingers, the highlights from her twisting blond curls reflecting in his dull eyes as he wiped his nose with the back of his blotchy fat hand. Oh, she was pretty, like... with nice hair, like...

He glanced about him, sending a ripple through the roll of fat around his neck. Cool, there was no one else in the aisle, which meant that if he wanted, like, he could go on lookin'. He allowed his eyes to rest for a while on the customer's posterior, forgetting the rest of her, her blond hair, her tiny perfect hands as they sifted through the mushrooms selecting only the whitest, only the purest, only the very best. He stared at the waistband of her tan tights, an inch of which was visible above her trousers. But then he looked away. It wasn't really right, like, to do that, to look at someone down there, like, when they didn't know. Slowly he moved away from her, taking his cardboard pallet with him.

He passed the plastic trough containing the peppers. They looked all right to him, now, like. There was no way, no way that bastard

Simon could tell him to do it again now. He felt a sudden pain in his leg and looked round to see that he had collided with a trolley being pushed by a young mother.

'Oh, I'm sorry! Are you all right?' she asked.

'Yeah,' he mumbled, bending to rub his chubby calf. As she passed him, he realised there was something he had forgotten to say, and the blood rushed to his cheeks. 'Yeah, thanks,' he said, glancing briefly up into her face.

'No, I really am sorry,' she smiled back at him over her shoulder, and pushed on with her trolley, her young son leading the way.

Some women were okay. Yeah, some were really okay, like. He picked up his cardboard pallet and slowly made his way over to the stockrooms at the back of the superstore.

The shift would finish, soon, like. Fuckin' fantastic. More fantastic than ever, like, cos today was sex dole. Get some grub for the dog first though. Yeah. So, it was like, grub for the dog, some tins for him, like, then sex dole - and he was really needin' that now after lookin' at that lady bent over them mushrooms. But he was always needin' that, like. Always needin' that. Sometimes it was like two weeks was too long to wait, really. But now it's like less than two hours to wait! Yeah, and nice one - after that, when he got home he still had two more Dr. Whos on that Dr Who tape to watch, and it was the white-haired one an' all, from when he was a kid, like, from when he was a kid ... which made it like not so bad having to, having to like, leave the woman at the sex dole and go home.

'Colin,' said the fresh produce supervisor standing next to a large stack of pallets crammed with tomatoes as Carlton ambled past.

'Yeah?'

'Have you done those peppers again, yet?'

'Yeah. I have.'

'Then come and show me, will you.'

Carlton turned and began shuffling back in the direction he had come, with Simon at his side. Fuckinell, Simon, the peppers are all right now. They're all right.

As they neared the pepper trough once more, Carlton was dismayed to see Simon start shaking his head. The supervisor lifted his hands and let them fall back to his sides. Carlton watched as Simon knelt down and picked up a pepper from the front of the trough. It was withered and marked with brown blemishes.

'You were told to remove stuff like this. This is the second time you've been asked to do this and it's still not done! Look, what's this? Another one! You've spent half the afternoon on this! Now get this mess sorted out. If I have to come here and tell you again I'm going to tell the manager, do you understand?'

Carlton sank to his knees and began slowly sifting through the peppers as Simon stood up and walked away.

Fuckin', fuckin' bastard.

He wiped his nose and dropped a reject pepper into his cardboard pallet, before looking round to see the sexy mushroom lady cross the far end of the aisle. His small eyes followed her until she was out of sight, and then he got back to work, concentrating once more on rooting out the bad peppers from the good, his plump, inarticulate fingers roaming listlessly across the trough of mostly shining red vegetables.

At the supermarket entrance, a crescent of young girls dressed in a mix of Camden Town retro styles made way for the heavy, almost lumbering, figure of Carlton as he exited the store, clutching a carrier bag full of dog food and crisps. One of the girls glanced accidentally into Carlton's tiny lustreless eyes, before immediately looking away again, tossing her long hair over her shoulder as he shuffled past. He knew this reaction well, had become used to the dull stabs of pain they engendered, and yet, despite this pain, he still found unconscious crumbs of enjoyment in these hurtful non-exchanges. Though he would not have been able to articulate it, at least he was for a second holding the dark pupils of a woman with his own - a tiny fragment of contact with the opposite sex of his species. And if it happened that his appointment at the sex dole office was still many days away, he would unconsciously build fantasies around these tiny glimpses into the souls of women beyond the benefit centre.

As he gained the pavement, swapping the cold strip-lights of the store for the weak daylight of the overcast Camden sky, he tried to calculate how much time he had before he signed on at the sex dole. His watch said 2:36. He signed on at 3. So that was ... that was more than half an hour. Or ... no, it was less, like. More like 25 minutes. Cool. Not long now, then, like. And in the meantime he could go and look in the comic shop for a bit. But actually, no ... never mind that, like. Better to just walk around ... look at the girls an' that. He liked to do that on a sex dole day, he could watch them and watch them and, like, let his sex feelings build up and stuff, and then it was okay cos then he could go down the sex dole and, like, let it all out and stuff. Let it out with a nice lady, like ... not just ... not just go home and wank, like. And it was all right to, like, look at the girls and ladies out here on the street, cos they were sort of movin' about and that, and it wasn't the same as starin' at that woman's bum in the shop while she was bendin' over them mushrooms, and him standin', like, so close to her ... an' that... That was different. And wrong, like.

As he came up to Camden High Street, two girls came out of the Underground station in front of him, and for the next five minutes, like, it was really fantastic cos he was walking along behind them, and their bums were, like, really really lovely. And he felt that warm feelin', and it made him feel kind of cool, like. And it was sound cos he didn't feel left out or anythin' either, cos soon he'd be at the sex dole.

He followed them across the road. It was so great watchin' their bums movin' from side to side, like. But then they turned into a shop full of weird stuff, leather gear and spiky collars an' that and they were gone. But that was okay, like, cos just comin' out of the next shop was another girl with, like really fuckin' nice tights on. Ah, yeah, fuckinell, nice one. Ah, imagine... touchin' them, like, or even ... even kissin' them - with your mouth, like. Fuckinell, yeah! And he felt the warmth getting stronger, felt the warmth between his legs somehow beating in his head at the same time. It felt nice and that.... It felt nice but like he'd better start watchin' the back of her head for a bit ... else he'd start gettin' big, like, and then he'd start walkin' funny and that'd ruin everythin'. Ruin everythin' if everyone started starin' at him like he was a twat, like.

He fixed his gaze to the back of the girl's head as she sashayed on down the street ahead of him. Her long black hair was tied up in some really weird knots, like ... really weird knots with weird fuckin' sticks and things ... bits of wood and that stickin' out of it. It was like loads of girls had stuff like that in their hair now, especially around here in Camden. But it looked too foreign, too fuckin' foreign, like. He didn't like it. Yeah, and if she came up to him and asked him to go out with her, he'd say, no, like, I don't want to. Yeah, that'd be cool! That'd be really cool. He chuckled aloud at the thought, but he knew that really he'd say, yeah, yeah, I'll go out with you ... but her actually, like, *sayin'* that, actually *sayin'* that to him? That was ... well, that was ... that was like fuckin' science fiction, that was! Might as well look for a job drivin' Thunderbird 2, or go into a red phone box, like, and expect it to be the fuckin' Tardis inside. But the thought didn't depress him. The girl walking along in front of him was like just a taster to get him goin', like, for when he got to the sex dole.

He just had time for one last look at the girl's tights before she disappeared into the doorway of a pub.

He ambled on, occasionally scratching a slight itch - to which he was entirely oblivious - somewhere in the inner region of his huge baggy-trousered thigh. Staring dumbly through the window of a trendy cafe at all the pretty girls drinkin' their posh coffee an' that, and then looking about the rest of the street at all the other girls and ladies about, he actually felt quite happy, like. Happy that he didn't have to try to ... try to talk to any of them. Happy that he could just go to the sex dole. But he had given up tryin' to talk to them anyway years and years ago, like. Actually, really, you were still supposed to try and talk to them. Some of the people down that sex dole ... some of the bastards, like, some of *them* would throw you off if you said you just didn't bother, like.

He began to drift away from the heart of Camden Town and began heading up Kentish Town Road in the direction of the sex benefit centre. Sometimes he thought he should try and talk to a woman again just so he wouldn't be lying when they asked him what he'd done to try to get a fuck, like, but it just hurt too much. He knew his fuckin' place. Knew where he stood, like, with the women. Knew where he fuckin' stood.

He let his chin sink into the mass of fat around his neck, as he noticed three girls in their mid-twenties coming along the pavement toward him. These girls here, goin' down Camden, laughin' and lookin' so pretty and that ... it was his job *not* to fuckin' talk to them! It was like ... like that was a rule life had given him. It was funny that the bastards in that place had this other rule, like. Like you've got to talk to girls an' that. Years back, in the days when he used to try, even if he talked to girls who weren't pretty, were ugly, like - even as fuckin' ugly as him - they wouldn't be interested either, tellin' him to piss off, or sometimes to fuck off too, so no way would he talk to these girls here. Ruin their fuckin' day for them. Ten years ago it would have killed him these girls here, with their nice lovely hair and everythin'... but now it's okay, like. Yeah, it's okay. Cos of the sex dole. Cos of the women in that place. They make life really okay, like. They're not really as lovely as these girls here, but they let you do it with them, like, and make you feel all right, like. So bye, Camden girls, bye, who needs you? Yeah. Yeah, and if he wanted to *talk* to someone, if he wanted to *talk* to someone, he'd talk to his dog.

As he neared the drab concrete building with its faded pollution-streaked panels, Carlton suddenly became aware of the soggy cardboard tray of half-eaten chips he was pushing along the pavement with his shoe. He stopped to shake it off and carried on, leaving a trail of mashed chip smeared over the pavement behind him.

He began to feel a bit nervous, now, like he always did when he got near to the sex dole, near to the building, like. But really excited, like as well, though. Ah, fuckinell, yeah, soon he'd have a woman, like, be really, be really goin' into her and that.... And he felt himself getting big again, like. But first though, he'd have to ... have to sit down at that desk, like, and they'd make him write his name on that piece of paper, and then sometimes they'd ask him stuff. He fuckin' hated that, like. That bastard, that fuckin' bastard with the glasses was always doin' that. And that was the reason he always got nervous, like, in case he got that bastard.

As he pushed open the door and entered the reception area, passing and ignoring the revolving stands of leaflets offering advice on self-improvement and contact opportunities, he looked over to the four signing-on desks. Yeah, there the bastard was. He was in today, like. Fuckinell. He lumbered up to the number dispenser, punched the button with his big soft finger, took the ticket, and shuffled across the room, before awkwardly lowering his great weight into the plastic seating of the waiting area, almost dislodging one of the other claimants. He let the carrier bag of dog food tins drop noisily to the floor, and sat gripping his ticket tightly.

He sat hunched over, staring at the stained carpet, occasionally glancing up at Williams, watching the quick, urgent movements of his head as he dealt with a claimant. He couldn't hear Williams' voice over the general hubbub of the room, but he could see his thin mouth moving quickly. For a moment he felt something like panic, but finally comforted himself - as he always did - with the thought that he was just as likely to see any of the other three claimant advisors. And yeah, cool, that black bloke was there, like. He was all right that bloke ... never messed you about ... never messed you about like that bastard over there. He hoped so much that he'd get that black bloke, like ... hoped so much that he'd get him. The other two were okay, like ... but they didn't ... they never ... they never looked happy to see you, like. But that bloke ... he'd even smile at you an' that.

He looked up and stared dumbly for a while at the LED counter, watched as it ticked off another number, calling another claimant to one of the desks. The black bloke's! He watched jealously as a small middle-aged man went up. You're all right, then ... you're all right ... home and dry, like. He looked down, unclenching his fist to look at his own ticket, which lay screwed into a ball in his palm. He had already forgotten the number. With clumsy shaking hands he struggled to smooth out the crumpled triangle of paper. 154. The LED counter said 149. So that meant there was ... another ... another five to go, like. He peered over at the four signing-on desks, at the four claimants sat before the four claimant advisors, glanced up again at the LED counter and then back down to the desks and Williams' head. He watched it make a sudden movement. Then watched Williams' hand write quickly across a sheet of paper while the claimant, a woman, looked on.

Well ... even if he got that bastard, like ... he'd, he'd get through it, like ... and then he'd go up the stairs. Whatever happened he'd be goin' up the stairs soon, like! And he felt the warmth return. As his dull eyes absently drifted back up to the LED counter, now reading 150, his fat blemished hand once more descended to his itching thigh.

Over at his desk, Williams turned the sheet of paper around for the claimant to sign. As she leaned forward to write, he stared at the crown of her head, at her thick dark hair, greying slightly at the roots. Good-looking woman. These lookers. Could they really not find it out there? Still, they never seemed to claim long-term. The woman looked up and pushed the claim sheet back toward him.

'That's fine, then, thank you,' he said, reluctantly taking his eyes from her brown-eyed gaze. He glanced at the range of available cubicles displayed on his monitor. 'If you'd make your way to number 11, please,' said Williams tonelessly, handing back the woman's SB40.

'Thank you,' she said quietly, putting the document back into her bag and rising from her seat. His eyes were caught by the movement of her trim posterior as she turned and put her bag over her shoulder. He watched her for a moment, his narrow lips parting slightly, as she headed across the room to the stairs. There's a nice one for you, Barry. You owe me a pint there, I think.

He pressed the button to cue on the LED counter and got up to return the claimant's file. Taking his seat once more, he watched as the next claimant approached. A youth, a tearaway by the look of him. While he waited, Williams quickly scanned the crew of waiting claimants, and became suddenly excited. There was a fat lad over there scratching himself in the groinal area. Definite possible breach of the hygiene conditions, that. Might be a chance of getting this one thrown off. Definite chance there. Have to check afterwards with the facilitator he sees.

Meanwhile, the tearaway had sat down before him. Williams took his SB40 and marched over to the filing cabinet.

Carlton watched as Williams returned and began dealing with the young man with the spiky hair and the leather jacket. Yeah, the bastard was definitely askin' him a few questions, like. And writin', like. Writin' stuff down. But what was the number on now, like? He glanced up again at the LED counter. 152. Which meant that ... which meant that if ... if the bastard finished with this bloke, before the others finished with theirs ... if he finished first, like ... then he'd push the button thing first and that counter thing would be 153. Which was the number before his, like ... and then there'd be almost no way he'd be gettin' him!

With a kind of animal desperation, Carlton's eyes moved as quickly as they could across the other desks, at the hunched over claimants and their advisors, at their moving mouths and moving pens. Slow down! Please, please fuckin' slow down! He looked back to Williams. Tell him to go, now, you bastard, tell him he can go. Come on, come on you fuckin' bastard. Come on you fuckin' fuckin'-

And the young man with the spiky hair rose from Williams' desk and headed for the stairs. The counter flicked over to 153.

Fuckin' yeah!! Oh yeah! Fuckin' sound! *Sound!*

It was as though all the joys of heaven and earth had been opened to him, and he looked on in secret bliss as a smart, erect young man strode over to Williams' desk and sat down.

Dressed in a crisp business suit, the fair-haired young man regarded Williams evenly from beneath a fiercely handsome brow, and leaned nonchalantly into one corner of the seat, at the same time opening up on Williams with a broad smile.

It amused Sacha greatly to encounter these prickly little underlings of the welfare state, to watch these drab cocks wield their wretched little power as if it mattered, which to him it could not, because he didn't need them, as the three girls he was currently shafting could testify to. No, he only came down to their sad little sex dole office for the pure fucking fun of it. And to top off the fun, the particular specimen in front of him was giving off a definite whiff of sexually frustrated bureaucrat.

'Your SB40, please.'

For a moment, Sacha wondered what he was talking about. Ah, yes, this sorry prat required his little document thingie. Better get it out for him then. The pathetic bastard looked so eager to scamper over to his important filing cabinet and pull out another bit of paper to scribble on, and thereby bestow on a young-stud-about-town another delightfully anonymous bit of afternoon poking. A bit of late afternoon stuffing to see him through till Sally at eight.

He pulled the document from his jacket and laid it on the table. Go on then, you petty little man, there's your precious bit of cardboard. Go and take it to your special and important filing cabinet like the good little bureau-twat that you are.

Williams picked it up, muttering a terse 'Thank you', irritated that the guy hadn't even opened his mouth, had just sat there smiling. Christ, the nerve of some of these louts. Because that's what the guy was, a bloody lout, and never mind the expensive suit.

As he made his way to the filing cabinet, he reflected on the character sat in the chair. There was something about this one. A bit of a shiny one. Definitely reckoned he was worth a bit more than the rest of us. Well, we'll have a look at you, chum. Put you through one. But first, we'll have a good long look for your file.

Sacha watched Williams march off to the filing cabinet. That's right, you desperate waste of sperm, go and get me my fuck, if you'd be so kind. He looked around the room, surveying the huddle of claimants clumped together on the rectangle of bolted-together chairs, and others, even sadder, who were wandering around actually looking at the boards with their fetid displays of untouchable personal ads. He knew that most of the people in here would probably be genuine claimants. But he almost couldn't believe it. Good Christ alive! What kind of foul infected leper did you have to be to come here and not be taking the piss? He himself was here for two reasons: one, he was paying for it out of his taxes; two, he was interested in sexual nourishment wherever it was to be found, even in a sewer like this, especially if it offered some rare spice such as the almost kinky anonymity of the sex dole cubicle. But these sorry fools here, this was all they had, the hopeless shits. What the hell was the matter with them? Some of them didn't look so bad. A couple of the women were even quite shaggable. He'd take them off the sex dole statistics himself if he weren't currently ramming superior fare. What were they doing here? Didn't they know they could walk into any club any day of the week in any part of town and be getting their brains screwed out within the hour? Maybe they were ripping the place off too, like he was, but somehow they didn't look the type. He moved his eyes once more across the group. Oh, here we are. A definite genuine case. Good heavens above, look at that. Hello, rolly polly gargoyle. You poor ugly mountain. Scratching away at yourself too, I see. You really are a real live leper, aren't you, my friend. Well, I freely grant you, there can be no other outlet for you, you big ball of sad sludge. I'm moved, pal. Truly moved. And I believe in charity. I don't begrudge *you* whatever part of my taxes gets spent on this place. In fact, they could put a penny on my income tax any day of the week, if they used it to build a little shag dole palace just for your own exclusive and private pleasure, my poor monster. You deserve it, you poor, sweating stain. Ah, they've called your number. Off you waddle then to your sexual alms. Alms for a leper. No-one can deserve it more than you. But as for all these other zombies....What was their excuse? Perhaps the men had negligible cocks and were scared of real encounters, or more likely they were just typical weak scum, falling onto the sour milky pap of the nanny state at the first opportunity. Or perhaps out of some deluded sense of respect for 'real' women they had come here rather than chat up a strange female in the street, the pathetic arseholes. But talking of weak scum, where was that useless prick who was supposed to be signing him on? Ah, here he came now. Just in time, old son, just in time.

Williams, having made a show of rifling in vain through the files, while all the time knowing very well the location of the relevant document, considered that he'd kept this Flash Harry waiting long enough - he must be stewing in his juice by now - and so with a satisfied inward smile, he slammed the drawer shut and strode purposefully back to the desk. But as he once more took his seat he was dismayed to see the scrounging jack-the-lad sitting calmly as ever. Well, never mind, he would make this one pay yet for his little roll in the hay.

'All right, as you've been claiming sex benefit now for two months, there are one or two questions I'd like to ask you before I sign you on. I must warn you that you must give me satisfactory answers or else you may forfeit your entitlement to benefit.'

You foreskin. You utter foreskin, thought Sacha, while keeping his body language as relaxed as before. All right, little man, I'll match you.

'Yes, of course, certainly.'

He deliberately leaned forward in his chair to appear more accommodating. I'll please you, you dreadful little maggot, I'll please you with my sweetly satisfactory answers, and afterwards you will wave me through to my little vulvar snack, my little tea-time pudenda before dinner.

Williams peered over his glasses, eyeing the young man critically. Yes, the clever bugger was definitely looking a bit more impatient now. Good.

'Right, can you tell me please what efforts you have made in the last two weeks to secure a sexual encounter?'

'Well. I went to a couple of clubs. Danced with one or two likely-looking girls. But they weren't biting. It's always the way. I have the worst luck. But I did get the number of a very pretty foreign student in an art gallery. Surprised myself there, a textbook case of successful cold-calling-'

'That sounds promising. You can call this girl then. Who knows? If something happens, you could be off our books by next week,' smiled Williams thinly, sitting back in his chair and folding his arms.

Hold your horses, you evaporating drop of piss.

'Ah, well, if only life were that easy. As I was about to say, I did call her, but it turned out she was on her way back to Sweden that very weekend so that was the end of that. This is it. This is the problem with London. You think-'

'Can you give me her telephone number, please?'

Brutal! This is one tenacious little tiny turd we have here. But, my friend, like all turds, you will be flushed away.

'You mean her number in Sweden? I don't know it. She didn't give it to me.'

'Then can you give me whatever number she gave you here in London?' Williams leaned forward once more, watching closely for any sign of hesitation or panic. If there were to be any, it would come now.

'Yes, I can,' said Sacha, pulling out his tiny silver mobile. He quickly selected a number from the phonebook and thrust it in Williams' face.

INGA 078803478913

'You can try it if you like, but it's dead. She's probably got a new simcard, now she's in Sweden.'

'No ... that won't be necessary.' Williams knew that the name and number in the phone didn't prove anything, but also that there was no further he could go with it. However, he made a mental note of the number - something he was very good at - just in case the lout tried to use the story again in the future. Meanwhile, there were other probes he could try. And other needles. Leave no stone unturned. 'You do appreciate, don't you, that you're not meant to be using this benefit centre as a holding ground while you look for highly desirable women?'

'I'm not.'

'I mean, I hope you're not just chasing beautiful young Swedish students. We might have something to say about that.'

'Well, I'm not.'

I'm not *chasing* beautiful young Swedish students, you stupid tit, I'm *fucking* them. Two of them. Ulla and Inga. Dear severely fuckable little Inga who could never keep possession of a mobile phone for more than a month before leaving it in a toilet or crushed to pieces on the floor of some Kings Cross club. He'd better buy her a new one: it was getting to be a pain in the arse trying to get hold of her at that filthy pit of a flatshare. The devil himself would have a job getting any sense out of that long-haired wankshaft that was always answering the phone there.

Williams regarded the guy for a moment. A slight abstracted look had come across the guy's face, and he was staring at the arm of his chair. Rude lout. The *characters* that came *in* here! 'So, apart from this elusive student, what other proposals have you made?'

You're beginning to get on my knackers now, you little wretch.

'Well, no actual proposals as such. But I was looking. I mean, I must have gone out nearly every night this week, but well, it just wasn't my lucky week.'

'Where did you go?'

'I beg your pardon?'

'The places you went to. The names of the places you went to,' said Williams, visibly irritated, looking at the table.

Tetchy!

'Why are you asking me that? Don't you believe me?'

'Well, I won't believe you if you don't give me the names,' snapped Williams.

'All right, I went to Bagley's Friday, 333 on Saturday. The Cross ... Thursday ... The End on Tuesday, I think....'

'These are all nightclubs, are they?'

'Yes, that's right.'

'And you say you don't have much luck in them?'

'That's right.'

'Then perhaps you should consider some other line of attack. Such as night classes, maybe. We've had one or two find their way back into a sex life of their own through that particular conduit.'

You'd better stop this shit now, you piece of refuse.

'Well, I'll think about it, but for now I think I'll stick to what's worked best for me in the past. I've only really been claiming for two months and, as I say, I think the quickest route out for me will be through the clubs. It's always worked fine in the past.'

Williams was pleased with this. The smart git didn't like that bit about night classes at all. If it had actually been in his power to send him to one there and then, he would have done so without further hesitation, but the bugger was still in the grace period. Still, he was satisfied now that he had ruffled the guy's feathers a bit, put him through one. That was enough for now. Next time he saw him he would put him out on a few dates. Warming himself with this thought, he wrote the date on the claim sheet, turned the sheet to the claimant, and rolled out the question.

'Okay then. Have you had a sexual encounter at any time in the last two weeks?'

About fucking time, you pustule.

'No, I haven't,' answered Sacha, taking the pen.

Carlton ascended the stairs, panting a little, yet flushed with the joy of his easy passage through the ordeal of the signing-on desk. He'd got that black bloke an' all. And the bloke had just smiled at him, like, when he sat down. Just asked him to write his name, like, and now here he was, like, on his way ... on his way up to a woman. And he was gettin' big again, now, like! Like out on the street ... like out on the street, only bigger.

As he gained the first floor, he struggled for a moment to remember which cubicle he was supposed to go to. Six. No, Seven. Seven, yeah, that was it, like. He peered down the long cream-painted corridor so familiar to him, his eyes no longer taking in the potted palm at the far end, and halfway along, the single cigarette bin with its tarnished chrome rim, the only furniture in this antechamber to the only really warm rooms he had ever known.

He moved eagerly down the corridor, though as awkwardly as ever due to his state of arousal. Finally he came to a door standing half-open.

Number 7. This was it, then, like. This was it! He made a pudgy ball of his hand and knocked on the door, proud of the fact that he had remembered to knock first, and hadn't just gone crashing through in his excitement, as he had done once, to the extreme annoyance of the facilitator within.

'Come in,' called a friendly female voice from inside.

Carlton shifted his great weight through the door and found himself in heaven.

SIXTEEN

The moment Angela Braintree saw the great slovenly figure shuffle its way into her cubicle she felt a shock of revulsion, which she immediately brought under control. It was pretty plain to her that this guy was not having an easy time of it outside; she noticed the plastic carrier bag of sad shopping. The following twenty minutes were quite obviously going to be the highlight of his week, and she didn't want to spoil it for him by looking disgusted. Otherwise there was no point her being here. The poor soul was one of life's dispossessed, and she was here to help.

'Hi,' she smiled, extending her slim young arm. 'Come over here, then.' She was sitting on the bed dressed in a loose flannel robe, with the lowermost curls of her blond hair resting lightly on the upper slopes of each half-exposed breast, her classically elegant head inclined in welcome.

As Carlton began slowly moving forward, she reflected that although lying down with him was going to be rather tough and physically more unpleasant than with other men, it would on the other hand in a way be more rewarding. It wasn't the guy's fault he was hideous, and for the next twenty minutes she would tend to his pain. A lot of the other girls and guys who worked here wouldn't really understand that - certainly the Latin-looking girl, Lucinda, hadn't, when she'd first spoken to her in the coffee-break that morning - but to her it was vital, the most important aspect of the job.

She knew that in the natural course of events, this guy would never, could never experience a woman with even a tenth of her beauty - unless he became rich - and there was something in this breaking of the received order that she found rather compelling and somehow extremely satisfying. She also rather liked the way these terminally unattractive ones knew and understood the immensity of the gift she was bestowing on them, in a way that other men didn't. Some of them would even begin to cry when they saw the scale of the beauty they were being given to enjoy. And she would stroke their poor unattractive heads in those moments; the charitable hit was as strong as giving a tramp a thousand pound note.

Still without saying a word, Carlton staggered on toward her, open-mouthed, unzipping himself as he went, but suddenly pitched forward, tripping over his trousers as he tried to pull them down, landing heavily on the carpet. He beat his fist on the floor, biting his lip in self-directed anger.

'Hey, hey, take it easy,' she soothed, rushing over to his side, as he pulled himself up into a kneeling position, his trousers and pants in half-hitched disarray around his massive flabby thighs. 'Don't be in such a rush!' she said softly, looking into his eyes. His poor wretched eyes, tiny and dull, brim-full of tears and disbelieving wonder. 'Let's shut the door first, shall we?' she smiled.

He smiled back.

'Okay?' She said kindly, inclining her head and glancing down at his mercifully not-that-big, half-erect penis, and as she rose she gave it a single reassuring stroke of her hand. She saw his poor wretched eyes close in ecstasy at her touch, and heard his shuddering whimper of pleasure. She went to the door and closed it softly before padding back to help him to the bed.

As she helped him to undress, sitting beside him on the bed, she felt like a 21st century Florence Nightingale ministering to some poor, bewildered, dying soul, a casualty of the sexual battlefield, shot to pieces on the first day, never having stood the ghost of a chance. Was it really like that? She watched him struggling with his vest. Probably. For him it probably was.

She took his vest and placed it with the rest of his clothes on the chair by the bed, aware of his eyes following her every movement. The poor guy looked as if he were in shock. Better try to put him at his ease.

'Okay?' she smiled again.

He managed a nod in response.

And then she untied the cord of her robe, allowing the soft garment to fall gently from her shoulders and settle on the bed. He stared at her breasts for a moment, then peered back up at her with a look of such disbelieving, heartbreaking gratitude, through eyes at once so sad, wretched and happy, that she couldn't help but draw his big unappealing head down onto her shoulder. She felt his wet eyelashes on her smooth skin, and then the first hesitant cupping of her breast in his hand. She cast her eyes over his unkempt, lifeless, brown hair, flecked with dandruff, steeled herself for a moment, then ran her fingers softly across it. 'There, my soldier,' she silently mouthed to herself. She knew that this tender style of hers went way beyond the recommended guidelines on emotional contact, but sometimes she just couldn't help it ... there was such suffering in their eyes sometimes.

'Okay, now,' she said, lifting his head from her shoulder and reaching over to the drawer. 'Can you put this on for me, do you think?' She handed him the little foil packet and stood up to disrobe completely. But as Carlton caught his first view of the discreet white triangle of her briefs nestling sweetly between her long thighs, he lunged forward as if to cradle his head there, as though to refuge there forever. Laughing good-naturedly, she gently pushed him back.

'Hey, come on, are you going to get ready for me?' she coaxed, indicating his solid erection and placing the condom packet back in his hand, while at the same time throwing her robe over the chair.

He glanced up at her, then back at the packet, and began fumbling about with it, before finally managing to tear it open. She saw his penis falter slightly as he clumsily turned the ring of latex around in his chubby fingers, trying to work out which side was which. He dropped it, picked it up, reaching past the rolls of his own fat to retrieve it. He was panicking, and his erection was vanishing, leaving a lame pink nub lost between the two white slabs of his thighs. She didn't want this; she wanted him to enjoy himself.

'Hey,' she whispered.

He made no response, so lost was he in his growing crisis, his head down, fumbling with the condom with one hand and with himself with the other.

'Hey,' she said aloud.

This time he looked up at her, his face crumpled with anxiety, his shaking hand holding the condom suspended above his sad, flabby groin.

'Watch,' she whispered, narrowing her big eyes provocatively, and calming him with a mellow smile. She moved round a little so she stood before him, holding her athletic pelvis directly in his line of vision, and began slowly moving her svelte hips from side to side, as if hypnotizing him with a pendulum made from the white 'V' of her underwear. She watched as his eyes narrowed in newly recovered sexual joy, watched as his lonely eyes began moving slowly from side to side in time with her hips. Then, partly to prepare herself, she began caressing her stomach, soon taking the caresses down between her legs. He let out a low shuddering moan of pleasure, and she saw the strength returning to his penis. She could move on now. She slowly pulled her pants down her legs, watching Carlton's open-mouthed delirium, and observing his almost fully-restored member. Stepping quickly out of her underwear, she knelt beside his lap, and began bringing his penis back to full capacity with long vertical strokes of her elegant, slender fingers. As she worked on him, she mused on the piece of him she was holding in her hands.

As a penis it was no less appetizing than that of any average handsome guy. It was no different. It was even quite appealing. She concentrated on its clean line, its confident upward slope and the strange bewitching contours of its purple head. That head, for which there was no real analogue: it wasn't really bell-shaped; she had never thought it quite looked like a helmet either; and in reality it looked to her like no fruit, vegetable or stone on earth. In fact it resisted simile and referred only and always to itself.

For a moment she deliberately put the rest of his body out of her mind, and focused entirely on his penis, using the atavistic power of its image and its form to work on her own erotic centre and so make it easier for her to take him. She was conscious of the irony of it: she would never lavish this much attention on the private parts of less repulsive-looking guys. Anyway, he was ready now.

'That better?' she smiled up at him, but, though she didn't show it, she was suddenly shocked all over again by the total lack of beauty to be found in his face. He was happier now though, and for her there was beauty of a kind in that. And it was time to make him happier still.

Deciding not to let him waste any more of his time in prophylactic bungling, she took the condom from his huge shapeless hand, and quickly had it in place.

Good, he was holding firm. She crawled onto the bed, her eloquent limbs flowing past the bleak white figure heaped on the edge. As she lay back on the sheet, she took care to spread her hair out across the pillow, before reaching her arms out toward him.

'Come on, my soldier,' she smiled encouragingly as he moved closer, the shadow of his great body slowly consuming her smooth lithe frame.

But she was beginning to have misgivings about her physical ability to give him what she wanted to give him. Her meditation on his penis had made her quite wet, but now, at the approach of his tragic ungainly face, and despite the best application of her will, she felt uncertain whether she would be able to hold herself open to him for long. Thankfully he had come up between her legs now, so she reached down and quickly guided him home.

He sank into her, his mouth falling open, and, closing his eyes, let out another shuddering moan. She felt him begin his prehistorically prescribed programme of forward thrusts, more ancient than man himself. It sometimes helped her to think in such terms for some reason, just as it helped that he was actually making some rather pleasant movements inside her.

But she knew she had miscalculated as she began to feel the sheer weight of him bearing down on her. She should not have chosen this position. That was stupid! Well, she would just have to hang on as he kept thrusting away. His poor, happy, ugly head was hanging over hers, and as the chafing of his belly across her own increased, she found herself fighting to overcome her revulsion at the grotesque mask the light was making of his face from this angle.

And suddenly she knew she couldn't look at him any more, she just couldn't look at the poor creature any more, or bear his weight either, or listen any more to his belly slap against her, or feel his breath on her face. She admonished herself for her weakness, but she had to get out of this. And there was a way. And without ruining it for him either.

'Hey,' she said softly, looking up into the heavy folds of his panting face, 'do you want to know what really drives me crazy?'

He nodded, his tiny eyes wide with interest.

'Being taken from behind,' she whispered.

He closed his eyes and she thought she could just discern the formation of a word between his silent lips, perhaps 'cool.' She felt him withdraw, but not quickly enough for her, and as soon as he was outside her, and she was free of his weight, she rolled onto her front, relieved but ashamed of her inability to keep the poor guy's face before her eyes. She breathed for a moment to regain her composure and then pushed herself up onto her hands and knees, wanting him in her again as soon as possible, for his sake, before her body lost the capacity to receive him, and to this end she began moving her bottom from side to side, the quicker to bring him on.

She heard him gasp, then swallow, and a moment later felt his stammering hands opening her once more, and she was relieved to feel her contracting flesh again give way to him.

As he resumed his happy thrusting, she found herself willing him on. Come on my poor outcast, come in from the cold, partake of a little luxury for once in your life. She was holding her chin in one hand, holding the corner of the pillow with the other, managing easily the moderate buffeting from behind. Although she was confident he was having a fabulous time with her bottom, it still broke her heart to think how he would feel if he knew her reason for presenting it to him. She felt so desperately sorry for him: she had turned from him, had in a sense rejected him like everyone else probably had. She had never felt the need to turn away from a guy before. It upset her.

And then she realised that he had stopped, but she was certain he hadn't come yet. She felt him release his tight grip on her behind, so that for a moment the only physical contact was genital, though suspended, stationary. She stared at the wall.

A sensation on her back.

He was touching her back lightly, incredibly lightly with his finger. There was a delicacy, a reverence in it she hadn't thought him capable of. Another sensation. On the back of her head. He was caressing her hair, with an infinite tenderness. And as she stared at the wall in front of her, she felt a tiny spot of wetness hit her back.

And another.

She turned her head to look at him. Then she reached her arm round and with the back of her finger she wiped the long track of tears from his cheek.

He was snivelling, afraid to look at her. But she caught his eye and smiled. 'Hey, come on, we haven't finished yet,' she whispered.

He nodded, returning her smile, and she held his tear-stained gaze as he resumed thrusting, held his eyes as he built up his speed, went on holding his eyes until he was banging into her so furiously, so violently, so wonderfully that she finally had to turn away and hang her head between her shoulders, alternately opening her mouth and biting her lip, as the blond curls at the edge of her vision shook and shuddered in harmony with the glorious pounding onslaught. He grunted like a Neanderthal, and she felt first one, then two, three, four ejaculatory spasms blurt out his final paean to her beauty.

She sensed him already diminishing, but she was amazed to find that she didn't want him to ... didn't want him to ... amazed that he had actually inflamed her own erotic need to such a pitch that she now had to use her fingers to fondle herself as he shrank and slowed to a standstill.

As he began to withdraw, she still had presence of mind enough to reach round and ensure that the contraceptive remained in place on his deflating member. She thought of his sadly tainted seed. Was there a womb anywhere on earth that would want it?

She sat up and smiled at him, taking her robe from the chair. It was painful to watch him remove the condom, trying not to spill anything. She watched him shuffle over to the pedal bin, the sheathful of cloudy fluid in his hand, and she reflected on his fate, which seemed to boil down to the same simple paradox she'd observed in other cases, namely that he'd been programmed by the order of nature to complete a task forbidden to him by that same natural order. And as he stood over the bin and dropped his seed into the only kind of receptacle he would ever find for it, she was suddenly struck, not merely by the cruelty of nature, but also by the sheer treachery of it.

As Carlton made his way home through the late afternoon rain, his head was swimming, assailed by a montage of image and sensation as he struggled to take in what he had just been through. She'd looked like a film star, a fuckin' *film star*, like! And when he'd cried like a twat, like, she'd wiped his face, *wiped his face!* No one ever ... oh and her bum, like, her lovely, lovely bum ... and she'd let him, like ... no one ever had -... no one ever ... and at the door, when he left her and he'd said, when he'd actually managed to, managed to speak, like and he'd said thanks, like, she'd smiled an' said it was okay an' then touched his head like before closin' the door ... and when they were doin' it from ... doin' it from - and she was lookin' at him, *lookin, lookin* in his, in his ... fuckin' eyes an' she was into it, fuckin *into it!* With *him*, like! And normally they never ... never really got into it with you, like, but *she* did! And with fuckin' *him!* And when she took off her ... took off her....

But above it all, as he lumbered through the rain, sobbing and smiling up into the clouds, he held before his eyes the image of her reaching to him from the bed and smiling as she'd called him her 'soldier'.

SEVENTEEN

Williams sat in the staff office, unscrewing the plastic cup from the top of his large tartan flask of coffee. Sandra peered up from her paper.

'I don't know why you don't just use the machine, Roger. Save you the bother of carrying that thing in every day.'

Williams sighed.

'The reason I bring this in is because the coffee from that machine is undrinkable bilge. Perhaps if they'd let us buy a kettle, I wouldn't have to.'

'Why are they going to buy us a kettle when we've got that machine?'

'Well, exactly, and that's why I'll have to go on bringing in this flask, won't I?'

'I don't see why you have to bring in such a large one, though. You look like you're on a camping holiday or something.'

'Look, Sandra, I don't want - I don't want to spend my whole break discussing my flask, having to justify my bloody flask, okay?'

'Sorry I spoke,' replied Sandra, looking down at her paper.

Williams sipped his coffee, one eye on Sandra, before allowing his gaze to drift to the table. He was furious about that smart git in the suit. He'd just ruffled his feathers nicely with that little grilling and had been about to send him up to dumpy old Pamela, the plainest facilitator, but she'd become occupied just as he'd been about to click on her box, and then at the same moment another two boxes had gone red, leaving him with no option but to send the scrounging slick bugger up to Lucinda, to bloody *Lucinda*.

He removed his steamed-up spectacles and placed them on the table, closing his eyes and rubbing the bridge of his nose. But there had been something earlier that afternoon, something good... what was it? Ah, yes, that overweight lad. Scratching away at himself. That's right; he was going to find out which facilitator he saw and have a word with them about it. If there was a personal hygiene breach there, there was a good chance of getting one off the books. Now would be a good time to do it, during the lull. Rising from his seat, he swigged back the rest of his coffee and strode out of the office, followed by Sandra's bemused gaze.

Entering the reception area he crossed to the signing desks, where he questioned Mills.

'Peter, did you sign on that overweight lad who was in earlier, about an hour ago?'

'No, I think Alex did.'

Williams glanced over at Harper's empty desk.

'Where is he?'

'He's taking his break. Said something about going out to pick up some photos or something.'

Williams went over to Harper's desk and examined the monitor, checking the afternoon's records. Let's see. 3.10. Carlton. That must be it. He took Harper's pen and made a note of the claimant's name and reference number. Now, who had Harper sent him up to? Angela. Who was this Angela? He'd noticed the name on his own monitor but hadn't heard of her, and hadn't seen her come in either. Must be a new regional facilitator. Well, anyway, he'd go up now and have a word with her, while she was unoccupied.

'Don't send anyone up to 8, Peter, for ten minutes. I'm just going up to have a word.'

'Okay,' replied Mills as a man in a purple shell suit approached his desk.

Williams knocked on the door of cubicle 8 and waited. A woman's clear well-spoken voice sounded from within.

'Come in.'

Williams entered the cubicle, and found himself looking at one of the most incredible-looking women he had ever seen. She looked like a Hollywood film star, but from years back, like Grace Kelly or someone! What in hell was Henshaw playing at, taking on women like this? And that couch potato had just been sent up to this woman?! Oh, we might as well *all* start claiming, then. And who was going to bother with the ruddy contact boards or follow their ActionPlans if they were being sent up to *this?*

'Hello,' said Angela, extending her arm, 'Come over here, then.'

Oh, bloody hell.

'No, no, no, I'm not a claimant. I'm the supervising claimant advisor - from the ground floor. The name's Roger. Hello.'

'Oh, I see, sorry. You must be the Roger Jenny was talking about. I'm Angela. A pleasure to meet you,' she said extending her hand, smiling disarmingly.

Williams shook her hand, struck now by the exquisite grace of her movements. And she spoke like an announcer on Radio Four. What the *hell* was she doing here?

'So, you work as a regional facilitator, do you?'

'Well, I did for three months, during my probation period, but now I'm hoping to get a full-time placement here, depending on how things work out.'

What? She was going to be here permanently?

'... on how things work out?'

'Yes, this is the first day of a two-week trial period after which, they - you - will hopefully take me in on a permanent basis.'

She was going to be here permanently! You can't have women like this working in sex benefit centres! Henshaw and Hopley must have gone out of their tiny minds! Henshaw's office was next on his list.

'Ah, I see ... well, I'm sure everything will work out.... Anyway, the reason I came up like this was to ask you something about one of the claimants you saw earlier. The overweight chap?'

'Yes?'

'As you can understand, for *your* protection, we have to be very strict about the personal hygiene of the claimants.'

'Yes, I understand.'

'Well - this is a little unsavoury, but that's the nature of the work we're involved in here - while he was waiting, I noticed the guy scratching away at himself in the groinal area, and I wanted to check with you to see if you noticed anything untoward ...'

'Let me think ... no, I don't think so.'

'No sign of a rash? Any fungal infection?'

'No ... not at all.'

'You're sure? Perhaps you didn't have the opportunity to make a... close inspection.'

'Actually, a situation arose where I had ample opportunity, and I can assure you he was completely clean.'

Williams felt his head swim at the thought of this ravishing beauty descending to the rank private parts of the specimen in question.

'I see. Okay, then.'

'The poor man was probably just scratching a passing itch.'

'Probably. Okay, I'll let you get on. Thanks.'

Williams turned briskly and left the cubicle, closing the door behind him.

Angela sat down on the edge of the bed, slightly perturbed by the conversation. There was something a little odd about this Roger fellow. He hadn't looked pleased at all when she'd told him she was hoping to be taken on permanently by the centre. And she hadn't liked his choice of language when he'd described the nature of their work here as unsavoury. And something in the insistent questioning about that guy had struck her as off-key too. She hoped he hadn't noticed the slight sharpness in her answers; she didn't want to compromise her prospects of a job here by getting into any ructions with the staff. But what had disturbed her had been the way he'd seemed to be *hoping* for evidence against the poor guy. And when he hadn't got it, he had definitely looked disappointed. And when she'd seen that disappointment, she'd felt vindicated in her decision not to tell him about the small slightly red area at the top of the guy's thigh, which had to her in any case looked completely harmless, in fact exactly like a simple reddening caused by a minor passing irritation, certainly nothing transmittable, not anything they had termed 'reportable' during her training.

She put the incident from her mind, picked up her book from the bedside cabinet and read for a while, until the next knock on the door.

'Come,' said Graham Henshaw. He peered up from the display of claim statistics on his monitor, as Williams entered the room.

'Ah, Roger, how's everything?'

'Fine, fine. Listen, Graham, I was wondering if I might have a word.'

Henshaw leaned back in his chair, and scrutinised Williams, 'Well, all right. I could do with a break from these figures. Fire away.'

'I just met the new facilitator.'

'Rather lovely, isn't she?'

'Well, I think she is completely unsuitable for the work.'

'Oh?' said Henshaw, raising an eyebrow. 'Why is she unsuitable, Roger?' He took his eyes from Williams and returned to his monitor.

'I thought that would have been obvious. Look, she's far too attractive, Graham.'

'She's one of the best qualified facilitators we've ever had in this centre,' replied Henshaw, his eyes on the screen before him.

'Look, if you start bringing in women like this you're going to double the figures in two months. Everyone's going to want a piece.'

Henshaw leaned back, stroked his beard and regarded Williams.

'Roger. I've been overseeing this office now for eighteen months, gaining a sense of how the system is weighted, getting a feel of how the *philosophy* of the system is being expressed by the people who work here. And it's quite clear the balance needs adjusting wherever possible. One of the problems with this place is that a lot of the staff don't really grasp the concept of welfare. Most of the facilitators for instance have backgrounds in escort work or prostitution, and are here for reasons of self-interest, principally the protection of the state, the pension, the health schemes and so on, and fair enough. But there is a new kind of facilitator coming through nowadays, Roger, people of social *conscience,* with no CV in the sex trade, because *trade* is not their interest. In place of trade, *charity*. This more ... *altruistic* sex worker is one that has so far not graced the ... cubicles of this centre. Until Angela.'

Henshaw rose from his seat and walked over to the steamed-up window.

'She has never worked as a sex worker before, Roger. She has degrees in sociology, theology, a Masters degree in gender studies. The title of her PhD? "Ethics and the Dialectics of Socio-Sexual Engagement."

'So what's she doing here? A sex benefit cubicle is not exactly the next step for a career academic, is it?'

Henshaw turned to face Williams.

'Roger, when you look at the claimant sat across from you at your desk, what do you see? I'll tell you: an object of contempt, a piece of social detritus. Whereas, Angela -'

'That's not true-'

'Whereas, Angela sees, and I'm going to use her words here, "a starving, thirsting spirit trapped in the unloved body, all hope exhausted but one - the Good Samaritan." That's what she wrote in her application letter. Note the language, Roger, the phraseology, the *Christian* phraseology. I freely admit, I'm very impressed with her. Now, after -'

Williams opened his mouth, but was waved down by Henshaw.

'You asked me how she came to be here, now please let me finish. After her studies she worked for a number of charities, and then... prompted by what she called.... experiences in her personal life, she became intrigued by the concept of sexual charity, something she had touched on only theoretically before. As she told it to me at her interview, she became enthralled by this "relatively new field of human compassion" - her words again - and decided that she had to, as she put it, take a job in the front line.'

'She'll swamp us in false claims.'

'That's your department.'

'I don't have enough power as it is.'

'Oh, I think you have more than enough, Roger.'

'Look, you're going to have every randy bugger between here and Margate wanting a crack at a looker like that. The system's wide open to abuse. We can't make half the checks we need to.'

'But you're doing fine, Roger. Last month's figures went down very well with the Department.'

'But it's not only that, is it, Graham! Charity is one thing, but this is like giving a beggar a villa in Marbella! It goes against all ... natural justice to let that lot down there have their way with a goddess like that. I mean, she looks like a ruddy film icon. Sex benefit was surely only meant to be a subsistence level handout, for Christ's sake!'

'Come on, they only get twenty minutes, and they're even forbidden to kiss her. And as for natural justice, well, of *course* it denies natural justice. That's the whole point of charity, Roger. *Natural* justice - the balance set by Nature - leaves the weak, the ugly, the unloved to rot in the gutter.'

'If they get used to a woman like that, they're not going to bother looking for it for themselves, it's as simple as that! Even if we do prevent a bloody tidal wave of new claims, you're going to see a massive drop in sign-offs, that's for bloody certain! And you might as well throw *away* the personal contact boards!'

'I don't believe that, Roger, the claimants have their obligations under the Charter. As do *we* - to treat them with a degree of humanity.'

'In my experience, the claimants will try anything to wriggle out of their obligations.'

'*Some* claimants, no doubt. And as I said before, I'm confident in your ability to weed out any undeserving cases. But as for the others, the true cast-offs of society's mechanisms of sexual engagement, these individuals are entitled to compassion and respect, as well as the basic physical release. This is what Angela brings with her. She raises the level of our game, Roger, raises the level of our *game*. Because she's not from the industry. She could have done anything, been anything - look at her CV, her personal charm and beauty - but she chose to come here and work as a sex facilitator because she felt called to it by conscience.'

'Then she must be a bit nutty, Graham, if you ask me.'

A slightly whimsical light came into Henshaw's eyes. 'Isn't that what they say ... *every* time a new saint emerges?'

Williams stared at Henshaw for a moment.

'If you don't mind my saying so, Graham, I think you've let her go to your head a little.'

Henshaw returned Williams' look. 'Well, who could fail to be moved by such a woman?' He sat down at his desk, taking his eyes from Williams and addressing his monitor. 'And now, I think you'd better be getting back, Roger - before our defences are overrun.'

'Well, I just wanted to register my concerns before any decision is made to take her on permanently.'

'I'll bear in mind everything you said, Roger,' replied Henshaw, glancing up.

Williams made a brief nod and left the office.

The whole thing was bloody ridiculous. The girl had to have a screw loose somewhere. Must have. And she wasn't the only one. What in God's name was Henshaw on about? Calling the girl a saint, no less! Going on about her 'Christian phraseology'! It was pretty clear the chap was already half doo-lally over the woman.

Coming to the first floor landing of the staff staircase, Williams glanced down the corridor beyond the double doors and noticed a claimant emerging from one of the cubicles. Instead of making her way downstairs, the woman - from one of the estates by the look of her, sagging, late forties - simply leaned on the opposite wall near the cigarette bin and started fishing about in her handbag. What the hell was she doing? He watched her bring out a lighter and a cigarette packet.

Oh, no, you don't.

He pushed through the double doors and approached her, covering the distance between them in long strides.

'Don't light that cigarette, please.'

The woman eyed him dubiously from her puffy, wilting face, her moribund curling hair tracing the outline of a possible past beauty.

'There's a cigarette bin 'ere.'

'There's been a ban on smoking in this building for years. This bin should have gone years ago. Anyway, I'm going to have to ask you to move downstairs, please. We don't want people loitering in this corridor.'

The woman put her lighter and cigarettes back in her bag, but showed no sign of moving on.

'I'm waiting for someone.'

'Who? What do you mean, you're waiting for someone?'

A door at the far end of the corridor opened, and a scruffy-looking girl in her early twenties emerged, head down, buttoning up a grubby white fleece. She looked up, her face twisting in irritation. 'I told ya not to fackin' wait for me, you stupid cah!'

The older woman simply looked at the floor as Williams addressed the girl. 'Please keep it down, and make your way outside.'

Ignoring Williams, the girl stepped up to the woman and snarled in her face. 'It's embarrassin' enough 'avin' to cam in wiv ya, wivout walkin' out wiv ya an' all!'

The girl ran off down the corridor, shouting, 'Don't you fackin' try to catch up wiv me!'

Williams put his hand on the woman's shoulder, the quicker to get her down the stairs, but she shrugged it off, glaring at him, and made her broken way along the corridor, as the loud clatter of the girl's flying heels reverberated up from the stairwell.

He watched her go. Christ, the rubbish that came in here. Give that fool Henshaw a week on the coalface and he'd soon shut up about compassion and respect and bloody "social conscience".

He made his way back along the corridor, and entered the landing. Passing the doors to the facilitators' relaxation area, he felt a curious pang and paused momentarily to peer in. But the suite was deserted: all he could see was part of one orange sofa and the corner of another. He pulled away from the door and gazed back over his shoulder along the corridor from which he had come. He felt a sudden flutter in his chest as he realised he had an opportunity here. After all ... after all ... he was entitled to his kicks too, wasn't he? He tried to remember if she'd have anybody in her cubicle at present. He couldn't be sure. But she didn't seem to be taking a break, so there was a chance.

He pushed through the double doors and strode quickly down to the fourth cubicle. He stopped and stared at the plain white door with its slightly off-centre numeral, and listened. She was possibly at it right now on the other side of that door. He thought of the smart bugger in the suit and felt like wringing the neck of whoever was in there with her now.

And yet he hoped to hear her. To hear what she sounded like when she was being done. Come on, come on. Sing for me, Lucinda. Sing for me. He listened with all his hearing, all his concentration, but no sound came.

Realising the door to the security guard's office was open further down, he swiftly turned and headed for the stairs.

EIGHTEEN

'Mike ... Hi, it's Carla. How are you?..... Good, thanks...........No, I'm not calling about the music. Actually, I've got a favour to ask you. A big favour, so you can say no if you want, but please don't. Maybe it's too much to ask, I don't know......'

She took a deep breath and exhaled heavily.

'Well, it's to do with the, er...the sex dole. You know I'm signing on, right?.......Oh..........I thought I told you...........Well, it's okay - not great, but I have my reasons............Well, I have my reasons, Mike...........Well, the thing is they can be a right bunch of fascists down there sometimes, like now, as a matter of fact..........Well, you're going to think this a bit rich of me, but I need someone, I need someone to reject me - or *pretend* to reject me...........You know, to show them I'm trying to get off sex dole. They've demanded to see some evidence of what I've been doing to get off, right? "*Get off*" - ho ho........... Mike, don't be like that........... Mike............................ All right, you have a right to be pissed off, but look, the reason - .... The reason I never slept with you was because you were - are - I hope, just such a good friend, like a brother - I didn't want the old sex thing getting in the way of that, I told you that at the time, and it's true, Mike............Oh, look, I'm sorry, I shouldn't have come to you with this..............Because I don't know who else to ask............ You're probably about the only guy I trust any more, practically the only guy I'm in *touch* with any more............................Well, that's really sweet of you..... If you're sure you don't mind....... Bless you, lovely.......... Well, if it's okay with you, then, I'll give them your number, and they'll phone you, maybe ask you a few questions...........It's just so they can see you exist, that's all...............Well...you'd reject me because you don't fancy me..............Well, because you've got a girlfriend, then............. They're not going to go prying into your life, Mike, they've got no right........... They might not even phone you at all...... I know it's ridiculous, but tell *them* that.....................Thanks so much, Mike, I really appreciate this, I'll buy you a pint next time....... All right, I'll let you go, then, but listen, I'll call you again tomorrow, because we'll have to get a little story sorted out.......Okay, bye, lovely, bye.'

She put the phone down and fell onto the bed. Poor old Mike. She felt awful. Was she using him? No, she wasn't *using* him, but whatever it was she *was* doing, it was leaving a shit taste in her mouth. You're quite a nasty, selfish little bitch when put to the test, aren't you Carla? And that was another thing: she hadn't even considered how it must make him feel to know that she was desperate enough to resort to the sex dole, but not desperate enough to resort to him. She'd tried to soften that by invoking all that platonic brother-love stuff, but the truth was she'd never really felt that connection to him either. God, *God!*

She lay on the bed, chewing her fingernail down and staring at the wall. She became aware of an odd taste in her mouth, and quickly pulled her finger away, frowning down at the sore stump of nail. It was bleeding. Oh, no, what a mess! She put it back between her lips and sucked, making her way to the bathroom, where she tore off a sheet of toilet-paper and wrapped it round her finger. Holding the tissue tightly to the ragged fingertip, she loitered in the bathroom and found herself gazing absently at a half-full bottle of shampoo. Should she wash her hair? Well, what for? She wasn't going to see anyone today... it could wait another day. Tomorrow. God, well, she'd *have* to do it tomorrow - she was doing an afternoon in the shop. And after that, the start of another four-day run in the place, another four days of living death, which meant that today was the last full day of life for a while. And what was she going to do with it? Was she really going to sort out those songs, as she'd promised she would to Holly? Or mope about all day in her nightie? In a way, the two amounted to the same thing; finishing lyrics tended to involve a lot of moping about, staring into space.

She began vacantly reading the label on the shampoo-bottle. Tearing her eyes away, she made her way back to her room, gripping her finger tightly.

Actually, she'd better make the *most* of the opportunity to mope about all day in her nightie, because next week the others would be back, and Sharona would be back on her case, all disapproving looks and little remarks, and her space, the boundaries of her realm would once more retreat to the door of her room. Holly was always on at her to take Sharona on, but she never seemed able to grasp the nettle, and would end up just burying herself in her room all day, rather than risk running into that interfering pain in the neck. Why did they have to come back at *all?* Without thinking, she flung her finger up to her mouth, causing the tissue paper to unravel and fall to the floor. Stupid idiot! She bent down and retrieved the red-spotted tissue, dragging a strand of hair away from her face as she stood up and padded into her room, a nagging guilt about Mike at the back of her mind, the depressing prospect of Sharona at the front.

She came to a listless halt before the bed, her lazy glance caught as it always was by the band of tonal contrast formed by the dark poster of Thom Yorke on her wall, and the complete set of white Beatrix Potter books running along the shelf beneath. She remembered again the poisonous remark she'd overheard Sharona once make about her books to some friend of hers in the kitchen: 'That shelf full of baby books says it *all*, really.' She realised she was almost shaking with anger at the memory, and let her good hand drop violently to her side, releasing the tissue a second time, which again fell to the floor. She glanced heavenward and sighed, before looking from the tissue on the carpet to her chewed finger. Well, it had stopped bleeding anyway. She looked back at the tissue. She'd pick it up later.

Her attention wandered to the curtains and she began unconsciously stroking her forearm.

After a while, it occurred to her that she'd been standing in the middle of the room like this for minutes on end. What was she doing? Ceasing the caressing of her arm as unconsciously as she had begun it, and with her head bowed slightly, she slowly cast her eyes around the room, scowling out at her world, her little world. Resting her glance on the jumbo acoustic guitar in the corner, she forced herself to lighten her brow, and shake herself out of this strange stop she had come to. She thought she'd managed it and tried to take a step toward the guitar. She didn't move. She tried again and found herself taking small forward steps until she was standing directly over the instrument. Big old Gibson. With your darling Maplewood body. But it's just not the same any more, is it?

And then she was crouching by its side, pressing her fingers to the soundboard. No, it *is* the same, it *is* the same! Sorry, wooden thing, I didn't mean it!

God, she sounded like a madwoman, or Fuchsia out of *Titus Groan*. She knew she'd read that book a few times too many. She stared at the guitar. Come on, stop talking to the damn thing and play it. Throwing a strand of hair away from her eyes, she picked up the instrument, holding it by the neck, its bulk dwarfing her small waist, and crossed uncertainly to the bed, where she sat down and began fingering a series of chords. The room reverberated for a few moments with her tentative strumming before once again falling into silence.

She remained sat on the bed, trembling slightly, the guitar in her lap.

Later.

She'd look at the songs later.

What she needed right now was a smoke. To settle herself down a little after the call to Mike. Slowly lowering the guitar to the floor, she leaned over to the bedside table and began rummaging through the clutter surrounding the night lamp, her hair falling forward around her face. Leaning back once more, the cannabis resin, papers and tobacco in one hand, a lighter and CD box in the other, she knocked the guitar, which went crashing to the floor, shattering the silence with a loud, blank, unresolved chord of bashed, playerless strings. Making no effort to pick it up, she gave the instrument a vacant look, listening to the extended, empty abstraction of the fading chord. Then, with a quick jerk of her head, she fixed her attention on the CD box in her lap, her fingers going to work with a Rizzla paper and a broken cigarette. Her long unwashed hair formed a curtain around the slowly assembled spliff, overseen by a face set in frowning concentration. Finally she lifted the somewhat uneven joint to her mouth, and flicked open the lighter.

Drawing the drug down into her lungs, she went on sitting on the bed, her eyes now back on the row of little white books over the headboard. Who shall we have today? Who shall we have today, Carla? Don't you want anybody, darling?

Peter Rabbit!

It's always Peter Rabbit with you, isn't it? Don't you want to try any of the others?

No! No!

She reached up to the shelf and took down the book, dropping ash on the crumpled, yellowing pillow. Turning the pages, she gazed down at the large, familiar type, not reading, simply casting her eyes over the friendly letters, and allowing the gentle tones of the illustrations to wash over her, the actual content of the images and the text having long ago lost the emotional hold they'd once exerted over her, the emotion having transferred to the object itself. The pale pinks and blues, the comforting layouts of the little paragraphs, mixed with the softening effect of the cannabis to smooth out her mood, and she began to relax.

But it was too quiet in here. She got up somewhat shakily from the bed, crossed the rug and knelt down next to a teetering stack of CDs. Luckily, *Waiting for the Moon* by Tindersticks was next but one from the top. She inserted the disc and crossed back to the bed, enjoying the feel of the centrally-heated air on her bare shoulders and limbs. Of course she had the heating on full. That would come to an end with the return of Sharona. So that settled it: today was definitely a nightie and central heating day.

Suddenly, she felt able to look at the lyric she'd been working on. Taking another drag on the spliff, she knelt on the rug and pulled her A4 pad toward her. Flipping through, she stopped at a page of jottings, and began reading. It didn't seem bad, and it didn't seem good, and she soon became distracted by a pleasant sensation on her knee. She was making small circles there with the back of her forefinger. She resumed reading but the pleasant circling went on. She sat up slowly, and taking her hand from her knee brought it up to her face. She continued the light circling caress on her cheek, closing her eyes.

And why not? Yes, Carla, why not ... why not explore all those caresses for a while, all those soft touches ... all those soft strokes that you didn't get down the sex dole ... She laughed an internal hollow laugh ... all that gentle contact the sex dole guys seemed forbidden to make ... and that all those guys from her past had been *incapable* of making ... She brought her other hand up to the side of her head and began slowly running her fingers through her hair, while continuing to stroke her cheek with her other hand. She felt her head swim, and she began to sway slightly from side to side. Then, leaning forward, she placed her elbows on her knees so as to be more comfortable, and went on caressing her head, moving the fingers of her left hand in a slow, lazy circle taking in her ear and the side of her neck. It occurred to her - and it caused her some amusement to think this - that while masturbation was kind of taboo it was just accepted that everybody was quietly getting on with it - no one would blame you or think you were crazy for doing it - but if you told someone you sat for twenty minutes just stroking your hair or fondling your ear like this, they'd probably have you sectioned or something. But there were certain *advantages* to it; it was a kind of self-love you could practise anywhere. If you wanted, you could just sit there on the tube, your eyes closed, caressing your hair with one hand, your neck with the other until it was time to get off. At Barking, of course, because naturally everyone on the train would think you'd gone completely gaga. When actually, you were just being good to yourself. Like the supermarkets were always telling you to be.

She leaned further forward, putting her head almost to the floor, and, moving her hair aside, began tracing gentle arcs on the nape of her neck, the fingers of both hands circling in mirror-image to each other. Her nose was touching her knees and she could smell them. She found the smell affecting, as she always did. She liked her smell. Was that strange? Who cared, she liked it. None of the men in her life had ever been moved sufficiently to say anything about her smell. She breathed deeply, and then, bringing her lips into a pout, she deposited first one, then a whole constellation of little kisses on her knees, brushing them with her lips, varying the pressure and duration of each little contact, experimenting with the sensitivity of her skin. Of course you couldn't expect this kind of pampering from the sex dole, but none of the others had ever bothered to kiss her like this either. None of *them* had ever bothered with anything but the standard kit of tits and bum and vagina, and even then never for more than five minutes, and with little grace or imagination, before they became immersed in their own gratification, virtually the whole of the rest of her body seemingly lost to them, as they rammed for

England, their heads buried in the pillow - ramming away with their long poles or their short poles, of which they were so proud or so ashamed, when, to her at least, that, the ramming, was never what really mattered. Well, of course it *mattered*, otherwise she wouldn't be signing on. It was just that it wasn't the be-all and end-all of the process. She'd just felt it had always ... needed *seasoning* with something.... But what? She had never known. Maybe it was something that just didn't exist - anywhere.

Still, a little prolonged tenderness might be a good place to start. She went on fondling the nape of her neck with both her hands, her touches gradually becoming ever smaller, ever lighter, ever more intense, until she was making microscopic little strokes, the localised sensations sending tiny waves of subtle pleasure spreading down her back. She drifted, alone with the caresses at the base of her skull.

After a while, she sat up again, her head filled with a sluggish intoxication, and reached for the spliff. Inhaling heavily, she felt her heart thump and her throat becoming thick, and then, letting her dizzy head hang forward, she gazed down at the hem of her baby-blue nightie, and beyond, the smooth skin of her thighs, where her legs slimmed out to the way they'd seemed when she was a little girl; she'd never quite gotten used to the pubescent swelling of her hips. A lump of cold ash fell from the spliff onto her leg. Oh well, never mind, she sing-songed to herself. She brushed it away with a violent darting movement of her hand, and stared at the resultant black smudge. Not so rough, Carla, darling! She returned her fingers to the spot and began covering the area with the same gentle sensations as she had bestowed on her neck, trying to make the little fingertip circles as light as she could. Again she drifted, the pattern of her nightie blurring, as minute ripples of pleasure went tingling round her thigh.

Pulling her vision back into focus, she moved her gaze to the shallow valley between the tops of her slightly squirming legs.

Well, she wasn't on any tube train now.

Raising the spliff to her lips with one hand, she pulled up her nightie with the other, and peered down at her pants, momentarily alarmed by the pattern of red spots. Red hearts. She'd forgotten she had these ones on. All the others were in the washing basket. She ought to throw these away; she'd never liked those stupid hearts. Christmas should be banned if mothers were going to buy daughters presents like this. Bunching the nightie around her midriff she took another heady drag on the spliff, before placing it shakily back on the CD box. She hung her head, her hair falling forward, enclosing her in a cowl of intimate self-communion. Bringing her hand to hover between her parted legs, she closed her eyes, preparing to touch herself as lightly as she had her neck and her knees. She waited a moment, allowing her closed eyes to relax completely in their sockets. And then through her knickers she felt the first faint, slow run of her fingertip, almost imperceptible but so excruciatingly perfect that she was already trembling, flowing inside in response to the tiny, tingling spot of perfection. Oh, God. Round and round ... Round and round the garden ... you can do that for a while yet, darling...

...she realised the CD had finished. She'd been doing this for nearly half an hour, and she could drift for a while yet, alone with this spot, and then later move her finger a little lower, and then still later perhaps try it with her pants off, playing with further gradations of touch, coaxing and teasing the delicate skin with a myriad little ecstasies. There was an infinity of possibilities, but all of them a world away from the limited sensual range of the men she'd known or expected to know. For a moment she allowed into her mind the idea of some delicate erotic guy who would have the sensual staying power to do this to her - stroke her hair for twenty minutes, stroke her down below for half an hour, more, do both at the same time, what heaven that might be! - and then she almost felt like crying, because he wasn't here, because it was just a level of happiness it was stupid to even contemplate!

She sighed, as if expelling in one go every breath she had ever taken. Pulling her nightie down, she jumped quickly to her feet, suddenly too upset to continue, and stormed off to the bathroom. What *they* could give, she'd get tomorrow. Tomorrow morning down the sex dole.

NINETEEN

1. What is your name?

No, no names. Let's have no names here. Brando never had to give his name to Maria Schneider in Paris in 1970. But ... well, all right, baby, if you insist.

He moved the cracked Bic to the relevant box and gave them his name.

2. What is your address?

They wanted to know his address and it seemed a harmless enough request to him and so he told them, writing it out for them in black ink, the black ink that for some reason was so important to them. Anything your little heart desires, babe.

3. What is your date of birth?

They enquired as to the date of his birth and he furnished them with this date.

4. What is your National Insurance number?

They appeared curious as to his National Insurance number, and with flashing movements of the biro he satisfied this curiosity.

5. What is your status?

They asked about his status, and it was a reasonable query, he had to admit, but he couldn't find the box that said 'pathetic sexual exile'. The broken Bic flashed over the box reading 'single' instead, the closest of the available options. The others were 'married', 'divorced' and 'widowed'. 'Married'? There was a note across from it:

> Sex benefit may only be granted to married persons in special circumstances. See SB31, section 12a.

What in fuck was that all about? Curious, Lawrence reached over his dinner-plate for the leaflet they'd given him, flicked to the relevant page and read. Oh, right, basically if, for example, you were a frustrated housewife, then they'd only give you some if you brought in a doctor's note to the effect that your old man's old chap was knackered, and a letter of consent signed by the poor bastard. Similar terms applied in the reverse situation. He flung the leaflet back on the table and went on to the next question.

6. Do you suffer from any disabilities?

Well, all my disabilities are of a very subtle, spiritual, moral flavour. And I doubt if even my mental one would show up on a psychiatrist's couch, but that's not really what you're asking about, is it, toots? No, no, I don't have any disabilities.

> 7. Are you currently involved in a sexual relationship? (By "sexual relationship" we mean any friendship or intimacy involving genital

contact of any description.)

Fucking stupid question! Presumably if you ticked yes to this they'd throw the form in the bin there and then. There was no point to it. Ah. But of course, it was one for the false claimers - if there were such a breed; it seemed hard to imagine what sort of fuck-up you had to be to go through all this piss if you didn't have to. But if you *were* such a twisted fuck, this question was presumably here to catch you lying on paper with a nice big signature at the end of it for eventual use in a courtroom. Well, honey, *I'm* not lying when I tickle your cute little 'no' box. My intentions are genuine. I won't two-time you, sweetheart.

8. When did your last sexual relationship cease?

Some time shortly after The Flood, I think. No, seriously, babe, it must have been ... March 1996. Jesus Christ....

9. Please give details of all your past sexual relationships.

For fuck's sake! And what the hell did they mean, give *details*? Surely they just meant names and dates. 'Details' was much too broad and unspecific. So much for the fucking 'Campaign for Clear English' award on the front of the form. Well, names and dates were all they'd be getting from him until they managed to express themselves more clearly.

10. When did you last have a sexual experience with another person? (By "sexual experience" we mean any encounter, however brief, involving genital contact.) If the answer is the same as to question 8 go on to question 11.

Well, sadly, it most assuredly *is* the same as to question 8, so on to question 11 go I.

> 11. Are you seeking only a long-term sexual relationship? (Sex benefit may in special circumstances be granted to those seeking only a long-term sexual relationship.)

Nope, I'll take anything I can fucking get - as that seems to be the way to your heart, darling.

> 12. Why did your last sexual relationship cease?

Fuck.... Never really worked that one out myself in point of fact. Ask her. Christ, they really knew how to put the boot in with the personal questions.

> 13. Who brought the relationship to a close? (We may need to contact your last sexual partner about this.)

Don't worry, it was her, not me. Why don't you trust me, babe? I told you I'd be straight with you all down the line. But if you must speak to her, lots of luck finding her. I couldn't.

> 14. What strategies have you employed since the cessation of your last sexual relationship or experience to procure another sexual relationship or experience?

I've tried just about everything under the sun, you bastards. But all right, you're asking about my 'strategies', my '*strategies*.' All right, I have employed a strategy of trying to get to know better all the girls who cross my path in the course of my daily round. I have employed a strategy of entering public houses, initiating unsolicited conversations with women who are entirely unknown to me. I have placed ads in the personal columns of newspapers and magazines; I have answered ads in the personal columns of newspapers and magazines. I have employed a strategy of entering nightclubs and attempting to dance winningly before groups of disinterested young women. I have pursued a strategy of pursuing every possible lead to the bitter end.

> 15. Would you consider yourself to be a) extremely good-looking; b) fairly good-looking; c) plain; d) ugly?

A clumsy attempt to gauge the punter's level of sexual credit, presumably to see if your aspirations in the marketplace were at all realistic. Well, it was a toss-up between b) and c), though he'd prefer to tick something in between. He stared at the question for nearly a minute. c) then, fuck it.

> 16. Would you rule out a sexual experience with someone on grounds of their physical type alone?

Oh, fuck. Here's a tricky one. The kind of question where a 'yes' might get your claim thrown out but might not. There was no way of telling. But fucking hell, 'physical type' could mean anything from hairy dwarf to sweating, elephantine slob. He'd risk an honest answer.

> 17. If you answered 'yes' to question 16 please give an indication of the physical types with which you would refuse a sexual experience.

Christ, how much more of this shit was there? He reached for his cigarettes, stuck one in his mouth, lit it and re-read the question. How in hell was he going to answer this? Maybe they were just trying to root out fussy tossers who refused to do it with anyone but slim young blondes. In which case it would be all right to admit to a certain natural aversion to the obese and the truly hideous. Well, he'd put that down. He couldn't really imagine that it was a condition of sex benefit that you be prepared to shag basically anything with a nervous system.

18. What kind of sexual partner are you looking for?

Well, what the fuck were you supposed to put for this? There was no way you could meaningfully answer this, and they probably knew it too, the fuckers! They just wanted to shit you up, run you around for a bit before handing you their little crumb of comfort. Or maybe it was just another idiot-question to trick thick dickheads into appearing too choosy. But of course, this question linked up with the one about how attractive you thought *you* were, so they could see if you were setting your standards too high. Sneaky bastards, splitting them apart like that!

Best option, go for vague: I'm looking for someone with a reasonable level of sexual appeal. Yes, this was the way through it. Just make the answers as meaningless as the questions, but give them the appearance of conscientious deliberation.

He wrote out his answer, and then felt a wave of vision-blurring fatigue. How much more was there? He flipped through the form. He was about half-way through the thing. The rest of the questions looked more like a dating agency form. They wanted to know what was your favourite gardening programme and whether your hobbies included smoking and all that crap, presumably so they could hook you up with some other saddo and get you the fuck off their books as soon as possible. Christ, he'd fill the rest of it in later.

Picking up the plate, he went into the kitchen where he dumped it carelessly in the sink and put the kettle on.

Leaning on the counter, he began thinking of Martina, poor depersonalising Martina. Well, she'd made contact finally. He glanced at the clock on the oven. She'd be on the plane by now. Back to mum and dad, or Mutter und Vater. Back to Zurich with a suitcaseful of depression. Where were her essays, her theses, her assessments now? It was just too fucking sad; come to London and lose your mind. He was going to miss her, he was *really* going to miss her. And yet they'd hardly ever met - well, he was going to miss her little telephone voice then, set in its perennial little miniature

London street.

Stirring his mug of tea, he went back into the living room. He'd been in a fairly bullish mood filling in the form, tedious as it was, but the business with Martina told him that the walls were really going to start closing in now all right. What faint hope he'd ever had of winning her had gone, while the more realistic prospect of the sex dole was finally heaving into sight. And not only that, a good friend was gone, a ray of light winking out of his existence.

He went to the table and stood over the claim form. Thinking about Martina had not been a good idea. Her loss only underlined the sheer fucking desolation of his current course of action. But he wasn't tempted to change it. It was as if the decision, once made, had been set in stone.

He moved the claim form aside and stared down at the medical form underneath, which he'd brought back from the doctor's that morning. Well, his sexual health was A1 anyway. One of the boons of a non-existent sex life. But the examination itself had been truly awful. Had he known that instead of a sex dole worker, the first person to touch his balls in two years would end up being his GP he might not have started on this sex dole crap at all. His GP: Dr. P. N. Kingford of the nicotine-stained moustache and similarly tainted fingertips. Could the tosser not have confined himself to a mere visual once-over? Best not to think about it. Bad enough having *zero* sex life without it dropping down to a minus value.

But maybe that boundary had been crossed anyway with his decision to sign on. No, not maybe. Fucking definitely. But so what? He'd been told by the forces that had formed him to get a fuck, and get a fuck he would. By the simplest and quickest possible expedient. It wasn't his fault. He'd learned now. He'd learned that it did no good to disobey orders given from below, orders written in that fluid white script, so deceptively clean-smelling, so ungovernable and so ancient. Ancient. That was it. You couldn't sit on top of a hundred million years' worth of lurching semen and expect to buck the trend! Because as an individual that was all you were, a painfully brief ephemeral husk being tossed about on a swelling primordial ocean of indifferent, mindless jizz. A roiling sea of spunk that never gave fuck *one* about you, never had, never did, never would, just went rolling along, pursuing its own mysterious agenda, as it had since time immemorial, with people - like the fucking dinosaurs before them -

being mere throwaway devices for its own eternal propagation.

Fucking hell, he was given to some pretty dismal perspectives on life. And yet they always seemed to have a sound basis in reason, ringing out with the clear, bell-like tone of faultless logic.

Sipping his tea, he sat down again at the table and continued filling in his form.

TWENTY

Sacha could not believe the evidence of his senses. All that night class stuff the other week had been bad enough, but now this four-eyed bag of flatus was becoming a seriously haemorrhoidal pain in the backside.

He leaned forward and switched on a smile. 'Can I ask you a question, please?'

'Go on,' replied Williams.

'You're saying I am *obliged* to arrange a liaison with one of the names on those boards over there?'

'Yes.'

'And if I don't?'

'If you don't I'll pick one out for you.'

'And if I refuse to take it?'

'Then I'll stop your benefit as of today.'

Are you *smiling* at me? It's hard to tell really, because your whole sour face looks like a pinched ringpiece, but if that *is* a faint smile I detect playing around that foul rectal sink-hole of a mouth, it would disappear pretty smartish if you could see who I had for breakfast today and who I had for lunch today and who I'll be having for supper tonight, you fucking drone. And it's not the same plate of vittals every time either, though each is better fare than you've ever tasted, or even sniffed at on the passing breeze, so don't start imagining, don't ever start imagining you're on the cusp of winning some sort of victory over me.

'All right, I just wanted you to make clear to me what my rights were. Why do I have fewer rights now than when I first started claiming?'

'Because we give you a few months to relieve your situation in your own way, using your own strategies. If you fail to get back on your feet in that time, as you have done, we will give you a hand. Now, if you're not going to go over to the personal contact boards I'll go over for you. And I may add, the fact that you haven't gone over already indicates to me that perhaps you're not serious about coming off benefit at all.'

'I think that's a little presumptuous of you actually, because you didn't really make any of this very clear to me when I started my claim. And the reason I'm not overly keen on the idea of personal contact advertisements is that in my experience they are a bad idea. I've never had success with them in the past -'

'Oh, I think you should give them another go,' said Williams, getting to his feet and crossing to the aisles of white cards.

And I think you should die of cock cancer, you insufferable open wound. Maybe it was time to call a halt to this whole merry sex dole lark. But last time had been rather superb though; stuffing that bit of Latino labia had in its way given even Ulla a run for her money. Not that she was anywhere near Ulla's class looks-wise, and that wide arse could never constitute the main course for any truly self-respecting sexual palate. Rather it was the way the bitch had ended up creaming all over the bed despite herself that had been so good. And he could see that she hated him, which of course made it all the sweeter. When he'd gone in, she hadn't even looked at him, had just lain there reading, barely condescending to take her pants off. But when he'd walked out the door, she was left writhing in a pool of her own juice, biting the pillow. If you can fuck a miserable whore out of her apathy like that, if you can set a desensitised shagged-out nanny-state vagina alight like that, even when she's looking at you with eyes full of loathing, then you *know*, you *know* that you have a certain winning way with the ladies. This was one of the great things about this bonk benefit kick; where else could you prove yourself like that without wasting money on prostitutes?

Sacha watched Williams moving up and down the aisles. Go on, then. Do your worst, nippleprick, I'm not leaving.

Williams selected a card and made his way back to the desk.

'Couldn't find any young Swedish students, I'm afraid, but try this,' said Williams, pushing the card across the table.

Overstepping your remit there with the old sarcasm, aren't you, shitwipe? Nevertheless, Sacha looked down and read.

> Me 41. Look for nice english man. Me interest much in sex. You can be how old. You have blonde hair. Peckham area. Telephone 07946778296.

There was a photo. Sacha removed his glance from the photobooth image of a plain, grinning, middle-aged, oriental woman as soon as he caught sight of it, and glanced up at Williams. You fucking weeping genital sore. He could walk out the door right now if he wanted. He might have to, because in order to go on claiming, he was somehow going to have to get this thing on the card to convincingly reject him. Certainly a challenge and a half. And yet. There were ways and means.

Holding Williams's eyes, he slowly picked up the card and placed it inside his jacket.

'I'll give her a call,' he said evenly.

'And we'll give her a call too. To see how you get on,' smiled Williams thinly.

The jumped-up wretch was enjoying this! And worse, the stinking little bollock was happy to let him see it. What tragic depths you could sink to if you were a no-life scraping of smegma.

Williams turned to his monitor, trying to conceal his joy. The look on the lout's face when he'd put the card in his pocket, trying to tough it out. He hadn't felt this good for weeks. He'd taken his time choosing that card. Taken his time and chosen well. The bit about the blond hair was perfect. You wriggle out of that, chum. Hope I'm invited to the wedding!

He ran his eyes down the cubicle display on the monitor. Unfortunately Pamela wasn't in today, but maybe Veronica would do.... Who else was there?... Tracy possibly ... Angela! Thank Christ she was occupied. It would've ruined everything if he'd had to send the lout up to that freak now. Rot that fool, Henshaw. And thank God

Lucinda wasn't in today either ... so no gravy for you there this time, mate.... Well, it looked like it'd have to be Veronica then. Well, that was at least better than last time; Veronica was no Lucinda. And anyway, hopefully this'll be the last we see of you, pally. Because when we catch you declining the sweet favours of Miss Naing of Peckham, we'll have your balls on a plate. In fact, you're already as good as off, sunshine.

He ran a ticket from the dispenser and handed it to Sacha.

'Number 11, then.'

'Thank you,' said Sacha as evenly as before, rising from his seat.

Williams watched him turn and head for the stairs. I got you. I bloody-well got *you*, you cocky sod. You should've looked at the boards when you had the chance! Should've looked at the *boards!* But no, you were too proud and look where it got you!

He allowed himself a brief smile into his lap. He'd treat himself to a little celebratory pint at lunchtime, if he could contain himself till then - he felt like getting on his desk and dancing.

From her seat in the waiting area, Rowena Fairgrove watched the attractive young man in the sharp business suit make his way to the stairs. She had been watching him since he sat down at the desk, and enjoyed the opportunity of weighing up the full-length view. Yes, he cut rather a gorgeous figure. Still, you had to be suspicious of a man like that in a place like this. He was either ridiculously shy, or up to something. Still, if she wanted, getting him into bed probably would not prove too difficult. But getting him to stay there and treat her as though she were some sort of equal partner might prove more problematic. That was always the snag with younger men. Even if you were still a babe at fifty, as she was.

She *was*, there was no point denying it; she had eligible young men forever bombarding her with compliments about her supple, slinky body, her elegant, well-preserved 'Nefertiti-like' profile, and large liquid eyes. But unfortunately it wasn't enough merely to look better than most of the women half your age. It wasn't enough to *look* half your age, you had to *be* half your age if you wanted a man to stay with you, to treat you with anything half-approaching respect, to invest any emotion in you. Because of course there was not much return to be made on investing in a beautiful property built on the quicksand of incipient decrepitude, no matter how 'elegant and well-preserved' it might appear. Very soon, it was all going to come crashing down, and the rotters all knew it. So when they came drifting over to her in bars, admiring her this, admiring her that, she knew that all they were really doing was sniffing around for a chance to drink from the rapidly emptying cup of her beauty, before running off into the night to look for other lampposts to piss on.

She glanced up at the counter. Two more to go. She hoped it would be the two women sat next to her, because their furtive bickering was becoming increasingly irritating. She stole a glance at the pair. They appeared to be related - and in the most immediate way. Good God, how awful. To have to come in on the same day as your daughter! Look at the state of them. She cast her eyes over the girl's greasy pony-tail, down the polyester tracksuit top to the stubby thumbs jabbing away on a mobile phone game, the foundation-caked mother wheedling in her ear, the girl sniping back in irritated half-whispers. For a moment, she imagined Leonora sat next to her - and shuddered. God, it was just too dreadful to contemplate. If Leonora ever found out she came down here ... well, the precaution of claiming at the Kentish Town office as opposed to the Hampstead one should prevent that unpleasant eventuality. Anyway, it was none of the little traitor's damned business.

Rowena's large hieroglyph eyes drifted from the mother and daughter, caught by the ambling motion of an overweight middle-aged man progressing across the room. He actually resembled Nick a little, though presumably his bank balance didn't, or he wouldn't be in here, because if you had the cash you simply plied some dense bimbo with diamond rings, or, if married, ditched the wife at forty-five and invested in fresh stock. Of the men she knew who were of her own age, all but one had over the last five years traded in their wives for a younger model, as indeed had Nick with her. That was what you got for giving your life to them.

On balance, you could actually say it was more dignified to come *here*. It *was* more dignified to come here than allow yourself to be buffeted from pillar to post by the fickle whims of those shallow, overgrown children. And at least there was the compensation of not having to put up with their slack, tubby little bodies - she had to admit she did have a certain penchant for the youthful physique herself! But it wasn't so important as to cause her to throw away a loving marriage for it. As Nick had done. She hoped Tina was enjoying the money, because Nick had really started to let himself go.

So, since she had been effectively thrown on the scrapheap, she may as well come here and indulge her little penchant. Not least because this too, having it off with the younger man, was, in a strange way, actually less humiliating here, less degrading: you didn't have to watch them pace guiltily about afterwards, or suffer the post-coital dead look in their eye when you caught them pondering the creases in your morning-after breasts and you could *see* them asking themselves if they really wanted to live with tits half a century old. And you didn't have to go through the pain of then watching them brighten up for a moment, so transparently offsetting the breasts against the Nefertiti head, as they came over to give you a hug, having made the internal decision to bravely hang around for a few weeks. And that was the *best* it could be; the others made no secret of the fact that they placed you in their debt for having condescended to favour an older woman with the blessed gift of their sexual attention.

Whereas here, no one sat in judgment on your shelf-life, they simply took you in their arms and quietly gave you what you wanted. Well, up to a point; it *was* the sex social after all, but it kept the wolf from the door, and did so without subjecting you to all that hand-wringing across the breakfast table, or all the missed birthdays and broken promises. There was a certain clinical quality to it, of course there was, but she actually tended to find a kind of serenity in that. If you approached it with the right frame of mind you could even find a certain meditative quality to it on occasion. Because ... yes, it was a retreat from the world. It *was*. And that was what she wanted; to retire from the dratted horse-traders' fair, and just be put out to pasture. Put out to pasture with the young men of the sex social!

Her number had been called. She uncrossed her knees and rose from her seat, screwing up her ticket into a little white ball. Her proud silhouetted profile glided past the windows as she dropped the ticket in the bin and approached the signing desk. She sat down, carefully tucking the hem of her faun cashmere coat beneath her, and addressed the grey-haired woman installed behind the monitor opposite.

'Good afternoon.'

'Hello,' came Sandra's flat response.

With her head held high on her long, perfectly angled neck,

Rowena smiled briefly and unclasped her small white leather handbag. She took out the slim plastic-sheathed document and placed it lightly on the desk.

Sheila Pedloe watched as the beautiful lady who'd been sat next to her leaned forward at the desk to sign her name. Look at her. Those big dark eyes. Looking for all the world like Queen Cleopatra or someone from one of them films. Well, it just goes to show. You can be posh as you like, even still be very pretty for your age - she must be over forty - and you'd still end up here, life could still end up driving you to a place like this. If it didn't drive you bloody mad first. She peered round to her left, and spoke.

'Tamsin, what are you doing later, love?'

'What? When? What are you tawkin' abaht?' replied the girl without looking up from her game.

'After. Are you still going over to Tottenham?'

'If you must know, no - though it's none of your business.'

'So you're not doing anything, then?'

'Look, shut up, right? No one else is tawkin' in 'ere, is they? And move up, shove over into that other seat, willya? There's no need for ya to sit so close now that posh bird's gone, is there?'

Sheila remained where she was, steeled herself for a moment then spoke firmly.

'You can come with me to the launderette, then.'

'You must be jokin'!'

'Come on, Tamsin, please.'

'Bad enough avin' to listen to ya goin' on in 'ere, and you fink I'm gonna cam and sit all arfternoon wiv ya in the launderette an' all? Leave it out, *please.*'

Sheila responded in a low, but furious voice. 'I'm not carrying them bloody bin-liners down those stairs by myself!'

'Then ya shouldn't buy so many clothes, then, should ya?'

Sheila drew back, softening slightly, and looked her daughter up and down. '*You* should buy some more clothes. Some nice ones. Put a bit of lippy on. At least *try* to smarten yourself up for the fellas. Then you wouldn't 'ave to come down *'ere*. I *'ave* to. But you, you're *young,* you -'

'Will you *fackin' shut up?'*

'Then you wouldn't 'ave to come down 'ere.'

'I *like* cammin' down 'ere!'

'I don't know as 'ow you can say that! I 'ave to come 'ere because I *'ave* to. A woman my age. But you, you're *young*.'

'It's disgastin' you cammin' down 'ere.'

'I have my needs too.'

'*Fackinell, leave it out, willya?*'

Sheila sat back, and watched as the posh madam over at the desk got up from her seat. High and mighty as you like. For all the world like an Egyptian queen. But you won't find no Mark Anthony up there darlin' and no Richard Burton neither. She turned her puffy eyes back to Tamsin.

'I can't carry them bags down those stairs by myself.'

'Get someone to 'elp ya then.'

'I don't know anyone else in that bloody place, do I?'

'Well, I dunno, phone Kenneth, then.'

'I told you never to say that name, young lady.'

'Ken, then, or Daddy, Farver, whatever the little bleeder's name is.'

'Oh, I could raise such a slap to you one of these days!'

'You ever touch me again, that's the last you ever fackin' see of me.'

'I'm sorry, Tamsin, I'm sorry.'

Tamsin made no response, and went on following the LCD blip darting around the screen of her mobile. Sheila merely stared at the screen too, following the shapes above her daughter's jabbing thumbs with vacant eyes. Suddenly, Tamsin stood up, shoving the phone inside her jacket, her eyes on the LED counter. But instead of crossing to the signing desks, she hesitated, then turned and leaned over the woman in the chair, fixing her mother with an intense stare, which Sheila found difficult to withstand.

'Ave you ever noticed anythin' abaht the blokes in 'ere?' asked Tamsin mysteriously.

Sheila looked about her.

'Nah, not dahn 'ere, ya fool. Upstairs.'

Confused, Sheila shook her head slightly.

Tamsin leaned closer and said quietly, 'They never *cam*. Or almost never. And they never go bare-back. Not like them selfish twats out there. Not allowed to. You wanna know why I cam dahn 'ere? So I'll never get pregnant. So I'll never make the same fackin' mistake as you.'

Sheila watched in silence as Tamsin turned and tramped off to the signing desk.

'Yeah, come in, yeah?' said Derek, throwing the paper on the chair, getting up from the bed and smoothing out the white sheet, his close-shaven head moving rapidly from side to side, making sure the cubicle was in order for the next claimant. Yeah, that'd do. That looked all right. He heard the door open and turned.

One of the coolest little darlin's he'd ever seen had just entered the room. But she had to be pushin' forty, had to be. But no worries, no worries. Slim, beautiful, really beautiful. Yeah, and she'd already clocked the wood responding. A little smile from her. Yeah, and no wonder, yeah? He smiled back and watched her undress for a moment. She was concentratin' on her buttons. She looked even fitter with that little look of concentration. Best get ready.

He loped over to the cabinet.

Placing her bra over the chair, Rowena watched the wiry young man as he pulled open the drawer. She observed his broad back, watching its changing, rippling surface as whole sets of different muscle groups were called in and out of play. She hooked her thumbs under the waistband of her briefs and paused a moment, staring at the fellow's charming young buttocks. A strong, sweet pain below her abdomen caused her to murmur slightly and she quickly pulled her knickers down her legs.

Derek turned. Right, he was ready to go. Protection in place and ready for the off. That's right darlin', get them little pink pants off and hop on this. Come to uncle Derek, though I'm old enough – er, young enough to be your son.

Rowena approached, noting the badly creased, unmade bed, the copy of *The Sun* on the chair, the football hooligan head of the young man coming toward her. But none of it mattered. It didn't matter at all.

This woman smelled good, yeah? She smelled really fuckin' sweet. And she knew how to shag, this girl, cos she *was* a girl, nah messin.' Straight up. She might've been forty, but she was diggin' her heels in like there was nah fuckin' tomorrow. And one minute her hand was on your hair, the next it was right up your jacksey. One cool fuckin' relaxed customer. And gettin' your arse felt by a little darlin' who knows what she's fuckin' doin' and gettin' paid for it deffo beat bangin' panels in that garage dahn the arches in King's Cross. And that old barstard wasn't payin' no pension neither. You want it darlin' I've got it. Here it comes, I'm ratcheting up another few rpms.

Derek increased the pace of his thrusting, as Rowena tightened her legs around him. He lifted his head slightly and peered down at the striking face below him. She had a kind of serious look on her face, yeah? as though she was concentratin' or somethin'. In another world or somethin'. As well she might be. But then the next minute she was just suddenly laughin', gigglin' really loud, yeah? as if she was havin' a fuckin' hysterical fit or somethin'. Almost cryin'! Cryin' with fuckin' laughter. Maybe she was takin' the piss, laughin' at him. What, was his cock not good enough or somethin'? He'd never had no complaints before.

'Kiss me.'

What? She wanted him to kiss her. He felt her hand on his head.

'Er, we're not allowed to, yeah?'

'I know. But you'd like to. Would you like to?'

'Well ... yeah, yeah. I would actually. You are one of *the* fittest birds I've ever -'

Rowena half-smiled, half-giggled and pulled his head down to hers.

TWENTY-ONE

The guy at the desk was bent forward writing, hadn't looked up at all. Probably demonstrating in his own little way his official power. Still, it was no small power he held; it was, after all, in his gift to bestow or withhold that all-devouring cosmic trick that men had learned to call: nookie. How's your father. Slap and tickle. A bit of the other. Well, you could try reducing it to the level of a seventies sitcom if you wanted but it still had the power to fucking tear you apart.

Clutching his sheaf of forms, Lawrence closed the door of the interview room and approached the desk. So here he was. About to beg for sex in earnest. Step one on the final leg to total self-abasement.

He found himself looking into the narrow eyes of a slit-mouthed bureaucrat, in fact one of the nastier-looking pieces of work he had noticed that first morning. That glorious fucking morning when he'd still been strong enough to walk away.

'Take a seat,' said Williams, peering up at the unshaven young man in the frayed camelhair coat. He narrowed his eyes in recognition. So we finally get to say hello, do we? For a second, Williams held the single dark eye glaring out at him from between locks of curling dark hair as the young man slowly sat down. Williams let his gaze drift across the growth on the guy's chin. Before coming in here and bothering *us,* perhaps you should try a barber's first. Or at least invest in a packet of razors.

'Bit of a high premium on razors these days, is there?' said Williams, holding out his hand for the forms.

'Sorry?' said Lawrence, widening his eyes slightly and handing over the documents.

Williams smiled thinly, opening the first page of the claim form. 'The girls might pay you a bit more attention if you shaved once in a while.' He began reading through the form, missing the ferocious glare boring into the front of his head.

Lawrence threw himself back in the chair and looked quickly about the small blank room as if appealing to some invisible audience, before once more resting his gaze on Williams. Fucking, fucking *hell.* Sarcastic *fucker.*

'Don't you think?' said Williams, without looking up from the form.

Lawence stared at the top of Williams' head. Christ, who *was* this tosser?

'My last girlfriend liked it.'

'But that was some time ago, wasn't it...?' said Williams, raising an eyebrow, his attention still on the form.

Lawrence struggled to keep the tone of his answer even.

'Sadly, it was. That,' he paused, '...is why I'm here.'

Williams had to admit that the guy had certainly stuck it out a good long while before coming in. Almost two years. A far more respectable interval than was managed by some - toerags who came in within a fortnight of ending years-long relationships. But on the other hand he was still just another scrounger. No, he was more than that - a bloody hypocrite was what he was. Williams brought back to mind the extravagant gesture of the guy that morning when he'd first come in, when he'd dismissed the leaflets with that supercilious wave of the hand and then glowered about the room before buggering off into the rain. You should've *stayed* out in the rain, chum.

Still, there wasn't really anything he could trip him up with on the form ... though his question 18 was a bit weak. Might as well give him a prod on that.

'You say you're looking for a sexual partner with a "reasonable amount of sexual appeal". What exactly do you mean by that?'

Lawrence weathered the sour look thrown at him from across the table.

'I mean ... basically anybody I find attractive.'

'Well, what kind of woman do you find attractive?'

'I suppose I don't know until I meet them. Don't you find that?'

Lawrence watched the narrow eyes slip disparagingly to a point somewhere on his chest, before returning to the form. This of course was the grim reality after all that slick bollocks in the leaflet about the public being entitled to 'friendly and courteous treatment'. But then what leaflet, what fucking marketing blurb ever matched up to the situation on the ground? You buy a cake, and it always looks shite compared to the photo on the box. So, how much worse the mismatch when you come to a dump like this where you don't even have the status of customer, where you're just a fucking beggar.

'Actually, we're here to talk about you, not me,' said Williams quietly without glancing up from the form.

Lawrence struggled for a second to make sense of the seeming non-sequitur, coming as it did so late after its proper place in the exchange, if it even *had* a proper place. Lawrence squinted at a patch of sandy hair at the side of the guy's head. The guy had been brooding on something there, hadn't he? - and so fucking intensely that he'd lost track of the time, and made a tit of himself. Lawrence smiled softly and examined the guy's downcast eyes. The unhappiness he found there provoked within him a momentary wave of empathy which caught him completely by surprise.

Williams put the claim form aside and opened the medical form. Lawrence cringed. As if it wasn't bad enough having that grabby arsehole of a GP write about his balls, he now had to suffer this poor sod of a middle-aged bureaucrat read about them as well. Lawrence shifted in his seat and watched as Williams slowly pored over the form. Come on, I'm clean. I'm practically untouched by womankind.

Williams closed the medical document and regarded Lawrence with a blank look.

'Your ActionPlan, please,' said Williams, glancing down at the desk and back up at Lawrence.

'I beg your pardon?' replied Lawrence, leaning forward slightly.

'Your ActionPlan.'

'I'm sorry, but I have no idea what you're talking about.'

'Look, you were told to bring in an outline of what you intend to do to go about securing your own liaisons.'

'No, I wasn't.'

'Yes you were. You were given an ActionPlan to fill in along with the claim form and the medical form.'

'No, I wasn't. There must have been ... some sort of *operational oversight....*'

Williams scrutinised the long-haired toerag leaning back in the chair opposite. "Operational oversight." Sounded like the bugger was trying to take the bloody Michael.

Lawrence sat up and leaned forward. 'I'm sorry, but this really is the first I've heard of any ... action plan.' He gestured to the documents on the desk. 'This is really all the woman at the desk gave me. Honestly.'

'Fine, well, you'll just have to write one out now, then.'

For fuck's sake, thought Lawrence, as Williams got up and walked over to a filing cabinet. How was writing out some anaemic little five point plan going to help when the fucking dog bastard worm-thing itself had been screaming at him for nearly two fucking years to "relieve his current situation". He watched Williams take a sheet of plain white paper from the cabinet. Still, if this was what it took to get into the knickers of this ugly three-storey glass-and-panel concrete floozy then write out an "action plan" he would.

Williams sat down and pushed the paper across the desk as Lawrence picked up the pen.

'So you want me to just write out how I intend to go about getting-'

'How you intend to go about procuring a sexual experience at the earliest opportunity.'

Lawrence held the pen poised over the paper. Christ almighty, this was about the single most humiliating experience of his whole life. To lay out his whole sorry sexual non-life for the perusal and judgment of some churlish office worker.

'But whatever I write it's just going to be a continuation of what I put for that question on the form about ... what was it? What strategies I've been employing so far....'

'Well, perhaps you'd better think of something else, then. Since your previous approach has ... failed to bear fruit.'

Lawrence glared up into the rectangular spectacles. The fucker never seemed to miss an opportunity to weigh in with a put-down.

He looked down again at the paper.

Well, what else was there? The options, the only courses open were clubs, pubs, whatever parties you get invited to –

'When you go into a club, what do you do?'

'What *can* you do except dance helplessly next to your target woman until she moves away.'

'And you don't talk to them.'

'No.'

'Why not?'

'Because it feels like harassment. Because it feels like I'm not respecting them as people. And to make some comment about the music, to ask them if they want a drink, to say anything to them at all seems to me as rude, as intrusive as if I were asking them there and then to go to bed - and of course that *is* the only reason I'd be talking to them, because naturally their... initial "being-for-me" is simply "sexual object". Basically I just end up feeling like a sexist bastard.'

Williams watched as the claimant, who had let his eyes wander to the wall, turned his dark gaze once more to him. Looked like the chap was a few shillings short of a pound somewhere.

'What you're really saying is that you're too shy to talk to them, isn't it?'

'No ... I don't think it is.'

'Be that as it may, you're going to have to undertake to be more forward in future.'

'Right....'

'Well, write it down then.'

Lawrence slowly lowered his eyes from Williams to the sheet of blank paper in front of him. Well, if that was what the guy wanted. He picked up the pen and wrote.

I undertake to be more forward in future.

He stared down at the line on the paper. It was about the most pathetic thing he'd ever seen in his life. He was a two-year-old again, being taught how to piss in a pot. And he was suddenly hit with a lucid sense of being in the process of committing some terrible crime against himself. The feeling was followed by a moment of numbing dissociation, as though he were no longer in the room, and he had to fight to bring himself back to the thread of the interview.

'... er ... do you want me to link this statement to what I put on the form about my ... ah ... current strategies?'

'It might be an idea.'

Lawrence let the sarcasm wash over him, and added a few more lines to the sheet of paper. He was going on with it. How could he not; his balls had him in a vice. So now that he'd started, he might as well make this daft fucking "action plan" as winning as possible. What else could he put that might get the git's juices flowing. Ah, yes, some toss about the internet might go down quite well. Never mind the sweet nothings, toots, I know *this* is what you want to hear:

> In addition I intend to put in place a programme of regular visits to my local internet cafe in order to peruse personal contact sites.

Well, Christ, that ought to do. What the hell else could you put apart from pubs and clubs and the internet? Oh, yes... he was forgetting the rich, fertile pulling grounds of London's museums and galleries. The only girl he'd ever approached in a gallery had given him such a look of mortal indignation at his offer of a coffee that he'd born the scars for weeks afterwards. Never, never would he do that again. Still, he added the category to the list, before turning the paper round and pushing it back across the desk. The titanium spectacle-rims glinted once more under the neon strip as the guy read through what he'd put.

'Have you thought about joining a sports club?'

No, he hadn't thought about joining a fucking sports club.

'Actually, I suppose that might be an idea... but, no, I just couldn't afford it.'

'What about your place of work. Surely there must be opportunities.'

'None whatsoever. I work from home.'

'Oh? And what do you do?'

'I make sculpture. I'm a sculptor.'

'Have you ever considered ... that you might increase your exposure to opportunities if you got a proper job?'

'It *is* a proper job. I do sell my work. From time to time.'

'But you don't make enough to join a sports club.'

'I thought I was applying for sex benefit not a mortgage.'

'There's no need to be sarcastic. This is all relevant to the point. You've deliberately put yourself at a double disadvantage in the sexual marketplace by your choice of career. That gives me something to consider.'

Oh, for Christ's sake! 'No, I didn't deliberately put myself at a disadvantage. I wasn't even thinking about the "sexual market-place" when I made the decision to pursue a career in art - because I was in a relationship at the time.'

Williams was staring at the sheet of paper. 'I want you to undertake to go out at least four nights a week, and approach four girls a night, and we'll see how you get on.' He pushed the paper back across the desk and gestured to the pen.

Lawrence stared at the paper for a moment, and then let himself drift with the shame of it all, and began writing, allowing the shame of it to claim him completely, his hand moving under the continued hostile gaze from the other side of the desk.

Williams lifted his eyes from the slender, writing hand, and allowed his glance to roam over the tousled locks of dark hair hanging forward over the furrowed brow and down-turned eyelashes as the guy leaned on his elbow to write, his cheek in his hand. If you want to be a sad case, chum, I'll make you *feel* like a sad case.

Lawrence finished writing and pushed the piece of paper across the table, but was halted by Williams, who pushed it back. 'Sign it and date it please.'

'Oh ... yeah. Sorry.'

Lawrence did as he was told, neatly signing his name and clearly writing out the date, before finally pushing the paper across.

Williams read through it one more time, before raising himself and crossing to a photocopier, running off a copy, and returning to the desk, where he placed the original along with the other documents in a manila file, and handed the copy to Lawrence.

'That's for you. Now, you agree to stand by those commitments under the terms of the Contact-Seeker's Charter, and we'll be making regular checks to see that you are so doing. Now, when you come into the centre, you will be expected before you go up the stairs to make good use of all the facilities located on the ground floor for your own encounter-search, these being principally the boards advertising personal contacts. Under the terms of the Charter you are not at this stage obliged to follow up on these, though this may change should we feel you are not doing enough to move on from benefit. You will receive your benefit once a fortnight from this centre. At your appointment you will be required to sign a declaration that you have failed in the intervening period to secure a liaison of your own, and that you agree to continue to abide by the terms of the Charter. Are you listening?'

Lawrence took his eyes from the length of white plastic casing hiding the electrical conduit running up the rear wall. 'Yes ... yes, I am.' He forced himself to keep his eyes at least on the bloke's face, but he was wandering, he was seriously wandering. He tried to listen, and watched the thin mouth working away, but fuck it ... the geezer's babble was just the same shit he'd already read in the leaflet. He nodded once or twice and ran a hand through his hair. Finally, the drone from the guy's little Cyberman mouth ceased, and Lawrence came partly back to himself as Williams opened a drawer and took out a narrow booklet encased in a thin plastic slip.

He moved slowly along the corridor, peering down at the slim document in his hand, at the time and date of his first session written in a box on the front in biro by the guy, and at his name, also in biro, trapped under the clear plastic sheath of the enclosing wallet, bisected by the passing vertical reflections of the overhead strip-lights. Unbelievably, despite the thorough humiliation and degradation sustained in the interview, and despite his half-formed desire to tear the SB40 to pieces there and then and fling them across the corridor, despite all that, the fucker in his pants was perversely aflame, extending along the top of his thigh, stirred to life by the sight of this passport to its next little harbour of long-awaited nothingness.

TWENTY-TWO

Carlton lowered his weight into the plastic seating of the waiting area and sat with his chin sunk into his neck, turning his ticket over in his big, round fingers.

It'd be cool if she was in, like. The angel. His lovely film star angel. Perhaps today, like. He'd hoped he might have had her again by now. But you never got the same one in a row, like, so really it was still early days cos it'd only been a couple of weeks. Since the best fuckin' day of his life, the best day ever. It must've been, it must've done somethin' *to* him, cos he'd thrown out all his fuckin' porn videos after. Though he was beginnin' to miss them again now, like. Well, because she wasn't there, because he couldn't have her. And after goin' with her, doin' it with her, like, the other sex dole women didn't seem as good. Not as good as they had before, like. But even before, he'd never sat up all night thinkin' about *them*, like he did with her, thinkin' about all kinds of daft fuckin' stuff to do with her. Like ... like what her fuckin' writin' looked like. Really weird, that. Even thinkin' about what kind of stuff she might have been into when she was a kid an' that. Probably not the same stuff as him, though. Probably not Doctor Who an' that. Probably Black Beauty, but no, she was probably a bit too young for that, like. And thinkin' about what she was doin'. He was always thinkin' about what she was doin' - at night, like - he knew right enough what she was doin' in the day. Fuckin' all these other bastards in 'ere. All these bastards were better lookin' than him, much fuckin' better-lookin' most of them, so by rights, like, they shouldn't be allowed to have her. They looked all right, so they should be made to fuck off, they should all be made to fuck off into the street and find their own women. She should be kept back just for him, like.

He peered up at the counter. His number had come up. But it was okay today, like, no pressure or nothin' cos he wasn't in today, the bloke with the glasses. Just that old cow and some other blokes who never messed you about much.

Raising his weight slowly from the seat, Carlton sought out the free desk. The old cow's. She could be a pain, like, but she'd never keep you more than a few minutes. Not like that other fuckin' bastard.

He shuffled slowly across the room, and awkwardly eased himself into the chair, before staring dumbly at the woman behind the desk. Come on, then, like, come on.

'Your SB40, please,' said Sandra tonelessly.

Oh, yeah, daft bastard, he was always forgettin' to give it to them, like. He reached into his coat and fumbled for a moment, his face affected by a fleeting panic, before finally drawing out a stained and crumpled document, one corner of which was almost torn off completely along with its plastic sleeve.

Sandra took the signing document from the great pudgy fingers, and rose from the desk. Making her way to the filing cabinet, she glanced down at the tattered item between her fingers. For the life of her she could never work out quite how some of them managed to get their SB40s into such states. Covered in filth. They ought to issue you with plastic gloves.

Returning from the cabinet, she sat down and placed the file on the desk. There seemed little point in putting the question to this particular specimen, but it was procedure, so she'd better trot it out.

'Have you had a sexual encounter at any time in the last two weeks?'

'... no,' mumbled Carlton as the claim sheet and pen were pushed across the desk toward him.

He picked up the pen and carefully placed his hand below the list of his signatures and began writing. Fuckinell, he'd gone over the box again, like. He always wrote his name too fuckin' big. And the cow was lookin' down at it all miserable, like. He finished the signature and began pushing the paper back across the table, avoiding the woman's eyes.

Sandra took the claim sheet and placed it back in the file, before turning once more to her monitor. She jerked the mouse around for a moment, the movements of her hand absently followed by Carlton's small eyes.

'Number 18, then.'

Carlton began to rise from the chair. He stumbled slightly and turned to the direction of the stairs, but was arrested by the woman's voice.

'Your ticket.'

Fuckinell. The ticket, like. He turned and took the small scrap of paper before once more turning to the stairs, but was stopped again by the flat voice of the woman.

'Your SB40.'

Fuckin' daft twat. He'd forgotten his SBthing an' all, like. He leaned round and picked up the dog-eared booklet lying on the desk.

'Can you please take more care of it in future. And try to keep it clean. Your SB 40 has to be handled by us as well as you, you know. Try not to get any more tomato ketchup on it in future, please.'

Sandra watched as the big ungainly lad lowered his eyes and nodded, before slowly wiping the document on his coat, turning and shuffling off to the stairwell. Sandra shook her head slightly. Heavens, where did they come from? Where on earth did they all come from?

Carlton pushed through the double doors and began hefting his weight up the stairs. Fuckin' cow. Old fuckin' cow. He couldn't help it, like. It wasn't easy keepin' everything tidy, like. If you've got to do it all yourself, like fuckin' washin' up and tidyin' and cleanin' and that, stuff's bound to get a bit out of hand in't it. Fuckin' bound to, like. It's all too much to keep track of, like. Apart from the dog. You've got to stay on top of the dog's shit, like. Cos of the fuckin' smell. The smell of rubbish is one thing, like, but you've really got to pick up that dog's shit as soon as it comes out, like. But with the other stuff, when you come back from work you're not gunna want to do all that stuff, you're just gunna open a can, like, and stick a fuckin' viddy on. And if your mum's dead, and your dad's gone, there's no-one, like, to tell you not to. No-one to tell you to turn off the video and fuckin' clear up. No-one to tell you to turn off the video. Which was cool cos he played tapes all night. Better than the telly. Well, it *was* the telly, like. Tapes of old telly. Cos old telly was better than new fuckin' telly, like, any day of the week. But if ... if *she* came in ... his angel ... and said right, turn off that fuckin' video and get this place - but she probably wouldn't swear like that, like - so, if *she* came in and said turn off that video and get this place cleaned up, like, then he'd fuckin' get it cleaned up then. Or what would be really sound would be like if she fuckin' cleared it all up *for* him, and then made him his tea and that, like his mum used to do for his dad. But no, he'd help her, like. And then after tea, they could watch Star Trek or summat. But she probably wouldn't be into it. But never mind fuckin' Star Trek, after tea, they'd go to bed, they'd go to bed, like, cos he knew she was into *that!* He knew that. He knew that from the way she'd looked round at him when he'd really been goin' into her hard, like. Fuckinell, if only he got her again, if only he got her again today, like.

He reached the first floor landing, pushed through the double doors and began shuffling down the corridor.

It was against the fuckin' rules, like, but if he did get her, then this time he might, like, might, like even try and kiss her. Not her face, like, cos she probably wouldn't like that, but her shoulder or her hand or summat like that. That'd be really cool.

He came up to number 18. Well, here he was, like. But even as he knocked on the door, he knew she wouldn't be on the other side.

'Come in.'

That *could* be her voice....

He turned the handle and opened the door. No, it was just one of the others, like, and one of the not so nice ones an' all, bit fat, like, but then *he* couldn't fuckin' talk, could he? Still, for a moment he just felt like going home ... but no ... sex was still sex, wan't it, like? But she didn't look very happy to see him. Not the way his angel had. *She* had held out her hand to him, like, but this one was just sittin' on the bed with her arms folded, lookin' fuckin' miserable, and fuckin' huffin' an' puffin'. Don't fuckin' like me, eh? Well, no one fuckin' *does*. But you're in *'ere*, an' it's your fuckin' job, it's your fuckin' *job*, like. Your *job* to fuckin' like me. So you might as *well* fuckin' like me, cos you're fuckin' *avin'* me!

He waddled slowly over to the bed, trying to unzip his coat as he went, but had to stop in his tracks and apply all his attention to the task. His lower lip hung open as he frowned down in concentration, tugging at the stubborn zipper.

TWENTY-THREE

Lawrence moved slowly from side to side in the swivel chair, his eyes on the drained white flesh of his slender fingers on the armrest, as the Jamaican guy returned from the cabinet with his file. Lawrence knew that his face probably looked as white as his hands, as it always did after a bout of speaking on the big white telephone. Christ, how he'd loved that phrase when his Dad had first told it to him. He'd fucking cried with laughter all morning over that shit. No laughter this morning, though.

Shit, to spend half the night throwing up because of some fucked-up unidentifiable emotional reaction to the coming big day.... Well, after all ... the crowning humiliation he was about to put himself through probably warranted it. And after he'd finished spewing his guts, his cock had wanted a go too, releasing its yellow stream into the big, flecked white womb, and as he'd pissed, he'd actually started talking to the thing in his hand. All right you ugly piece of crap, you've won, and tomorrow you get to release your *white* stream, your shitty white stream, inside your preferred channel again, cough it all up one more time in your favourite venue. Because I've done it, you bastard, I've found someone - though I don't know who she is yet, and I'll *never* know her name - I've found someone in whom you can trust, in whom you can upchuck every last drop of your life-starting bile.

The Jamaican guy had returned with his file. Lawrence stared at the manila envelope as the guy drew out a crisp sheet of paper and pushed it across the desk toward him. Lawrence ran his eyes down the page of descending rectangular boxes, all awaiting his fortnightly signatures, a dismal graphic forecast of a prolonged future of continued sexual failure. The sight should have prompted a bout of dark laughter in him somewhere, but it didn't.

'Have you had a sexual encounter at any time in the last two weeks?'

Lawrence glanced up into the bright, brown eyes, unprepared for the nakedness of the question, and instinctively searched for some quirky reply, but checked the impulse - because he was a fucking loser, and he was fucking lost, and to pretend he were anything otherwise would only make him look even more ridiculous.

'No ... I haven't,' he said quietly, his eyes held by some oddly comforting quality in the calm, yet intent face on the other side of the desk.

'Aall right, then. If you'd just sign your name there for me, please.'

Lawrence nodded faintly and took up the pen.

'Okay,' said Harper, as Lawrence passed the sheet to him. 'Now, this is your first time, innit? There anythin' you want to ask before you go on up?'

'No ... it's okay, thanks.... I read the leaflet.'

'Aaall right, then. Take this ticket and show it to the security guard over there at the stairs, then go on up to cubicle number 12.'

'Er ... that's on the first floor, is it?'

'Yeah, that's right. First floor and down the laang corridor.'

'Thanks,' said Lawrence as he got up from the seat, somewhat unsteadily, his knuckles showing white on the armrest of the chair.

'You aall right?'

Lawrence stopped and smiled weakly. 'I'm just a little bit nervous.' For some reason he couldn't quite fathom he felt no embarrassment at the confession.

'You'll be aall right.'

Lawrence nodded, his dark eyes on the back of the monitor, and moved away from the desk.

He drifted over to the stairwell like a sleepwalker, gazing down at the stained carpet. He knew he was looking at the carpet, he could see it passing beneath him, but the fact surprised him - because he wasn't there. He didn't know *where* he fucking was, but it didn't seem to be there, crossing the floor of that rancid sex dole office.

Dissociation.

Yes, a little touch of dissociation, and a little dab of derealisation. And what better place for it? In fact, in the present situation it was probably a *bonus*. Here's the security guard. But are you and your brown uniform actually there, pal? Well in case you are, just in case you are, here's my ticket. My ticket to ride.

The guard passed his bored glance over Lawrence's ticket and waved him through to the stairwell.

As the double doors swung closed behind him, Lawrence began climbing the stairs, his footfalls landing heavily on the concrete steps. He was here all right. Christ in heaven. The sound of his steps clattered around the stairwell, reverberating up through the building. Well, he was inside the fucking great concrete tart now, sure enough. He watched his hand moving up the shiny black handrail. An image of the Belgian girl from the pub, Francoise, passed through his mind - her fucking hand on his coat - the last fragment of any real-world erotic life he'd experienced. And although it had been virtually nothing, *some*thing had been carried in that fleeting moment ... some small passing happiness. If he could ... if he could grasp the feeling of that moment, and somehow hold it in his head through the event to come, it might ... there might be some joy to be found in that. But no, it was ridiculous, and anyway, fuck it, this wasn't about joy. Joy had no role to play in this.

As he reached the half-landing, a triangle of white feminine underwear exploded in his mind with stunning force, as though his cock were reminding him and itself of what they were both there for. As if it were grasping, for the first time, the glad reality of the situation, which reality being that *a fuck,* that dodgy Holy Grail, that iffy be-all and end-all, that dubious light fantastic, was now just minutes away.

As he stepped up onto the first-floor landing and slowly leaned into the swing doors, he felt the slug-like flesh in his pants already drawing itself out. Fucking hell. He didn't want to turn up at this fucking cubicle thing with a bloody hard-on. He didn't want to knock on that door sporting such a blatant fucking badge of his desperation. He stopped and stood in the corridor, wincing, trying to fight the growing stimulation, but to no avail as ever. He sighed hard and went on, wrapping his coat around him.

He scowled at the passing cream-painted wall on one side, and the row of doors on the other. So this was where it all went on, was it? Looked like a fucking hospital or something. Christ almighty, what was he doing here? Well, we know what we're doing here ... we've gone over it a hundred fucking times. Nothing to say now, nothing to think now ... nothing to do now but get fucked.

Number 12 must be about halfway down. Shit, look at that. On the wall. Two framed prints roped into a naff attempt to cheer the place up. A nude by Modigliani, and a Robert Mapplethorpe torso. His 'n' hers. Jesus Christ. A coy and ill-judged attempt to tastefully reflect the business of the place. And it was a fucking failure. The images didn't relate to each other; the male and the female had been plucked from separate worlds, to hang lost in the off-white expanse of the wall. Hmm. He smirked sourly. Perhaps there was some thought behind it after all.

But here was number 12. He drew himself up and stared for a moment at the numeral, aware that his arousal had mercifully slumped somewhat. He turned a white knuckle to the door and tried to knock. Fuck; it was as impossible as cold-calling women in pubs: instead of smashing the glass pane of his loneliness over some poor girl's head as she drank at a bar, he was now about to drop the concrete slab of his uselessness in the lap of some poor girl closeted in a sex dole cubicle. But no more fucking *arguing* and analyzing and comparing and contrasting, knock, you tosser, knock and be fucking done with it.

But Christ, what if Martina could see him now, or Sophia, or Laura, or Bibi? Or Anna, Jane, Zoe? But fuck that, they were the reason he was *here*. Hadn't they all one way or another left him to the mercy of the blind, craning worm? They hadn't wanted to get involved with the fucking thing, hadn't wanted to be bothered with it. Whereas he had no choice. They'd rather pretend the thing wasn't there. A luxury not given to him. And so they had no right to judge him. Even as he formulated the thought, he knew it was a banal and stupid chain of flawed logic.

A woman's faintly irritated voice sounded from within as he rubbed his knuckle, so hard had he been knocking.

'Yeah, come in.'

He drew in a breath. Okay, this is it. Come on, pull yourself together, you arsehole.

He opened the door and stepped inside.

The girl was more attractive than he thought she'd be, which was good, but it didn't make a scrap of difference to the pure, distilled embarrassment of the situation. She was lying on her side, dressed in a white robe, absorbed in a book. Maybe he should go. But he took a step forward, waiting for her to say something. She hadn't even fucking looked at him yet. Was it because he'd knocked too loudly on the door? Already, the sight of her thick swirl of shiny black hair and smooth olive thighs had conspired to extend his cock painfully up and away toward his hip-bone, and his balls were responding powerfully to the knowledge that for the next twenty minutes the woman on the bed was all theirs.

She looked up from her book. Fuck. She definitely looked pissed off about something.

'Well, aren't you going to get undressed?'

The question was rhetorical, and together with the look in her eyes it said: look, I'm not getting paid to fucking talk to you, and I'm not getting paid to help you through this. If you're going to fuck me, then fuck me, otherwise piss off. All of which seemed entirely reasonable to Lawrence. Nevertheless, he'd rather talk to her, though he had no interest in her as a person; would rather ask her what she was reading, though he had no interest in that either.

She removed her fierce gaze back to her book. In so doing, it seemed to Lawrence, she contemptuously glanced at the dumb fucking mound in his trousers. Which was also fair enough. Shit. What in Christ's name was he *doing* here? He wanted to go, but instead of heading back to the door, he was easing off his coat. No, he should definitely fucking *go*. Because who *was* this person? And who was he to just fucking walk in here and throw one up her? How had he come to believe in this fantasy that the fact that he was a sad, desperate, wanking, tossing twat somehow gave him the right to just swan in here and plug this stranger? The fact that everyone else seemed to go along with it, including her, was surely no excuse. He held on to his coat. He'd better just get the fuck out.

He was about to put his coat back on when he was caught by a sudden movement on the bed. The girl, while still frowning down at her book, had suddenly flung open the robe around her hips. And it was as though the whole room had come instantly under the influence of some other presence. Suddenly there was nothing else in the world but that simple fucking triangle of damned white cotton disappearing down between those curving olive surfaces. He stood, transfixed, held to the spot by a simple geometric shape; diverted from his chosen, correct path by a simple abstract form. It was wrong, it was all fucking wrong but a team of proverbial wild horses couldn't have dragged him away now from that insane white expanse and its even more insane cargo. Insane because it would once have been one of the most beautiful sights in the world to him, but had now somehow lost ... its ... its *meaning* ... though *none of its power*; every millimetre of his cramped moaning cock was crying out to make contact with it.

He let his coat drop to the floor where he stood, the realisation that the soft wedge in front of him was his for the taking suddenly hitting him like a new layer of consciousness; the desolation, the fucking scorched earth desolation that had been his sex life was past. It was past if he wanted it. He quickly pulled off his jumper and dropped it on top of his coat.

He was out of the Gobi desert now, or at least at an oasis. Well, maybe not your actual tree-lined pool kind of oasis, more like a fucking muddy hole in the ground. But in drinking the mud you drink the water and - Christ Jesus, she was slowly pulling her panties down - while still reading her fucking book! He began undoing his jeans, wincing with unwanted pleasure as his hand accidentally brushed over his groin, his eyes fixed on the girl's lowering knickers, as the whiteness made way for the darkness, the thick fuzzy darkness. And there was the slit. The fucking Golden Chalice. The prize at the end of the egg and spoon race. But ... as Bibi might say, what was it? Nothing more than a simple line.

A fucking black line, that's all it was.

And for the want of this short black line he'd driven himself half-mad for two fucking years?

His hand was motionless on the zipper of his jeans.

He'd thrown Sophia out of his life because she had withheld from him this simple, short fucking black line.

He realised he was breathing in short gasps.

Ah, come on, come *on*. For fuck's *sake!* And now the girl was looking at him like he was some sort of nutter. And she was probably right to.

Forcing himself on, he undid his zip and stepped out of his jeans as the girl dropped the book on the bedside cabinet, opened the drawer, and pulled out a square sachet which she tossed to the foot of the bed.

He stepped hurriedly to the edge of the bed, instinctively stooping his body forward over the erection sticking out of his underwear. Well, she sure as Christ didn't want to have to look at it, did she? But she was looking at her nails anyway, and then away over to the door, with the same irritated sneer she'd had since he'd first come in. But never mind that. Just get this fucking johnny on.

He tore off the top edge of the packet, and pulled out the medical-pink latex ring, its translucent skin like the outer membrane of some bizarre, self-devouring earthworm, the coating of fake mucous causing it to slither between his fingers. Squinting in concentration, he examined the inner edge, trying to work out which way the thing had been rolled. He held it up to the light. Fucking thing! No, that must be it. Forcing his glance down to the mute, brutal stare of his cock, he lowered the condom, compressing the sealed teat, seeing it as a sort of sick inversion of a real nipple, designed to *receive* white fluid, rather than to release it. He began rolling the thin artificial skin down over the taut surface of his glans, momentarily caught up in a fantasy of suffocating the fucker, throttling the bastard once and for all for having dragged him to this pass, to this fucking cubicle, this execution chamber of his self-respect.

Turning to the girl, he was relieved to see her lying back on the bed; he didn't want to meet her gaze. In fact, he didn't want to look in her eyes ever again. It made it difficult to objectify her, and that was what he had to do if he was going to get through this - harness that insidious male capacity for objectification. It always came so naturally when looking at women on the street, but here, where it was truly needed, he was simply afflicted by an acute awareness of the girl on the bed as a thinking, living, dreaming, perceiving individual. He crawled toward her, trying to banish from his mind his sense of her as a repository of a whole private universe of feeling and sensibility, concentrating instead on the black maw between her legs. As he came up to her parting knees, he glanced over at the bedside cabinet in an effort to avoid her eyes, his attention alighting on the cover of the book lying there. Instantly and involuntarily, he read the title. It was a work of philosophy. *On Human Nature,* by Hume.

Christ... Christ alive.

He positioned his hips before hers and peered down at his cock, now so anaemic-looking wrapped in its latex shroud. But for all its gagged, muffled appearance, there was no muzzling this fucker, this wanked-out fucker, and no reining it in; it had the leash between its jaws as it waited there poised before the dark nest of the girl's pubic hair. This region of hers - now more public than private - this state-run private/public pubic region of hers ... How the hell was he going to enter it? No matter how gently he might try to prise her apart, it seemed an unthinkable outrage, to just touch her down there, without so much as -

The girl quickly brought her hand down and with a perfunctory movement of her fingers, simply held herself open for him. How was it that he was here doing this? He inched forward, praying to God and all his angels that the girl didn't mind too much. Insanely, he was hit by a flashing mental image of Lady Penelope, the puppet's blond head tilting impossibly on its fulcrum, as his glans nudged the girl's labia, the contact causing him to gasp in pleasure despite himself. And then he was in, *it* was in, the piece of shit was in, held by - he had to admit - a delicious uniform pressure. He moved the hair away from his eyes and began moving his hips slowly, lowering his upper body to hers. She was staring at the wall, her face blank apart from the habitual faint sneer, one arm thrown back over the pillow. He denied himself an examination of her breasts - she wasn't a fucking piece of meat for his entertainment. Granted, he was fucking her, but he could at least make it as civilised as possible for her. Besides, he just wanted to get his head down and out of sight. He rested his head on the pillow beside hers, but turned away, his chin lightly touching her shoulder. Somehow, this contact seemed more intimate than the slow fucking, and therefore even more outrageous. She felt the same way, it seemed, because she suddenly shrugged the contact away. Well, no wonder - he hadn't fucking shaved for days, had he! Thoughtless, stupid bastard. It might have been all right for Laura in the old days, but this woman probably thought he was some sort of fucking vagrant. And she was obliged to let him fuck her. Christ, he had to say something to her. He had to.

He struggled to find his voice, and then spoke.

'Er ... sorry, I ... er ... meant to shave this morning.'

'Don't worry about it,' came the toneless response.

'Well, I'm sorry, anyway,' he said, trying to sound as friendly as possible.

She made no further reply. Fucking hell. The brief exchange, followed by the absence of a reply, was a depressing echo of his usual failed approaches down the pub! Jesus, he might as well *be* down the pub, crapping out with some girl at the bar! He should have kept his fucking mouth shut. Yeah, but hang on, this was the sex dole for Christ's sake. What the hell do you expect? Just shut up and lie quietly while the lower half discharges its sorry fucking primordial mission. That's all you're fucking here for.

Lucinda lay comfortably enough, absorbing the guy's motions, occasionally even stirred to small pleasures, but as usual, her mind was on other things, drifting from the paragraph she'd been reading before the guy had come in (this Hume geezer seemed to have a sound head on his shoulders, but she just wished she could be more sure what he was actually on about) to the steps she'd learned at the dance class the previous night, to the gift she still had to buy for her sister's little brat. Bloody kid had everything already. And never showed a single sign of appreciation. Which at eight years old you'd expect by now. And, God, the bloody family celebration was coming up. Christ, why should she have to drag herself all the way out to Epping just to commemorate the birth of that little monster? So they could all play bloody happy families? At least the little tyke's father wouldn't be there this time. Incredible it had taken Maria this long to see sense and finally ditch the rotten bastard. How many punches in the face does it take, for God's sake?

It was high time women started dishing them out for once! Starting with Roger Williams downstairs. She couldn't believe she'd seen him skulking around outside the lounge a second time! Well, if it happened again she'd go straight to Jenny or Graham. What the hell did he think he was doing? And the stupid bloody fool obviously imagined he couldn't be seen ... *and* he was married ... they were all the bloody same ... and that claimant the other week … that bloody *smug* dickhead in the suit, with those bloody cocksure blue eyes. She'd clocked him instantly as clearly being a nasty bastard, and she'd wanted to show him that that big dick of his didn't count for shit in her cubicle. And *despite* that, the bastard had managed to arouse her all the same. She could have bloody killed him for the look on his face when he'd left. And she still wanted to give him a good kick in the balls for having given her that orgasm she never wanted, that awful overwhelming orgasm. *Bastard!* At least this guy here had some manners, was keeping his movements pretty gentle, and was keeping himself to himself - apart from his stupid apology for not shaving! Sure, shave. It's better for us if you shave, but if you forget to, don't draw *attention* to it! Don't go *on* about it! You may be inoffensive, but you're still a fool, like all men. Even our friend over there on the table, Mr. Hume, for all his jolly and grand ideas, probably when you get down to it - just one more lost clown.

The guy's curly hair was beginning to get in her face, and she pushed it aside.

She could get something for the kid from Camden, probably, this afternoon. Some bloody computer game crap should do the trick; she wasn't going to waste her day-off tomorrow going into town all for the sake of that little sprog of Maria's! And no way was she -

She felt a sudden swelling of the guy's dick. Good, he was coming. Quite copiously, she couldn't help noticing. But at least he wasn't a shouter like that ridiculous character before him. The silly fools should be banned if they were going to roar in your ear-hole like that. Actually, that was something to remember for next time Jenny came round with her questionnaires. Thank God this bloke was making an effort to remain inconspicuous; she'd just about had enough for one day.

Anyway, what had she been thinking about? Yeah, yeah, no way was she going to spend more than 15 quid this year on that brat. Let Maria complain to dear Mama as much as she likes. In fact why not go further and get a really *obviously* cheap and shit present? Or at least one the little sod will be absolutely guaranteed not to like. A jumper or something. She smiled in satisfaction as she pictured the boy's misery on feeling the soft material through the wrapping paper. Yes, a jumper would do nicely!

The guy's dick was shrinking now and he was pulling himself out.

Good. Another one down ... how many to go? About four more, and then : home James for a hot bath, a couple of Bacardi's, and for later, let's see ... a big tub of Haagen-Dazs in front of the box. And half a packet of Paracetamol.

Lawrence screwed his eyes shut and opened his mouth, twisting his head in a silent scream as the semen jolted out of his body, paralyzing his movement, as though his glans were gripped helplessly by the very earth, trapping him. He crushed his head against the pillow, teeth clenched, his spirit reduced to nothing but a fleeting arena for the mindless bedlam of orgasm until the final bolt of fluid ripped up through his vas deferens, his body made a single hard jerk, and he was released. He let out a shuddering breath and collapsed his weight, his cock slackening as the empty parts of him began filling up once more with an excruciating, killing shame, and a hopelessness deeper than before. For a moment he lay shaking, trying to keep his breathing quiet.

He lifted his head slightly. The girl still had her arm thrown back over the pillow, and she was still looking over toward the cabinet. In fact, her body had barely shifted at all since the beginning of the whole sorry procedure.

He became aware of a post-coital twitching of his hips, and sneered at the automatic movement - more suited to the palpating of a severed insect thorax than to the self-control of sentiency. Jesus Christ, what the *hell* was he doing here?

At least he'd kept it from her, his orgasm, his sweet pollination, his beautiful fertilisation of the rubber-sealed void in the end of the condom, kept it between him and the pillow, him and his own groin. But now he had to lift himself from her and get out. Which would involve facing her to some extent. And he hadn't even thought about this moment before coming in here. God, what a fucking farce.

He raised himself onto his forearms, just in time to see the girl's blank expression break into a half-smile, though directed as ever into the side of the cabinet. What? Was she laughing at him? Or, more incredibly, had she enjoyed it? No, neither. As far as she was concerned he wasn't there at all. It was just some part of her inner life breaking out onto the surface. If he were lucky, maybe she would just go on staring at the cabinet until he'd gone.

Raising himself a little higher, he carefully drew back his hips. A small sucking sound announced his exit from the girl's body, causing him to wince in embarrassment. He sat up and glanced down at his lap while the girl lay on the bed still, a soft look in her eyes as she went on staring at the bedside furniture. He noted the slight softening in her face, but knew that it was not for him, and let his eyes drift back to his lap. For all his desire to be gone, he paused a moment, held by the sight of the diminishing flesh between his legs.

His fucking cock. A somewhat reduced figure now. A ridiculous figure, suddenly too small for its silly plastic environment suit. Looked like the bastard had thrown up inside it. What happened, then, shithead? The ride too rough? Well, I hope you made the most of it, because you're not coming back. You listening, you nasty little bastard? You're not dragging me back here again.

The girl put her legs together and swung round to a sitting position on the bed, forcing Lawrence to move backwards suddenly to make room for her. He glanced nervously at the side of her head. Her eyes were closed tightly, and she was rubbing her temple. Before he could stop himself, he asked her if she were okay.

'What? Yes,' she replied, flashing him a look of burning irritation, before adding in a grudging mutter, 'Thank you,' and reaching for the drawer of the cabinet.

He watched the back of her head for a moment. Christ, let's just get the hell out of here. Now. He glanced down at his lap.

Shit.

What was he supposed to do with the johnny? He couldn't see any tissues, and there didn't seem to be a bloody bin in evidence either. Don't say he was now going to have to ask her for a tissue. He scanned the room, aware of a slight panic building in his chest. For fuck's sake! He was just going to have to speak to her again. Fucking impose himself on her again.

He turned to her.

'Er ... sorry, but er ...'

She fixed him with an impatient look.

'... I mean, I'm sorry to butt in on you again, but what do I do with the ... what do I do with this ingenious little device here...?'

With a distracted air, she handed him a tissue from the drawer, and went on massaging her head.

'Thanks.'

He quickly pulled off the condom, wrapped it in the tissue, and looked in vain once more for a bin. Jesus Christ! He looked again at the side of the girl's head, saw the fingers under her hair now slowly massaging her neck. He didn't want to break in on her again. But there was nothing for it. Fuckinghellfire. All the forces of the universe should be fucked in the throat for forcing him now to disturb her yet again.

'Er ... sorry, but do you have a bin in here?'

'It's over there,' she said, without looking round or indicating any particular part of the room.

'Sorry, where?'

'There!' she sighed, indicating a corner obscured by the cabinet.

'Oh, right, thanks. Sorry,' he said, getting up.

Why the hell hadn't he thought of looking in this corner?

He stood over the bin and depressed the pedal. The lid banged up revealing an off-white mess of tissues and slowly leaking condoms. The sorry leavings of sorry men. He dropped his own contribution on top, and slowly lowered the lid.

Crossing over to his clothes, he pictured some poor cleaning woman at the end of the day emptying the bins. Emptying them one by one into a black bin-liner she'd be pushing down the corridor on a little trolley stacked with brooms and cleaning fluid.

No way was he ever coming back here.

He dressed quickly, glancing warily at the girl, who was now sitting cross-legged, still massaging her neck, but now reading the back of her book, which she held on her knee. So she was into Hume, was she? What might it be like to discuss the old Scottish empiricist with her? But he was getting it all wrong again; he could discuss philosophy any time he liked with Sophia, or, at least until a few days back, with Martina.

He watched her concentrate as she read. Why was she reading the back of it when she was already half-way through the thing?

But she wasn't reading it; she was simply staring at it.

She was waiting for him to get out.

He pulled on his coat, all the while looking down at her, fighting an urge to mutter some word of thanks, some word of farewell. But he knew she didn't want it. She simply wanted him gone - obviously so he'd cause no hold-up on the sad wanker conveyor belt and keep her here any longer than needed. He turned and headed for the door. But ... should he say something after all? Fucking goodbye at least.

'Well,' he smiled from the door. 'Bye, then.'

'Yes, bye,' she replied, without looking round, actually waving him away with a small dismissive gesture of her hand.

He stood for a moment, stunned, and was gone from the room.

Closing the door behind him, he proceeded along the corridor, furious with himself for having pushed her too far, for having forced his society upon her. Why the *fuck* would she want to exchange word one with the losers who came to her in that cubicle? Especially one who hung around afterwards wasting her time and making such a palaver out of disposing of the condom.

He quickened his pace down the corridor. It was only the consoling thought that he'd never set foot in the place again that prevented him from putting his fist through the glass panel of the swing door.

A moderate rain fell steadily through the blackness outside the kitchen window as Lawrence took his coffee and cigarettes through to the living room and sat down. He turned his hands over, examining the powdered residue of dried clay caked into his palms. How long had he been out there? Normally, he couldn't take the cold out in that shed for more than a couple of hours. But this new figure based on that accidental pose in the bathroom that time was showing promise. There was something to it. There must be for it to have held him half the night in that freezing fucking shed.

He stuck a cigarette in his mouth, flicked open the lighter and inhaled deeply. So he'd had a fuck, then. A dismal and sad one, certainly. But a fuck was still nevertheless a fuck. Well, then ... did he feel any better for it?

He exhaled slowly, resting his head on the sofa back.

Well, in truth, if he were honest ... then some fundamental, cold, hurting part of himself did feel as though it had been bathed momentarily in a kind of lukewarm water. Which was at least something. The dog bastard was a little calmer for having had its head stroked. And though he hated the idea, he might as well admit to himself now that, despite all that had been lost, despite the shame and the wretchedness, and despite his resolve to the contrary in the cubicle, and if nothing else turned up in the meantime, then it was obvious he'd be going back.

TWENTY-FOUR

Sacha ran his gaze across the bar of the exclusive West End club, his severe eyes by turns raping or dispatching, always assaulting, this or that member of the female clientele, until finally meeting the sceptical look of the attractive smoking brunette sat in the overstuffed leather armchair across from him.

'Ten thousand quid,' he said, his sharp, handsome features breaking into a smile which the woman in the armchair always found too sudden and too intense.

'Stop it, Sacha. There's no way I'd do that to Brent. Or to Sally either, for that matter.'

'I'm serious, Lorraine. I'll give you ten thousand pounds if you'll let me fuck you.'

'I think we'd better talk about something else,' said Lorraine, glancing over at her friends at the next table.

'Ten grand would certainly keep certain wolves from your door.'

She glared at him, sipping her Chardonnay.

'I'm serious, Lorraine.'

'And so am I. Think about something else for once in your life, Sacha.'

All right, I'll think about the miserable look on your face when your sad little Hampstead boutique finally goes to the wall. If you want to lose your business to save your precious, uppity, under-exercised little snatch for that tedious hippy scrotum you call a husband, then far be it from me to stop you.

'I don't know, Lorraine, you could be doing yourself two very big favours, here....'

'If you were any kind of a real friend you'd do me the second favour anyway.'

'Come on, you know it doesn't work like that.'

'Not with you, it doesn't, I'll grant you that much.'

'Just a small, little fuck, Lorraine. What's the harm?'

'No, thanks, Sacha.'

All right, rot in peace with that pea-knobbed old stoner, then. Fuck you.

Placing her empty glass on the table, Lorraine reached for her handbag and rose from her chair. 'I'm going to the ladies. I'll be back in a moment.'

Quarter of an hour, more like. Enjoy it, Lorraine. That's the last you're getting from me for a good while.

Sacha watched her cross the deep red carpet, hating the way her streamlined hips blended into the potent swell of her rear; hating it because he'd not now be fucking it. Nevertheless, he let his eyes track the provocative rotation of her taut bottom past the gilt mirrors, glass cabinets and indoor palms all the way to the ladies toilet, before switching to the rich display of women at the bar.

He mused on the press of girls, a forest of long, bare arms and long tinted hair surmounting a broken horizon-line of low-riding trouser waistbands and exposed panty-elastic. A good half of this girl-flesh was certainly mountable; it was a good night. The private clubs were a good draw for high-end vulva, though much of it was, of course, irritatingly uppity. But that was only natural; why else were they queuing up to pay a ludicrous six quid for a glass of wine? The value wasn't in the wine; it was in the price itself: it kept the lepers out. Which was of course partly the reason for his own presence, though he was not averse to coralling starving undergraduates - so long as they were basically genetically superior, that was all that mattered. But some of the bitches in here, particularly the three young fillies currently looking down their decaying noses at the slow-moving bartender, had clearly ruled out all cock not attached to a big pile of cash. And yet, all three of these W1 sluts came fitted with rumps which, while clearly worth exploring, were nevertheless a notch or two short of what you'd call top-flight. Still, he'd give them a go; he had cock, cash and coke enough for the lot of them. Though not the time, unfortunately. The world-beating flesh of Ulla's arse with its heaven-forged geometry was waiting for him up in Hackney. Still, it might have been nice to have fit these three in before somehow, but it would have taken hours to get anything off the ground there. And then, after you'd fired into their cervixes a few times, you'd be plagued till well into the next morning with three different kinds of bullshit. That was another advantage to that welfare brothel up in Kentish Town: it fit quite nicely and discreetly into the middle of the day.... Christ, hell, he'd almost forgotten. He'd better do something about that leather-faced troglodyte the bastards had set him up with. How long had it been? A week? And he'd still not called her. Better take care of it soon, before that spectacled jobsworth clitoris or one of his minions got in touch with her and discovered his ... well, how would they term it? His 'failure to capitalise on opportunities afforded by the centre' or some such turgid rubbish. Shit, he'd better take care of it now. But it seemed a pity to sour the evening by speaking now to that thing, that foul antithesis of sexual allure, and besides, it was late. But on the other hand, that benefit arsehole clearly had it in for him. And if he left it till he got up tomorrow, there was a danger the arse might get to her first. If he hadn't done already. Still, it was late, and she might be asleep. Well, the chinky old trout would just have to wake up, then.

He brought out his tiny silver mobile and selected a number, but on seeing Lorraine emerge from the toilets, thought better of it, cancelled the call, and rose, making his way toward her.

'Something's come up, Lorraine, I'm afraid,' he said, smiling brilliantly. 'A bit of business. Must dash.' He deposited a quick, malign caress on her cheekbone, then headed for the exit, leaving her to stare after him. She turned in disgust and returned to her friends.

Passing the elegantly liveried bouncer stationed at the door of the first-floor cocktail lounge, Sacha descended the smart staircase, reflecting on the fortnightly afternoons spent up in Kentish Town. How much were they were worth to him? How much was it worth to him, the oddly appealing, random kick of the bonk benefit cubicle? An afternoon with a Park Lane whore? Two? Ten? He smiled to himself. Easily. Even playing the pathetic games of the drones on the desks could at times provide rich amusement. On the whole, it was a pretty pukka set-up and worth protecting, but this pig he'd been set up with had the power to put the kybosh on the whole thing if she weren't managed correctly. Obviously, she'd have to be coached to tell the benefit centre that she hadn't fancied him. She'd have to be coerced. He grinned. After all, why not? He had ten grand going spare now that Lorraine had failed to see sense. One phone call should take care of it. Although, no, perhaps not. Money wouldn't be enough. Not to shut her mouth properly. Not to be *sure*. He'd need her address too. He could put somebody on it, but no, there wasn't the time. Well, then, there was nothing for it but to *meet* the piece of shit.

Crossing the foyer, he brought out his phone and emerged into the street, sweeping back the sharp cut of his straight fair hair. He flipped open the lid of the mobile, dialled and waited, pacing between the lampposts and peering up at the orange canopy of city-lit cloud cover, before turning his head quickly back to the pavement.

'Hello, I'm responding to an ad you placed with the sex-benefit centre in Kentish Town................Yes, yes..................Yes, look - ....Look, if you're interested in meeting.............If you're interested in meeting -............. Can you stop speaking for a moment, please?...........Thank you, I'm sorry, but I'm very busy and don't have much time, so if you'd like to meet..........What?...........I'm 32.......... Then I suggest we meet tomorrow afternoon.............How about your end of town? You're in Peckham, aren't you?...........Well, I can come down to Camberwell, say....4 o'clock..............Okay, do you know a café called "The Ship"?.............Good, right, well, I have to go now............ I have to g-...............Yes, see you tomorrow then........... Yes.................Yes, that's what I said..............Yes...........Goodbye.'

Jesus Christ, shut up, you stupid gook slob. Shut up and let me get to my sweet Scandinavian slit if you know what's good for you, you excrement.

Slipping the mobile phone back into his jacket, he strode down the street, his thoughts racing ahead to Ulla. Delicious as she was, she'd become slightly irksome of late. She'd better have sorted out all that nonsense with the rent and bills at that flatshare. He didn't want to sit there drying any tears to*night*. You'd better have sorted it, Ulla, because the strong sweet smell of your cute little quim is already in my nostrils and I want to fucking feast on you tonight.

Drawing up beside the low-slung profile of a sleek red sports car, he casually aimed the electronic beam of his key-ring and gripped the chrome door handle, unconsciously warmed by the feeling of security offered by the cold metal.

The young Greek waitress removed the two empty cups from the small round table and returned to the counter, her swift, elegant motion carrying her deftly past the other tables, almost all of which appeared to be peopled by students from the art college, a group to which the waitress herself almost certainly belonged.

Sacha watched as she went, his eyes on the small of her back. The proximity to the art college and its fund of loose, arty fluff was of course the only reason for his acquaintance with this particular shit-hole. Cafés like this were a nice little shag source. Still, a conquest made here never beat the sheer magnificence of what could be achieved at the degree shows. Nothing quite matched that master-of-the-Earth feeling of walking into the exhibition space of some pretentious little mixed-up minx, buying up every last one of her daft canvases or preposterous fucking cardboard box installations and knowing you'd be screwing the daylight out of her by the end of the week; and then revisiting the show with her, the faces of her tutors like slapped arses to see her on your arm, because you'd been where they'd only wanked over in their imaginations, and there *you* are with the taste of her delicate, perceptive, avant-garde, angst-ridden little arsehole still on the tip of your tongue.

Hell, he was getting excited. Which was a little unfortunate because he was in fact staring, if unseeingly, at the truly unappealing head of Miss Li Naing, 41, Peckham area. It was still spouting, in broken English, the woman's tedious life history. So, you've been living in England for seven years; so you should speak English better than this by now, then, shouldn't you? So you're "assistant manager" at a launderette in Catford. A truly wonderful achievement, that. Whoooah, don't smile like that! Your face is a cracked sewer as it is, we don't want it breaking up completely. We don't want our pretty young waitress stooping to clear up a mess like that. Also, don't smile, because in your awful smile I see your hope. Your hope for a better life; because it's not just a fucking you're after, is it? Well, you're not getting either. Neither the fucking, nor the better life. But if you play your cards right, you troll, you'll get a big consolation prize. Oh, God, don't start talking about your parents. All right, that's enough. Time to cut you off.

Putting a finger to his lips, he reached his hand to her, steeling himself for the contact, flinching inwardly nevertheless as his fingers enclosed the loose, lined skin of her spindly hand. He forced himself to look into her small, narrow eyes, disgusted by the expectancy, the joy, he found there, and also the idiocy. How could she seriously believe he was interested in her? Could she not see that she occupied the lowest end of the desirability spectrum, while he occupied its highest?

He caressed her index finger, which he noticed was trembling slightly. And for a moment, he almost felt sorry for her. But on peering up at her once more and noting evidence of awful, hanging breasts, he was filled with a renewed hatred: for 41 years her lack of beauty had been a stain on the world and now she was staining him with it.

Time to get out of here.

'I think we should go somewhere we can be alone for a while. I'd suggest my flat, but it's over an hour's drive from here. So...'

'We can go my place.'

To your place, you stupid dink sow. Don't they *have* prepositions in the fucking Philippines or whatever paddy field swamp it is you so unfortunately crawled out of?

He removed his hand, and stood up abruptly, dropping a five-pound note on the table. 'All right, let's go to your place.'

Realising he may be letting his hatred show, he flashed her a smile, and cringed inwardly as she happily, gratefully returned it.

He strode off to the door, leaving her to scramble for her jacket and bag.

The charmless sprawl of a Peckham Rye housing estate spread below him, brokenly visible through the concrete slats of the urine-soaked stairwell, as Sacha trudged wearily and angrily up the steps. The animals that lived in these blocks *deserved* poverty. They deserved it for having trashed that elevator and pissed in this stairway. Ahead of him, the dreadful rear end of that woman toiled on up the stairs. How much further, you bloody flat-faced, rat-arsed boot, you fucking sexual write-off? But at least the exertion of the climb had forced her to shut her mouth for a while.

She was turning left out of the stairwell onto a bleak open-air walkway. About time. They must be on about the sixth floor. Following her out onto the long grey terrace, he saw that she'd stopped in front of a battered red door. Presumably the entrance to the rat-hole she called home. And there was the number: 68.

68 Brentford House, Brentford Road, Peckham.

She was fiddling with her keys, smiling at him a little uncertainly. Was there a trace of shame in her dismal slitty eyes? He didn't bother smiling back. No need now.

The door swung open and he followed her inside.

Closing the door behind him, he ignored her entreaty to go through into the living room, and remained where he was in the cramped hallway, thanking Christ that he would not be venturing any further into this fetid rabbit hutch. He watched her disappear through a side door and waited a moment for her puzzled head to reappear.

'You okay?' she was saying, 'You no come through?'

He regarded her with his serious blue eyes, hands in his pockets.

'The answers to your questions: yes, I'm okay; and no, I'm not coming through.'

She was squinting at him, her head on one side like some confused dog. 'Why? What - what you mean?'

'I mean that I find you deeply unattractive.'

She gazed up at him, pain filling her eyes.

Oh, don't look so sorry for yourself. Take that look off your face before I take it off for you.

'I thought you - I thought you like me....' She began stroking the back of her hand and lowering her head.

'No. I'm afraid not. Now listen carefully to what I say.'

Her shoulders were shaking.

'Right. Now this is the -'

'Why you come here?'

'I'm about to fucking tell you, aren't I!'

'Who are you?' she said through her tears.

'Shut up!'

There was fear in her face now. Which was good, but he'd better soften up a little; he didn't want her getting hysterical. He forced himself to take the edge out of his voice.

'All right, now just listen carefully to what I say. The situation is this: I'm prepared to give you a lot of money if you do exactly what I tell you. Do you understand?'

The woman's streaming face was a confusion of puzzlement and fear.

'I said, do you *understand?*' She seemed unable to speak. Fighting his disgust, Sacha reached into his lapel pocket and drew out a white silk handkerchief. 'Here, look, it's all right, dry your eyes with this.'

He watched her take it.

'Why you want … why you want to give me money?'

'All right, first, can you tell me if you've received any calls from the sex benefit centre in Kentish Town?'

'No. No calls. They no call.'

'Good. But they will. Now this is what I want you to do: when they call, I want you to tell them that you met me, but that you found me … not to your liking sexually.'

'What?'

Sacha raised his voice. 'I want you to tell them that you refused me, that you didn't want to sleep with me!'

'… and you give me money … for this?'

' A lot of money, that's right.'

'… why?'

'That's none of your damned business!'

She jumped at his shout, visibly terrified once more.

'Would you like to see how *much* money?'

She nodded her head slowly.

Sacha removed his wallet and took out a sheaf of fifty-pound notes.

'There's twenty of those there. That's one thousand pounds.'

'… You really goin' give so much money…?'

'Yes. It's yours. If you'll do that one little thing for me.'

'All right … I do what you want, I tell them what you want.'

'Come over here, then.'

She stepped forward slowly.

'Hold out your hand.'

He watched as she raised her hand, her face flushing with cautious joy as her fingers closed around the wodge of notes. Take it then, you awful yellow hound. You can get your nasty little fingers around my cash - I invite you - but never will they go round anything else. How could you…? How *could* you ever have entertained such a hope? With your hope you've insulted me.

'There, that's it. You're a thousand pounds richer. Now, when they call, tell them that we met in the café up in Camberwell, that you decided you didn't want me - that you didn't like my eyes or something - and that after an hour or so, you said goodbye to me and came home. All right?'

'Yes. I tell them.'

'Good.' Sacha allowed his eyes to wander over the low, narrow ceiling of the hallway. 'Good. Now, you do understand … you do understand that I have your address, now, don't you?'

He fixed his eyes on her.

'… why, what you goin' do?'

'Nothing. If you're good. But if you take my money and tell them or anybody else about this conversation, then -'

'No, no, no, I tell them what you want! I tell them -'

'Bloody stop interrupting, will you? Just shut up! *If* you tell them or anybody else about this conversation, I will pay some people to come here and pay you a visit. They will come up those stinking stairs, enter this stinking flat, and pay you a little visit. Do you understand?'

She was nodding, though she appeared almost in shock.

Christ, she might lose it and go to the police anyway.

And for the first time in years, Sacha too felt something like fear rising up inside him.

Better mollycoddle her for a bit.

'But look, nothing's going to happen,' he said, switching on a smile, 'I don't want it to. That was just ... security. For my own peace of mind. So that I can trust you. All I want is for us to do this little bit of business. All right? Look at all that money in your hand.'

A vague expression of relief competed with the fear in her face as she peered down at the roll of banknotes. Finally, the deep lines around her mouth shifted into a weak smile.

'All right?' smiled Sacha.

'Yes … it all right. I tell them … don't worry.'

'Good … okay. Good, then I'll be off now.'

He turned to the door, but stopped himself.

'Ah, my handkerchief.'

'What?'

'My handkerchief, please.'

'Oh, I sorry. Yes. Here.'

Without another word, he opened the door, and stepped out on to the concrete parapet. Striding quickly down the walkway, he barely noted the sound of the woman closing the door behind him.

Now to just get out of this filthy scum-encrusted warren. And mix with his own kind. Find a woman with a superior grade of DNA and soothe his offended cock inside her.

As he was about to enter the stairwell, he paused, and in irritation, pulled out the handkerchief, unfolded it and stared at the damp patch in the centre. Moisture from that woman. He didn't want the moisture of that fucking weasel.

He continued down the stairs as the square of white silk floated down across the face of the tower block.

TWENTY-FIVE

'What do you mean, you still haven't found it?' shouted Williams. 'I've been on at you for two days!'

Mills shifted in his seat in the staff office, placed his coffee on the table, and glared up at Williams.

'Look, Roger, there's been a lot on.'

'Well, do it now, will you!'

'Can I finish my coffee at least?'

'There's too much sitting around in here drinking coffee. I suppose you realise, don't you, that we may have lost a chance to bag a fraudulent claim because you can't pull your ruddy finger out! Now get out and check that file, please.'

The junior claimant advisor sighed and slowly got to his feet.

'Right ... the personal contacts file, was it?'

'That's right,' said Williams, already halfway to the door.

'And you seriously want me to go through the whole file?'

'Well, there's no other way, is there? If the card had been filed correctly in the first place, there wouldn't be any need, would there? But since -'

'Okay, okay ... what was the name again?'

'Oh, for heaven's sake, Peter. Naing. Li Naing, Peckham.'

Mills lamely followed Williams out of the door, taking his coffee with him.

Slamming shut the lower drawer of the filing cabinet, Mills got to his feet and walked over to Williams' desk.

'All right, I've found it,' he said, handing over a small white card.

'About bloody time. Where was it?'

'It had been filed under M for some reason.'

'Well, what the hell was it doing there?'

Mills shrugged his shoulders.

'This number should have been called days ago. Sometimes, you know, you lot are nothing short of bloody useless. All right, Peter, get back to your desk,' said Williams, reaching for the phone.

He stabbed out the number and waited, staring over at the stains from the heating units on the far wall.

'Hello?......Yes, I'd like to speak to Miss Naing, please.......Ah, hello, I'm calling from the Kentish Town Sex Benefit Centre. You recently placed a contact ad with us, and we subsequently put you in touch with one of our claimants?..........Well, this is just a quick follow-up call to see how you got along..................Aha.......Ah, I see....................Really?........Okay, well, that's fine, then, thank you......Thank you for your time......Goodbye.'

He slammed the phone back into its cradle. Jesus Christ. You stupid bloody woman! What do you mean, you didn't like his *ears*, you silly bitch? He's English, he's got blond hair, that's what you said you wanted on your card – and what was the *matter* with his bloody ears, anyway?

He ran his hand through his thinning hair, his eyes still fixed on the opposite wall. Incredible! It was just incredible! Unless the flash git had somehow gotten to her... but it was impossible to prove... and yet this business about the lout's ears was so preposterous it almost had to be true.

He removed his glasses and rubbed the bridge of his nose.

All right, chum, you got away this time, but next time I see you I'm just going to put you out on another one. And if you get through that, another. And in the meantime, there's a workshop coming up and your name's ruddy-well going on the list, sunshine, ruddy-well going on the *list*.

He sprang up from his chair, and crossed to Sandra's desk.

'Sandra, I'd like you to put a note in one of the files for me next time you're up. Notification of an LSW.'

He stared down at her slowly nodding grey-bobbed head.

'Actually, no, forget it. I'll do it myself.'

He marched quickly off to the staff office as Sandra turned back to her monitor.

'Whatever you say, Roger,' she sighed.

TWENTY- SIX

'Mr. Carlton, the purpose of this interview is to enable you - and *us* - to take a fresh look at your situation, to see how things have been going. That's why we call it a "Fresh Look Interview". Though I'm sure you're familiar with the procedure, being as you've attended quite a few of these interviews in the past. Okay, now let me just bring up the rest of your file and we'll see how you're doing.'

The young woman behind the desk looked into her monitor, as Carlton shifted his weight nervously, his chin sunk into his neck.

It was good he'd got this one, like. She didn't seem too bad. And he liked the look of her an' all. Liked the look of her all right, but he'd rather have her up in one of them cubicles than down 'ere givin' him all this crap ... all this crap they're always givin' you, like ... interview *shite!* They should interview all them other bastards, but he should be left alone, like. Left alone.

'Okay. You've been signing on at this office now for almost ten years. Now, I know that's rather a long time, but the important thing to remember is not to get depressed about it.'

I'm not ... fuckin' depressed about it. The only thing ... the only thing wrong, like, is where's my angel? What've you done with my angel?

'I'm sure if we have a look at your situation from a different perspective, I'm sure we can find some way of improving that situation. Now, to give me an idea of how things have been going perhaps you can tell me what strategies you've been employing recently.'

He wanted to say, what strategies, like? What fuckin' strategies can *I* employ? But he knew he'd better just lie, like, though he didn't like to. But he'd got them ready and to hand, like, his lies. He'd been up all night on them, getting them straight in his head, like.

'Er ... spoke to a woman at the bus-stop, like ... the other week.'

'Good, yes. And what did she say?'

'Said she didn't want to come. For a coffee, like. I asked her if she wanted a drink of coffee with me.'

'I see.'

'And the other day, like, the same thing in the video place....'

'What happened in the video ... place?'

'A girl, like ... asked her if she wanted to watch a viddy ... she'd bumped into me, y'see.'

'I'm sorry, I don't understand. You mean you already knew her. She was an acquaintance of yours?'

He could see that she believed him, like. The stuff about the girl bumpin' into him made it *sound* real.

'No, she bumped into me ... an accident, like. I didn't *know* her. She said sorry. So *then* ... I asked her if she wanted a pint, like. Well, not a pint ... some wine. Down the pub.'

'And what was the response?'

'She didn't want to.'

'I see. Well, what you're telling me about here are random approaches on the street.'

'No, it was inside, like. In the video place.'

'I know. But what I mean is that your approach in these cases was bound to fail because of the context of each encounter. What we've got to do is get you thinking in a more focused way about the approaches you make. Where you make them. When you make them. And to whom you make them. And this is what we mean when we speak of strategies.'

Fuckin' strategies! Always on about fuckin' strategies, but what good's strategies to *me*? Fuckin' women are never gunna want a drink with *me!* No matter how fuckin' ... fuckin'... *focused* I am. And you know it! Yóu fuckin' *know* it ... so why don't you leave me alone ... just fuckin' leave me alone. Bring me my angel and leave us alone....

'For instance, it's always a good strategy to make approaches in an environment which gives you a certain accreditation. For example: your workplace, or a social gathering or group to which you belong. That way, you don't present yourself as a total stranger. Women can find that a little off-putting.'

I know that, like. I'm not fuckin' daft. You only think I am, like, cos I'm playin' you clever ... playin' you clever.

'Okay, let's start with your workplace. From your records I see you were working in a supermarket. Are you still there?'

'Yeah.'

'And what do you do there?'

'Stack shelves ... fruit, like. And vegetables.'

'I see. And do you have many female co-workers?'

'Well ... erm... there's one or two. But, you know, they're old ... and married, like.'

'Only one or two? I would've thought there'd be a lot of women working in a supermarket. What about on the tills?'

'Oh, aye, there's a lot on the tills.'

'And is there anyone there you have considered approaching?'

'I like some of them, like.' He began shifting in his seat.

'But you wouldn't consider approaching them,' said the young woman, eyeing the claimant's lowered head. He was wringing his hands.

'No ... and why do you *fuckin' think?'*

He'd fuckin' said it out loud.

'All right, all right, there's no need for language.'

Yes there is, yes there is, yes there *fuckin' is.*

The woman continued in a gentler tone, 'But as for … I mean the question of your … personal appearance, I was going to come on to that, but as you've … raised the issue, I have to say that your personal presentation does perhaps leave a little to be desired. Now, it easily happens when we're feeling stuck, or in a rut. Little things, like washing our hair, changing our clothes may tend to go by the wayside. But there are things we can do to change that.'

Fuckin' leave me alone ... you cow, you fuckin' cow ... wash my hair, an' it's all gunna be cool is it? Fuckers-like, is it!

'It's all about taking a more positive approach. Now I know these can be difficult things to discuss, difficult things to face up to, but if you're struggling with your ... personal grooming, then there are little pieces of advice we can give you, a few handy hints. In fact, I think it would be really good for you if you were to go along to a workshop.'

... fuckin' no way ... no *way* ... *not again....*

'Now, we have a LiaisonSearch Workshop starting on the 14th. I think this would be a good idea for you, because it incorporates a grooming module into a broad structure taking in all the other things we've been talking about. Now, it's a full-time two-day course, so you'll have time to go into real detail with the instructors. So. I'll put your name down, then, shall I?'

'I've already bin on one.'

'Oh? I don't think you could have. We've only been running LSWs for about three months, and there's nothing in your case file about your attending.'

'I've bin on one though. And it didn't do much good, like.'

'Well, when was this?'

'About two year back.'

'Well, then. That would have been an Encounters Workshop. You've never been on a LiaisonSearch Workshop. LiaisonSearch is a completely different concept. I'll put you down for -'

'Look, it'll just be ... it'll just be the same, like ... do I *have* to...?'

'It won't be the same, Mr. Carlton. I've told you. It's a thoroughly updated program. Actually, it's tailor-made for people of your needs.'

'I don't want to go, like.'

'I'm sorry, but you've ... you've been claiming for ten *years.* I know you've been having problems, but ... you have to make an *effort.* I'm sorry, but those are the rules. Now, I'm putting you down for Saturday the 14th at 9 a.m. Okay? And please attend, won't you? Because, I'm sorry, but I have to warn you that if you *don't* attend, your benefit will be automatically suspended. You understand that? Your benefit will be suspended.'

... no ... no, don't do that ... I'll go, like....

'Okay, now here's a leaflet about LiaisonSearch to take away with you. I'll just write the time and date on it for you as a little reminder, and the address of course! Which is... let's see now... Jetstream Training, 27b Junction Road, Tufnell Park. Okay. So. You're all set. Now. Is there anything you'd like to ask me before you go?'

Carlton lifted his chin slightly, and shook his head.

'Okay, that's it, then.'

Stuffing the already crumpled leaflet into the side pocket of his grubby anorak, Carlton rose from the chair and shuffled off to the door, his exit unobserved by the woman behind the desk, her whole attention once more claimed by her monitor.

TWENTY-SEVEN

Sacha pushed open the swing doors and entered from the street, bringing with him the sound of an idling queue of traffic which was cut short as the doors swung to behind him. Crossing leisurely to the ticket dispenser, he took a number and sat down, scanning the signing desks and brushing the sleeves of his suit.

The breast with the glasses appeared not to be in today. A pity, that. Might have proved rather enjoyable watching the cock squirm in the face of his defeat. Because he, Sacha, clearly *had* prevailed; he would have heard from these bastards by now if that gook warthog had blabbed.

Mercifully, there weren't too many people in front of him; it was always a little nauseating waiting around down here with these scrapings. There was that tubby shit-sack again. Perhaps, after all, the thing to do with these slobs if they really couldn't find vagina would be to simply cut their worthless little balls off. No more frustration. And a great saving to the taxpayer. Simple, really. Still, he would *miss* these fortnightly romps.

His number had been called. The free desk appeared to be manned by some sort of awful old bitch.

He strode over and took a seat.

'Good afternoon,' he said, flashing the woman a smile, wondering about the true extent of his power. Could this smile, for instance, right now in some small way be moistening the drawers of this rank old crone? Did he have *that* power? The power to resurrect the dead?

'Good afternoon,' said Sandra flatly, taking his SB40.

To Sacha's annoyance, she didn't look at him again, merely rose and drifted off to the filing cabinet. He tracked her with his eyes. Come on, you wreckage, *look at me*. No? Then die of ovarian cancer. But hurry up with my file first. How slowly you open the drawer. Come on, move it, you tweed-skirted bastard.

Sandra closed the drawer and crossed back to the desk, file in hand. Sacha's eyes flashed to a handwritten note clipped to the top of the manila envelope.

She sat down, running her eyes over the note.

'Right, well. Before I sign you on, I have to tell you that as you've been coming in for several months now, it's been decided you should attend a LiaisonSearch Workshop.'

What are you talking about, hag?

'It's a weekend course, starting on Saturday the 14th. Now, the course will be taking place at a training centre in... Tufnell Park. You're to report at 9a.m sharp -'

'Hold on a minute. What are you talking about? I'd like you to explain to me please exactly what on earth it is you mean by these three rather bizarre words, "Liaison Search Workshop" which you seem to have pulled out of thin air.'

'Well, I'd've thought it was self-explanatory enough.'

'Ah. Well, you see, I don't. I'd like you to explain it to me.'

'Well. It's a course for claimants who seem to be having problems in moving on from benefit. You'll join a group of others like yourself and be taken through a series of activities designed to help you rethink your strategies for securing liaisons.'

'I see. Well, presumably I have a choice as to whether I attend or not.'

'Actually, no. You do not. If you fail to attend, you will lose your entitlement to benefit. And actually, I must say, you don't strike me as being very keen. Perhaps you've already decided you'd rather not attend. In which case we can dispense with your claim forthwith.'

She began returning Sacha's signing sheet to its file.

'I never said I wasn't keen. I merely asked that you explain it to me.'

'Then why did you ask if it were compulsory?'

Sacha felt a simple, human, honest need to boot her in the crotch.

'Well, because ... All right, to be honest with you, I'm never keen on these group sessions, whatever the field of human endeavour. But, if you think it could be of value in this case, then ... I'll give it a go.'

'All right, then,' said Sandra slowly, once more removing the signing sheet from the file, and sliding it toward him. 'Have you had a sexual encounter at any time in the last two weeks?'

'No. No, I haven't,' replied Sacha, taking the pen.

Mounting the stairs to the first floor, Sacha was almost shaking with fury. At that moment nothing in the world seemed so foul as the grey desiccated object sat behind that desk in the reception area. She was worse than that testicle in the glasses. A malicious, rotting husk. Dead from the neck down, but still dangerously quick off the drawer. What was this faeces she'd sent him to? He removed the leaflet the woman had given him. Where was this fucking place? "Jetstream Training"... some company they'd farmed the shit out to. Some piddling little 'consultancy' hiding out over a parade of shops in Tufnell Park ... an unconscionable waste of his time ... but then, if he didn't go...

... well, after all, on the other hand, it may well prove rather amusing to watch the sad onanist brigade being put through a few hoops; to look down from the lofty pinnacle of his own prowess onto these pathetic turds reduced to grubbing about in some dog piss workshop because they were all too weak or ugly to just take the pussy that was lying around all over. No, when looked at it in those terms, the prospect began to sound rather appealing. He could do with a good laugh.

A series of beeps from his mobile announced an incoming text. Inga, probably. He drew the tiny phone from his pocket and opened the message. Sally. Reminding him to be home by nine. It was *his* fucking home, he'd be back to it by any time he liked. Might have been a bad call having her move in, after all. Though the arrangement had its uses. At least he didn't have to drive halfway across town in the middle of the night if he woke up needing a poke. And she had her charms. Her height, principally. He'd always thought that Ulla and Inga, while they had the edge over her in most departments, could do with an extra inch or so.

Another message. Sally again. This time telling him that she "loved" him. Not the name of the game, Sally. The word, as used by me, is merely a password allowing me access to your sweet *fundament*, my dear. I don't love you; I fuck you. And you'll get a good one when I get back - at a time of my choosing - but first, I think I'll get a little practise in, if you don't mind.

He gained the landing and strode down the corridor. What number had that harridan given him again? 8, wasn't it? And what little morsel lies behind number 8 today? The pieces in here ... not top-drawer, of course, but there was always something you could get your teeth into. Number 8. Here we are, then. He came to a stop and put his hand in his trouser pocket, before rapping on the door with the other.

He was struck by the eloquence of the answering voice, a clear, well-spoken voice, as the woman bid him first wait a moment, and then come inside. He turned the handle and entered.

Well, well, well ... what was the world coming to? There, sat on the edge of the bed holding out her arm to him, was nothing less than a fucking *Porsche*. A *Bentley* of a ride, with everything, absolutely everything, in place.

What were they doing allowing those things downstairs up to a luxury item like this?

'Hello,' smiled Angela.

'Yes. Hello,' said Sacha, fixing her with his own smile.

He moved toward her, unbuckling his belt.

TWENTY-EIGHT

Shaking slightly, her blond hair falling around the classical, angular beauty of her face, Angela stooped to pick up her underwear from the floor, telling herself that it was all right, everything was all right, that he'd gone now. But the strange violence of that smile was still flashing away behind her retinas. With her knickers in her hand she tried to stand up, but remained squatting on the floor, her shoulders trembling. Clutching the nylon tightly in her fingers, she burst into tears.

She remained there for several minutes, crying, until finally, she wiped her nose with the back of her hand and got unsteadily to her feet. Taking a tissue from the drawer, she blew her nose and sat down on the bed, her shoulders still affected by a persistent tremor. She forced herself to stop shaking. Come on, she had to be professional about this. What, after all, had he done?

She pulled on her underwear and tied the cord of her robe, but it was no good; the sight of her still shaking hands brought on a fresh bout of tears. She shook her head in an effort to bring herself under control, and reached for another tissue.

Perhaps she should have called the guard ... and told him what? The guy had not technically acted improperly at any time ... and yet she felt like she'd been raped. Well, if she felt like that, then she should have called the guard.

She sat forward, holding her sides, shaking now more than ever.

She wasn't cut out for this. It shouldn't feel like *this*.

Was it *her* fault? He certainly hadn't liked the fact that he'd failed to arouse her, that she'd needed lubrication. That was unusual for her, but there'd been something that ... had fazed her. He'd ... he was too handsome ... what was he doing there? And those cold eyes, bright and blue ... fierce ... yet at the same time lifeless, lifeless. And he'd been too big and it hurt - like being impaled. She should have stopped him at that point. She should have stopped him. But she'd let him go on ... it was as though he'd paralysed her. With something in his face.

He had raped her after all. But not with his penis, since she had allowed him entry...

... but with his face. With some kind of ... hypnotic *violence* in his smiling face.

Her body was shaking dreadfully.

Suddenly consumed by an uncontrollable nausea, she got up from the bed and staggered to the door. Realising she'd never make it to the facilitator suite, she turned, glanced around in panic then knelt before the bin, depressing the pedal with a small bone-white hand as the sweat broke over her brow. But the bin was a mistake; before her lay his used condom. Too late. She retched three times.

Picking herself up, she reached for another tissue, wiped her mouth and dropped it in the bin, before kneeling down again to tie a knot in the plastic bin-liner. She fell back against the wall, and wept quietly.

She'd been kidding herself. She couldn't do this job. She couldn't handle it, after all. She couldn't do it again anyway, after *that.* She clearly didn't have the required toughness. Lucinda was right; you had to be tough. And she'd had the arrogance to think that her sensitivity had actually made her a better facilitator than Lucinda. Well, perhaps she *had* given them something that Lucinda and the others couldn't. She knew she had really helped some of them ... some of those poor souls ... she'd seen it in their eyes ... wasn't that *worth* something? That was valuable social work ... a *moral act....*

She began wiping her eyes again.

... she shouldn't just give up on it ... but no, she didn't have the strength ... that man....

... she'd helped *them*, but she'd left herself open to that man ... that terrifying man ... Good God, if she stayed, there was a chance she'd receive him again in time.

She should report him.

For what, though? For smiling? For smiling too much?! She couldn't think straight. Maybe she should go through to the ... through to the suite and get a cup of tea ... she'd had a shock and she needed ... but she didn't want to let the others see her like this ....

She banged the floor with the palm of her hand and shook her head.

She just wanted to go home. Home to dear, dear Tom.

He'd told her she was "bloody mad" and he was right, he was right... she thought she'd ... she thought she'd got it straight in her head, but clearly she hadn't. No, no, she couldn't *do* it. She just couldn't do it again after this.

TWENTY-NINE

This was good. He'd been talking to this girl now for nearly half an hour. Her face was sweet, her mind interesting, and he liked her crazy clothes; the white lace petticoat worn over the shredded jeans. Also, she was smiling a lot and occasionally leaning her head in towards him. Like now. Although, he had seen her doing that with the guy further along the bar earlier.

'So,' she was saying, 'if you do sculpture, you must have an opinion on Amish Kapoor.... I love his stuff.'

Lawrence smiled. 'Well, I quite liked that big red thing he somehow managed to cram into the Tate Modern.'

'That was fantastic, that was! What was that called again?'

'Marsyas. But I only liked it because it was so big. And I think that was the only reason anyone else did.' He drew on his cigarette. 'Let's face it. If that thing had been only two foot long, no one would have given a shit about it.'

'Well, maybe, but the whole point of that thing *was* the size, wasn't it? Wasn't it part of the concept?'

Lawrence smiled broadly. 'Yes, I think maybe it was. *Is*.'

The girl was about to say something when she was hailed by a group near the door. 'Yeah, I'm coming!'

She turned back to Lawrence, at the same time raising herself from the bar stool. 'Oh, sorry. My friends are leaving. It was fun talking to you!'

Jesus, don't go.

'Listen, Louise - it *was* Louise, wasn't it?'

'Yes.'

'Listen, Louise, that was a lovely conversation we had there, and it might be nice if we had another one day. And so - sorry about this - I humbly ask, beg, and implore you for your telephone number.'

'Ah. Well, I don't think that's such a good idea.'

'All right. Fair enough.'

'It's not a personal thing. It's just that I don't do that. I make a point of it. But me and my friends are always in this pub -'

You don't have to lie.

'- so we're bound to bump into each other again, anyway. See ya.' She slipped off her stool and hurried to catch up with the two exuberant couples exiting to the street.

He calmly absorbed the blow of her departure, taking a slow sip from his glass and lighting a cigarette. As Martin used to say a couple of years back, when they'd both spent a night and fifteen quid each getting nowhere in some deafening shit-hole of a club: oh, well, only thing to do now is, walk home, sausage sandwich, bed, and hope for a better tomorrow.

But good Christ, how many fucking tomorrows had there been since then? And actually, fuck the sausage sandwich. Brown sauce had long since ceased to cover up the taste of disappointment.

Still, for him to have even *thought* of repeating Martin's stoical phrase - instead of just storming out - showed how the edge had been taken out of his desperation in the two months since he'd started signing on. It was like valium or something, a session in that place. It was incredible how, even that, a bleak fuck once a fortnight, could round out the awful physical restlessness; in some small way, soothe the pain. Then again, it was pretty depressing to think that the reason he wasn't quite so depressed was because he was on sex benefit, a "blowjob-seeker" according to the latest bit of graffiti sprayed on the wall of the building. A nice joke, but not strictly accurate; the state didn't do oral. Plenty of written, though, and plenty of verbal. Which was probably what they'd got lined up tomorrow at this workshop bollocks.

When they'd told him it was compulsory, his first idea had been to sign off there and then, but he hadn't. He just hadn't been able to. He'd grown accustomed to the fortnightly shags, joyless as they were. Christ.... No, not accustomed, rather he'd acquired a cold physical addiction to them. He'd finally got his rotten knob stuck into something, and, not trusting him ever to come up with anything else, it didn't want to come out again - and after tonight's performance, who could blame the bastard?

And so, tomorrow at 9, under the maleficent guidance of his cock, he was due to trudge up to Tufnell Park and deliver himself up to the marker board hell that would inevitably constitute this "LiaisonSearch Workshop" fuckwittery; hand himself over to whatever deathly private contractor it was that called itself this "Jetstream Training" dogshit.

He drew on his cigarette.

But, hang on, he was probably being too negative, as usual, because surely, once he'd been trained by these fuckers, he'd assuredly be flying through the stratosphere on the jetstream of a perfect and complete sexual fulfilment, dipping in and out of all manner of casual affairs, dirty weekends, trysts and full-blown romances. Yes, tonight he could rest easy, because in the morning he would surely harvest a bounty beyond compare, gaining access to pearls of an almost Talmudic wisdom, guaranteed to bring the bearer the gift of woman's compliance. All this and more awaited him the morrow up in Tufnell Park.

THIRTY

Wicked.

Saturday. He could lie in.

Get under the duvet, watch a bit of MTV. Mum'll do the room-service ... ah, fackinell ... no, he couldn't. He had to go to that fackin' thing today. Why'd they have to do it on the weekend? They were fackin' *barstards* down that sex dole! Do this, do that ... give up your weekend to go and listen to a lot of bollocks. Fackinell!

Pickford threw off the duvet and got to his feet, scratching his messy tuft of yellow hair, before adopting a somewhat leaden martial arts pose in front of the mirror, learned not from a class so much as cadged from a Jackie Chan video. Next, he pulled down the waistband of his boxers, and began swinging his cherubic penis from side to side until it began to thicken and lengthen. He'd been getting some good *training* in down that place. Be a shame to mess that up and get thrown off for not goin' to this bladdy thing this morning. He smiled down at his erection. All right, I'll do it for *you*, sunshine. Not that he really needed to *be* on the sex dole. It was just a training ground till the *real* birds came along. Made sense, really. If you thought about it.

He stepped out of his boxers and into a fresh pair, before loping off to the bathroom.

'You up already, David?' called a voice from downstairs. 'I was going to bring you up your breakfast.'

'Got something to do today, Mum,' called Pickford as he urinated, swinging the stream from side to side around the pan. 'But do us a slice of toast, yeah? Then I'm out the door.'

His cheeks flushed by the cold morning air, Pickford marched past the parade of shops that formed Junction Road, checking off the numbers, the little finger of his left hand sticking out in unconscious imitation of MTV rap stars.

Cam on. Where *was* the fackin' place? He was at 29 now. Where was 27? He backed up a few steps. Right. There it was. But this was a bladdy launderette! Better have another look at the piece of paper. Oh, right. 27*b*. Well, where the 'ell was 27b, then? Oh, there's another door there next to the launderette. But it doesn't say naffin' about this fackin'... jetstream ... trainin' shit. Door's open, though. Staircase ... Oh, well, naffin' for it: up the stairs we go.

He made his way up the steps, the large red tick emblazoned across the back of his tracksuit following a similar tick on his cap up into the darkness.

Emerging onto a small landing, he was confronted with a single door fitted with a pane of frosted glass. Not even a fackin' sign on the door. The door was ajar. Looked like a bleedin' school classroom inside. *Shit*. He'd had enough of that bollocks for one lifetime.

He tentatively pushed the door open and stepped inside. Rows of desks. Some posh geezer sat behind one of them. Sharp-lookin', though.

'Scuse me, mate. This the right place for the er ... sex dole, yeah? The workshop job?'

'Yes, I believe so,' answered Sacha, adjusting the sleeve of his casual suit.

'They should put a sign on the door or samthing,' said Pickford, taking a seat at the end of Sacha's desk.

'Yes. Perhaps they should,' smiled Sacha.

Pickford put his hands on the desk and rocked backwards slightly in his chair, peering about the room. Another couple of punters were just coming in. He turned again to Sacha.

'Seen anyone in charge, then, yet, mate?'

'They're in there, I think,' said Sacha, indicating one of the two closed doors flanking a centrally placed white marker board.

Bill Masters slowly climbed the stairs, his face sunk into his beard as he wiped the condensation from his glasses, the white neck toggles of his anorak swinging from side to side.

One could only presume this was the place they meant.... Well, it must be, surely. It said 27b on the door. Quite unequivocally. Still, all the same, you'd think they'd put their name down there somewhere. He stepped onto the landing and approached the door. Well, that looked like it ... desks and so on ... a poster about sex benefit on the wall.... God, what a bloody depressing prospect this was, though.

He paused for a moment and sighed, then gently pushed the door open and put his head into the room. 'Excuse me ... you're all here for the ... er ...'

'The sex dole workshop, mate,' answered Pickford.

Masters made a brief nod and looked at the floor, quickly moving off to a desk near the back of the room. Good God. That lad ... the lad that had answered him - one of those bloody ruffians he'd had that run-in with that time on the street. Still, the boy hadn't recognised him, though. An accidental benefit of the youth of today: a short attention span and no powers of observation.

He pulled out a chair, and sat down quietly, his hands in his pockets. After a while, he brought out a small notebook. He might have time to distract himself with a small mathematical problem if they weren't going to get started immediately.

Sacha watched Masters for a moment. Grey beard, green anorak. A sinking geriatric claiming a few last shags before the retirement home and death. The boff dole was probably a good racket for these corpses. Doubtlessly so, especially if they got anywhere near that blonde from the other week. Actually, they really should reform the system and ban these old cocks; they'd *had* their go on the savannah. It was only right that the labia of the world should now close for them, just as isolation, sickness and despair should now claim them.

He turned his attention to the door. Another loser coming in. Some sort of Bohemian waster in a tatty long coat. The fellow didn't look too happy to be here. My friend, if you took the simple expedient of getting a haircut, you wouldn't have to keep pushing it out of your face like that. Yes, I'm looking at you. And you're looking at me. What, would you like to fuck *me*? Given up on the girls, have you? That's right; go and sit down. The teacher will be along soon to teach you how to hold your prick. Lesson One: "Pussy hates Tramps; Get a Shave."

The door to the left of the white board opened, and a smiling man in his early forties emerged.

'Ah, hi! We're beginning to fill up, I see. Good. Okay. Good morning. I'm Ken, one of your two course leaders this weekend, the other being Sue, who is, ah ... unfortunately still back there battling with the software - sorry, we've had a couple of problems this morning. Anyway, I can see we haven't quite got a full complement yet, so we'll give the others another five minutes or so to turn up, and then we'll get started.'

From his desk near the front, which he'd taken because he simply hadn't been bothered to proceed far into the room, Lawrence watched as the man called Ken turned and went back into the small office. Bye for now, then, "Ken". See you in five minutes. Lawrence leaned back in his chair, stretched his legs out under the table, crossing them, and clasped his hands across his stomach, his expression vacant. Through a gap in the door to the office, he could just make out a woman's wrists working away on a keyboard. Presumably the "Sue" that had been spoken of. He exhaled heavily. The only humanly possible way to get through this was going to be to take it one minute at a time.

As far as his neck would allow, he cast his eyes over the room. Apart from the desks and a few posters for sex-support initiatives tacked up here and there, and the ominous presence of a video and TV set up on a trolley in the corner, the place was completely barren. And not very well kept up either: dark stains running up the walls from the radiators; peeling paint in a corner of the ceiling. Whoever these jetstream fuckers were, they didn't seem too house-proud. But then this place was probably just a stop-off as they ducked and weaved through a string of London properties, looking for the cheapest rental. Or else the whole thing was part of some dodgy tax write-off for some shadowy parent company, and for that reason, they needed to be constantly on the move. Moving so fast, they never even got time to screw a nameplate on the door.

He cast his eyes quickly across the desks. More punters had arrived. Youths in baseball caps, a few old boys, a smattering of casually dressed but clean-cut professional types, a couple of Asian and African-looking guys ... one or two rough types leaning on the wall by the door ... and that slightly weird fucker in the suit. And no women.

The door to the office opened again, and Ken appeared, followed by a somewhat bland but alert-looking woman dressed in a black trouser suit. Ken spoke first, accompanying his words with expansive gestures of his arms.

'Okay. Hi, everyone. Good morning. Well, as it looks like we're almost all here, we'll make a start. I'm Ken - as the early-comers will have already gathered -' At this point he bent forward slightly, laughing a little through clenched teeth. 'And this is Sue....'

'Hello,' nodded Sue in greeting, her eyes quickly summing up the various elements in the room.

'And we're your course leaders for the weekend - something else which the early-comers will have heard before, but never mind,' laughed Ken.

Lawrence stared at the edge of his desk. This was going to be even harder than he thought.

'Now, the first thing to do is get you all registered, so if you'd please sign the sheet of paper that Sue is handing out to you ... and pass it round the room.... Actually, you're going to need a pen later, so if you haven't got one, we have some biros up here, so -'

'I've got one, mate,' called out Pickford, smirking slightly.

Sue zeroed in on him, smiling. 'Fine, then you won't be needing one of ours. As for the rest of you, come up and get a pen if you haven't already got one.'

Sacha looked on as several men slowly got to their feet and drifted over to a small pot of pens indicated to them by Sue. This was beautiful. Go and get your pens, then, since you don't know how to use your penises, you cripples. No, this was truly beautiful. The only thing was, he didn't know if he'd be able to keep a straight face for all 16 hours of it.

Still slouched in his chair, Lawrence slowly removed his own black biro from his inside pocket, placing it with an exaggerated precision centrally before him on the desk. He watched vacantly as the others made their way back to their desks.

Ken addressed someone to Lawrence's rear.

'Excuse me... er... you two standing by the door. Do you mind taking a seat, please.'

'There isn't anywhere, yeah?' answered a bull-necked man in his thirties with a shaved head and a cross of St. George tattooed in the middle of his forehead.

'Well, what about over there?' said Sue, indicating the desk occupied at both ends by Pickford and Sacha. 'Sorry, do you mind moving along there?' she said, addressing Pickford.

'What?' said Pickford, taking his pen out of his mouth.

'Could you move along toward the other gentleman, please, so these two can sit down?'

With a surly look, Pickford shifted across to the seat next to Sacha.

Sacha moved his chair slightly toward the wall, away from Pickford. He glanced at the side of Pickford's head, and was oddly reminded of being on safari; you got that same feeling of unease when the animals came too close.

'Okay,' called Sue, 'Has everyone signed their name on the register?'

A handful of faint yeses sounded through the room.

'Is there anyone who *hasn't* signed?'

Silence.

'Then whoever has the paper, can they pass it to the front please.'

As the register was slowly passed over the desks, Ken stepped forward. 'And by the way, we do have the heating on, so do take off your coats if you like.' He jutted his chin forward, laughing. 'Try to look as though you're *staying,*'

Lawrence stared at the white board, unmoving. From behind, came the sound of the slow disrobing of one or two coats.

'Okay, fine,' continued Ken, 'Let's kick off. Welcome to LiaisonSearch. Now, I'm going to begin by outlining the program for you. Okay, the workshop is broken down into a series of -'

He broke off, his attention taken by the large, wide head which had appeared behind the window of frosted glass in the entrance door, and which remained there, a blurred pink mass looking in. Several heads turned to look as the door handle finally turned and a large, untidy figure shuffled uncertainly inside and off toward the back of the room, head bowed.

Pickford leaned in to Sacha conspiratorially, and giggled. 'Fack me. Talk about *fat*.'

Recognising Carlton from the benefit centre, Sacha answered with a faint movement of his eyebrows.

Pickford chortled, and turned to watch Carlton.

The newcomer was hailed by Ken. 'Er ... excuse me....'

Carlton stopped and looked round, excruciatingly conscious of the roomful of watching faces.

'Excuse me, but you do realise you're over twenty-five minutes late.'

Carlton struggled to speak, looking from Ken to Sue, his mouth working silently for a moment. 'Couldn't ... couldn't find it, like ...'

'Well, you're here now,' smiled Sue, 'So if you'd like to find a seat.... There's one over there at the back, look.'

Carlton nodded faintly and turned from her, his vision once more moving across the staring faces. Stop fuckin' lookin'... y'fuckin' *fuckers*.

He made his way to the desk, and sat down awkwardly, watched continuously by Pickford, as Sue went over with the register for Carlton to sign.

'Right. Okay', resumed Ken, 'As I was saying, the workshop is broken into a series of individual units, each of which will deal with a different aspect of your situation. The first unit is entitled "Obstacles"; the second is entitled "Taking Action"; the third, "Self-Projection"; and the fourth, "Action in Practice." Now, to help keep a clear distinction between these themes, the course is colour-coded.'

Lawrence lifted his eyes to Ken. Colour-coded ... Christ help us....

'That is,' continued Ken, 'each unit has been designated with a colour. Red for "Obstacles", green for "Taking Action", yellow for "Self-Projection", and blue for "Action in Practice". You see, there's a logic to it. And we'll -'

Lawrence had put up his hand, his head cocked to one side.

'Yes?' said Ken, his face suddenly cold.

'This colour thing. I'm sorry, but where's the logic in having yellow for "self-projection"? I mean, red for "obstacles", I can see that. But yellow for "self-projection"...?'

'Well, yellow is positive, sunny ... and that is the view of ourselves which we should aim to project.'

'Is it?'

Sue was glaring at Lawrence. 'Well, we'll go into that later in the relevant unit.'

The relevant unit, yes, thought Lawrence, nodding acquiescently.

'Okay', continued Ken, 'We'll be giving you fact-sheets printed on the relevant coloured paper for each unit, and also coloured notepaper according to the unit we're working on. Now. You've all got pens. Okay ... Sue is coming round now with sheets of red paper for you to jot down notes on. We're going to give you files this afternoon for you to keep these papers in, so if you could just look after them the best you can until this afternoon. Right.... Okay. Obstacles.'

He went over to the white board, picked up a red marker and wrote "Obstacles," underlining it twice, before turning and looking meaningfully around the room. 'What is stopping you from reaching your goal? What is preventing you from securing your own liaisons? I'm asking you. Come on, let's throw a few ideas around.'

Silence.

Ken pointed at an Asian man in his thirties. 'Hello. You there. Can you help me out? What sort of obstacles have you encountered?'

'Well ... the girls I meet always.... They always seem to have a boyfriend already, you know?'

'Okay, thank you, that's good,' said Ken as he wrote "lack of single women" on the board.

'What else?' said Sue. She indicated Lawrence. 'Hello, can you think of something?'

He shot her a dark look. 'Well... how about *devilish bad luck*.'

'Can you be serious, please?'

'I *am* being serious,' replied Lawrence with a look of wounded innocence. 'I think devilish bad luck is the main *obstacle* to my *liaison procurement*.'

'Well, I think we're looking for something a little more specific than that.'

Sacha had been watching Lawrence, impressed. At least this bohemian arsehole knew how to take the piss. If the fellow threw away that scruffy coat and cut his hair, he'd probably cut a reasonably attractive figure; his features were genetically quite strong.... Perhaps he *was* getting laid, and was claiming falsely for a laugh, as he was.

'Can anybody else help me out?' asked Ken, his eyes roving round the desks.

The room remained sullen. 'You, there. Hello. Our friend who came late.'

Carlton looked up with small, shocked eyes. Once again, the room had turned in on him. With pudgy fingers, he began creasing the corner of his piece of red notepaper. 'Er....'

'Just name an obstacle you've come up against.'

Carlton was looking down, shaking his head.

'You can think of something, surely,' said Ken.

'... gettin'... gettin'...,' managed Carlton, before falling into silence.

'Sorry?'

'... gettin' them to say yes, like...'

Pickford tittered audibly, along with the shaven-headed guy on his left. Sacha smiled into his lap, restraining his laughter.

'All right, settle down,' said Ken. 'It's actually a very good point. How *do* you get them to say yes? And we'll come onto that later in "Taking Action." But for the time being, we're still looking for the obstacles that are actually causing this unsatisfactory situation. Well, as you don't appear to be able to think of anything - in which case I don't see why you don't all walk out the door right now if you encounter no obstacles in securing liaisons - then I'll tell you some of the obstacles that have been put forward by other groups. Here's one for you:' He paused. 'Shyness. Something, I would suggest, we have all just witnessed right here in this room from the lot of you.'

Ken stared about the room for emphasis, before writing the word up on the board.

The man with the shaved head spoke up.

'Yeah, well, I'm not shy. I tawk to who I bleedin'well like, but - and I don't mind admitting this - they – women, right? - don't want to bleedin'well talk *back*. And you know why? You know *why*? Because *they* are bladdy *ignorant*. It's them who've got the problem, not *us*. It's them who should be in 'ere, being taught sam bleedin' *manners*.'

He looked about the room, the tattooed red cross on his forehead distorted by an angry crease.

'Well,' said Sue, 'if this language is an example of *your* manners, then I'm not surprised women don't respond to you. But we'll talk about all this in Self-Projection.'

'Self-protection naffin'! Who do you think you are, tawkin' to me like *that?* I don't have to bladdy put up with this!'

'No, you don't; you're free to leave any time you like,' said Ken. 'But we are obliged to inform your benefit office if you do.'

The man glowered at him for a moment, before falling silent, sulkily shrugging his shoulders.

'Okay,' resumed Ken. 'So far, on the board we have "Lack of

Single Women," and "Shyness". Now, here's another one that crops up....' He began writing on the board. 'Poor social life. Right. Let's start with these three. Now, I'd like to get you to share your experiences. That's part of the aim of the workshop. Let's begin with lack of single women. Apart from our friend here, who else has had a problem with this?'

The room was silent.

'Well, how about you with the baseball cap. Have you found this to be a difficulty?'

Pickford looked up. 'Well ... I dunno ... yeah ... I suppose so...'

'You suppose so?'

'Well, yeah ... yeah, you can be there chattin' up some bird and then ten minutes in they start talkin' about their bloke an' that.'

'And this has happened to you on several occasions, has it?'

'On several occasions, yeah.'

Another youth in a baseball cap spoke up. 'And sometimes, right, you can be tawkin' to them for two hours, yeah, and you think you're in there, yeah, and you've even bought them a few drinks, yeah, and then sam boyfriend turns up. Yeah? And you've even bought them *drinks!*'

'Well,' smiled Sue, 'buying a girl a drink doesn't entitle you to sleep with her.'

'I didn't buy her *a* drink, I bought her three!'

'Yes, well, the point still holds,' said Sue over the laughter.

'All right, I'm not sayin' she should've slept with me, I'm just sayin' she was well out of fackin' order, yeah? Lettin' me buy all them drinks! '

Pickford let out a piercing giggle, causing Lawrence to glance up momentarily from the doodle of a black dog he had begun in the corner of the red notepaper.

Ken was smiling patiently at the youth who had spoken. 'Sorry, could I ask you to watch your language, please?'

Lawrence concentrated once more on his drawing, framing the dog's head with a human pelvic structure as the voice of Ken went on. One of the youths began speaking again. Lawrence smiled to himself and added a baseball cap to the dog. He was carefully outlining the brand logo when one of the older men at the back of the room was coaxed into speaking. Lawrence began strengthening the dog's snarl, finally losing track of the discussion completely. When he next looked up, Ken had returned to the board and was pointing at the second item on the list.

'Okay. Shyness. Who can tell us something about shyness?'

There was no response.

'Hello, the artist,' said Sue.

Lawrence met her look.

'Would you say you are shy with women?'

'... No,' said Lawrence, 'I would say ... I was *polite* with women.' He laughed into his lap. '*That* is the problem.'

'What do you mean?'

'Well, I mean I don't know if it is a question of shyness. Shyness ... implies fear. And it's not about fear. It's more ... it's more a case of having been inculcated with the idea that you simply do not have the *right* to speak to a woman you don't know.'

Pickford muttered to Sacha, 'What's he on about, eh?'

Sacha ignored him and stared at Lawrence. Oh dear. You mean it, don't you? Looks like I was right about you the first time - well no, it's worse than that. You choose to be weak where you could be strong. You *choose* to live like a fucking worm. That makes you something worse than this other detritus littered about the room.

'Well,' laughed Ken, 'you're going to have to get rid of ideas like *that.*'

Lawrence regarded him evenly. 'So you're saying we have the right to just barge in on any woman in a bar having a quiet drink?'

'Well, not "barge in" exactly,' said Sue. 'But you have the right to make a polite and civilised approach.'

'*Do* I, though?' said Lawrence, screwing up his face, and tilting his head on one side.

'Yes, you do,' replied Sue, turning to the rest of the room.

'But I don't know, though,' continued Lawrence, 'I mean, where do you draw the line? At what point does a woman start feeling harassed? I mean take yourself. Supposing you were approached over the next two weeks by all the men in this room -'

'All right, all right,' broke in Ken, 'There's no need to get personal with this.'

'I'm not getting personal, I'm just making a point.'

'Yes, well, we've got the point, thank you very much.'

Lawrence shrugged and fell silent.

'The point is,' resumed Sue, 'that of course you have the right to approach, so long as you remain courteous and treat the woman with respect.'

A middle-aged man near the window spoke up. 'I think the chap at the front has a point actually ... I mean how can you be treating them with respect if you've already refused to respect their right to privacy?'

Lawrence gave a single nod in his direction.

The man with the shaved head spoke. 'But they don't *'ave* no right to privacy when they're dahn the bleedin' pub, do they? 'Ow can they? It's like the jungle, yeah? And they're animals – no, they *are* - well, not *animals*. But they're there, yeah, for us to *take*. They should be there for us to *take!'*

He glanced at Pickford who was sat to his right, nodding sagely.

'Am I right, mate?'

'Fackin' spot on, mate.'

'And *my* point is sam-one should bladdy tell them!'

'Yes,' said Ken, 'Well, I think you're going a bit too far in the other direction there.'

'Look,' said Sue, addressing the room generally, 'the way you should be thinking is this: so long as you are courteous and polite you have the right to approach members of the opposite sex in public places and there's no need to go tying yourself in knots over questions of privacy and harassment, but on the other hand don't over-egg it the other way by imagining you're *entitled* to a positive response. And certainly don't start regarding women as animals to be taken. You won't get very far that way.'

Won't you, indeed? thought Sacha.

'Okay,' said Ken, 'Let's have a look at poor social life. Then we'll have a short coffee-break.'

At his desk at the rear, Carlton wiped his nose with the back of his hand and went on staring at his lap in an ongoing instinctive attempt to protect himself from the potential ravages of the room.

One by one, plastic cups of coffee in hand, the group began to distribute itself once more around the desks. The door of the room on the right stood open, revealing the top of an external flight of steps which led down to a bleak yard behind the building. Ken was visible at the top of the steps, calling a handful of smokers inside. Pickford appeared first, sharing a joke with his new shaven-headed friend, while Lawrence came up last, his hands in his coat pockets as he followed the others back into the room and took his place, falling into an immediate slouch in his chair.

'Okay,' said Ken, 'Let's move on to our second unit, and "second unit" is an appropriate name for it, really, because we're going to be showing you a short film!'

He looked out over the sea of blank faces.

'You know. Second Unit. Films. No? No takers? Oh, well, stand-up comedy was never my thing. I suppose that's why I'm here doing this.'

'Too right, mate,' sniggered Pickford, his laughter echoed by the guy with the shaved head.

'All right, settle down', said Ken, wheeling the TV trolley into the middle of the room. Sue leaned against a wall and folded her arms as Ken loaded the video.

'Okay, we've talked about obstacles. Now let's talk about taking action. There's some good advice in this video, so have a look, and afterwards we'll go over what it has to say.'

Lawrence watched blankly as Ken bent down, started the tape and crossed to the wall to join Sue. Lawrence let his eyes drift to the monitor, cursing his groin yet again for leading him to this perdition. Dull graphics unfurled across the screen. Music. A bloke appeared; some kind of cheeky-chappie presenter tit. Looked vaguely familiar.

'Ere, it's that geezer from Eastenders!' called out Pickford.

Lawrence noticed Ken nodding enthusiastically. Jesus, he was actually *proud* that this Z-list fuckwit had agreed to lend his 'kudos' to the video.

''Allo!' grinned the face of the actor, filling the screen. 'So you reckon you're 'avin' problems with the ladies. Gettin' them to notice you. Gettin' them to speak to you. Well, don't worry, son. You're not the only one. We've all been there at sam point in our lives. But the good news is that there *are* things you can do about it. Take a look at this.'

The scene changed, revealing the actor now standing in a pub. Behind him sat a woman at the bar. The actor glanced round at her, and then smiled at the camera. 'Not bad, eh? Let's say you fancy her. As who wouldn't. But what are you going to do about it? Eh?' The actor paused, frowning. 'Well, I'll tell you what you are going to *do* about it. You are going to approach her and intro-*duce* yourself to her. But you are going to do it in a certain *manner*. Ah, but maybe you're afraid to go over. Nevertheless, go over you will. Why? I'll tell you why. Because she's already on her way out of your life, so you've got nothin' to lose. Speaking to her is your one chance of keeping her *in* your life! So whadda you care if she turns her nose up and walks aht the door? She was going anyway! All right. So, you're going to approach her. Okay. First, here's what you *don't* do.'

Lawrence looked on as the actor went over to the woman and delivered what amounted to a hopelessly clumsy entreaty for sex followed by a sexist harangue which actually elicited one or two chuckles from somewhere in the room, to the visible dismay of Ken and Sue. Lawrence glanced round. It was that blond-haired dick in the baseball cap again.

From his desk at the rear of the room, Masters peered nervously over at the youth who had laughed. He let his face sink back into his beard. How had this all come about? How had he let this happen...? How had he, a head of mathematics, come to be here ... as though in the same class as the very type of bloody hooligans that had cost him his job...? Watching this preposterous video ... Oh, God ... Oh, God .... Julia, why did you ... why did you have to *bloody die*?... all right, well, I know ... because the course of things - nature demanded it be so, I know ... but please understand, my sweet girl, as I understand you, then please understand me in turn ... that nature also demands that I go to that dreadful place, that I sit now in this dreadful room. But *I do it for you*, you know that, you know that, don't you? *You have to know that.* I -

He was interrupted by another guffaw from Pickford and looked up as though dazed, the open locket clutched tightly in his hand. He found himself staring at the face on the TV screen, if for no other reason than that his eyes had been attracted there by the moving light.

'... so you approached her,' the actor was saying, 'and she didn't want to know. Okay, it happens all the time. Now, ordinarily you'd probably conclude that that was the end of the story, and have a little cry into your pint, but no, this is not the end. This is just the beginning. Because this was simply job number *one* on your things-to-do-list for the night. Because what you are going to do now is find another little lady - there are hundreds of thousands of them in a town like London - and you are going to go through the whole process again. And if *she* ain't interested, you are not going to *mind,* and you are not going to be dis*heartened*, the reason being that she was only job number two, and you have plenty of jobs on your list to*night*. Perhaps you're wondering how many. Well, I'll tell you how many.' He held up ten fingers to the camera, his expression fierce. 'Ten. That's right. You 'eard right. Ten. Because this is a numbers game, my friend. It is *a lottery*. And like the lottery, you increase your chances of success the more tickets you buy. Now you might think you have a very small chance of winning the lottery no matter 'ow many tickets you fork out for, and you would be right. But you will be happy to learn that where the *ladies* are concerned ... your prospects are a good deal brighter. Did you know that it is a fact - a *fact* - that recent surveys have consistently shown that single males on average secure a bunk-up for every ten approaches they make. You put ten in, you get one out. That's not actually a bad rate of return. But it requires persistence, perseverance, and persistence again. What I call the three P's. Sure, you will get rejected. No one's saying you won't. You will get rejected. A lot. But deal with it. Accept it as samthing to be got through. Because do you know what? Somewhere out there is Miss Yes and she's waiting for you to walk up to her bar stool and offer her a drink. But you ain't going to find her sat on your arse at home or staring into your beer over by the dartboard. It's like any other game in life. If you want results, you gotta get out there and do the spadework.'

He strode over to the woman at the bar, placed his arm around her, and once more addressed the camera. 'So there you have it. Remember the three P's. Persistence, perseverance and persistence again. I've got faith in you. *She*'s got faith in you.' The woman smiled into the camera and raised herself from the stool. The actor winked at the camera. 'Now get busy.'

The pair turned and walked off, arm-in arm.

Ken stopped the tape and went over to the white board where he wrote "spadework" in capital letters and underlined it twice, before turning once more to face the room.

Carlton stood in the street, finishing his hamburger. Further up the road, he could make out a few of the others making their way back. Fuckinell, was it time to go back already, like? That bloke had said an hour. He looked at his watch. Yeah, it's time. He looked up the road. Some more of 'em goin' back. That bastard with the cap, the one that'd laughed at him. And that other one, the fuckin' skinhead. He felt a pain in his gut, and pulled a face as he swallowed the remainder of his burger. Only the afternoon to go, like. But there was still tomorrow. But don't think about tomorrow. Better be gettin' back, now, like. He didn't want to be late. He didn't want to be late for that bastard ever again. But better let them *fuckers* get inside first, like.

He stuffed the hamburger carton in a nearby bin, and at a slow pace made his way up the road.

From behind his newspaper, Ken watched as the last few members of the group returned from lunch and filed back to their desks; the clever-dick in the long coat; the overweight lad. He glanced at his watch, folded up his paper and went out into the room.

'Okay, I trust you all had a good lunch, and have come back refreshed and ready for action. Right. On to unit three: Self-Projection.'

The door opened, admitting Sue and a second, somewhat matronly woman, laden with bags.

Lawrence eyed the new arrival with deep suspicion. He couldn't fathom her purpose, and he didn't like the look of all the bags. He began bracing himself.

'Ah, just in time,' laughed Ken.

'Sorry, I had a little trouble finding it,' warbled the woman cheerfully, 'Thank heaven for mobile phones!'

'Not to worry,' smiled Sue, 'Anyway, if you'd just like to come through here.' She led the woman through the door on the right of the white board, and closed it behind them.

'Okay,' said Ken, 'Self-Projection. In this unit we're going to look at matters relating to how others perceive us, how we come *over*. Are we doing enough to make sure we are projecting the sunniest side *of ourselves, the best we that we can be* ?'

Lawrence, lying almost prone in his chair, put up his hand.

'Yes?' said Ken.

'How is that even moral?'

'What do you mean?'

'Well, to "project the sunniest side" of myself would surely be an act calculated to deceive.'

'What?' said Sue.

'Look, what you're saying there is you're asking us to mask off the crap side of ourselves, and thereby gain something from another party by false pretences.'

Sacha observed Lawrence with disgusted fascination. Good God, you get worse by the minute, don't you?'

'I think you'll find that people have been doing that since time immemorial, and probably nowhere more so than in the matter of finding sexual partners' replied Ken.

'Yeah, well, that doesn't make it moral, does it?'

'We're not here to discuss morality, we're here to help get you lot back to satisfaction' countered Sue. 'Now, can you please stop these irritating digressions and allow the group to proceed with the programme?'

Lawrence threw a look at the ceiling and fell silent.

'So', breathed Ken, 'to get back to it. Are we doing enough to make the best of ourselves, presentation-wise? Now, to help us in this, we've engaged the services of a personal make-over consultancy - which explains the lady you saw just now - and we're going to treat you all to a little one-to-one session. That's right,' laughed Ken, 'we're going to make you all beautiful!'

Lawrence bored his gaze into Ken's neck. Christ on a fucking plate....

A few low groans sounded around the room.

'What, you're gonna put make-up on us?!' called out someone at the back.

'Not make-up, *make-over*,' corrected Ken.

Pickford peered round at the overstuffed figure of Carlton, then caught the eye of his skinhead friend, and smirked.

Carlton saw it, saw the skinhead turn and look. Fuckinell, don't ... don't ... fuckin' *bastards*... He could see their mouths moving, and hear them when they laughed. He felt the blood pumping across his chest, and lowered his eyes to his lap.

'Okay, calm down,' said Ken, 'it's a bit of fun, that's all. But it will help you to get a better perspective on your personal presentation. Now, while you're waiting to be seen, you can be looking through some pamphlets I have for you in the office. And when you've *been* seen, you can write down notes on what Mrs. Furlow had to say about you on the yellow notepaper I'm handing out now. Oh, I was going to get you your files, wasn't I -?'

Sue's head appeared at the door. 'Okay, we're ready.'

'Right,' said Ken, 'We'll start from the front.' He looked at Lawrence. 'Okay, can you go through, please?'

Lawrence made no move.

'Can you go *through,* please?'

Lawrence planted his palms heavily on the desk and slowly pushed himself up. He stood for a moment glowering at the side of Ken's head, before slowly walking over, watched with amusement by Sacha. The door was ajar, and Lawrence entered without knocking. Sue appeared from within, and closed the door behind him.

He found himself stood across from a small table covered with jars and creams. Before the table sat the make-over woman, adjusting a small mirror. Opposite her was another chair. To the left of the table stood Sue, eyeing him critically. Lawrence made to sit down, but was stopped by the make-over woman.

'No, don't sit down yet. We're going to take a look at your general deportment first. Can you just stand for us for a moment, please?' she rapped out, unsmiling.

Lawrence stood for them, amazed that the bubbling conviviality the makeover woman had shown to "Ken" and "Sue" was not now to be wasted on him.

Both women scrutinised him in silence, running their eyes over him slowly. Any attempt to defend himself with the ferocious look he directed toward them was nullified by the combined force of their cool observation of him. He realised he was experiencing a level of humiliation that went far beyond that of the signing-on desks, even beyond that of the sex dole cubicle itself.

'Well,' said the make-over woman finally, her eyes somewhere around his knees, 'the first thing is the coat.'

'My thought exactly,' agreed Sue, looking down at a frayed hem.

What the fuck *was* this?

'What's the *matter* with my coat?'

'Well, it's clearly seen better times,' said Sue.

'The early1970s by the look of it,' rejoined the make-over woman, frowning. 'Do you wear it a lot?'

'All the time.'

She began shaking her head.

'Actually,' began Lawrence, 'it may interest you to know that the last time I received any truly positive attention out *there* was on account of this very coat. "I like your coat", she said. And she actually reached out and touched it. Even asked me where I bought it.'

'And when was this?' enquired Sue.

'A few months back.'

'It's probably put *off* a good deal more girls since.'

The make-over woman was still shaking her head. 'No, you're going to have to think about investing in a new coat.'

'Well, think about it is about all I can do. I can't afford a new coat. Even if I wanted one.'

'All right. Well, then ... we'll move on to your posture.'

'You'll move on to my *what*?'

'Can you try putting your shoulders back a little for me.'

'What the hell are you talking about?' He took a step backward. It was one thing to sit at a desk and let a lot of bullshit wash over him, but *this* -.

Sue stepped in. 'I'm sorry, but this is for your benefit and if you don't change your attitude, I'll be obliged to put in a report to your benefit centre. Now, come on. Can we see you put your shoulders back please?'

Lawrence remained as he was, his eyes almost wild. He could not let these fuckers do this to him. He glanced over to the door. He could leave. Now. Just say 'fuck your sex dole' and leave.

But the dog wasn't going to let him.

The fucking dog bastard did not want to be booted back outside into the cold. It would rather see him sacrificed to these two demons.

As he stared at the two women, an unbidden image of their groins came into his mind. He chased it out as best he could, but the ghost of a white triangle remained behind his eyes. A hateful, shimmering white triangle disgorging its cargo of darkness; black coils of hair unfurling like wire before the skinned head of the dog.

He knew he wasn't going anywhere.

Gradually, very gradually, he felt his shoulders move back, as the women had commanded, until he was standing upright and erect. And the rebellion in his eyes fell away from them to the floor.

With the eyes of the room on him, Lawrence closed the door and made his way back to his desk. In his pocket he held clutched in his hand a small tube of cream they'd given him for the bags under his eyes - which was going straight in the bin the minute he was on the street. What about the bags under *their* eyes? But he knew he had no argument; they weren't signing on. They'd told him to cut his hair. He'd reminded them that it wasn't the 1950s. That in fact many girls liked long hair. Had done for several decades now. Look at all those bastard rock stars and so on. They'd kindly pointed out to him that he wasn't a rich rock star, and he'd decided the hell with it, he couldn't be bothered to argue with them any more, and fobbed them off with an empty promise to cut his hair.

'Ere, he don't look no different!' laughed Pickford.

Lawrence eyed him and sat down.

Ken joked, 'Maybe she thinks he's beautiful enough already.'

Lawrence laughed aloud sourly. This was a fucking nightmare.

'Okay, next!' ordered Ken.

A middle-aged man next to Lawrence wearily stood up.

The room fell into a relative silence, and stayed that way for a while as the group indolently looked through the pamphlets, and one by one went in to the make-over woman. The quiet was broken only by the occasional sniggers and furtive chatter coming from Pickford's desk.

The man with the shaved head emerged from the examination room, the red cross in the middle of his forehead wrinkled in agitation.

'What'd she say, mate? asked Pickford as he sat down.

'It's just a lot of bollocks, innit! Like that shit on the telly where they tell those geezers what gear to wear an' that.'

'Yeah, but what'd she say?'

Pickford was answered by a furious glare. 'I *said*, it's a lot of bollocks!'

'All right, I only asked,' replied Pickford quietly.

Ken snapped his fingers at him. 'All right, can you go up, please?'

Pickford rose sluggishly and made his way past Sacha's chair. Sacha watched as Pickford's somewhat bow-legged gait took him up to the examination room. As the youth disappeared inside, Sacha beamed to himself. The whole thing was delightful, simply delightful.

After some time, the door opened, and Pickford emerged, looking slightly disconcerted. As he made his way back to his desk, it became clear he was carrying something in his hand, despite his best efforts to conceal it by holding it close to his side. The guy with the shaved head leaned forward and grabbed it from him, read the label and burst into laughter. 'Acne cream!'

One or two others, including Sacha, shared his amusement.

Pickford snatched the jar back, and then, red-faced and frowning, took his seat, whining, 'All right, all right, leave it out.'

'Okay,' said Ken, 'Can you calm down over there? We've had enough disruption from you pair for one day, thank you very much.' He looked at Sacha. 'All right, you're next.'

Sacha nodded graciously and went up.

Less than five minutes later, the door opened and he was once more strolling back to his desk, watched curiously by Pickford.

'What'd they say to you, then?' asked the red-cheeked youth.

'They didn't say very much at all,' smiled Sacha broadly. 'In fact, we talked about the weather.'

At the back of the room, Carlton sat and stared unseeingly at the pamphlet he'd been given, slowly turning the pages with fat, sweating hands, as the group continued to go up one by one to the make-over woman. For some time, he hadn't dared to look up. Best not to, like. In case those fuckers at the front were lookin' at him again. He turned a page of the pamphlet to reveal a graphic of a scruffy cartoon bear. This was all just fuckin' shit, like. Make-over *shite*. Might do for a fuckin' cartoon bear, like, but if you were a human and you looked like the fuckin' back end of a *bus*, then it's ... it's gunna take more than some fuckin' make-over woman's shite to make any difference. The only thing ... the only thing you *could* do, like - because he'd been over this a lot in his head, like - was die, and hope to come back handsome.

He became aware of someone speaking to him. The bloke.

'... hello, is there anyone there? You, yes, hello,' said Ken shortly, 'Can you go up, please. You're the last one.'

Carlton found himself looking into a wall of faces. He cast his eyes down and got up awkwardly, before shuffling off past the desks. As he passed Pickford he made an attempt to stare back, but the glee in the youth's face was too much for him. He concentrated instead on where he was going, but he could still feel their looks pricking the flesh on the back of his neck.

Lawrence watched as Carlton knocked on the door with a pudgy fist and entered, hefting his weight into the room. Poor fucker, thought Lawrence as the door closed behind him. He began defacing the wretched bear character in the pamphlet, replacing its eyes with torn black holes.

After some time, the door opened and Carlton struggled out, his lank hair now combed forward and matted to his forehead with gel, both hands gripping an assortment of jars and creams. Pickford took one look, began tittering and nudged the others. Carlton moved forward, dropping a tube of moisturiser, causing Pickford to laugh out loud. In stooping to retrieve the tube, Carlton nearly dropped the rest, but finally succeeded in righting himself without further disaster. He looked up. It seemed a long way back to the comparative safety of his desk. He shuffled forward through the hail of laughter.

'You'll be all right with that lot, mate!' barked the guy with the shaved head.

Pickford turned to his sidekick and giggled, 'All the birds are gonna want to shag him now with his new trendy hair - I don't think!'

'All right, I've told you two to calm down. Now, will you calm down, please!' shouted Ken.

The laughter subsided as Carlton made his tortuous way past Pickford's desk. Ken watched the bleak, shambling figure as he reached his chair and sat down heavily, contemptuously dropping the products onto the table. A plastic tub of skin cleanser skittered off the edge to go rolling across the floor. Ken strode over to retrieve it and wordlessly placed it back on Carlton's desk. He made his way back to the front of the room. 'All right. I think we'll take a break for coffee.'

There came the sound of pamphlets being snapped shut and chairs being pushed back as the group relaxed and began dispersing to the coffee machine. Sue and the make-over woman emerged from their room, allowing Pickford and his small group to drift through the back door exit to the yard. Descending the steps, they glanced back into the room, sniggering and removing their cigarette packets.

Lawrence watched them go, and sat for a while, unaware of the sharp blue eyes trained on the side of his head. He turned to look around the room, his glance finding the slumped figure of Carlton. Lawrence stared at the ridiculous mess of gelled hair, which the guy had since ruffled up in a misguided attempt to undo the work of the make-over woman. He was now busy trying to stab a hole in the side of one of the tubes of cream, the roll of blemished fat around his neck vibrating with each quick stab of the pen. Lawrence looked away and stared at the white board for a moment, before slowly pushing his chair back, feeling for his cigarettes and making for the exit to the yard.

At the top of the steps he lit up and glanced down at the group around Pickford, which was beginning to break up. One youth was making his way back up the steps, followed by the guy with the shaved head. Lawrence descended to the yard and regarded Pickford, who now stood smoking alone, his cheeks even redder with the cold, shoulders hunched.

'Hey,' said Lawrence.

'What?' replied Pickford warily.

Lawrence simply stared at him in response.

'What?' repeated Pickford.

'Nothing,' smiled Lawrence genially. 'I was just going to say ... that big bloke, the fat boy. Pretty amusing, eh?'

'Yeah,' giggled Pickford, 'What a hopeless fat twat!'

'Yeah,' laughed Lawrence, swinging his gaze up into the white sky, 'But then when you think about it, he's been shafted right from the word go, hasn't he? I mean, he's basically been cursed from birth by the whole fucking universe.'

'Yeah,' chuckled Pickford uncertainly, trying to read the smile on the guy's face.

'So that's *his* excuse. But what's yours?'

'What?'

'What's *your* excuse for being a hopeless twat?'

'You fuckin' what?'

'I *said,* what's your excuse for being a hopeless twat? And what's mine? You're in there laughing at that guy but what you don't seem to grasp is that we're *all* fucking losers here.'

'*You're* a fackin' loser, I wouldn't argue with that, mate.' He screwed his face up and moved closer to Lawrence. 'And who the *fack* do you think you're calling a hopeless twat?'

'You, clearly. And me.' He drew on his cigarette. 'You and me are both stupid, hopeless, clueless twats otherwise we wouldn't fucking be here, would we?'

'Look, mate, I'm just playing their fackin' game, right? I'm shacked up with a few birds outside this set-up, don't worry about that.'

'Are you now?' laughed Lawrence. 'If I thought that were true, I'd not hesitate to shop you to those two bright sparks in there. Honestly, I wouldn't. But since it's clearly bollocks...'

Pickford stared at him for a moment, faltered and looked away, wiping a hand across his nose, before once more resuming his hostile stance. 'All right you hippy piece of *shit,* I reckon you're a bit funny in the head, so I'm gonna walk away from this, but no one calls me a twat, right? But I'm gonna let you off, yeah? Otherwise you'd be fackin' dead!'

'Thanks very much.' Lawrence bowed his head. 'Much obliged.'

Pickford took in one last lungful of smoke and prematurely discarded his cigarette, throwing it vehemently to the floor before turning and trotting back up the steps into the building.

Lawrence turned and called out amusedly, 'Hey, who the fuck are you calling a hippy?' but Pickford had already disappeared into the building.

Lawrence faced the yard once more, his cigarette in his fingers, staring over at the bundles of barbed wire lining the dark brick wall of the tatty compound. He imagined, for no reason at all, trying to scale it. Well, why would he be scaling it? To break into some godforsaken outpost of Carphone Warehouse to nick a load of mobile phones? No. To escape this fucking gulag of a workshop? Maybe. He pictured himself making the attempt, imagining how his jeans would ultimately get snagged, and, losing his balance, how he would land on the barbs with his full weight, stripping and lacerating the ugly sleeping flesh between his legs. He pictured the ripped head of his cock and the ruptured sacs of his pointless, vapid balls emptying Ballard-like over the vicious black metal. Well, it would serve the fuckers right, all three of them, for dragging him down to this purgatory.

He finished his cigarette and dropped it to the floor. He was just turning to re-enter the building when he stopped and, as if in shock, stared again at the barbed wire curling angrily across the blank sky. An image had come to him. And he knew he shouldn't view it. But he stared at the wire. And let it come.

The Belgian girl was there, perched on the wall, crouching in distress over the wire, her short skirt hitched up by raised trembling knees, the soft triangle of her knickers poised millimetres above a tense coil of cruel serrated barbs.

She slipped.

As metal teeth disappeared into smooth nylon, he stopped the tape, turned and hurriedly climbed the steps up into the building.

Entering the room, his shock at the unwanted vision in the yard was compounded by the sight of Ken and Sue standing impatiently before the already assembled group.

'Come on, we've been waiting for you,' said Ken. 'What's the matter? You look like you've seen a ghost.'

Pickford whispered to his skinhead sidekick, 'I told you I shitted him up!'

Lawrence heard and sat down, raising an eyebrow in Pickford's direction, before glancing up at Ken and Sue. 'I did see a ghost. A very beautiful and sexy ghost. That's why I was a bit late. I thought I'd try and do a little *spade*work with her. And so, remembering my three P's, I -'

'All right, there's no need to be clever,' snapped Ken.

Lawrence smiled down at his pamphlet, shaking his head, drumming his fingers on the table, unaware that he was being observed keenly from behind by cool blue eyes. Under Sacha's merciless gaze, Lawrence let out a single loud laugh, coughed and brought himself under control.

Sacha eyed him curiously. You really are something of a tragic wanking basket case, aren't you? Weak, sad - and mad.

THIRTY-ONE

Sacha had awoken early, his semi-erect dick nudging Sally's sleeping backside. He had been about to throw one up her when he remembered it was Day Two of the "workshop" and that he had to be up in Tufnell Park by nine. Foregoing the first shag of the day had put him in a bad mood, and now here he sat in the middle of an already darkening Sunday afternoon, listening to this Ken penis droning on about "not setting your standards too high". Ordinarily, by now, he would have set Sally up with the usual golf lie and be on his way over to Ulla's. He looked about the room. The first day had been amusing in its way, but now he'd had enough. Sunday afternoons were for rutting, not sitting about over a launderette with a load of witless muff-spongers. On a Sunday afternoon any discerning male in his right mind should be taking his high-quality Swedish goods and getting her leg up over the bathroom sink.

'Right, then,' said Ken. 'So, to recap. Targeting. Don't aim too high. Be clear about what qualities you respond to in a sexual partner, and what qualities you have to offer them. Now, I'd like you to write out - on your *blue* notepaper, please - a list of these two categories: what you like in a sexual partner and what they may find to like in you. Now we don't want any graphic details, thank you. Just general qualities. Okay, we'll give you twenty minutes for that. Off you go.'

There was a murmuring sound of reluctant bodies leaning forward to write. A few quiet sniggers broke from Pickford and his skinhead friend.

At the back of the room, Carlton sat, his pen motionless in his fat hand, while at the front, Lawrence slouched low, writing lazily with his pen held at arm's length to reach the desk.

At last, Ken called time. 'Okay, fine, let's see what you've put.'

Sue stepped forward from where she had been standing in the corner. 'We'll begin with what qualities you look for in a sexual partner.' She had Pickford in her sights. 'Can we hear what you've put, please?'

Pickford glanced round at his sidekick. The pair giggled.

'Well?' demanded Sue.

Pickford read out: 'Big tits,' and burst into laughter.

'Really?' smiled Sue. 'How fascinating. And have you put down anything else?'

'Couldn't really think of anything else.'

Sacha laughed.

'Then you're lucky, aren't you?' continued Sue. 'You should be easy to please. After all, there are many, many women blessed with an ample bosom. They come in all shapes and sizes, all ages. With such a large crowd to go at, you should have no problem!'

'Well, hang on a minute! I don't want no old women! They've gotta be fit, yeah?'

'What do you mean by "fit"?' put in Ken.

'I dunno - *attractive*.'

'Then write it down on your list, please,' said Sue shortly.

Pickford glanced heavenward and began writing, as Ken looked over the room. 'Excuse me. You, the older chap at the back.'

Masters, who had been sitting in contemplation of the zipper of his anorak, peered up at the course leader.

Ken smiled. 'Can you tell us what you've written?'

'The qualities I look for in the fairer sex, you mean?'

'Yes, please,' encouraged Sue.

Masters swung his head to face her. For a moment, he held his mouth open, a small dark recess in his copious grey beard. He looked down at his piece of paper and read.

'A warm ... a warm, generous nature. A gentle, relaxed disposition. A certain grace and poise that I can't put my finger on.... I'm sorry.'

He lowered his gaze to his beard and pushed the paper away from him.

'No, that's very good. Thank you,' smiled Sue. 'It's nice to see we have at least one gentleman here, anyway.'

Masters made a vague, troubled nod of gratitude.

As Sue looked away, he peered down at the portrait in the locket held open in his hand under the desk. *I wrote about you, Julia. I wrote about you.* You know that I want nobody but you, my sweet girl, that I speak to no woman but you. That I go in that cubicle so that I should never have *cause* ... So that no woman can *take* me from you ... while you're *away. You* know that, love. You ... *know* that.....

... and my kisses, my kisses are only and forever for you.

Sacha couldn't be sure but he thought he could make out wetness in the eyes of the wreckage in the anorak. Amused and repulsed, he removed his gaze and turned back to the front.

Lawrence had been steadily glaring at Sue, having taken as a personal insult her designation of Masters as the only gentleman present. She caught his stare and, undaunted, smiled back at him. 'And can we hear what *you've* put, please.'

'You mean what I like in a woman? Or do you mean what qualities I like in me?'

'The former, if you don't mind.'

'Sorry, it's just that you asked us to write down both categories. And for a moment there, when you asked to hear what I've put, I was uncertain which list it was that you desired to hear - a confusion shared by the older gentleman, I believe.'

'Well, I did make it clear a few minutes ago that to begin with, I wanted to hear what qualities you look for in a sexual partner. Now, can we hear what qualities you look for in a sexual partner, please,' replied Sue.

Lying back in his chair, Lawrence picked up his piece of paper and read in a slow and deliberate voice.

'Sloth and arrogance.'

'I beg your pardon?'

'Sloth and arrogance.'

Ken gave him a cold look. 'And that's what you look for in a girl, is it?'

Lawrence regarded him darkly. 'Yes. Absolutely. I find the combination captivating.'

'I think you're having us on.'

'Not at all. In Mediaeval times sloth was regarded as a condition conducive to promoting randiness. It's in Rabelais. One of the characters alludes to it.'

Pickford muttered to the guy with the shaved head, 'What's he on about? What's fackin' sloths got to do with it?'

'I see,' said Ken dubiously. 'And what about arrogance? Is that in Rabelais too?'

'No, I just like that.'

'Why?'

'I don't know. It just turns me on, that's all,' replied Lawrence.

Sue rejoined. 'And that's all you have to show after half an hour's deliberation on this subject? For instance you make no conditions on a woman's physical make-up?'

Lawrence held her look for a moment before leaning forward to peer at his piece of paper.

'Sorry. There was one thing.'

'And that is?' inquired Ken.

Lawrence carefully read out from the paper. 'No anus.' He peered up at Sue as expressions of puzzled bemusement spread round the room.

'What?' spat Sue in a low, quiet register.

'No anus. That's what I demand from my women,' replied Lawrence with a mild look. He gave a hollow laugh. 'But maybe that's where I've been going wrong.' He banged the table with his palm. 'I've been setting my standards too high! I can see that now from the insight I've gained from this brilliant workshop!' He fixed Sue with a furious glare.

There was a smattering of uncertain laughter, in which Pickford did not join. Instead, he put in an aside to Sacha, 'He's a fackin' nutter, this barstard. What's the matter with girls' arseholes?'

'It's his idea of a joke, I think,' replied Sacha tersely, suddenly put into doubt as to whom he hated more, the pussy-whipped prepuce at the front or this shit-thick scrotum sat next to him.

Sue was laying into Lawrence, 'You'll be asked to leave in a minute if you don't *change your attitude!*'

Lawrence looked over at the wall, as though appealing for salvation, then folded his arms and stared at his lap, his mouth moving as if in conversation with himself.

'I told ya. Look at him. He's a fackin' nutter,' whispered Pickford to both Sacha and the guy with the shaved head.

Ken removed his gaze from Lawrence and began searching the room once more. 'And how about you there at the back,' he asked, craning his neck. Several heads turned to face a sick-looking Carlton.

'... er ... I haven't written anythin', like ...' answered Carlton quietly.

'Yes, you have. I can see from here,' laughed Ken. 'Come on, what have you put?'

Carlton remained silent. Ken gave Sue a quick glance, and strode over to Carlton's desk, while Sue picked out another claimant. The attention of Pickford and his skinhead friend, however, remained on Carlton as Ken knelt by his desk and quietly read out from his paper. '"Pretty and nice. Like an angel."'

Pickford heard, and twisted his face in a fit of silent giggling.

Ken looked from the piece of crumpled blue paper into Carlton's small, sad eyes, as ever nervously averted. 'Fine,' said Ken quietly, looking down again at Carlton's inept scrawl, 'that's very good. But you must try to ... try to get a little more *reality* into your ... responses. Okay?'

Carlton made no answer.

'Just a little more reality,' said Ken, smiling. He brought himself upright, and caught Pickford and his friend smirking in Carlton's direction. 'All right, you two. You just pay attention to the rest of the group, please,' he admonished, returning to the front of the room. 'Right, everybody, we'll move on to what you've listed as qualities *you* have to offer.'

Lawrence drifted, toying with the image of first Ken, then Sue tearing their collective jetstream groins on the barbed wire out in the yard. But it wasn't as amusing as he thought it would be - too messy - and he pushed the idea from his mind and shifted restlessly in his seat, fixing his vision on a stained patch of paint on the wall. From the random smudges he began reconstructing views of his dog-loined sculpture, distracting himself for a while with Leonardo da Vinci's's old game of seeing images in walls of flaking paint.

When he next came back to the room, Ken and Sue were outlining some fresh assault on his shattered dignity. From out of their mouths were coming the words, 'role', 'play' and 'exercise'.

A new darkness came into his eyes as he regarded them, and

without reservation now, he began hurling the two course leaders legs akimbo onto the barbed wire fence.

'Right,' Ken was saying, 'In the past we've had a lot of fun with this closing part of the course. Now, the lovely Sue,' he laughed and jutted his jaw forward, 'will be playing the girl in the bar. Meanwhile, I'll be picking people out to come up and demonstrate what they've learned over the two days, by having a crack at her, so to speak! Now, to simulate the feeling of a real bar, and to make it a little more fun and give you a bit of incentive to come up and show us what you can do, we're going to provide drinks for the actors! Sue has got her vodka and tonic, and I've got a few cans of lager for our suitors!'

Sue sipped from the glass she had brought from the office and walked to the whiteboard, where she leaned an elbow on the shelf and waited.

'Okay, you're first up,' said Ken, picking a young Asian man, who reluctantly began to drag himself out to the front. Ken handed him a can of lager, and pointed him in the direction of Sue. 'There you are. You see a nice girl in a bar. She looks your type. What are you -'

'She don't *look* his type,' muttered the guy with the shaved head savagely.

The young man turned. 'What do you know about what my type is?'

'Well ... she's not Pakistani like you, mate.'

'What on earth are you talking about?' demanded Sue.

'Yeah, what the hell are you trying to say, man? And I'm not from Pakistan!' shouted the young man furiously.

'Well, wherever you're from, I'm sayin' you lot should stick to your bleedin' own! Takin' our bladdy women!' He declaimed to the rest of the room, 'No wonder there's none left for us!'

'Well, maybe you just don't know what to give them, my friend!'

'Oh and you do, I suppose! So what the fack are you doin' *'ere*, then, eh? I'll fackin' 'ave you outside in a minute, mate!'

'All right, that'll do!' shouted Ken. 'You. As of now, you're on marked time, do you understand? One more outburst like that and you're *out*.'

The guy with the shaved head sat back in his seat, receiving a look of solidarity from Pickford.

The young Asian man was still staring at his antagonist.

'All right,' said Ken, 'now let's continue.'

'No, I'm not doing it!' yelled the young man, thrusting the can of lager into Ken's chest and storming back to his seat. 'I don't perform in front of racists!'

Ken was about to insist but was stopped by a cautioning look from Sue.

'All right, let's have somebody else,' ordered Ken, visibly irritated at being thwarted. 'Come on. Let's have you at the back there, seeing as you've contributed almost nothing at all so far to the workshop.'

Carlton looked up, blinking in panic.

'Come on,' said Ken, urging him forward.

The large figure slowly rose and began moving forlornly to the front of the room.

'Go for it, Elephant Man,' jibed Pickford quietly as Carlton passed him.

Carlton heard, and came to a halt, staring at the floor.

'Now look,' said Ken, 'if I don't get a little more cooperation out of this group, I'll be forced to put in a bad report to the centre. And you know what consequences that may have for your benefit. Now, come on, please.'

'Now wait a minute,' smiled Sacha, *'I'm* not being uncooperative. Why should I be penalised?'

'Look, can we just get ON, please!' exclaimed Ken. He beckoned Carlton forward.

Carlton resumed his shambling progress to the front, Lawrence watching him as he came to a stop before Ken. Why couldn't they just leave the poor bloke alone?

Ken smiled encouragingly and handed Carlton a fresh can of lager. 'That's it. Just think of it as a bit of fun, that's all. Now there she is over there.' He turned Carlton to face Sue. 'What are you going to say to her?'

Carlton raised his eyes from the floor to Sue and dropped them again, shaking his head. 'Dunno.... ah dunno, like....'

'Why don't you have a sip of your lager,' suggested Ken patiently. 'Try to relax, and it will help you to get into it.'

Carlton nodded faintly, and began fumbling with the ring-pull on the can, the rolls of fat around his chin trembling as he struggled.

'Don't shake it about too much -' cautioned Ken.

The can exploded, causing foaming lager to dribble quickly all over the floor.

Pickford laughed.

Ken stepped forward, 'Here, let me take that. We don't want the floor wet.' He took the can into the office.

'Come on,' said Sue, the gesture of a smile on her face. 'Surely you can think of something.'

Ken emerged from the office. 'Come on. You're in a bar. There's the girl. What do you do?'

Carlton stood, lost.

'Well, first, I suggest you move closer to her. You've got about ten feet between you there.'

Carlton shuffled closer.

'Now you have to engage her. How are you going to *engage* her?'

Carlton's face remained blank, as he went on dumbly staring at Sue.

'What do you say to get her interest?'

Carlton wiped his nose with his hand.

'Oh, come on, think of something, *anything*.'

At last, Carlton opened his mouth. 'Do you like ... do you like dogs...?'

The room erupted in laughter, Pickford's squeals rising above the rest.

'All right, calm down,' shouted Sue, putting down her glass and rounding on Pickford. 'You. Since you think you're such an expert, perhaps you can improve on this line from our friend here.'

'Er ...' began Pickford, still laughing. 'Er ... do you like dogs, *darlin'*?' he spluttered, overtaken by another paroxysm of laughter.

'Just pack it in and simmer down, will you!' said Ken, trying to calm the room, before turning to Carlton, who was standing hunched over, as though trying to lose himself in the floor. 'Okay, why don't you just ... go and sit down ...'

As Carlton returned to his desk Pickford muttered to his neighbour, 'Why do they bother with 'im, yeah? I mean who'd ever want to fackin' go out with *that*?'

'Yeah,' said Lawrence, without looking round, 'when they can go out with a herd-instinct tosser in a baseball cap instead.'

'I've fackin' told you once, mate!' snarled Pickford.

'Told me what?'

'You!' shouted Ken, pointing at Pickford. 'Stop swearing, will you!'

Pickford dropped his pen loudly on the table and fell back in his seat.

'Now -' began Ken, but was interrupted by the shaven-headed guy suddenly leaning forward and jabbing Lawrence in the back. 'You're out of *fackin' order*, there, mate!'

'Piss off,' enunciated Lawrence in an irritated tone, pulling his shoulder out of range, surprised by the recklessness of his response.

'I'll *fackin' bury you,* you fackin' TWAT!'

'All right, that's it!' yelled Ken at the guy with the shaved head. 'I've had as much as I'm going to take from you, and I'm asking you to leave the group, please! '

'You what?'

'I'm asking you to leave, please.'

'Now hold on -'

'If you're not gone in two minutes I'm going to call the police.'

A large tattooed hand ran back across the shaven scalp as its owner considered his position.

'All right, I'm goin'. Who needs this shit? Who *needs* it? I'll go out and get some bird to fuck me to*night*. Whether she wants to or not! I don't need your fackin' shag dole!' He got up and looked round the room, the tattooed red cross on his forehead contorting with hatred. 'I reckon you're all a load of sad tossers sitting here listening to this *shit.*'

He kicked his chair out of the way, sending it skidding across the room, before storming off to the door and slamming it behind him.

Meanwhile, Carlton, in a somewhat agitated state, had sat down again and was breathing loudly through his nose, his head down. Lawrence had his eye on him, watched his shoulders rise and fall in time with his breathing until they suddenly broke into a faster pace: the tell-tale sign of silent weeping.

Ken was about to pick out another unwilling participant for the role-play exercise, when a grunt-like sob from Carlton seared the room. For a moment, Ken attempted to continue, but was arrested by Masters, who had tentatively raised his hand, and now spoke quietly from his place at the end of Carlton's desk.

'Er ... excuse me, I think this chap is in some distress, you know.'

Ken looked from Masters to Carlton, and then round at his colleague. 'Sue ... could you ...?' he requested, gesturing toward

Carlton.

Sue quietly drew in her breath, and made her way to the back of the room, where she knelt next to Carlton's desk.

'Now, come on, now,' she said with a mixture of tender loving care and impatience.

Convulsed by sobs, Carlton moved his head slowly from side to side, in his torment increasing the pace until he savagely threw his cheek to one shoulder and held it there, snivelling. 'Just fuckin'... f-fuckin'... l-leave us alone ... f-fuckin'... f-fuckin'...' He broke off, the words and the movements of his face trailing away to leave a silent, shaking mask of pain, eyes screwed shut, mouth held open in a soundless cry, his whole tragic head cruelly delineated by the overhead strip-lighting.

Embarrassed, Ken looked at his watch, and then once more regarded the room, most of which was engrossed in Carlton.

'Er ... well ... as there's only fifteen minutes to go ... I think we may as well call it a day.'

A murmur went round the room, including an audible 'Thank Christ for that,' as people began rising from their chairs.

'Okay, now don't forget your files, will you?' counselled Ken.

Lawrence remained seated, watching Carlton and Sue, as Pickford drifted past on his way to the door. Lawrence caught the youth's eye, glanced over at Carlton, then back up at Pickford and winked. 'Nice work.' Feeling Ken's eyes on him, Lawrence gave the course leader a meaningful glance as though to signify the comment was meant for him too, while Pickford, subdued since the ejection of his friend, threw Lawrence a final, morose look, muttered ''Snot my fault, mate,' and left the room.

Ken strode into the office, leaving Lawrence to observe Carlton, who had been momentarily abandoned while Sue had gone off in search of tissues. For a moment, Lawrence felt an impulse to go over himself, but really ... what the fuck could you do for the poor bastard?

Sacha, who was also still seated, waiting for the room to clear, finally rose and began crossing to the door. In passing Lawrence, he gazed down at the crown of his head. So long, then, you mentally deteriorating tramp, you weak, fucking fool.

Lawrence glanced up briefly at Sacha as the latter passed, and then looked away again to Sue returning with a tissue. Sacha dismissed the loser in the camelhair coat and strode off to the door, a film of his dick sliding in and out of Ulla's rear already playing behind his eyes.

With the room now almost empty, and leaving his file on the desk, Lawrence too rose from his chair. He took a last look over at Carlton, who was now silently wiping his face, Sue having forsaken him to begin wiping the marker board. He turned and headed out the door, feeling for his cigarettes.

Ken emerged from the office, put his hands on his hips, sighed and began collecting in the abandoned files strewn across the desks.

THIRTY-TWO

Drawing her dressing gown tightly around her, Carla walked slowly out of the kitchen into the hall, taking her tea with her. She could hear Sharona and Ian laughing in the lounge, probably watching some rubbish on the telly as usual. Carla decided she'd go through anyway; she'd seen enough of her room for one day. Resolving to weather Sharona for as long as she could, she quietly entered the living room.

Ian lifted his head from Sharona's shoulder, 'Hiya.'

'Hi,' said Carla, sitting down in an armchair.

'Have you only just got up?' asked Sharona by way of a greeting.

'Yes.'

'Some of us have been out to work all day.'

'It's my day off, okay?'

'It's always your day off.'

Carla said nothing, and sipped her tea, observing blankly the unconvincing emotional soap-crisis playing out on the TV. Her attention drifted past the yelling actors to the set they were standing in front of, to the pictures on the walls. Who had chosen those pictures? Who had knocked the nails in the cardboard wall to hang them from?

Sharona was speaking again. 'So if you've only just got up, I suppose you haven't defrosted the fridge, have you?'

Carla breathed in. She'd forgotten all about it. 'Sorry, it completely slipped my mind.'

Sharona shook her head and fumed silently.

Carla pushed a length of hair over her ear, sipped her tea and stared ahead as the credits to the thing on the telly began rolling up the screen and into oblivion.

Ian spoke up. 'Oh, yeah. Heard something funny today. You know Dania? *You* know, Sharona, you met her at Jackie's thirtieth.'

'With the red hair? Used to go out with Mick?'

'Yeah, that's right. Well, you know she dumped him -'

'*She* dumped *him?'*

'Yeah. Thought she could do better for herself. Only it didn't quite work out the way she expected, because apparently she's on sex benefit now.'

'No way!' laughed Sharona. 'Well, it serves her right.'

'But,' chipped in Carla, 'maybe she *has* found something better for herself.'

'Don't be stupid. You'd have to be a pretty sad case for that. Anyway, I don't approve of that. '

'What?' asked Ian.

'Being dependent on benefit.'

'Some people probably have no choice,' said Ian, laying his head again on her shoulder.

Sharona shook her head. 'Then they should all be made to shag each *other*, or be forced to go out and find someone! Or do with*out*. I mean, why should I as a taxpayer subsidise the sex life of some anti-social saddo? I mean, it's ridiculous.'

Carla stared hard at the carpet for a moment, her lips pressed tightly together. She rose suddenly, and stormed out of the room, her tea sloshing wildly over the rim of her cup.

'What's the matter with *her*? You'd think *she* was on the flaming sex dole,' said Sharona, looking at the door.

'Maybe she is', whispered Ian.

'What?'

'Well. I mean, she hasn't had a bloke up there for months. So maybe she *is* on the sex dole.'

'She'd better not be,' said Sharona, turning back to the TV.

Carla stood in the hall, furious, and completely undecided as to what to do with herself next. With disgust she noticed her ring-finger was in her mouth again. She pulled it out and decided that, after all, she'd better get *some*thing inside her; two days was really too long to go without eating anything - not that there *was* anything, some peanut butter, maybe - and besides, she really didn't want to go back up to her room again just yet. Actually, she felt like going back in *there* and just declaring in clear, strident tones to Sharona that in fact she *was* claiming sex dole, just to piss her off, and point out to her that one of the reasons she was *on* the sex dole was so that she wouldn't have to stay up half the night arguing with some selfish dolt of a boyfriend, at which point she would glance significantly at Ian. It was a pleasant dream, but with of course no chance of realisation; Sharona would simply use the revelation as another stick to beat her with. She turned listlessly and tramped off to the kitchen.

The doorbell rang.

Carla stopped and peered over her shoulder at the blurred outline of an older woman battling with an umbrella on the other side of the frosted glass. She froze for a second, glanced toward the lounge and then ran to the front door, opened it and hissed, 'What are you *doing* here?'

'I've come to see how you *are*.'

'Why didn't you just *call*?'

'I *have* been calling. But you haven't been *answering*, have you.'

'I was probably just out or something!'

'For a whole week? And what about your mobile phone? We've been worried sick about you,' admonished Carla's mother, stepping into the hall, removing her gloves and heading for the lounge.

'Don't go in there!' hissed Carla, putting a hand to her head. 'We'll go up to my room.'

Her mother peered grimly at the ceiling, and made for the stairs, examining her daughter's attire as she passed. She assumed the dressing gown was due to her daughter's having just taken, or being about to take, a shower. Then she noticed the nightie underneath.

'You haven't got dressed today, *have* you.'

'*Shut up!*' whispered Carla furiously, bustling her mother up the stairs.

'Carla, what's the matter? Why aren't you dressed?'

'*Nothing's* the matter! I'll ... I'll get you a cup of tea. Just ... wait for me in my room.'

Carla hurried down the stairs and into the kitchen where she quickly filled the kettle, slammed the plug in, dropped a teabag in a mug and leaned on the counter, chewing her nail. She pictured her mother in her room. She'd better not be rooting around in her things. Well, she wouldn't have to! Everything was just lying open all over the place anyway! Thank god she'd run out of smoke, otherwise that'd be spread all over the carpet too. But her notebooks, her diaries, they were just lying all over! Why did she have to come *round?*

Anxious to get upstairs, she glared at the kettle. Come on, boil, you bloody thing, *boil!*

Carla pushed open the door to her room, the mug of tea steaming in her hand.

'Here,' she said, proffering the drink to her mother, who had cleared a pile of books and clothes off the single chair, and was sat down, peering with distaste around the floor.

'Thank you,' said her mother, sipping the tea, becoming once more absorbed in the floor, which was almost a foot deep in clothes. 'No wonder you haven't got dressed. It doesn't look like you've done any washing for weeks.'

'Why have you *come?'* cried Carla, her voice rising hysterically. 'You've no right to come round here without warning and just start poking about in my space, in my private space!'

'Carla... this isn't right.' replied her mother, looking over at the unmade bed, at the empty wine bottles strewn about the room. 'What's the matter? What's going on, love?'

'Nothing's "*going on*"! Will you just stop it! Stop going on!'

She let out a tense, agitated laugh at the repetition of the words "going on," and flopped down on the bed, muttering, 'all right, something *is* going on. You. *You're* going on. And on. God!' She jumped up again, suddenly disgusted with herself for the lame wordplay.

'Why don't you come *home* for a few days?'

'No way! Anyway ... I'm too busy. With Mike. With the music,' lied Carla.

'Oh, so that's going well, is it?'

'Yeah, we've got a few gigs coming up,' she lied again, sitting down on the edge of the bed.

'Wasn't he keen on you at one stage?'

'Yes, but I wasn't keen on him.'

'Oh,' she paused, 'And you're ... still not seeing anyone, then?'

'No.'

'That's a shame. I think you could do with someone. Someone to take you *out of yourself.* I mean ...' she gazed around the room again, '... it's not healthy, being shut up in here by yourself all the time.'

'And you wonder why I don't call you! Listen to you. You're going on as if I were still thirteen years old! It's always the *same!* I mean ... it's like ...' She caught sight of a pair of knickers on top of a heap by the door. She went over and picked them up, displaying the pattern of red hearts. 'This is what I'm talking about! I mean, what kind of a present is that for a mother to give her grown-up daughter?!'

'They were just a stocking-filler, love. Save you spending your money in Marks ... I thought they were pretty....'

'Pretty disgusting, more like.' She dropped them on the floor, and went back over to the bed.

'Don't be so ungrateful.'

'There you go again. I don't like them, Mum. Take it.' She looked up at her mother and added in an airy voice, her gaze wandering up to the ceiling, 'Deal with it ... accept it ... get over it ... live with it ... come to *terms* with it -'

'Don't... talk like that. You sound like you're going bonkers.'

'I'm not going bonkers, I'm just trying to survive ... *this!*' She sighed, letting her arms fall heavily onto the bed.

'Survive *what*?'

'Nothing. This conversation.'

'There's no need to be rude to me.'

There was silence for a moment.

'Your brother's getting on all right. He phoned last night. Says Montreal is fantastic. He sends you his love.'

'What good's that? *Sending* it to me. Why didn't he phone and give it to me himself?'

'He said to tell you he'd call you soon.'

'He hasn't called for months.'

'He's just very busy. He hasn't called *us* for months either.' There was another pause. Carla's mother looked about the room again and caught sight of the row of little white Beatrix Potter books running across the shelf over the bed. The set was complete and fastidiously lined up in order. She smiled. How Carla had *loved* those books when she was little. She felt a warmth breaking over her, and looked over at her daughter, who was staring at her lap.

'Anyway, I thought, perhaps, if you like, we could go and eat out somewhere.'

'I don't know ... no, Mum, I just don't feel like it.'

'Perhaps another time. Perhaps next week, then.'

'Yeah ... maybe.'

'A woman came into the shop the other day - actually I've got to know her quite well - and she was telling me about her son. He's a musician too. Plays the electric guitar. It turns out he lives just at the bottom of Archway Road, and I thought, well, that's literally just round the corner from my Carla -'

'God, Mum!'

'Well,' said her mother defensively, 'I thought that was a funny coincidence. Two mothers up in High Barnet with their kids both living practically next door to each other in Archway.'

'What's so incredible about that?'

'He's on his own, too ... and we thought, well ... perhaps they should get together ...'

'*What?*'

'Well, maybe you'd ... *like* each other.'

'You're mad!' shouted Carla, jumping up. 'You're completely *mad*, aren't you? You'd better not have given her my number....'

'No, I knew you wouldn't like that -'

'Of course I wouldn't! You don't know anything about this person! He could be *anything!* I can't believe it!'

'Well, that's why I didn't *give* it to her. Anyway, she gave me his. To give to *you.*'

'And what do you think *I'm* going to do with it? Even if I were *interested* in this harebrained scheme - yeah, I'm really going to just phone up some guy I've never met! Some guy I know absolutely nothing about! And even if I *did* call, what would I say? "Oh, hi, you don't know me, but your mother gave my mother your number and ..."? You're just daydreaming, Mum, forget it!'

'He *might* be really *nice.*'

'Yes, and he might be an obsessive, dangerous psycho, an abusive, psychotic -'

'Now, look, you're just being silly. His mother is very nice.'

'You can't tell what a bloke's like just from looking at his mother!

You're *insane!*'

'Well, anyway, I'm going to write it out for you, and you can think about it.'

'You're not listening to me, are you? You don't want me to spoil your little game with that woman. That's it, isn't it? Well, I'm not some doll for two old ... old *fish*wives in a supermarket playing at matchmaking!'

'Oh, don't be so bloody rude! I'm just trying my best to help you, that's all -'

'I don't need any help in that department, thank you very much. I'm all right on my own,' said Carla wearily, sitting down on the bed again.

'All the same,' began her mother, removing a pocketbook and a pen from her handbag. 'I'm going to leave you his number anyway.'

'Well, I don't know why,' laughed Carla emptily, shaking her head.

Her mother tore a page out of the notebook and leaned forward on the table to write, pushing a pile of papers out of the way to clear a space, when suddenly she stopped, her attention held by the top half of something revealed by the dislodged heap of paper.

Carla was watching her. What was she looking at?

'What?' asked Carla.

'What's this?' said her mother quietly.

'*What?*' repeated Carla, suddenly panicked.

She watched as her mother picked up her SB40 from the table. Oh, no. No! She thought she'd left it in her bag! She must've tipped it out onto the table when she'd been looking for her purse!

'How... *could* you?' said her mother, searching Carla's face, her own features crumpling into indignation and pain.

'It's no big deal -' began Carla weakly.

Her mother stared at the signing document, swallowing lungfuls of air.

'What ... what have you *done to yourself?* To *us!* Look at you, Carla. You're young, you're beautiful, you should *be* with someone. A girl your age should be thinking of ... marriage ... children ... not begging - begging for a hand-out from some stranger in some filthy *cubicle! We had such hopes for you!* And you say you won't phone my friend's son because you don't know him! And yet you'll go *there* ... let some total stranger ... *do that* to you -'

'Yes, because at least it's safe -,' countered Carla with dwindling conviction, almost at the point of tears.

'You stupid, stupid girl! Those places are for the ... the dregs of society! For people who can't do any better! Is that what you *think* of us? Have you no *respect* for us? For *yourself?* We didn't break our backs and our hearts bringing you up just so you could throw yourself on the scrapheap! Because that's what you've *done*, my girl! That's what you're *doing!* You're *throwing yourself away!*' She burst into tears.

'Mum....' pleaded Carla.

'And heaven alone knows what your father's going to have to say about this!'

'Oh, don't tell him, Mum! Please, please don't tell him!'

'No, no, no, I'm telling him!'

Carla fell forward to her knees.

'No, don't! Don't!'

Weeping, her mother looked off to the window.

'Mum, listen, let me – the ... the *reason* I'm claiming -'

'Claiming!'

'You don't understand! It's – guys ... out there ... I just -'

'Oh, *shut up!'* cried her mother, flinging the SB40 at Carla, and rising from her chair in a fresh wave of tears. Astonished, Carla watched as she gathered up her gloves and her handbag, and with no further glance toward her daughter, rushed sobbing from the room and down the stairs.

With the slam of the front door, Carla rocked forward, finally succumbing to a storm of tears, her grimy white dressing gown forming a sobbing hill amid the jumble of clothes.

Eventually, she pushed the wet hair out of her face, and, still wracked by sobs, peered over to where her SB40 was lying on the floor. With a trembling arm she reached across and picked it up, slowly forcing herself to sit upright. Holding the document in one small shaking hand, she brought up her other to join in the grip, and with a determined look, made as if to tear it in two, but a doubt creased her brow and she flung it back onto the table, fell back, turned and buried her face in the bedsheets.

THIRTY-THREE

Lucinda forced herself to stop reading. The last claimant of the day had long since dropped his doings in the bin and cleared off. Glancing up at the clock, she realised she'd been lying there for nearly twenty minutes past knocking-off time. That was the trouble with this Hume geezer; you just got lost if you broke off reading while the fellow was in the middle of making a point.

She closed the book, got up quickly from the bed, and, switching off the light, stepped out into the corridor, closing the door behind her.

The others would probably have already left by now. Which was a pity; she could've done with going for a few beers with Toby before slogging off down the road to the tube. God ... it better have bloody stopped raining.

As she'd expected, the facilitators' suite was empty. At least, there was no one in the lounge - though it sounded like someone was taking a shower. She was about to make her way through to the dressing rooms when Charles emerged from the kitchenette.

Lucinda never thought Charles quite fitted in. His age didn't help. At 45, he was older than most of them. Or maybe it had something to do with that rather martial, upright bearing of his. According to Elaine, he'd been a sergeant major in the marines or something and Toby was always coming up with hilarious theories as to how he'd wound up in a sex benefit centre.

'Hello, Lucinda, you're a bit late tonight.'

'I know. I couldn't put my book down. Stupid, really. Have a good day?'

'Fair to middling, I suppose. But you know, I do wish some of the girls from those estates would wash their bloody hair from time to time. They should do something about it downstairs. Send them home if they can't keep themselves clean.'

'God, tell me about it. It's the same with the blokes.'

'The problem *is*, you see, no one has any self-respect these days.'

'Well, if they did ... we'd probably be out of a job.'

'Yes. You may well be right,' grinned Charles. 'Anyway, I'll see you tomorrow. Cheerio.'

'Oh, has Toby left yet?'

'About a quarter of an hour ago.'

'Oh, okay, thanks.'

'Till tomorrow, then.'

'Yeah, night-night,' returned Lucinda, and continued through to the female dressing rooms.

Opening her locker, she was hailed by Elaine, who had just stepped out of the shower, and was now padding over, wrapped in a robe and wringing out her thin blond hair. 'Hi, are you still here?'

'Yeah, I just can't bear to leave.'

Elaine laughed and plugged in a hair-dryer. Becoming suddenly serious, she turned quickly to Lucinda, and spoke in the low rapid voice she reserved for gossip.

'Listen, Lucinda, have you heard?'

'Heard what?'

'The new girl. The raving beauty. Angela,' said Elaine darkly, switching on the hair-dryer.

'No. What about her?' asked Lucinda, becoming impatient.

'Jenny just told me upstairs. Apparently she's quit. That's why she's not been in. Just put a note in Graham's office, and - out the door.'

'You're joking!'

'No joke.'

'Why?'

'No one knows. It's weird isn't it? I mean, she was so *into* it.'

'Well, maybe that's why,' replied Lucinda, removing her clothes from the locker. 'She was too intense about it. You can't be intense in this work. You have to let it wash over you. She was nice, though. I was beginning to like her.'

'She *was* nice ... but just a little *strange*, yeah? I mean, all those ideas she had about the "lost souls" and all that.'

'Well, exactly. All that charity stuff. She was connecting with them too much. You can't do that. Not *wise*.'

'You mean she was getting attached to them or something?'

'No, I mean she was probably too open to their ... *sadness*. You know, that awful bloody sadness some of them give off. Probably feeling it too much. Couldn't take it.'

'Oh, and I'll tell you something else,' began Elaine, putting down the hair-dryer and pulling on her clothes. 'Jenny told me that she had no history in the business. No *previous experience*.'

'Jesus *Christ*! Well, there you are. No wonder she couldn't hack it. You can't just leap in at the deep end. What was she doing before?'

'Would you believe, studying?'

There was a pause. 'Oh....'

Elaine fluffed up her hair and reached for her coat. 'Anyway. I'm off, yeah? You're in tomorrow, aren't you?'

'Uh-huh.'

'Want to go to that salsa place again after? Have a bit of a larf?'

'Sure, why the hell not?' smiled Lucinda broadly. 'Maybe drag Toby along.'

'But then Derek'll tag along, too.'

'Yeah, good point. Just us, then.'

'Yeah, just us. Girls' night out. Well, got to dash, yeah? Dinner with Bob's sister. See ya tomorrow. Don't forget your glad-rags!' sang Elaine, heading for the door.

'I won't! Take care, babes!' laughed Lucinda, throwing her mane of shining black hair over her shoulder and stepping into the shower.

Williams watched from the staff office as Elaine emerged from the stairwell, crossed the room and exited to the street, her blond hair glinting briefly under a street-light before vanishing into the rain. That was all of them, then.

So. He'd finally got lucky. Apart from the cleaner, he and Lucinda were the only two people left in the building. So now it was just a question of waiting for her to come down. He'd better make himself look busy.

Stepping toward the door to the reception area, he was halted by the sound of the staff toilet flushing behind him. Bloodyhellfire! Who the hell was that?

Sandra appeared, pulling on her coat.

'Staying late again, Roger?'

'Yes ... just going over a few things. For the morning.'

Sandra gave him a curious look. All the computers were off, all the files put away.

'I see. Well, see you in the morning, then. Goodnight.'

'Goodnight.'

Williams watched her cross the room and disappear finally into the street. Goodnight and good riddance.

Right. Look busy.

He went out to a desk, switched on a computer, opened a drawer and pulled out a pile of claim forms, dropping them on the table next to the monitor.

Well, after all. He had the right, didn't he? Briony had bloody asked for it. Quite apart from anything else, that couch was playing ruddy murder with his back. He had the right.

He peered over at the empty plastic seating of the waiting area. If those jokers all had the right to it, then so did he. Still, he was nervous. No good denying it, he was bloody nervous. But anyway, he was thinking too far ahead. He'd be lucky if he got her even to agree to come with him for a drink at this stage. One thing at a time, boy, one thing at a time.

Hell, here she came.

Lucinda burst through the swing doors, and cut across the room. He felt the usual faint weakening of his bowels that he always felt now when she appeared. Controlling it, he forced himself to speak. He'd waited a bloody long time for this opportunity.

'Ah, Lucinda ... could I borrow you for a second?'

She stopped and looked at him, frowning. 'What is it?'

'I was just going over tomorrow's rota ... I wonder if you could just help me out for a minute.'

She sighed and went over.

'Does this check out with what you have upstairs? Peter forgot to check it with Jenny ...'

Lucinda leaned over the desk and peered round at the screen, enabling Williams to lose himself in the crown of her head. He could smell her hair, even see the pores on the white skin of her scalp she was so close. Christ, her hair was incredible, just incredible.

She stood up. 'Yeah, that looks okay.' She made to turn.

'So, you're off home now?'

'That's right, yes.' She turned again.

'Don't rush off,' he laughed gently, touching her shoulder, but at her look, instantly withdrew his hand. He began speaking rapidly. 'Listen, I was thinking, we never get a chance to *talk*, you and me. Which seems silly, since we're actually colleagues here. Look, I'm about to knock off myself - I was just going over a few things for the morning, just a few things - but, and so, why don't we walk along the road together? Perhaps, you know, we could pop into the pub for a drink.'

'I don't think so. I have to get back.'

His hand went up once more to her retreating shoulder. 'Well perhaps tomorrow, then.'

She pushed his hand away and turned to face him, her eyes blazing. Glancing down at the desk, she grabbed a thick sheaf from the pile of blank claim forms and without warning threw them with real force at his head, shouting, 'If you want to fuck me, Roger, I suggest you *fill in one of these like everyone else!*'

A storm of white paper hit Williams full in the face and fell to the floor, littering the carpet with forms.

After the initial shock, he floundered for a moment, his pinched face betraying his shame for a second before quickly adopting a mask of righteous outrage. To Lucinda the fakery was obvious.

'Christ,' he spat, 'I only asked you to join me for a drink after work! What's the bloody matter with you?'

'Listen,' answered Lucinda, speaking low, but in a voice thick with anger. 'I've seen you lurking around outside the lounge. If there's any more of it, I'm going straight to Jenny and Graham. Do you understand?'

'What are you talking about?'

'And you're married. You should be bloody ashamed of yourself!' she shouted, marching off to the door.

'What are you on about?'

She gave him one last vicious look over her shoulder before punching open the door with the palm of her hand and disappearing into the street.

He descended to the floor and began furiously retrieving the forms.

Bitches. *Bitches!* Was there one of them anywhere in the world that wasn't just a vicious stinking bitch from hell?

THIRTY-FOUR

The man in the green rubber suit flailed his rubber tentacles and lumbered after Sarah Jane through the laboratory of the research station, as Carlton looked on and opened another bag of crisps. But it was no good, like. Even Dr. Who couldn't take his mind off it - even this, Seeds of Doom, one of the best ones. Actually, it was just makin' it worse, like, because wasn't he, wasn't he just a bloke in a fuckin' monster suit himself, like? With fuckin' women runnin' away screamin'. Only, *his* suit didn't come *off*. And those bastards ... those laughin' fuckers, those fuckers at that shite had made him feel more sewn up inside that fuckin' suit than ever.

And now ... now ... this. And now, fuckin' *this!*

He crammed a palmful of crisps into his mouth and tried to get back into the video, but it was like he wanted the green tentacled thing to get Sarah, like. Get her and fuckin' give 'er one or summat. But that was a bit fuckin'... weird, like. And like, it was weird not to be - not to be on Sarah's *side* ... not to be on the Doctor's side.

But why *should* he be on the Doctor's side? *Fuckin' doctors!*

Because of that fuckin' doctor, he might never see *her* again. He'd only ever seen that angel once - and it was bad enough, like, not seein' her again in all this time ... goin' in, hopin', and never gettin' her - but he might never see her again at *all* now. He might never see *any* of 'em again.

He punched the arms of his chair and let out a low, broken moan, his voice mixing with the gurgling sound effect of the creature on the screen. The small, aged terrier curled up tightly before the radiator pricked up its ears and lifted its head, watching with mucous-filled eyes as Carlton pushed himself up out of his seat and shuffled over yet again to the table, where for three days now, the form from his quarterly medical test had lain open amongst the detritus, silently damning him with its cold, red-inked testimony.

He stood over the table, his face working, and peered down at the document, at the little red tick in the box opposite that long word that he couldn't read, because the itching wasn't there, it wasn't there, and the fuckin' doctor had got it all wrong, like. There was nothin' there, he was clean, and this doctor was just makin' it up because he didn't want him near women, not even sex dole women, because this fuckin' doctor had it in for him, like, had it in for him like all the rest of the bastards had it in for him.

All right, it was a ... a ... a bit red down there, but it was never fuckin' *fungus,* was it? Fungus grew in forests, not between your legs, like. But that's what the bastard had said. A nasty fungus infection he'd said. But he was fuckin' lyin', cos it was just a red patch that's all, and flat - not like there was anythin' growin' there, and surely ... surely you'd see summat growin' there if it was fungus, like. Fungus was like mushrooms, wan't it?

That doctor had fuckin' lied.

And that red tick ... that red tick in that box by rights shouldn't be there.

He turned and waddled back to his chair for his can of lager, then returned to the table to stand over the medical form once more.

But maybe it'd be okay, like ... but no ... no way. A tick like that'd get him thrown off for sure. He could chuck it away and hope they forgot to ask for it. But no, they were always on at you to bring in your form every three months, like.

He took a sip of his lager, but again felt that stinging in his eyes, because just the taste of it, like, just the fuckin' taste of it was enough to take him back and it was like he was there again in that room when that bastard had made him stand at the front an' talk to that fuckin' woman. When it'd bin like school again, fuckin' school, where he'd dreamed of just ... just tearing everybody to pieces. If he were at school, now, like, he'd get that bloke from that workshop an' that woman an' that bastard in the cap an' that skinhead bastard and get them in the metalwork room, get their ‘eads under one o’ them big drills and just fuckin’ drill their eyes out.

But maybe, maybe it was the dog’s fault, like. The dog’s fault for makin’ him say that stupid, daft shite about dogs that they’d all had such a laugh at.

He turned and looked at the small terrier which had now fallen asleep again in front of the radiator. No ... he was all right.

‘You’re all right, boy. You’re all right, like.’ He felt his eyes well up at his momentary denunciation of the animal, but forced himself not actually to cry, because he’d done nothin’ *but* cry for days. ‘At least you ... like lyin’ against me sometimes.’

He turned and again stared down at the medical form.

What if he ... well, what if he *changed* it, like? He could ... use some liquid paper or summat to get rid of that red tick. Yeah, *yeah*, that’d fuckin’ do it! His mum used to have some of that stuff somewhere. Kept it for her crosswords an’ that. But it’d probably be all dried up now, like. But maybe not.

He crossed slowly to the sideboard and began rummaging about in the drawer. All her old photos. Photos of her when she was young, like ... a few of him as a baby, which was about the last time he’d looked like everyone else, the last time he’d fuckin’ fitted in, and she’d known it, like, cos she hadn’t taken many photos of him since ... like that fuckin’ school up in Durham shouldn’t have - look at ‘im, just a big fuckin’ blob on the end of the row.... But where was that fuckin’ liquid paper?

His pudgy hands moved through the photos, pens, bits of thread, pins and sellotape. Ah, there it was. But was it still wet, like?

He fumbled with the top for a moment, before succeeding in unscrewing the cap. Magic, it was still all right!

He shuffled back to the table, and sat down. Then, holding the pot in one hand and the brush in the other, he leaned forward over the form and concentrated. That was a fuckin’ small box. Better not get any of this stuff on the sides, like. Come on, hold your fuckin’ hand still ... that’s it, that’s it ... cos everythin’... *everythin’* depends on this....

As carefully as he had ever done anything in his life, he began lightly brushing the paper, his heart surging with relief as the red slash gradually disappeared beneath the white fluid.

He sat back and smiled, as much from amazement that he hadn’t messed it up and got liquid paper all over the form. Breathing out in satisfaction, his eyes on the clean white box, he made to screw the top back on, but dropped the bottle on the table. *Fuckin'* - but it was okay. It had spilled on the cloth, but the form was okay. And who cared about the fuckin' cloth any more?

With more care this time, he screwed the top on and sat back, staring down at the box again. He laughed aloud and took a sip of lager. Everythin' was gunna be okay, like.

And as if to confirm it, the comforting voice of Tom Baker came to him from the video, and he turned his head to the screen, back on side once more.

THIRTY-FIVE

Lawrence picked over his dinner of sardines and eggs. As dinners went, it really was about the most pathetic he'd scraped together yet. But at least he had culinary finesse enough not to have it all mixed up on the same plate: here were the two fried eggs on a side plate, and the sardines on a larger dinner plate. But the problem was that the two separate elements of this repast in *themselves* were enough to turn his stomach. And yet, the sardines had seemed a reasonable enough proposition in the supermarket...

He threw his fork down and lit a cigarette.

Christ. How long had it been since he'd seen anyone? Three days? No, four.... Who? Jesus, it must have been that poor, bland, dumpy woman he'd *done* it with, last time down the fuck dole. He couldn't believe he'd gone on with that ... but beggars couldn't be discerning selectors and all that, and you got what you were given ... otherwise you were off. And much as he longed to be off, it just wasn't an option... not at the moment.

Right, so the last time he'd seen anyone, they'd been lying under him in a sex dole cubicle. Fine. So when was the last time he'd *talked* to anyone? Must have been the day before that. In the pub with Neil. Five days ago. Five days!

The walls were crowding in now, sure enough. The days when Martina used to ring up and talk about God now seemed like *halcyon* days ... empty as they'd been.

He peered down at the phone. It was like the fucking thing had died. Well, apart from the occasional call from his parents, bless their cotton socks. *Should* he go back to the family seat for a while...? No, no, no, not back up there.... Better to drown here.

But he *had* been *trying*.... He'd just ... tailed off the last two weeks or so. You could only take so many lonely nights out on the pull no matter what that cockney wideboy had said on that video. Christ, to think that he'd actually started listening to that crap! And of course it hadn't done any good. And meanwhile, whatever was left of his self-respect went on ebbing away from him drop by drop, leaking out of him every other Thursday into the end of that fortnightly, government-issue condom.

Maybe those two harpies from the workshop were right ... maybe it *was* his coat.

He smiled weakly, letting his head fall dangerously close to the plate of sardines. Pulling himself up just in time, he threw his head back and stuck the cigarette in his mouth.

Ah ... fuck.

'*Fuck!*' he shouted aloud, throwing himself forward again, jumping up and taking the plates out to the kitchen. He thought better of scraping off the leavings and simply dumped the plates, cutlery and all into the bin. Well, he was the only one here, what did he need all these fucking plates and forks and knives for?

He stood over the bin, smoking hard. The honeymoon was over now all right. The desperation was back, the edginess was back, that was plain.

Still standing over the bin, he pulled the cigarette out of his mouth and exhaled.

Okay, his cock was happily sunk into shag benefit, and at least it kept the fucking thing quiet, but what about *him? What about him for Christ's sake?* He needed, he needed ... to claw back a little *dignity* ... If knob he must, then let it at least be with a woman who *wanted* him to knob her.

But *again* ... why did he have to knob at all? That thing between the legs of the girlies; that little nick made from on high by old Goddy with his rusty cosmic penknife; that little trough; was it really so amazing that it warranted all this ... *day-in, day-out, soul-wearying, fucking nonsense*?

Thou shalt not fornicate. Fine. I don't want to fucking fornicate. So why did you cut the girls down there, and why did you stick your dangling unholy trinity on me? If you don't want us to fornicate, why not reproduce us with a click of your heels, instead of leaving us to this crudity, this messy little process you devised, which is at best absurd, at worst, sick and ugly. All this brutal in-and-out penetrative compulsion ... are you *insane*? Is that the best you can come up with? And then on top of that, you have the brass neck to say you're going to throw us in a torture chamber for ever more for doing it, as if the whole bloody farce were something *we* came up with! Well, it was your idea, mate, don't blame *us*!

He flung the cigarette in the bin, and then in a furious passion, stepped up onto a chair and yelled at the ceiling, 'In fact get down here now, you tosser, and bring your penknife with you, and cut this, cut this ... *fucking thing off me!* Because you shouldn't have put it there, you shouldn't have put it there in the first place! Mad *bastard!*'

He banged a cupboard with his fist and half-slipped, half-fell off the chair to the floor, where he sat back against the oven and laughed bitterly, groping for his cigarettes. He had just invoked his Creator to cut off his cock. This was surely something approaching madness.

There came a loud thud from upstairs followed by heavy footsteps moving overhead along the hallway.

Oh, fuck. That biker greaser in the flat above.

He pulled himself to his feet as steps sounded outside the door. The bell rang. And rang.

Shit. He went out to the hall and opened the door to a bulky man with a pony-tail dressed in leather and chains.

'All right, mate, what are you fuckin' raving about?'

'Er ... sorry about that. I was talking to myself.'

'Really? Sounded like you were talking to me.'

'No, I er ... no, I wasn't. Really.'

'Yeah? Well, I can hear everything you're fuckin' saying, and next time, I *will* bring my penknife down. Okay?'

'Yeah. I'm really sorry. I was just having a bit of a mad moment. Nothing to do with you. Really.'

'You want to see a head doctor mate before you get into trouble,' said the neighbour, turning and heading back up the steps.

Lawrence closed the door and stood for a moment in the hall. The guy was right. He'd better try and just sort himself out. He really had better ... get out more. Starting now. Yeah ... why the hell not ... just go out. And see what happens. Probably the usual generous helping of fuck-all ... but what the hell ... a bit of fresh air and all that crap.

He went back into the lounge, grabbed his coat and headed out the door.

Taking his regulation pint of lager and packet of cheese and onion crisps from the bar, Lawrence went and sat down at one of the long, narrow tables of the crowded Camden music pub, observing the musicians and their entourages drifting in and out of the back room.

He'd probably made the right decision to come out. He did feel a bit better, but the longer he sat here not talking to anyone, the worse it would gradually get. Still, he could probably stick it for one pint, maybe two.

Most of the musicians were kids in their late teens, early twenties, their hair studiously cut to styles from the 1960s and 1970s, styles worn yesteryear by their heroes from the history of rock - that was to say, their masters, their *elders and betters*. Lawrence was just musing on the harmlessness that this gave them, and of how that in turn lent them a certain gentle appeal, when a girl's midriff crossed his view, activating his loins immediately. He heard a voice just above his head and looked up. She was speaking to him.

'Excuse me ... do you mind ... do you mind if I sit here?'

She was indicating the single space next to him.

'No, not at all. Please ... do.' All right, don't get too excited, there probably isn't anywhere else for her to sit. No, fuck it, *get* excited. This was an opportunity. For the love of heaven, recognise that. Recognise it and work it.

He watched as she eased her way somewhat unsteadily round the end of the table. She was pretty and very young, the bones of her face soft, as though still forming themselves, as though yet undecided in which direction to take her seductive, baby-like features, while her big eyes had been emphatically marked out in thick eyeliner, as though she were afraid that without it they might disappear altogether.

As she sat down, Lawrence could not help but notice that her shredded low-riding jeans were slung somewhere half-way down her behind, revealing an expanse of pale blue underwear. The adjoining area of skin was so smooth and of such a delicious complexion that he felt a clutching spasm in his heart, and a fleeting sense of the world opening out briefly, as if onto a bright row of summer gardens.

But it all closed up again just as suddenly, the stress of the coming campaign rolling over him as he peered up at her profile and began to concentrate. Well, first off, since she had spoken to him first, and had sat down next to him, he surely had more of a right to speak than usual. She seemed pretty drunk, her head apparently just a little too heavy for her as she sipped her wine and let her eyes wander about the room, wandering anywhere, it seemed, except toward him. She pulled her cigarettes from her bag, stuck one in her mouth and began battling with a cracked, and clearly spent, lighter. Lawrence felt for his own lighter, relieved that smoking - that beautiful social ice-breaker - had come to his rescue once again. He could forget about all that opening line horse-shit.

'Er, here ... allow me,' he smiled, flicking open the flame.

'Oh, thanks,' she smiled back, as Lawrence drank in the soft modelling of her face, noting the black roots of her long purple-dyed hair, the sunglasses pushed to the crown of her head. 'You're very kind.'

You're very kind. Well, that sounded good. Right. Let's start with the sunglasses.

He looked up at her head and grinned.

'Er ... I didn't notice the sun in evidence much today.'

'Sorry?'

Fuck. Maybe he'd sounded a shade too sarcastic. Laugh genially and explain.

'Your sunglasses. The sun hasn't been out for weeks.'

'No, it was! This morning!' she said, wide-eyed, as though anxious not to be accused of doing something stupid. 'Not for long though. For about twenty minutes.'

'Oh, when was that? I missed that. Shit.'

'About 8 o'clock. When I left the house.'

'Ah, well, there you go. I was asleep. The best twenty minutes of the year so far and I missed it because I was *asleep*!' He banged the table lightly with his hand and her laughter came to him, so welcome that he could almost feel it on his neck like soft, soothing balm. 'So... er, where were you going so early in the morning. Some sort of *work* type of thing, was it ?'

She looked down at the table. 'Therapy, actually. I'm in treatment. Full-time psychotherapy.'

'Oh right....' said Lawrence, suddenly saddened. Make a joke out of it. Somehow she looked like she could take it, that it would be the right thing. 'Full-time, eh? So you're just fucked up from 9 to 5?'

'Yeah,' she laughed, 'Like any other occupation!'

'Right!' he laughed with her, lighting a cigarette. 'So ... what's the problem? If you don't mind my asking?'

'No, not at all. Well, here's the list, then: borderline personality disorder, depression, derealisation, dissociation, depersonalisation.'

Fucking hell. Poor thing. 'All the D's,' he said gently.

'Yeah, all the fucking D's!' she laughed, her eyes wandering.

Lawrence sucked on his cigarette, touched by how conscientiously she had recited the symptoms of mental fracture, as though at pains to be honest and open, or as though she hoped to keep the demons at bay by cataloguing them and keeping them constantly in sight. He was hit by an almost fatherly concern for the girl, and forced himself to ignore the powerful arousal her nearness had caused in him. She was vulnerable, struggling to keep herself together, and he had to put away his lust, because to do anything else would just be... *feral*. No, his role here, if anything, had to be Good Samaritan, father confessor, big sister.

He took a sip of his lager. 'I've had a touch of that myself in my time. Not the personality disorder, I mean depersonalisation.'

'Yeah?'

'Yeah, I'd depersonalise for a bit, feel like I just didn't exist at all, then after that derealise for a bit, you know, like *I* existed, but now nothing else did. Like I was watching everything on a giant screen or something.'

'You should try it all at the same time, depersonalising, derealising and dissociating all at the same time.'

'Jesus.... Yes,' said Lawrence, humbled.

'It's a fucking nightmare.' She let out a low, shuddering laugh. Lawrence caught its note of utter mental exhaustion. He peered sadly at her soft cheek.

'So ...' said Lawrence, 'have you come for one of the bands tonight or something?'

'No, I'm waiting for my friends.'

Well, there you go - he wouldn't have gotten anywhere anyway.

She turned to him. 'So, er, what's your name?'

'Lawrence,' he smiled, a warmth flowing through him, despite his platonic resolve. 'What's yours?'

'Well, it's kind of *mad.*'

'Like mine then. Go on.'

'Drusilla.'

'Wow.... I see what you mean.... It's beautiful, though. Still, shouldn't you be wearing a toga or something with a name like that?'

'I do ... at home. As I order my slaves about,' she laughed, making an expansive gesture of her arm.

'And these slaves.... Would they be your parents?'

'Yeah,' she said, still laughing. She looked at him for the first time in a while and raised her glass. 'You seem like a good bloke, Lawrence. Pleased to meet you. Cheers.'

Jesus Christ, this was nice. 'And I'm very happy to meet you too, Drusilla. Cheers.'

'Actually, my name's Drew, but I wanted to lengthen it to Drusilla.'

'Well, I think you did the right thing.' He watched her for a moment as her eyes wandered around the room, and she began mouthing the words to the song on the jukebox. He was impressed that a kid like this knew all the words to *Oliver's Army* by Elvis Costello. She had taste ... and intelligence ...

'I must say - I hope you don't mind me saying this - but you seem remarkably ... *compos mentis* considering the problems you've got to contend with.'

'I told you. I'm only a nutter from 9 to 5. Actually, it's because I'm really drunk. I can deal with it better when I'm pissed. Actually, I'm drinking more than usual at the moment.' She looked deep into her wineglass, 'Since that bastard last week.'

'Sorry?'

'My boyfriend.... I broke up with my boyfriend last week.'

'Ah.... Sorry about that.'

'You love these bastards ... and what do you get...?'

'Yeah ... well ... it's just one big bloody mess if you ask me. This whole ... men and women business.'

'Yeah,' she laughed, still staring into her wineglass.

'I mean, sometimes I get the depressing sense that we're nothing more than sacs of fluid just milling about waiting to reproduce.'

'It seems like that sometimes,' she laughed sourly, 'and it's like we're just condemned to it.'

'Drusilla, how old are you?'

She whispered in his ear, her closeness thrilling his entire nervous system, 'Eighteen in June.'

Seventeen! Jesus, she was fourteen years younger than him! He'd put her at about twenty or twenty-one. Well, that was it. He'd definitely better stop fancying her. Thank God these friends of hers were coming soon.

Again she leaned right into his head and whispered, her lips this time brushing his ear, 'But don't tell anyone or they'll throw me out.'

What the hell was she doing? Was she aware that her lips had touched him? Was it deliberate? Or was she just so pissed she didn't know what she was doing?

'Well, don't worry, your secret's safe with me. Besides, I want you to stay and talk with me till your friends come.'

There was a pause before she spoke, as if she were considering something. 'Actually, I've got a confession to make on that score.'

'Oh?'

'Yeah... I'm not waiting for any friends. I've come out by myself. Do you think that's sad?'

'Not in your case. It is in *mine.* I've come out by myself, too. I'm a professional sad bastard, you know.'

'I find that hard to believe.'

Lawrence felt a massive involuntary surge in his pants. 'Er ... why did you say you were waiting for your friends, then?'

'I ... I didn't want you to think I was sad....'

'But why do you care what *I* think? Look, you're getting our roles mixed up here. *I*'m the sad old git; you're the pretty young girl.'

'I wanted to come and talk to you.'

Holy shit.

She glanced up at him with nervous eyes, 'I liked the look of you. I could see you were a nice person. You get so many psychos in London.'

'But I'm just a fuck-up like everybody else. More so probably.'

'No ... I can trust you.'

'What? You don't know anything about me.'

'I can see it in your aura.'

'My what?'

'Your aura. I was reading your aura from the bar. A person's aura tells you all you need to know.'

'Ah....' Maybe she *was* nuts after all. 'Ah ... but I have a *fake* aura. So people will like me. A bloke in Clapham fixed it up for me. Cost a few bob, though.'

'Don't take the piss,' she laughed, swaying to one side.

'I'm sorry. Actually, I'm flattered, *touched*. Look, er ... do you want another drink?'

'Sure, thank you. Glass of white wine.'

Lawrence rose, and squeezed past her, his legs brushing hers as he moved round the table and forced his way through the throng to the bar.

Did she fancy him? Probably not. She had called him a 'nice person', which definitely had a platonic ring. But anyway, anyway she was too young and clearly in a very unstable state. To do it with her would be to take advantage of a very psychologically disturbed person barely out of childhood. And on top of that, she was drunk and her boyfriend had just left her. He shouldn't even be buying her alcohol.

Still, this was the first time in his life that a girl had approached *him*, and therefore this was still a truly golden and momentous event. And she was gorgeous. And she *had* said she liked the look of him. Maybe she *was* into him! It would be absolutely typical of his fucking luck if she was. That non-existent tosser upstairs was probably having him on again, winding him up as punishment for his little speech earlier. But no, come on, for Christ's sake, he was flattering himself. There was nothing, *nothing* to really suggest she wanted anything sexual from him. But her lips had brushed his ear - though, no, that was probably accidental. She'd simply come over to talk to him, because he looked like a 'nice person' - which meant *harmless* person. And when she said she trusted him, she probably meant that she trusted him not to make a move on her.

Bitterly amused to find himself actually *relieved* that a sexy girl didn't want to fuck him, he put in his order to the bartender.

'Well ...' said Lawrence, stepping out of the pub and pushing up his umbrella, 'I'm heading off up Kentish Town Road, then. Where are you going?'

'Er ... I'll get a bus outside Camden Tube.'

'All right, I'll walk you there. Wait with you till the bus comes. Fend off all the psychos for you.'

'Cool,' she said, looking at the floor. It seemed to Lawrence that a quietness had come over her during the last half-hour, her movements and gestures increasingly belying some inner turmoil. 'Come on, you'd better get under this umbrella.'

'Thanks,' she said, glancing up at him nervously, and then down at the floor again, as they moved off into the rain.

He felt her slip her arm into his, causing an unwelcome downward rush of blood to his knob. Again, he was shocked by the mindless immediacy of his sexual response. Yet despite his dismay, he allowed himself to feel the simple, yet enormous pleasure of a girl's arm in his, even though it was almost certainly a mere gesture of friendliness - as indeed he hoped it *was*.

When was the last time a girl had willingly touched him like this? Well, it was probably Sofia ... months back when they'd walked arm in arm out to the shed ... and of course, the gesture had meant nothing then, just as this meant nothing now.

The short walk to the bus stop was conducted almost in silence, Drusilla occasionally murmuring fragments of songs from the jukebox, though still seemingly preoccupied, her attention on the pavement, her balance at times precarious. Lawrence observed her soft profile. Well, okay ... infuriatingly, she wasn't the answer to the sex problem - but she could perhaps be a friend, and Christ knew, his address book needed a bit of topping up ... and after all, who knew what might happen in the future -

'Okay, this is it,' she said quietly, looking up, as they came to the bus shelter. 'Oh, here's my bus!' she cried, looking over her shoulder. 'Well, it was lovely to meet you, Lawrence -'

'It was lovely to meet you too -'

She craned her head up to his and kissed him on both cheeks, then drew back, glancing round at the bus pulling up behind her, before looking back up at him again, a sudden, aching desperation in her face.

He was about to speak when her head was launched toward his once more, her eyes closing. And then she was kissing him on the mouth, her tongue immediately forcing open his lips. Stunned, he abandoned himself to the violent probing of her tongue, and a low joyous moan sounded somewhere down in his throat, so long had it been since he'd been kissed. Her tongue went on squirming around inside his mouth as the bus pulled away from the kerb and moved off again into the rain. He blinked the wetness out of his eyes - her desire to kiss him had already unlocked his tears - and stared at her lowered eyelashes, so long and so luxurious, as she crushed his lips with her young jaws, and the apple smell of her shampooed hair filled his head. Dear Jesus Christ in Heaven. He knew, fuck it, he *knew* he should stop this. But he stroked her cheek instead, and she moaned aloud. She had her hands inside his coat and was pulling his jumper and T-shirt up. Oh, *Christ*. As her fingers found the flat of his stomach, he heard his excitement break from him in a small uncontrolled whimper. He was embarrassed at the sound, but she seemed to like it, because her cheeks drew back in a little smile, as she went on rolling her tongue around his mouth. He was home.

But she was seventeen. A minor, drunk on the alcohol he'd bought her.

But ... to *undress* her, smell the skin of her back ...

No, no... She had psychiatric problems; her boyfriend had left her only last week -

Oh, come *on*, you arsehole. There's no debate to be had here! You can't have this. Pull back. Now.

Because this is *you*. And *you* don't get fulfilment. You get sex dole. You get *torment*. You are here to be teased and mocked by everlasting bad luck. Now put this vulnerable little girl, this *child*, down.

He took hold of her shoulders and gently eased her back. Her eyes opened reluctantly and she closed her mouth, standing uncertainly before him. 'What?' she said, the languor of the kiss making her more unsteady on her feet than ever.

'Look, er ... I don't think we ... should ... I mean, you are incredibly attractive and I would love to go on doing this with you, but....'

'But what?'

'I - well. I don't think it would be fair on you -'

'Listen, you're coming *back* with me!' she shouted furiously at the pavement, her eyes suddenly wild.

He regarded her cautiously, before replying. 'I just don't think that's wise. I mean, look, I'm a lot older than you-'

'You don't fancy me. Fine,' she snapped, turning from him.

'Bollocks. That kiss was the best thing that's happened to me in fucking *years!*' declared Lawrence with passion.

'Then come *back* with me!' she cried, whirling round, with what now seemed like the pleading face of a twelve-year old.

'Listen, Drusilla, look, I - I don't think you're thinking straight. To sleep with me so soon after splitting up with your boyfriend would be a ... a desperate act. I think you should -'

'Don't fucking tell me how to live my life.'

'Look, why don't you give me your number, and -'

'Look, just don't bother, okay? Forget it! You've had your chance!' she shouted, shaking her head wildly, and lurching off to the other end of the shelter.

He felt an actual weakening in his knees at the idea he might never see her again. But then, the reaction wasn't so incredible; she had already given him so much. It really had been the happiest moment of the whole of the last two years, probably longer.

'Hey, Drusilla -' he began, but was interrupted by a bus juddering to a halt alongside the shelter.

'Okay, I can get this one,' she said, running to the vehicle as if to her salvation.

'Please. Give me your number -'

'No fucking way! I'm not making any more of an idiot of myself!' she sobbed, without looking round, and half-climbed, half-stumbled onto the bus.

He took a step forward, but the doors closed behind her and the vehicle moved off into lamp-lit drizzle. Through the steamed-up windows, he could just discern her small figure making its unsteady way to a seat on the far side. She dwindled rapidly to a grey blur, leaving him to stare after the rear window of the bus as it disappeared up the road, finally to merge with distant traffic.

He fell against the shelter and lit a cigarette. Jesus Christ. What madness. What utter madness. Maybe he'd done more harm by turning her down.... No, no, surely he'd done the right thing. Jesus, she'd be okay.

At least he could be happy she'd gone for him in the first place. Yes, but ... *had* she fancied him? Actually, now he thought about it, there had been a sickness somewhere in that long, beautiful, yet somehow *bruising,* kiss. Perhaps she just picked up random blokes every night ... and it was a sort of symptom of her 'disorder'. Maybe.

But even so, she'd still picked him over every other punter in that pub.

No, fuck it, he'd pulled. He'd *pulled*, for Christ's sake! He should celebrate!

No. No, he shouldn't. He'd pulled, but he'd pulled forbidden fruit. Which was as good as nothing. It didn't count. It didn't fucking *count*. He was still left standing in the rain, empty-handed. No matter what he did, the end of the night would always see him standing empty-handed at some bus shelter, some tube station, some hotdog stand. He felt a sudden sickening sense of entrapment, as though discovering only now the true extent of some invisible barrier laid out all around him. Even when they *wanted* him, even when they wanted him to *fuck* them, even *then*, it seemed the girls had been fixed by unseen laws to remain on the other side of that vicious piece of glass.

And then before he knew what he was doing, he was bellowing 'FUCK!' into the night air and punching the bus shelter like any other good Camden nutter on a Saturday night.

Realising he'd been hitting the Perspex panel for far longer than was reasonable, he came to a stop and fell silent. He stood quietly for a moment, rubbing his bleeding knuckle, staring at the patch of ground where he and Drusilla had stood and kissed. Finally, he stepped wearily out of the shelter and, not bothering with his umbrella, marched off down the street, the slow rain gradually washing the lingering scent of apple-shampoo from his wet hair, from his neck and from his tired, scowling face.

THIRTY-SIX

Lawrence glanced up at the LED monitor, screwed his ticket into a ball and looked for the free desk, noting with a sigh that it was being manned by the petulant git in the glasses. He rose slowly and went over.

As he neared the desk, Lawrence watched as the guy stood up and extended his arm toward him, looking him in the eye. Lawrence was perplexed by the gesture. It appeared for all the world as though the bloke wanted to shake his hand. Maybe it was some new approach or something.

Feeling slightly awkward, though pleasantly surprised, Lawrence extended his own hand.

Williams pulled his hand away quickly and muttered, 'No. Your SB40. Your SB40.' Only when Lawrence had withdrawn his hand did Williams extend his again.

Jesus. You miserable fucking -

Lawrence pulled out his signing document and handed it over. Williams took it from him wordlessly, and strode off to the filing cabinet as Lawrence lowered himself into the swivel chair and waited. Christ, this bloke was absolutely extraordinary. He followed the titanium rims of Williams' spectacles back to the desk. All right, I'm scum for coming here, but you have no right to treat me like that.

Williams took the signature sheet from the file, and intoned flatly,

'Have you had a sexual encounter at any point in the last two weeks?'

'No.'

Lawrence received the sheet from Williams, signed his name and pushed the paper back across the desk.

'And what *have* you been doing in the last two weeks? How is your LiaisonSearch going?'

Jesus, the *tone* of this bastard. I *am* trying to get off this shit, you son of a bitch.

'Well, actually, last week, I came very close with a girl in the pub.'

'Very close?'

'Yes, but she was ... she had - she was very drunk for one thing, and quite disturbed psychologically.'

'Go on.'

'Well ... she was in therapy. Full-time psychotherapy. Personality disorder, clinical depression etc. Very attractive though. But young. Seventeen. She wanted me to go home with her. But I really don't think she knew what she was doing ... and as well, her boyfriend had only just left her the previous week. So ... as you can understand, I very reluctantly said no. You know, in view of her vulnerability, I thought it was best to just put her on a bus home.'

'How did you know she was sexually interested?'

'How? She practically jumped on me at the bus stop.'

'And you didn't go home with her?'

'No.'

'Okay, I'm suspending your benefit.'

'What?'

'I'm suspending your benefit. You declined an encounter.'

He felt a weakness in his knees, just as he had when Drusilla had turned from him in the shelter. 'Look, the girl was messed up. I would have been taking advantage of her.'

'All right, it was a messy situation. But life is messy. Didn't anyone ever tell you that?'

Lawrence stared at Williams, amazed.

'You should have slept with this girl.'

'For Christ's sake, I don't believe this!'

'Look, the world's tough. If you want to act like a saint out there, that's your look-out, but don't expect the state to shoulder the burden for you.'

'Are you serious?'

'Of course I'm serious. The Contact-Seeker's Charter takes no view on where an offer comes from. An offer is an offer. To decline an offer is by definition to admit that your need is not sufficient to merit the receipt of benefit. And you declined an offer. So I have no choice but to suspend your claim. Anyway, you obviously don't need us if you're getting offers from attractive young girls.'

'It was the first such offer I've had in my life, and I'm under no illusions about getting any more any time soon. And besides, she was off her head. Plus she was only seventeen!'

'One whole year over the age of consent.'

'Jesus Christ almighty!'

'Listen. You've broken the terms of your contract with us. Be advised by me. Go home. Give this girl a call. There's nothing more we can do for you here,' said Williams, taking Lawrence's file and rising from the chair.

'I couldn't even if I wanted to. I didn't get her number.'

'Well, that wasn't very diligent of you, was it? I mean, that's almost grounds enough in itself for me to stop your benefit. I'm sorry, but there's nothing more I can do. That's it. Now, if you'll excuse me, there are a lot of claimants waiting.'

'Hang on a minute, that can't be it, just like that! I want to know exactly what happens now. There must be some process, for God's sake!'

Williams sighed. 'All right. All suspended claims go to an adjudication panel. They have the final decision, and I can assure you that in a case like this, where a claimant has openly turned down an encounter, the recommendation will be to issue an SB13, notification of cessation of benefit.'

'But I must have some right of appeal.'

'Well, you can appeal their decision of course, but it would be pointless.'

'All right, well, how do I do that?' asked Lawrence, finally getting to his feet.

'You'll be notified of their decision in two weeks. Then you can send in your appeal.'

'Right. And how do I send in my appeal?'

'The forms are on those stands over there. Now if you'll excuse me.'

With great anger, Lawrence looked him in the eye. 'To have done it with her would have been immoral. You know that.'

Williams lowered his gaze to Lawrence's chest. 'As I said, we're very busy in here today. Excuse me.'

Williams turned and marched off, leaving Lawrence to glare after his receding back. Stunned, Lawrence drifted slowly away from the desk himself.

Williams leaned on the filing cabinet, took out his pen and wrote out a brief note for his report to the adjudication panel. He clipped the note to Lawrence's file, which he then dropped in a drawer. Another one off the books. And a good catch it was, too. Be good to see the back of that scruffy smart-arse. There he was over there, by the stands. Go on, get out of it, you scruffy pillock.

He watched until Lawrence was safely out onto the street. Bye, then, chum. You should've shagged her. You should shag them when you *can*. And if you haven't got the balls, then don't come crying to us. Don't come crying to *me*. Why should I wipe your backside with a silk handkerchief every two weeks? No one's there to bloody wipe mine!

He turned and headed into the staff office. Grabbing his tartan flask, he poured himself a plastic mug of coffee and sat down.

He took a sip, wincing at the heat. No one ever puts their bloody arms around *me*! Lucinda, you seem to fail to realise that I arrange things here. And I'm going to bloody arrange things for you, all right.

Harper came in. 'Aall right, Roger?' beamed the Jamaican.

Williams looked up.

'Yes. Fine, thanks,' he replied, blowing on his coffee.

THIRTY-SEVEN

Carlton fumbled with the key to his letterbox. Come on, get in, get in, like. The key rattled in the lock. He opened the flap, peered inside and drew out the single brown envelope. It was from *them*. From the fuckin' sex dole. There it was, then.

He reached inside, closed his big, soft fingers around the letter and drew it out.

He was tempted to open it there and then, but no, he'd go up, first, like. Wouldn't be good to open it here ... in case ... it hadn't, hadn't worked. But it must've done. It must've done! You couldn't see anythin' through that liquid paper stuff.

Still, he felt his guts churning over so much, that in a minute, he was gunna let off, like and it'd probably be a bad 'un, an' all. Better get in that lift quick, before it comes.

He shuffled over to the lift, stepped inside and pressed the red button, breaking wind as the door slid shut. Through the gap he just managed to make out a young couple who had just entered from the street. Thank fuck they hadn't got in this lift with him, like.

As the cabin ascended, he stared down at the letter in his hand. Better pray, now, then. But it's too late for prayin', now in't it? Whatever's in that letter is in that letter. How can fuckin' prayin' change it? Prayin'... Fuckin' prayin' never does *nowt* any road. Like with his Mom. All that prayin'... and God and Jesus had still killed her, hadn't they? Must've bin cos they wanted to, like ... stinks in 'ere now.... Good job them two hadn't come in, like.... But the letter'll be okay. The bastards couldn't see through liquid paper! It'll be okay. They'll just tell him to come in same as normal, like.... But what if they'd found some way *to* see through it? Or phoned that doctor and checked! They could've phoned that fuckin' doctor and checked! Or just held the paper up to the fuckin' light or somethin'...!

The door grated open, spilling Carlton's bulk onto the fifth floor. He hurriedly moved his weight over to the door of his flat, found his key, dropped it, picked it up and after a moment of trouble with the lock, entered the flat.

Ignoring the shivering dog that had come out to greet him, and which was now making a slow, silent circle around him, he pushed the door shut and began tearing at the envelope, at first ineffectually and then frantically, showering the dog's head with scraps of brown paper. Finally he had the corner of the letter between his finger and thumb and pulled it out, unfolding it clumsily.

Department of Health and Social Security.
Kentish Town Sex Benefit Centre.
276 Kentish Town Road.
London NW1 4SD

Date 27.2.04
Reference: 098367
Direct Lines:0207 972 5518/4673
Fax:0207 972 5523
email: sexben@dhss.gov.uk

Mr. Colin Carlton,
Flat 43 Larchwood Estate,
Malden Road,
Kentish Town,
London.

Dear Mr. Carlton,

You are hereby notified of your disqualification from receipt of sex benefit (See form SB13 [enclosed]). This has been decided in light of irregularities discovered in the medical form SB20 recently submitted. It has been decided not to proceed with a criminal prosecution in view of the relatively harmless nature of the condition you attempted to conceal. However, as you have been caught in an active deception, you are permanently barred forthwith from any further entitlement to sex benefit. This decision is final and binding, there being no appeal in cases of active deception.

Yours Sincerely
S. Barnes. (For Graham Henshaw. Manager.)

He blinked, almost staggered into the dog, steadied himself for a moment, shook his head as though trying to shake off some physical encumbrance, and stumbled over to a chair, falling face forwards onto the cushion.

Over by the kitchen, the shaking terrier looked from its empty bowl over to the heaving shape piled against the chair, and back to the bowl again.

THIRTY-EIGHT

'Sally, it's just not on,' said Sacha gravely, resting his head on the iron bedstead and crossing his legs under the grey silk sheets as the tall, lithe figure of Sally emerged from the *en suite* bathroom.

'All right, all right!' replied Sally, tying the cord of her robe. 'I've just said we won't invite them, haven't I?'

'That's not the point. Frankly it's just not acceptable that you could even have dared suggest it in the first place.'

'Sacha, don't be -'

'I'm not having old people hanging round the flat.'

'Old people! They're my *parents*, Sacha!'

'Precisely... A pair of old people whom I don't know. And whom I don't care to know.'

'Fine, well, they're not coming now, are they?' replied Sally quietly, dragging a brush through her short blond hair.

Sacha peered down at his chest, examining the firm ledges of his pectorals. 'When I agreed to your moving in here, I told you I wanted all this filthy family stuff kept well away from me. And what happens? Two months down the line, you start wanting them round for dinner.'

'I simply wondered if perhaps you'd changed your mind. What's so awful about that?' she asked, turning to him.

However, he was staring from the bed over at the wide plate-glass windows, beyond which spread a broad panorama of misty London skyline. She waited for him to speak.

'But that's not all, is it?'

'What do you mean?' she said, putting down the brush.

'You gave them this number, didn't you?'

'What? Why? Did they call?'

'*She* called,' said Sacha deliberately, his gaze still fixed on the windows. 'Last night, while you were out.'

'Oh,' breathed Sally, 'I'm sorry.'

She watched as he slowly turned his head to her. There was a pause before he spoke.

'When I have a night in on my own, Sally, I want to relax, I don't want to be dragged out of my chair to listen to that putrefaction go on about her bloody grandkids for ten minutes, do you understand?'

'All right, I'm sorry. But I wish you wouldn't talk that way about her, Sacha.'

'Then don't give me cause!'

'I'll tell her not to call again. I'm sorry. I told her only to call here in an emergency. She knows she's only supposed to call me on my mobile.'

He turned back to the window.

'Look,' began Sally placatingly, 'I'll go and make us some coffee, okay?' She moved toward the door, but halted again at his voice.

'I don't know, Sally. You're failing me.'

She turned to find herself looking straight into the bright blue eyes trained on her from the bed, oddly aglow in an expression that was otherwise dead.

'Don't say that, Sashy. *Please.*'

'You're failing me *now.* Even as you stand there. And I do believe you don't even realise it.'

'What ?'

'Look at you. What do you think you're doing? Where do you think you're going? You don't know whether you're coming or going, do you?'

'I was going to make some coffee -' she began, perplexed.

He shook his head and stared at her, coldly brandishing a dazzling dental smile. 'But you've forgotten your first duty of the day.

Incredible, really. First you want to fill my home with your parental stink, and then you throw aside basic morning etiquette. What *is* a fellow to think?'

'I-'

He dropped the smile. 'Where do you think you're going, Sally? Where do you think you're going with your *mouth*?'

He threw aside the sheets.

'Where are your bloody *manners?*' he enunciated softly.

'But -'

'But?'

She swallowed hard. 'But ... you want me to do it two, three times a day -'

He didn't want to argue about this, he wanted his cock sucked. Well, there was always the quick way. 'That's right. I do. Because I can't get enough of you. Because I love you,' he soothed, engineering a certain softening of his face.

For a moment, she stood staring at him from the door. 'Do you, Sacha? Sometimes, the things you say -'

'What?' he protested, using his warmest smile.

'Oh … nothing,' she said with a half-smile, crossing the rug.

She climbed onto the bed and began crawling toward his groin. He watched as her blond head briefly smiled up at him before lowering into position between his legs. Love, nothing, Sally. It's a simple exchange. One roof for another, you might say: the roof over your head for the roof of your mouth.

'Okay … you can make the coffee, now, if you like,' said Sacha, taking his hand from Sally's head and stretching his legs out under the sheets.

'You bastard!' cried Sally, raising her head from his abdomen.

He grinned. 'Just my little joke, darling.'

She regarded him warily, before breaking into a cautious smile and moving her face slowly up to his.

Sacha closed his eyes and took her long, warm kiss. Yes, Sally, this is all very nice, but there are *other* mouths ... always other mouths to 'feed' ... other holes to fill ... other slightly sweeter holes to fill...

As she went on kissing him, whispering declarations of love in his ear, he glanced over at his jacket, suddenly impatient to check his mobile. Gently, he eased her off, and spoke, ensuring that he filled his voice with a reassuring warmth, 'But I really could do with that coffee, now, baby.'

'Okay, baby,' she laughed, patting his stomach, then lifted herself from the bed and padded from the room. He watched her disappear down the corridor, before reaching for his jacket and removing his phone.

Two messages. One from Ulla, and one from Inga. Better not be any cancellations. He'd been looking forward to this afternoon; first, Ulla in Islington, then over to Inga in Hackney.

He checked each message in turn.

Good. Just the usual love drivel.

He put the phone away, rolled onto his side, and lay gazing out at the white sky.

Love. No risk of any of that twaddle with the coitus dole. It was a curious fact that that concrete khazi on Kentish Town Road was about the only place where a chap could reliably expect to bang in peace.

THIRTY-NINE

Carlton sat unseeingly before the TV as the *Dr. Who* theme music washed over him for the hundredth time that month, the tune now, however, having almost lost for good its ability to comfort and console. The grubby carpet around his feet was spread with a litter of boxless video cassettes, but this accumulation of science fiction and hardcore pornography was also fast losing any ability to soothe.

With tiny eyes, he followed the long brown hair of Sarah Jane around the screen, completely deaf to the long exposition being delivered by the Doctor. Her hair. Her fuckin' lovely, lovely hair ... just to touch ... just to touch a girl's hair, again ... even just their hair, like....

That fuckin' liquid paper!! If he'd only just left it alone, he'd still be goin' down!

He began violently rubbing his knees and staring wildly round the ceiling.

... it was like when his Mum had died! Only worse. When she'd died, the fuckin' pain had gradually got a bit better, like, in time. A bit better each day. But not this. Every week it was just gettin' worse....

He was never gunna go up them stairs again. Never go through them doors again...

He pushed himself up from the chair, and stood, bewildered,

rubbing his hand. And the full stomach-churning weight of his loss hit him again as though for the first time, though it kept hitting him every day.

Without that place ...

... he'd probably never get another fuck again in his life.

... after all, like ... he'd never in his life had a fuck outside it.

He stood in the centre of the room and let the tears come. The dog peeked up at him from under the table and yawned, waiting to see if he would go into the kitchen.

Presently, he wiped his eyes and shuffled through a scattered pile of rubbish to the kitchen, followed by the expectant terrier.

... and today at work in the supermarket ... all the lovely women and girls in the supermarket today... The sex dole used to help you to bear that, like. It meant that when you were in the street, or at work in the supermarket you could bear all their lovely hair, their faces and their little hands ... you could bear it cos you knew at least that you'd be goin' down the sex dole at some point ... that you weren't fuckin' *left out* ... but now ... how was he supposed to fuckin' bear them, now? How was he supposed to bear the fuckin' sight of them and their hair and their eyes and their lovely bums an' legs *now?* Workin' in that supermarket was gunna be just fuckin' torture from now on. But workin' *any*where'd be torture - women were fuckin' everywhere!

He began crying more loudly, allowing himself to slowly slide down the side of the refrigerator to the floor.

... he was *out.* Just a piece of, of fuckin' shit thrown out on the street. Of course, he'd never, *ever* been *in*, like ... But without the sex dole, he was more out now than he'd ever been in his fuckin' life. Just a piece of shit in the gutter. But no, people didn't stare with fuckin' disgust at shit. They just ignored it, like. Women didn't give shit angry looks, like they did with him. He was *worse* than shit. No wonder them fuckers on that course had laughed. They were right to! They were all fuckin' right to! And they'd laughed cos he was stupid, and they were right there an' all! That rubbish he'd said about the dog! Do you like dogs! Only a daft twat like him would've come up with that shite!... and only a daft twat would've messed about with *fuckin' liquid paper on that form!* All of them were right, like, he was nothin' but a daft, fat, ugly bastard!

He snivelled for a while, trailing his hand around the floor.

But the angel ... oh, the angel ... the angel....

... she ... s*he*'d liked him.

He bent forward and sobbed, wracked by the memory of that single luminous encounter. How she'd helped him when he'd fallen over his trousers. How she'd made him king of all the fuckin' world when she'd looked at him over her shoulder and kept on lookin' at him as he was doin' her from behind. How she'd been *into* it ... Oh, how she'd been *into* it, like ... and now never again ... and how she'd held his head near her lovely tits, like....

Filling his head with the smell and the sight of her blond hair tumbling past his face to her breast as she had cradled his head on her shoulder, and summoning her hand to stroke his hair once more, he cried himself to sleep against the fridge.

He awoke in the cold kitchen with a pain in his arm, and the dog staring at him from over by his bowl. He propped himself up against the fridge and squinted at the clock, momentarily confused by the time. Two hours had passed. So it was still Friday night, like ... but it was better asleep ... she'd been in his dream ... the only one who ever....

He sensed an idea groping toward him.

... if *she*'d liked him ... if she'd liked him, like ... then maybe ... maybe someone *else* would ... somewhere ... but maybe that's mad, like, but maybe not ... but even so, like ... that'd mean, that'd mean *tryin'*, like ... goin' out there ... and *tryin'*... but that'd just be a nightmare ... but what else was he left with…? He had to face it, what else could he fuckin' *do*...? If he didn't, didn't try out there, then what - what was he gunna do? Just watch Sarah Jane on that fuckin' video for the rest of his fuckin' life…? Out there ... there, there was a *chance* ... only a fuckin' *small* one, though ... but, but he couldn't go on without - he just couldn't ... he had to face that, like... why not be brave, why *not* try, like ... like ... like they'd said at that workshop shite ... only do it right... do it *right,* like ... and not just stand there and ask 'em if they liked dogs ... maybe if you just said the *right things* to them, the kind of things the sex dole were always on at you to say.... Maybe if he read that leaflet they'd given him ... but fuckinell, any girl he spoke to would probably just fuckin' walk away, as usual - no way could he just go out there and - … but he had to try, like ... there was no *other* fuckin' way ... and, and there might be *another angel out there* ... he had to face up to it, like ... it was time now to fuckin' face up to it.... - He could put that stuff on his hair that woman had given him, put on *all* that stuff she'd given him. She hadn't given him that shite for nothin', and they hadn't said all that stuff for nothin'... it must work or they wouldn't say it, they wouldn't say it, like! Maybe all this time, like, all this time he'd just been too ... too negative, and what he had to be was positive, like. Positive, *positive!* Like they said on the course ... on that video an' that ... that was it, think positive, like! *Yeah!* Positive, *positive!*

He picked himself up and walked out to the lounge, rubbing his arm. Coming to the table, he rummaged through the pile of bills, comics and fast-food cartons until he found the pamphlet and crumpled notes from the workshop. Making a space on the table, he laid them out carefully, then shuffled over to a plastic carrier bag in the corner of the room, picked it up and carried it through to the bathroom, where he emptied the contents over the floor. Bending down, he began rummaging through the pile of health and beauty products he'd been issued with at the workshop, glad now that he hadn't been able to sell them at the market. He found the jar of hair gel, stood up and turned to the mirror.

Carlton moved uncertainly toward the bar of the Camden pub, displaying to the groups of young people drinking at the tables the large smear of dried ketchup on the back of his grubby beige jacket. Overhanging the collar at the back of his neck were straight lengths of mouse brown hair, missed by the gel locally massaged onto the front of his head.

There were some lovely ones in 'ere, like. But he must be fuckin' mad thinkin' any of 'em would want to talk to him. But come on, you've got to try, got to fuckin' try, like. One of 'em might be kind, like the angel.

What he had to do, like, was get their interest like that bloke on the course had said. And like in that leaflet, where it said that it was good to, like, watch them for a bit first to see if there was anythin' about them you could talk to them about, like. Like, if they were readin' a book or somethin', a book *you'd* read an' all, and could talk to them about. But it'd been a bit since he'd read anythin', like. Any road, it didn't look like any of the women in 'ere were readin' anythin', anyway. They were all talkin' to their fuckin' mates an' that.

The bloke behind the bar was lookin' at him. Better tell him what he wanted to drink, like.

'Er ... pint of lager, like.'

'What kind of lager?'

'Eh?' grunted Carlton, unable to hear over the noise of the bar.

'What kind of lager do you want, mate?' repeated the guy behind the bar.

Momentarily panicked, Carlton read from the first pump his eyes landed on. 'John Smiths.'

'That's bitter, mate.'

'Well, that's what I want ... I've changed my mind, like,' replied Carlton weakly, as the bartender nodded dubiously and moved off to the pump. Carlton watched the guy's well-toned forearms as he pulled the pint. Bastard. But never mind that bastard, like. He looked round again at the bar.

Another thing it said you could do in that leaflet was help them, like, if they were havin' trouble with somethin', bags of shoppin' or summat like that. But none of these women seemed to be havin' any trouble with anythin'. And they definitely didn't have any fuckin' bags of shoppin' you could help 'em with....

... but what else had it said in that leaflet? He should've brought it with him. But no, that was a fuckin' daft idea! Yeah, he'd look really cool standin' on his own in the pub readin' a fuckin' sex dole leaflet! Come on, just try and remember the things it said, like.

The bartender returned with his pint. 'That's 2.80, mate.'

Carlton fumbled with his money. 'Oh ... and a packet of crisps an' all.'

'What flavour do you want?'

'Salt an' vinegar...... no, cheese and onion,' corrected Carlton belatedly, forcing the bartender to replace the packet of salt and vinegar.

Taking the cheese and onion crisps, Carlton avoided the eyes of the bartender and handed over his money, before looking round again at the crowd.

So what else had it said in that leaflet, like?

A girl approached the bar and took up a place next to Carlton, trying to catch the attention of the bar staff. She was pretty, like. But not as pretty as the angel. But still really pretty, though.

He watched as she lit a cigarette and craned her head over the bar, letting out a long, curling line of smoke.

Smokin'!

That was somethin' it said in the leaflet. It said you could offer them a fag, or ask for one of theirs, like, or give them your lighter. But even if he *had* any fags, that wouldn't be any good cos she had her own, like. He could ask her for one of hers, then ... but he didn't fuckin' smoke.

He put a handful of crisps in his mouth, then looked thoughtfully down at the packet as he munched.

He could offer her a crisp, like!

But it didn't say anythin' about crisps in the leaflet... maybe cos it was a bad idea, like.

Still waiting to be served, the girl watched the bartender with annoyance. She began looking agitatedly around her, and threw a comment in Carlton's direction. 'They certainly know how to keep you waiting in here, don't they?'

'Yeah ... er ... do you want a crisp, like?' blurted Carlton before she could look away.

'Yeah, don't mind if I do. Thanks, I'm bloody starving.' She reached over to the packet. 'I'm waiting for this bloke to sell me some bloody Pringles.' She looked back to the bar.

'D'yuh like Pringles, then?' asked Carlton.

She turned back to him with a slightly puzzled look. 'Well, yeah. That's why I want to get some.' She turned again to the bar, but continued speaking. 'The problem with Pringles, though, is that they fill them with chemicals so you can't stop eating them.'

She leaned forward as the bartender passed, but he'd been hailed by a girl further down the bar. She muttered, 'Fucking hell!' then turned to Carlton and, without a word, took another crisp from his packet, before resuming her monitoring of the bartender.

'Er ... you can have some more if you want,' said Carlton.

She turned, smiled, took a handful of crisps and turned back to the bar.

She'd smiled at him! She'd fuckin' smiled at him! And she was eatin' his crisps an' all. He didn't need that leaflet. He didn't need any fuckin' leaflets.

'Er ... what flavour Pringles do you like, then?'

'Well, it's got to be sour cream and onion, hasn't it?' she replied without looking round.

'I dunno … I like the barbecue ones, like.'

The girl made no reply, having finally engaged the service of the bartender. Carlton watched as she took the pipe of Pringles, collected her change and began moving away from the bar. Over her shoulder and almost as an afterthought, she called out, 'nice talking to you!' and began picking her way through the crowd back to her friends.

Having had no chance to reply, Carlton had to content himself with staring after her as she went. Her hair was long and lovely, like, and just lookin' at her bum in those trousers was makin' him feel a bit dizzy. But he shouldn't stare at her down there … not when she'd been so kind to him, like. Cos she *had* been kind. That was cos he'd said the right kind of things to her. He'd done all right. Okay, it was just stuff about crisps, but she'd still been into it, like. If those bastards in that workshop were 'ere now and they'd seen that, they wouldn't be fuckin' laughin' now.

He watched as she sat down next to two guys in their mid-twenties.

So those were her friends, were they? Blokes. It *would* be fuckin' *blokes*, wouldn't it? And they were thin, as fuckin' usual, like.... Bastards. And they were helpin' themselves to her Pringles, like, really diggin' in to that pipe… fuckin' pigs… didn't they know she was starvin', like? Can't they see she's waitin' for them to take their hands away so she can have a turn? No, of course not, cos they're too busy, too busy talkin' to their fuckin' selves, like! They're ignorin' her, *ignorin'* her, an' eatin' all her fuckin' Pringles! All right, *now* they're talkin' to her … an' she's laughin' … but now they're talkin' to each other again an' she's got no one to talk to again, like! An' now she's tippin' up that pipe to get the last crumbs out, like, cos them pair o' bastards have scoffed all the fuckin' rest!

How could they just sit there an' ignore her, like… ignore a pretty girl like that? How could you just ignore her an' *eat all her fuckin' crisps?* Fuckin' pigs didn't know … didn't know they were *born*, like.

She'd been havin' a better time when she was talkin' to *him*.

He turned back to the bar, missing the long kiss on the mouth shared by the girl and the guy on her right.

What did it say in that leaflet? See if there was somethin' you could help them with.... Well.... there *was* somethin' to help her with here, wan't there…?... if they'd had all her crisps … then she must still be starvin', like.

His small eyes sought out the bartender, who, being presently unoccupied, acknowledged him with a weary flicker of the eyelids, and approached.

'Erm … can I, can I have some Pringles…please?'

'What flavour?' intoned the barman flatly.

'Erm … sour cream an' onion….'

The bartender fetched a tube of Pringles and Carlton handed over his money.

He turned and looked over again to the girl's table. The two blokes were goin' on to each other again and leavin' her out. This was sound, like … he could make her feel better … he could show them up….

Gripping the pipe of Pringles in one hand and his pint in the other, he began moving away from the bar. However, after a few steps he halted, and stood, blinking, as the noisy crowd seethed around him.... It was what he didn't do, like … goin' up to a girl. What was he *thinkin'*? But, hang on, she'd already talked to him, so it was all right, like, *and* he was helpin' her like it said in the leaflet.

He moved on toward the girl's table. He had no need to attract her attention because for the last few feet she watched his approach, unsmilingly, her face only softening at Carlton's own instinctive smile of self-defence.

'Hello again,' she said guardedly as Carlton came to a stop over her. The two men peered up momentarily from their conversation, casting dubious looks over the newcomer, before once more becoming absorbed in themselves.

'Erm … d'yuh want some Pringles, like?' asked Carlton, thrusting the pipe forward.

The girl peered over the top of the tube, and said, 'But you haven't opened them yet.'

'Well, they're for you, like.'

'I'm sorry?'

'I bought them for you, like. They're sour cream an' onion.'

'Oh … well, thanks but I'm fine.'

She turned her face, and began listening to her companions.

'I just thought I'd get them for you, like, cos you said you were hungry an'-'

'Well, I'm all right, now, thanks,' she replied without looking up.

'But … how can you be?'

'What?'

'I bet you're still hungry. I bet you're still hungry, really, aren't yuh?' persisted Carlton with a loud nervous laugh.

The guy to the girl's right looked up. 'You all right there, mate?'

The girl added, 'Look, I don't want any. Ok*ay*?'

'But I saw yuh, like. Y'didn't -'

'Saw what?' asked the companion.

Carlton addressed his reply to the girl. 'Y'didn't get to eat hardly any of them Pringles y'bought, did yuh? *They* had most of 'em, like, an' I saw, an' so I got some more for -'

'This is really weird,' laughed the girl nervously, drawing back.

'You've been watching us?' asked the guy.

'You pair ate all her fuckin'' crisps an' she was starvin'!'

'Jesus Christ!' said the girl, shaking her head, and keeping her eyes off Carlton.

'I think it might be for the best if you were to piss off, now, mate,' said the friend.

'And ignorin' her! You were ignorin' her! Don't fuckin' ignore her!' shouted Carlton with wet eyes.

'All right, mate, just fucking piss off, now, yeah?'

'Fuckin'… fuckin' skinny wankers!'

'You're the wanker, mate,' said the second guy quietly.

The girl snarled, 'Look, just *fuck off*, you fat bastard!'

A tremor ran through the roll of fat around Carlton's neck, and he raised his glass slightly in an unconscious gesture of aggression.

An arm appeared from behind him, snatched the pint-glass out of his hand and slammed it on the table. At the same time, the pipe of Pringles slipped from his other hand and knocked the girl's wine into her lap. He was gripped from behind. 'All right, *out*, you arsehole!' shouted a shaven-headed bouncer dressed in black.

The girl looked down at her trousers and wailed 'Fucking he-ell!' as Carlton was shifted round by the bouncer, put into an arm-lock and marched off to the door.

'I just wanted, wanted to give her some crisps, that's all, like, that's fuckin' all, don't -' pleaded Carlton in tears, appealing to the side of the bouncer's head as they passed a row of bemused faces at the bar.

'Shut up, twat!'

The bouncer leaned into the door and walked Carlton out into the street. Carlton saw the man's leg come quickly across his own and felt himself pushed from behind so that he tripped over into the gutter.

Standing over him, the bouncer yelled, 'You can count yourself fuckin' lucky I don't get the old bill down 'ere! Now fuck off!'

As the bouncer pushed his way back into the pub, Carlton got slowly to his feet, rubbing the bits of grit from his grazed hands, trying to keep his tears as silent as he could. He stood bent forward slightly, rubbing his hands and wiping ineffectually at a brown mark on his trousers.

A group of female Goths came past, making their way down to Camden, and he watched them go, weeping in silence as they went by, their long, stockinged legs filling him with a new, almost unimaginable level of pain.

FORTY

Lawrence stared down at the brown envelope on the doormat. Here it was, then – the fuckers' final decision. Bending to pick up the letter, he reflected sourly that even if the adjudication panel had now decided in his favour, it would be the hollowest of victories; even if, after considering his appeal, they had reversed their initial decision that he should fuck off, then the restoration of his self-respect, which had been an effect of his suspension, would also be reversed. He should have recognised that in throwing him off, they'd been doing him a favour. He should've fucking seen that, instead of spending two entire days throwing his heart and soul across four pages of A4, like some desperate, misunderstood lover and then sending this masterpiece of eloquent persuasion off with his appeal form. He smirked unhappily. The petition had been a masterpiece all right, considering it had been composed by the stinking, sweating triumvirate in his trousers.

He tramped slowly through to the living room, lit a cigarette and half-heartedly tore open the envelope.

Department of Health and Social Security
Adjudications
Kentish Town Sex Benefit Centre

Kentish Town Road
London

Date: 2.3.04
Reference: 110997
Direct Lines: 0207 972 5518/4673
Fax: 0207 972 5523
email: sexben(a)dhss.gov.uk

Mr. Lawrence Richards
Garden Flat
33 Wellington House Road
Kentish Town
London

Dear Mr. Richards

I'm pleased to inform you that your appeal to the adjudication panel has been successful. Your claim has been re-activated as of the date at the top of this letter.

Yours Sincerely

B. Hatfield

For David Flint
Adjudications Supervisor.

Lawrence drew on his cigarette and allowed the letter to go spinning to the floor.

So. The stupefying, insidious half-solution of the crap sex dole shag once more lay open to him. If he wanted it. But he knew better than that. It was immaterial whether he fucking wanted it or not. The simple fact of its availability meant that he would be taking it.

And of course, how *could* he deny his baby now that she had come back to him?

The lost fortnight was over and she was calling him back to her, through her mouthpieces B. Hatfield and David Flint, calling him back to crawl beneath her concrete skirts and finger once more the white paper triangle of her numbered ticketing system....

He realised he was staring at a blank space on the wall, and was gripped by a sudden terrifying notion that he would never again be able to look away from it. For almost a whole minute, he was utterly lost in the conviction that this single square inch of magnolia paint was destined to form his entire visual landscape up to the moment of his death; more, that it formed the boundary of the entire universe, though it was only ten feet away.

Panicked, he tore his eyes away and began glancing round the room in an effort to suck reassurance from the rest of his surroundings, but no such reassurance came, the sight of his bookshelves, on the contrary, unaccountably making his legs go weak.

Come on, come on, easy does it, now, you fucker ... *easy fucking does it....* Don't. Don't, you mad bastard, there's no reason to ... *no fucking reason to ...*

He looked down at the hand holding the cigarette.

... no ...ah, no....

It was on a screen.

It was just a hand on a fucking screen. Like before. He was just watching everything on a screen! None of it was really there. It was all just on a distant screen he was watching from inside some depersonalisation multiplex of the soul.

Overcome now by a growing nausea, and feeling unable to get out of the chair and over to the ash tray, he managed to crush the cigarette out weakly on the wooden armrest. With both hands he held on to the sides of the chair. Before his eyes, all the things in the room around him one by one began losing their emotional resonance, until each object was reduced to a frightening abstraction. He shut his eyes, only to be confronted by something worse.

Suspended against a strange dull whiteness hung the cruellest abstraction of all: a huge dense wire mesh structure mapping the infinitely subtle triangular scallop-shell sweep of the female pubis, its natural mystery now heightened to unbearable, screaming enigma, pummelling his psyche with the full, shocking, killing force of the brain-splitting void. He opened his eyes again but the object remained, drifting terrifyingly across his vision, the mesh becoming ever denser until it resembled fabric, a huge white triangle hanging in the room. A chain of mad connections flashed instantly through Lawrence's agonised mind. The room-filling hallucination was like a painting by Magritte - Magritte was Belgian - The Belgian girl, Francoise - her hand on his coat ... her hand on his coat - He threw his head about furiously, trying to dispel the image; felt a sickening punch to his temple and gazed down bewildered at his own white-knuckled fist. He lurched to the patio door, his breath ripped up by the violent ravages of panic attack. He pushed open the door and thrust his head outside, only to see the overcast sky fragmented by the cover of skeletal winter trees into a great mosaic of triangular shards of white. He fell back into the flat, gagging. Swallowing hard and glancing wildly about the ceiling, he sat down heavily on the floor, the jolt bringing his vision once more in line with the nameless stack of horizontals that had formerly been his bookshelves. Cowering on the carpet, he shot a look of pure dread at the objects in the room, at the chairs, at the tables, at his hands, every item now completely stripped of any shred of association or meaning. He shut his eyes, and pressed his knuckles into his eyeballs. But waiting behind his eyelids was the triangle, a vast, perfect, inverted equilateral triangle, its colour a single, subtle grade short of pure-white.

... fuck, he was going this time ... he was really ... really going to go over this time....

With a low whimper in his ears, and forcing himself to keep his eyes open, he gradually edged back to the wall, and huddled against it, weakly beating the carpet with slow-motion fists, his whole body shaking as he gazed about him in wide-eyed horror.

FORTY-ONE

Lucinda closed the *Time Out* and made room on the couch for Elaine as the blond facilitator padded over from the kitchenette, coffee in hand.

'You okay, Lucinda?' queried Elaine, a concerned look on her face.

'Yeah ... yeah, why?' replied Lucinda, frowning, reaching for her coffee.

'I don't know ... you look a bit preoccupied. A bit drawn. Is anything up, love?'

'No.'

Elaine was not satisfied, as she indicated with a sceptical tilt of her head.

Lucinda looked around the facilitator lounge, saw that Toby, Charles, Pamela and the others were safely engaged in their own conversations.

'Actually,' began Lucinda, staring ahead of her, and then turning to Elaine, 'actually, I'm thinking of going back to the street.'

'*What?*'

'And not the street exactly. Mayfair. Executive class.'

'Don't, Lucinda. Don't go!'

'I'm not sure that I will, yet,' smiled Lucinda.

'But have you done anything about it? Have you got a contact? It's not always easy getting the big clients, you know. I mean, there's a lot of competition out there, yeah?'

'I know some people ... I don't know, I think I could get a foot in the door.'

'But *why*, Lucinda? It's easier, here ... *safer* ...' She added in a low voice, 'You *know* that.'

'The money's better.'

'But you were the one who used to say that a bit of peace of mind was more important -'

'That was then, Elaine.'

'But what's changed?'

'I want more money ... I'm thinking of finishing my degree. And I can't pay for it if I stay here.'

Elaine sipped her coffee, watching Lucinda's face.

Lucinda continued. 'And besides, if I'm going to put out for a load of ugly slobs I may as well get as much dough for it as I can.'

'But they're not *all* ugly slobs who come in here. Not by a long way.'

'I don't know.... That's all I seem to get these days.'

Elaine put down her coffee and turned full-face to Lucinda. 'Look, babe, just do me a favour and think long and hard about this before coming to a decision, yeah? Remember Jean -'

'Elaine -'

'I'm serious. I don't want to read about you in the papers all messed up on heroin and -'

'I'm not going to start taking heroin, for God's sake!'

'No, well ... just think before you leap, that's all. That's all I'm asking, Lucinda.'

Lucinda simply stared down at her lap, her lowered eyelashes watched by Elaine.

Elaine reached her hand to Lucinda's forehead, and lightly brushed a thick wave of shining black hair away from her temple.

Lucinda squeezed Elaine's hand and smiled tiredly. 'Of course I'll think about it.'

Returning from the filing cabinet, Williams examined again the overweight lump sat waiting for him over at his desk, drawing pleasure from the unappetizing lengths of red hair coiled up on the guy's shoulders and the shocking misalignment of his lower jaw. All told, a rather splendid specimen. All right, chum. Not long now. Just have to wait until she gets back from her coffee break.

Williams sat down, gripped his mouse, and began moving the cursor across the screen of his monitor.

'Er ... excuse me ...' ventured the claimant. 'Why do I have to answer all these questions every time I come in now?'

'Because we're keeping your case under special review.'

'Oh ... right.' The man frowned at the desk for a moment, then looked up. 'But why? Why is my case under special review?'

'Because you've been coming in for years,' replied Williams flatly, staring at his monitor.

'Oh ... right. I see.'

Williams made no further reply, his attention fixed wholly on his monitor, where the cursor hung over the red square box marked 'Lucinda'. The claimant sat uncomfortably, while Williams waited, unmoving, staring at the screen. The box turned green. Instantly, Williams stabbed his mouse and the box turned back to red. He quickly ran off a ticket from the dispenser, and with a flash of his titanium rims, shot a look at the claimant. 'Number 9, then.'

The man took the ticket, got up and walked away from the desk, presenting Williams with a rear view of the lank, red hair hanging down his wide pear-shaped back, the shirt hanging out of the back of his battered leather jacket. Off you go, then. Enjoy her. She's all yours, pally.

He sat back, smiling inwardly. Another prince for you, you bloody bitch. He watched the guy go through the double doors, then leaned forward to cue on the LED counter.

Well, all in all, it was going very well. Even that pain in the neck, Harper, hadn't suspected anything and had just gone along with the note he'd put in the files of all the real walking disaster areas, referring them at all times to his desk. That had been the difficult part. But having got the junior advisors to send all the truly repulsive cases to him, it was a fairly simple matter then to keep them hanging about, asking them questions until her box turned green. And it appeared to be having the desired effect. She was really beginning to look as though she'd had some of the fight knocked out of her! Well, it damn well served her right. Served her ruddy-well right. It was just a shame bloody Briony couldn't *join* her up there.

He sat forward again, preparing to receive the next claimant.

FORTY-TWO

Undaunted by the leaden January sky, the huge press of market-goers surged slowly through the labyrinth of stalls spreading out from Camden Lock, some of the girls displaying their navels, as though by so doing they could somehow hasten the end of winter.

At the end of one narrow alley of stalls and shop-units stood a group of teenage girls slowly turning a revolving stand of hosiery, examining the array of fashion tights and knee-length socks dyed various shades of fluorescent pink and green. Across the way from them, an attractive young woman in a red beret and fishnet tights lingered before a stall of imported carved wooden Buddhas. Between her and the group of girls, the crowds continued to flow and swell: tourists clutching cartons of takeaway noodles, tall blond women with glinting studs in their bellies running their hands across racks of leather bags and musty vintage clothing. At the hosiery stand, one of the teenagers, an elfin girl in white fur boots, selected a pair of hooped pink and orange tights, only to wrinkle up her face and put them back again, to the annoyance of her friends, who were now impatient to move on.

The woman in the red beret also now appeared to be on the point of making a purchase. After exchanging a few words with the stall-holder, she indicated her preferred statuette, and was about to reach into her knowingly kitsch purple handbag, when she paused, glancing off in the direction of some commotion or other somewhere further up the narrow alley of stalls. However, unable to make anything out through the crush of people, she continued with her purchase.

The girls at the hosiery stand had also turned to look, caught by the sound of distant shouting, though their line of sight, too, was blocked by the crowd. Frustrated by the inability to see, the girl in the fur boots turned back to the stand while her friends remained on tip-toe, craning their heads up the alley and swapping comments. It sounded like some bloke was up there yelling something over and over again.

Holding her Buddha in one hand, the woman in the red beret stood waiting for her change, somewhat alarmed by the growing proximity of the hoarse, slurred shouting. Jostled suddenly by a girl backing away from the oncoming commotion, she turned and squinted through the crowd, catching a glimpse of the fat, snarling head of a man yelling something in the face of a petite hippy girl in a floppy hat. The girl stumbled to the side, and the view closed up once more.

All the girls by the hosiery stand were now craning their heads in the direction of the trouble, when the crowd in front of them suddenly parted and a large overweight figure came lumbering toward them. The elfin girl in the fur boots moved sideways and backwards but made the mistake of catching Carlton's eye. He swung his head in her direction and bellowed in her face, the earlier shouted phrase now becoming clear.

'*Give us a fuck!!*'

The girl swallowed in panic, a drop of spittle on her eyelid, and looked to her friends, but Carlton had already bowled past, his small eyes finding the fishnet tights of the woman in the red beret. Snorting like a wounded bull, he half-shuffled, half steamed across to her and thrust his face so far into hers she fell back on the stall, scattering the floor with little round statuettes. In a hoarse, deep-chested roar, the obscene imperative once more rent the air.

Open-mouthed, the girls by the hosiery stand looked on as Carlton moved off down the alley, repeating, like some foul deranged mantra, the same four words in the face of every female in his path. The woman in the red beret also looked on agape, until finally the crowd closed around the lumbering figure and he became lost to view.

FORTY-THREE

'......No, Holly, I didn't go in today...' sighed Carla into her mobile, her hair hanging forward as she sat cross-legged on the floor, making a long looping doodle in blue biro on the cover of a dog-eared pad of A4.

'......Because I'm going to stop going in altogether. I'm going to stop signing, *that's* why........'

She frowned and looked up at the ceiling, the phone pressed to her ear.

'..........Because it's the only way my Dad's ever going to speak to me again!.............Holly -.........Look, I'm *not* letting them boss me about!..........It's my decision, okay?...........'

She leaned forward again and continued doodling as she listened, occasionally rolling her eyeballs at the ceiling.

'.......What do you mean, they don't respect me? You know, maybe they're right? Maybe it's me who's not respecting *them?* I mean -........'

She bit her lip and fell silent, glaring down at the looping pen in her hand. Suddenly, she furiously increased the pressure, tearing a hole in the cover of the pad.

'..........Look, they're *my* parents, just let me deal with it how-.........I'm not being ungrateful!.............look, you can be pretty overbearing, sometimes, you know, Holly! Just -...........Right!............

Fine, let's just -............Let's just not talk about it any more, then...............All *right,* all *right! God!*..................I don't know, I might go out tonight................Some friend of Amanda's, someone on her course, reckons she can get us into some posh club. It doesn't really sound like my kind of place, but -..............I'm not sure, Holborn or Bloomsbury or somewhere.................Well, if I'm not signing, I've got to start seeing what's going on in the real world, haven't I?................Well, no time like the present, as they say......... ....Yeah, yeah, but to be honest, I am a bit nervous, though. I haven't been out for nearly two months. But I don't know, maybe it'll be good for me, you know?............Why don't you come along? Clare really liked you and -...............Well, what are you going to *do?* Just stay on the sex dole *forever?*..................No, I'm not going out on the pull exactly, but ... if there's anyone nice, well, you never know, maybe it's time to give it a try again, I mean, they can't *all* be frontals, I suppose.............I'm *not* telling you what to do!............. And I'm not *criticizing* you! God!...............And it's not just because *of my Dad, Holly!* -..............Well, because I think I really should, should try to do without it, I mean -..............But I'm not getting at *you!* You do what you want!...............Right, and you're sure you don't want to come tonight?............Okay, see you Tuesday, then...... ....Bye.'

Carla gripped the handrail of the escalator with a small, mittened hand, and began moving up to the station entrance, peering out from beneath her wary brow at the endless file of people descending opposite her. It was weird how when she'd been small she used to love deep stations like this. How she and Andrew used to love trying to stand perpendicular to the handrail of the escalator, to make all the people on the other side look as though they were bending backwards! What did Andrew use to call it? Yes, the 'gravity alteration game', that was it. It used to drive their Mum up the wall when they did that. And then they'd rush back up to have another go. But now, she just wanted to get out. It'd been a long time since she'd used the tube. She wasn't ... used to it any more. And she'd better concentrate when it came to stepping off.

As she came up to the ticket hall, she held the rail tightly, and, looking at the floor, raised her foot and stepped forward onto the concourse.

Now, where was Amanda? Ah, there she was, by the entrance.

Carla walked quickly over to a tall, yet somewhat shapeless girl with a blond bob, who turned at Carla's approach.

'Carla, hi!'

'Hi!' replied Carla, as Amanda embraced her.

'It's so good to *see* you! You shouldn't hide yourself away so much!' laughed Amanda, finally letting go of Carla's shoulders.

'I know, well, I'm here now,' smiled Carla. 'How are you?'

'Great, thanks, but what about you? Look at you! As gorgeous as ever!' gushed Amanda, as they turned and headed to the street.

'What's the name of this club again?' asked Carla, ignoring the compliment, as they stepped out into the night air.

'Actually I don't know. I've forgotten!' laughed Amanda, a little too loudly it seemed to Carla. 'I've only got the address. But it's not far. So tell me. What've you been up to?'

'Well, nothing much. The shop. Been working on a few songs ...' She became distracted by the sight of her reflection in the dark plate glass facade of a looming finance building. God, her nose. If only she could just push it a little to the left. Fighting an impulse to put her finger to her nose, she reminded herself she was supposed to be in the middle of a conversation, and looked at Amanda.

'But anyway, what about you? How's it going at work?'

'Oh, the usual. They're still driving me up the wall. Well, it's that Trevor, mainly...'

Carla watched the pavement move beneath her feet, and tried to listen to the diatribe Amanda proceeded to deliver against her workmates. However, the pavement proved more absorbing, and after a few minutes Carla was ashamed to realise that she'd barely taken in a word Amanda had said. But then again, Amanda never *really* listened to anything *she* said, either.

As Amanda came to the end of her rant, Carla murmured an appropriate-sounding 'God,' and shook her head slowly.

'Yeah, I know,' said Amanda, 'Anyway, we're here!'

Looking up, Carla saw that they were approaching the shining black front door of a four-storey Edwardian terrace building. A smart couple were making their way inside, passing an attractive blond girl in a black fur waiting on the step. The girl saw them and called out, 'Hi!'

‘Hiya!’ called Amanda as she approached and embraced the girl. Amanda broke the hug, turned and presented Carla. ‘Carla, this is Ulla! Ulla, Carla!’

‘Pleased to meet you,’ smiled Carla, shaking the girl’s hand.

‘And I am very happy to meet you too!’ said the girl in what seemed to Carla to be a thick Scandinavian accent.

‘So!’ exclaimed Amanda, looking from one girl to the other. ‘Here we are, then!’

Ulla laughed apologetically to Carla, ‘Sorry, but we have to wait for my boyfriend. We cannot get in without him, you see. He has the membership.’

‘That's all right,’ said Carla. ‘Anyway, thanks for inviting me.’

‘No, no, I always like meeting Amanda's friends!’

Amanda addressed Ulla. ‘Oh, before I forget, I brought the notes from that lecture last week. I've put them on a floppy for you.’

‘Oh, great, great! Thank you, Amanda!’

As Amanda rooted through her handbag, Carla became aware of a car pulling up to a stop across the road, slamming into reverse gear and backing into a parking space.

‘Ah, he's here!’ exclaimed Ulla, taking the floppy disc from Amanda.

Carla watched guardedly as the door of the red sports car opened and Ulla’s boyfriend stepped into the street. As he closed the door and came over to them, Carla's first impression was that everything about him was shocking: his extreme good looks, his teeth, his smile, his blue eyes - visible as blue even from this distance. Every feature was sort of freakishly perfect. And his smile.... It seemed as if it were somehow moving ahead of him, like an advance guard, clearing everything out of his path, as though he cleaved his way through life with it. Like ... a snow-plough or something. But no, that was a stupid image! Better to stick with the advance guard idea.

‘Hi, baby,’ called Ulla, taking two steps toward him as he came up to them.

‘Hi, darling,’ he said, slipping an arm around Ulla’s waist, and kissing her hard on the mouth. Then, as he drew back from the kiss, Carla was astonished to find the crystal blue eyes boring deep into her own.

'Hello,' he smiled graciously, ignoring Amanda's attempt to greet him.

Ulla gestured to Carla. 'Carla, this is my boyfriend, Sacha. Sacha, this is Carla.'

'Hello,' smiled Carla, putting her hand forward to be shaken. However, her strategy of avoiding any unwelcome kiss met with failure, as Sacha deftly twisted her hand round and up to his lips.

'Delighted to meet you, Carla.'

Carla kept smiling, though her discomfort was plain in her creased brow. She drew her hand back quickly, but he went on looking into her eyes. Not wanting to be seen to actually look away, she concentrated on some harmless part of his cheek until he was finished with her.

She watched as Amanda effected her greeting, and the group began moving towards the door. Sensing that Sacha's head was once more turning in her direction, Carla made sure she was looking at her shoes as they entered the carpeted foyer of the club.

Sat in the round sofa of the circular booth Sacha had picked out for them, Carla quietly sipped her wine, content to observe the surroundings and let Ulla and Amanda soak up Sacha's conversation. From where she was sitting at the far end of the couch, she couldn't really hear him anyway, which suited her fine. Before she'd drifted from what he was saying, he'd been going on about what a great rower he'd been at university. Why did guys like that still need to show off even when they'd got a really attractive girlfriend? And just look at Amanda.... Lapping it all up. Wow, so the guy could row a boat. Off you go, then. Row, row, row your boat, merrily down the stream....

She looked out at the well-heeled little groups occupying the other booths, at the slender debutantes standing around the bar, a lot of them actually looking just bored or miserable. Some of those people looked absolutely *deadly*. Deadly boring and deadly effective at whatever ruthless business it was they got up to in the day. What was she *doing* here? What exactly was supposed to be the big attraction of this place? She wanted to go home, but that would be rude to Ulla, who was actually really nice ... and she was probably being too hard on her boyfriend, who was probably okay, too, really. At least he'd stopped trying to catch her eye now. And it wasn't every day you got a chance to see how the 'elite' managed to struggle through their evenings. She should just sit back and take in the spectacle, see it as a kind of anthropological field trip. Of course, if she really concentrated, really concentrated on her observation, she'd probably find enough material here for a whole album of songs. But which no one would ever listen to, of course. Still, that really thin girl over there, so full of apparent life whenever her friends are talking to her or when she's talking to them, but who looks so lost when they leave her out, you could really imagine Joni writing something about her. In fact everybody in here looked like they'd stepped out of an English version of *The Hissing of* -

'I said, what do *you* think, Carla?'

She turned to find herself looking straight into Sacha's smiling eyes, trained on her from across the table.

'Sorry?'

'Come on, Carla!' giggled Amanda.

'Sorry, I haven't really been able to hear what you've been saying.'

'We were *saying* ... - oh, never mind,' replied Amanda, shaking her head and reaching for her drink.

Carla looked at her, missing Sacha's steady observation of herself.

Glancing from Carla's faint scowl to Amanda's expression of mild irritation, Ulla took Amanda's hand, smiled at Carla and got to her feet.

'Come on, let's have a dance.'

Amanda allowed herself to be pulled up, a wide grin on her face.

'Are you coming, Carla?' asked Ulla.

'Er, no ... thank you. But you guys go ahead,' she smiled for Ulla's sake, including Sacha in her reply.

'No, it's a bit early for me yet...' said Sacha. 'But have a good workout, girls,' he laughed, as Amanda and Ulla squeezed past.

Carla watched the back of Sacha's head as his eyes followed the girls to the dance floor. Go on. Go with them. You don't have to sit here with me.

She just had time to avert her eyes as he swung his head round to face her.

'So, Carla,' he said, sipping his champagne. 'What game are you in?'

'You mean, what do I do?' replied Carla, reaching for her drink, an unconscious tactic to delay looking at his face.

'Yes,' smiled Sacha broadly. 'I mean, what do you do?'

'Well, I work in a shop -'

'Dear oh dear oh dear!' said Sacha, his eyes wide. 'But, if you don't mind my saying so ... your beauty and your intelligence clearly mark you out for something a little ... better than that.'

'Well, that's very kind of you. But -' - should she say this? Yes, why not – 'But why do you say I'm intelligent? I mean, we haven't - I don't think we've spoken enough for you to get any idea of my level of intelligence.'

'Good point. Good point. However, it's quite plain simply from the way you hold yourself ... and from the wonderful way the muscles of your face move. Like now. Look at that.'

Carla gave him a dubious look, and reached for her glass again, now suddenly worried that her last remark might give him the idea that she *regretted* the fact they hadn't spoken much yet.

'So, Carla, what is it? If you're stuck in a shop -'

'I'm not stuck in a shop.'

'You're stuck in a shop. What's the story? You have a passion, don't you, Carla? It's written all over your face. Passion. And it's not for working in a shop! What is it? Art? Acting?' He sat back and regarded her. 'No ... it's music, isn't it?'

'Actually, it is, yes,' replied Carla, looking up and trying not to appear too impressed by the lucky guess.

'So how's it going?'

'I'm stuck in a shop. How do you *think* it's going?' frowned Carla into her glass.

Sacha grinned and lit a cigarette. 'I could put you in touch with some people if you like. That is, if you're any good. Are you any good?'

'That's not for me to say, is it?'

'Come on, you're going to have to do better than that! If *you* don't say it, no one else is going to. I'll ask you again. Are you any good?'

Carla held Sacha's look. The guy was irritating, but he was right. She *needed* to be spoken to like this.

'Actually I am. I'm *bloody* good.'

'I'm glad to hear it. You know, I'd like to listen to something at some point.' He leaned back. 'If that's all right with you.'

Carla's eyes dropped from his to the safer region of his cheekbone. He obviously fancied himself rotten, but maybe he *could* help. No, this was what she had to do. Like Holly was always saying. Get out there. Take advantage of every opportunity that came along. Well, here she was - out there. And here was an opportunity. Of sorts anyway.

She reached into her bag. 'Actually, you can hear something right now, if you like. Oh, but I don't know if you'll be able to hear over the music in here. Maybe if you press the phones right into your ears.'

'You have something on you? Excellent. I'd love to. Let's give it a try.'

'It's a pretty ropey demo, though.'

Carla handed over her CD player, and watched as Sacha pressed the phones to his ears and began listening. He made an appreciative nod, and heard the track through, Carla watching his face despite herself for more signs of approval. Finally, he handed the player back, with a deferential nod.

'You've certainly got something there.'

'Thanks ... er ... so you know someone in the business, then, do you?'

Sacha gave her a brilliant smile, and paused before answering. The pause was so long it seemed to Carla as though he were teasing a child by withholding a bag of sweets.

'I know one or two A&R people, yes.'

'Really" said Carla in a low register, immediately annoyed with herself for sounding so impressed.

'Yes. Plus I know a couple of guys who run various nights in town. If you like, we could -'

Ulla had appeared behind Sacha and now flung her arms around his neck. 'Come on, baby. Come for a dance now.'

Carla watched as he laughed and craned his head back to be kissed.

'Carla, come too!' invited Ulla, as Sacha got to his feet.

'Oh ... no, thanks, it's all right. Maybe later.'

'Back in a moment,' said Sacha with a significant look, before moving off with Ulla to the dance floor, where a limply gyrating Amanda was inspired to fresh vigour by their arrival. Carla observed them for a while, almost embarrassed by Amanda's transparent efforts to impress, and reluctantly admiring the sharp, powerful movements of Sacha – he looked like a professional dancer.

A presence lowered itself into the seat beside her. 'Hello, hello, he*llo*....'

She turned her head quickly.

A large middle-aged man was peering at her through heavy-lidded eyes. 'Forgive me, but I just had to come over...'

Carla looked away and reached for her glass. 'Well, there's somebody sitting here. They won't be long.'

'That's all right. It won't take me long ... it won't take me long to tell you what I ... what I came over to tell you...'

Carla looked ahead and sipped her wine slowly, as though by keeping the glass to her lips she could avoid replying.

The man's head suddenly lurched closer. '...You're bloody sexy, aren't you…? You do know that, don't you?' The head pulled back. ' ... *Fucking* sexy...'

Putting the glass down, Carla bit her lip, and remained staring ahead. 'Right, I see. Thank you very much. But I think my friends will be back in a minute.'

'... No, it's all right, you see ... I'm not going to take up any of your ... any of your time, I just wanted to tell you that you are the most beautiful girl in the house ... absolutely fucking beautiful...'

Carla stared at the table, considering whether to get up and leave. Maybe that was a bit drastic. The bastard would go in a minute. She reached for her glass again, saw that her hand was nevertheless trembling with anger. Well, if he didn't leave in a minute, she could always escape to the toilet.

'... You've almost finished that.... Let me get you a top-up...'

'I thought you said you weren't going to take up my time.'

'... Let me just get you a little top-up.... Can't have you running dry, now, can we? Tell you what. We'll have a drop of the fizzy stuff... Now, where's that champagne waitress...?'

Just *clear off,* you *bastard!*

'Look, I'd rather just wait on my own for my friends.'

'... What, do they have exclusive rights ... exclusive rights or something, eh? ... No, no, I insist that you have a ... drink.... After all, we haven't even been introduced - '

'She just told you she'd rather wait on her own for her friends.'

Carla looked round, filled with relief to see Sacha standing over the man.

'Ah ... ah ... and you're one of them, I suppose....Well, let's not fall *out,* heh, heh.... I only came over to say hello to this *charming* creature ... now why-'

'Oh, it's "charming", now, is it?' said Carla fiercely, her voice shaking. 'Before, it was "fucking sexy".'

'Well... yes, well -' spluttered the man.

'Will you leave our booth please?' said Sacha, his smile edged with violence.

Carla peered up at him, oddly thrilled to see his aggressive confidence wielded in her defence.

'... Look, I'm sorry I spoke the way I -'

'I don't think you realise your place, do you?' smiled Sacha. 'So let me spell it out for you. *You,* you see ... *you* are a foul, worn-out piece of refuse. And foul, worn-out pieces of refuse do not mix with charming creatures.' He held out his arm, indicating the way out from the booth.

It seemed to Carla a slightly strange thing to say, but it appeared to do the trick.

The man said nothing, merely rubbed his eye for a moment, and then slowly raised himself from the seat, as though the insult had reminded him of some solemn truth. As he passed Sacha, he paused, and said in a subdued voice, almost in deference, '...the girl was on her own - I just thought I'd...' He dropped his eyes and moved on.

'Thanks,' said Carla, looking up as Sacha moved round to sit down next to her.

'Don't mention it,' replied Sacha, lowering himself into the booth.

Making space for him, Carla observed his profile, for the first time half-consciously finding something to admire there. Thank God he'd come back when he did.

Sacha caught her glance, parted his lips in an all-powerful smile, and reached for his drink. Taking a large mouthful, he replaced the glass and picked up his cigarettes, turning to Carla once more.

'You know, I've been thinking. Why don't you give me that CD of your music now? I mean, why wait? I could start putting it around a few people tomorrow, if you like.'

'Well ... I don't know.... If you're sure....'

'No problem.'

'Well... okay, thank you! It'd be brilliant if you could.'

'Like I said, no problem,' repeated Sacha.

Carla drew the disc from her bag and handed it over, watching as he slipped it into his jacket pocket. She quickly put her hand forward. 'But be careful with it. I mean I've got other copies but that's the best version.'

'I'll guard it with my life,' assured Sacha, as Amanda and Ulla returned from the dance floor.

Carla listened with growing fatigue as Amanda, leaning past her so as to be heard by Ulla and Sacha, related yet another sexual misadventure from her past. Sipping her wine, Carla allowed her eyes to drift to where Sacha's hand was resting on Ulla's leg. She had to admit he had interesting fingers, strong but articulate, and yet there was something disturbing about the actual hand. Something stone-like. The way it was just immobile there on that girl's leg somehow seemed to give it great weight. As though it weighed several tons. She imagined the weight on her own leg and flinched inwardly, though keeping her eyes on the hand. Why was she staring at his hand? Did she fancy him? No. No, she didn't. Her gaze flitted to his crotch and then quickly away. Because what would he be like in bed? Pig-like, probably. No, definitely pig-like! The hand told you that. *Everything* told you that. Still, Ulla seemed to really like him, though; she was always touching him and fondling him.

She watched as Ulla ran her fingers across his neck, and felt a strange, unexpected wave of jealousy. But not because of Sacha, she realised thankfully, but because of the air of ... *fulfillment* Ulla gave off. That was what Ulla had that she wanted, and, her eyes dropping to Ulla's jeans, Carla allowed herself to imagine a similar fulfillment in her own body. It was so intense that she underwent a sudden, vicarious clenching between her legs, and had to put her glass down, her frustration threatening to overwhelm her.

She twisted suddenly in her seat, crushingly aware of everything that was missing from her life. Damn it! *Damn it!*

Putting her fingernail to her mouth - something she never did when out - she forced herself to turn and listen to Amanda's prattle, all the while pressing her legs tightly together under the table.

Glancing at Sacha, she was shocked to see him looking right at her. And God, she still had her nail between her teeth! She dropped her hand and turned quickly back to Amanda, filled now with a desperation to go home. But she'd have to wait for Amanda to stop talking first, so she could decently make her excuses and leave. Come on. Stop. Just stop talking, Amanda. Come on, it's quite easy. Just put your lips together and then don't move them again for a while.

As if by magic, Amanda concluded her speech and sat back in her seat, tittering.

'Well,' smiled Carla, after waiting a respectable five seconds, 'I think I'm going to head off, actually.'

'You're not going already, are you?' frowned Amanda.

'Yeah, I don't know, I'm really tired. Are you coming?'

'No, the night's young, Carla. I'm staying.'

'Okay, well....'

'But you can't walk on your own to the tube,' threw in Sacha.

'I'll be okay.'

'No, no, I'll run you round in the car.'

'No, it's all right.... I don't want to drag you away.'

'It won't take a moment.'

'Go on, Carla,' urged Ulla, 'Better to be safe, no?'

'I insist,' added Sacha.

'Well ... okay. Thanks.'

Picking up her bag, Carla rose and smiled at Ulla, 'Well, it was nice meeting you.'

Ulla stood and kissed Carla on the cheek. 'See you again soon.'

'Yes, I hope so. Well, Amanda, I'll give you a call soon, okay?'

'Yeah, take care,' replied Amanda, as they shared a brief embrace.

'See you in a minute,' said Sacha, kissing Ulla, and rising from his seat.

Carla waited for him, and then with a final goodbye to the others headed for the exit, Sacha one step behind her.

Carla pulled the fur trim of her coat into the car, closed the door and lay back awkwardly in the passenger seat, slung so low she felt as though she were lying on her back in the road.

'Comfortable?' enquired Sacha, as the engine purred to life.

Carla nodded and peered out of the side window as they pulled away from the curb. A nod would do. Well, he'd become pretty uncommunicative himself as they'd come down the stairs into the street - though he'd been smiling away as ever, of course. But he hadn't really wanted to talk much more about the music, just kept assuring her that he'd definitely call some guy called Nigel. Actually, he hadn't really wanted to talk about *any*thing, and had just shrugged off her compliment about Ulla.

She watched the orange-lit pavement slide past the window. Still, it wouldn't do to actually appear ungrateful. Better think of something to say to him.

Turning from the window, she peered cautiously at the side of his head, a silent, smiling silhouette crowned by the forward stab of his sharp forelock and backlit by the orange glow from the empty street. Why wasn't *he* saying anything? He was just sat there staring ahead and smiling.

Her eyes drifted to a pool of light moving down across the instrument panel, following it till it encroached on some pulsing thing near the steering column. In shock, she realised she was looking at the swollen head of Sacha's huge rearing penis, craning up well past the lower rim of the steering wheel.

Without looking round, he broke into laughter. 'I thought you'd never notice!'

Carla removed her glance to the door handle, swallowing hard, fighting a sensation of drowning in thick vomit.

Sacha laughed. 'I don't want to sound immodest, but it's not exactly a dick you could *miss*, is it?'

Carla found the strength to reply.' I wonder it doesn't interfere with your concentration.'

'Good point! I'd better pull over, then.'

'Just take me to the station, please,' demanded Carla, aware now of the quivering in her voice.

'No, in view of the road safety concerns you've just raised, I think I'd better pull over.'

As the car slowed, Carla got ready to try the door handle, but, in sudden fear of violence, prepared herself to be as discreet as possible in case he'd locked it.

As the car drew up, she pulled quietly on the handle, but in vain, her panic increasing with the realisation that they had come to a stop in a desolate back street.

She wanted to scream at him to open the door, but imagined the back of his hand crushing her face.

'Well, here we are...' said Sacha softly, shifting round in his seat, the side of his face edged by the orange light falling from the streetlight onto the dashboard.

God, oh god. Keep him talking, *keep him talking.*

'What about your girlfriend?' Carla heard herself say in a choked mouse-like voice.

'I'm sacking her.'

'So she's not actually "sacked" yet, then?' replied Carla, showing anger despite her fear.

'No, that moment comes with my first glimpse of your knickers. A moment long overdue, but a deliciously incipient one....' he chuckled. 'Nothing like the coming moment!'

Carla said nothing, and, shaking, forced herself to scan the dashboard for the door-lock, keeping her eyes from the brutal lump rubbing up against the steering-wheel, but nevertheless perceiving his hand moving up and down in the darkness.

'No, with my first look at your pants, Ulla gets her p45.'

Carla found the door-lock, but realised she'd never reach it *and* get back to the door without him grabbing her. She could hit him really hard in his disgusting prick - but no, he'd just kill her, he'd just kill her -

Now he was whispering. 'Isn't it the most thrilling thing in the world, Carla? To be on the threshold? And you and I are most certainly on the threshold.... Show me your pants, Carla, and for you, just for you, I'll throw Ulla on the scrapheap....'

With his left hand he reached toward her. And then the weight of it was on her leg; the ten-ton weight, just as she'd imagined, now pressed down on her thigh. Her breathing was broken in her ears, and a scream was building in her throat. If she let it out, someone might come, but more likely, she'd just get the weight of his other hand across her face. And then, as though for the first time, she realised it was really going to happen. She was going to be raped. She was overcome by a strange sense of knowing all her life that one day this moment would come. That it had always been coming.

As Sacha brought his other hand over and began pushing her coat up her legs, she lashed out violently, knocking his hand from her leg with a wildly flailing arm, and catching him in the shin with the heel of her boot.

He pulled back slightly and sighed. 'Now, come on. Don't mess me about. I would remind you that this was your idea.'

'*What?*' said Carla, shaking, pulling down her coat.

Sacha sat back in his own seat. 'It was your idea to leave the club.'

'Look. I just wanted to go home. *You* asked me if I wanted a lift!'

'Little looks,' said Sacha from the darkness.

'What?'

'What about all the little looks, Carla?'

'This is completely crazy! Crazy and insane!'

'Come on. You know the game.'

'What are you *talking* about?'

'You've been playing it all night.'

'Let me go. Just let me *go*!'

'I'm not stopping you.'

'Why have you locked this door, then?'

'For your travelling comfort and safety, of course,' said Sacha, unlocking the door. 'Why else would I lock it?' he added with an undertone of anger, taking his cigarettes from his jacket.

Carla gripped the door-handle. She could go.

Sacha lit up. 'You'd bloody-well better not be insinuating what I think you're insinuating,' he breathed, exhaling.

She paused.

'Well, why did you stop here, then? In this back street with no one around?'

'You'd rather fuck in Oxford Street?'

'I don't want to fuck *at all!*'

'You could've fooled me,' said Sacha.

Her hand still on the door handle, Carla fell silent, trying to work out if she was in some way to *blame* for what had just happened. In confusion, she peered up at Sacha, meeting his eyes. He wasn't smiling.

'Go on, you little fool, get out.'

He leaned forward, pulled her hand from the handle and opened the door himself.

'Hang on, I don't know this street -'

'You should've thought about that before you accused me of attempted rape.'

With a feeling of shame, which she knew was insane, Carla began pulling herself up out of the seat.

'Oh, and before you go, two things. Firstly, in future, keep your eyes in your head if you're not grown up enough to follow through on what you start. That way you'll save serious players a lot of wasted time and trouble.'

She stepped numbly out of the car into the street.

'And secondly.'

He smiled. 'Don't, as they say, give up the day job.'

The CD flashed from Sacha's hand and went skittering across the pavement as he pulled the door to and sped off down the road.

In a daze, Carla slowly walked over to where the disc had come to a stop by the kerb. She stooped, picked it up and held it in her hand, staring down at her miserable reflection in the scratched mirror surface. Stupid, stupid, STUPID!

She flung the disc back to the pavement, where it bounced once on its edge and rolled to a stop several yards down the street.

Her eyes filling with tears, she ran over to where it had come to rest, stooped again to retrieve it a second time, and stuffed it into her bag.

Hurriedly drawing herself upright, she felt a sharp thrill of fear and gave a sudden wild look about the street. With the threatening silence of the dismal, empty backstreet suddenly pushing the nightmare of Sacha to the back of her mind, she broke into a panicked run toward the light of a busier street at the far end of the road.

As the platform picked up speed, and the rushing posters and benches were replaced by black void, Carla sat staring at the chain of woollen rabbits circling her mittened wrist. She looked up, caught her own frowning reflection in the window of the tube train, and dropped her eyes back to her mittens.

Why had she come out? *Why?!* She should've stayed at home. Where it's safe. Better to be safe. Ha. Like Ulla had said.

She would have *been* at home, as well, if it hadn't been for *them.* If they *cared,* if they *really* cared, they would have respected the reasons why she'd been signing on, or at least tried to under*stand* them, but no. No, not them. No, they'd rather act like they have no daughter! They'd rather send her out to be raped on the front seat by some bastard *bastard animal!!*

Yes, to all intents and purposes, they had *sent* her into the clutches of that pig bastard tonight.

Well, they could just bloody go to *hell!* If she wanted to claim sex benefit, then it was none of their *bloody business!*

She tasted wool in her mouth, and pulled her hand away, letting it fall heavily in her lap.

Why, why hadn't she gone *in* today?! She should've gone in. She shouldn't have *bloody stopped signing!*

But … she hadn't actually *told* them anything at the centre. She hadn't actually signed off on any official paper or anything … she *could* just go in tomorrow and say she'd forgotten to go in, that she'd made a mistake and got the days wrong or something. Hadn't Holly done that once and it had been all right? Yes, she'd do that. She'd go in tomorrow -

If Andy Pandy baby brother had been there in that street, that pig bastard would have been sorted out.

Again, the wool was between her teeth, and again she pulled her hand away.

What had *she* said last time they'd argued on the phone…? 'I didn't bring you into this world so you could waste yourself on that living death!'

Well, if this was bloody life out here, she'd take the living death any day of the week. Every other Tuesday to be precise.

The mitten went back up to her mouth, and this time, it didn't come down.

FORTY-FOUR

Lawrence weakly pulled the front door closed behind him and stepped out into the cold air. He felt the deep chill, though faintly, as though it were coming to him from three lifetimes away. He trudged slowly, almost gingerly, up the steps, realising from the experience of the last few weeks that the dissociation from the cold was in fact the unwelcome herald of another little psychotic wave rolling in. He mentally braced himself and tried to carry on as best he could, concentrating hard on the placement of each footfall. He was halfway up the steps to the pavement when it broke over him: the sickening vertiginous sense of never having existed at all.

He knew it would probably pass, that it was just another low aftershock from the weeks of crushing depersonalisation, but the feeling was still cruel enough to keep him halted on the steps. He told himself it was all nothing but an illusory blip, that he was momentarily caught suspended between modes of perception, but the truth was he was struggling to ride it out. He fumbled for his cigarettes and lit up, anxious to feel the heat in his chest, to use the burn in his lungs as evidence that he did in fact possess some physical central core.

He inhaled evenly, and, calming slightly, took the remaining steps up to the pavement, but, catching sight of a weathered fire hydrant, became convinced that if he existed at all, then he and this object formed one indivisible unity spreading out across the whole of time and space.

His breathing threatened to race out of control.

Tearing his eyes from the hydrant, he tried to regulate himself with long, measured inhalations of cigarette smoke. The strategy worked; he found himself taking long strides and making progress down the street.

Settling shakily back into himself, he reflected on the banal orthodoxy of death as the only certainty. To get to death you first needed life, existence, and as events had just shown, how could you actually be *certain* of *that* shit? And if life was not a certainty, then neither was death.... Descartes reckoned he'd proved his existence by the mere fact of his ability to think ... but right now, it seemed to Lawrence that proof of *his* existence was more to be found in the fact that, despite the pitiable state of him, his balls were *even now* still capable of dragging him down the road to the fucking sex dole.

Descartes was full of shit. Fuck thought. Fuck thinking. All that *thinking* stuff was just a glorious red herring. Because what, in evolutionary terms, was the *original purpose* of thinking, of *intelligence*? How had it fucking come about in the first place? Well, sadly, hadn't it come about as just another tool for the survival and procreation of the organism? For that and no other reason? Unhappily, all the evidence pointed to this sorry conclusion. And the sheer *strength* of the sex instinct was exhibit fucking A; the intelligence was utterly powerless to govern it (witness him now!). Intelligence had been irrevocably placed in the service of survival and procreation ... and of the two, procreation was king, because what was survival? Simply a means of hanging around long enough to deliver sperm to egg.

All of which led to the nightmare conclusion that intelligence, and with it, all higher consciousness, had been spawned by the blind, mechanistic compulsion to reproduce; which meant in turn that all endeavour in the field of higher reflection and creativity, all poetry, art and music, all philosophy, all *insight*, the whole mighty canon of human thought was nothing but a meaningless by-product: the foaming dribbled froth hanging from the mouth of the slavering, mad bastard dog.

And it all fit. It all fit. Because look, as soon as you reached an age when you couldn't fuck any more, when you couldn't shoot a good arc of white piss any more, the universe ordered your *destruction*. It wasn't interested in any *thoughts* you may still have to contribute!! Why should it be? It never cared a single, solitary damn about any idea or perception you articulated while alive, just as it never gave a single, isolated shit about the insights and achievements of Plato, Lao Tzu, Shakespeare, Michelangelo or Beethoven. As with them, the only thing it had ever wanted out of you was your *jism.* That was its sole interest in you. And when you've shot your lot, that's it for you, pal, crawl off and die, and take your tenth symphony with you, we're not fucking interested, because your creativity, your intelligence, your *sentience,* was never anything more than a tool in the service of showering the planet with your seed.

He let his shoulder collide with the wall as he walked, and with such force he felt his skin grazing through his coat. For several yards he marched on, leaning hard into the brickwork, his hands in his pockets.

... and the triangle ... that little triangular flash between their legs ... the white triangle ... finally ... in the last analysis ... when all was said and done ... what *was* that fucking white triangle if not a fucking signpost, a spunk-white arrow pointing down to death?

He made white-knuckled fists of his hands, heard his breath coming almost in snorts.

His right hand encountered a ball of screwed-up paper in his pocket. His white triangular ticket from last time he'd gone in. He pulled it out and chucked it in the road, his face contorting wildly.

...and white was the colour of the seed, and white – spunk white - was the colour of life, the *blankness* of life, the true symbol of a vacuity for which black was too strong. The vapidity of all existence was to be expressed not in the velvet depths of the void, but in the lactescent highlight on a cooling drop of generative fluid; in every haphazard, pale, blurted streak ever summoned by a despotic wedge of nylon; in the colour of semen, which was the colour of impenetrable cloud, the colour of the cataracts in the eyes of the dead.

He heard a bitter gallows laugh, and hunched up his shoulders against the wind as he made the turn into Kentish Town Road, bringing into view the dismal glass-and-panel structure of the sex benefit centre just beyond the garage. He approached, staring grimly at the pollution-streaked concrete support pillars.

Jesus *Christ.* No wonder he'd begun finally to lose it completely. No wonder he'd been breaking apart and depersonalising to fuck knew where and back again....

... if you ... if you acted against your nature ... aha, *no*.... If you acted against what you knew to be your *best judgment*, as he had by ever coming here in the first place, then it was always, *always* bound to fucking do for you in the end.

He passed the garage, his tired eyes on the faded blue panels lining the ground floor of the three-storey building ahead.

Reaching the entrance, he lifted a pale, thin hand from his coat pocket, and slowly pushed open the door.

A low grunt sounded in Lucinda's ear, accompanying the tell-tale culminating pulse inside her. Well, thank Christ for that! She sensed an immediate diminishing of the guy's dick, and began shifting awkwardly underneath him, impatient for him to be off her. She gave him a few seconds, then began forcing him upwards.

'Er... yeah, all right... sorry, love...' said the man, easing his considerable weight upright, his eyes on his fat, meaty hand as he scratched his hairy belly.

Lucinda stared at him in disgust as he squinted down at the dangling condom and reached for his glasses. He put them on slowly, the sticking plaster holding them together at the bridge once again coming stupidly into position in the middle of his porridge-like face.

He tugged ineffectually for a moment at the condom, before reaching up to lay a few strands of specially-grown hair hanging from the side of his head back across the top of it. As if to cover his embarrassment, he gave Lucinda a grin, allowing her for the first time to see the hideous state of his teeth.

She felt her fury grow, and watched him with burning eyes as he looked down and began tugging again at the condom, now dangling from a penis which had shrunk to little more than a small cone of concertina foreskin, overhung by a wide pasty ledge of stomach.

She stood up quickly and pulled on her robe, firing a withering dark look down on the top of the guy's head. How many repulsive bloody slobs like this had she been sent this week alone?

The condom finally came off in the guy's hand, and he grinned up at her.

She stared back, on the point of exploding.

Lawrence screwed up his ticket and crossed to the free desk. He sat down across from the middle-aged woman behind the monitor and lightly placed his SB40 on the table. Smiling faintly, he gave her a polite nod in greeting.

Sandra acknowledged by merely looking the ashen-faced, ghostly young man in the eye as she took his signing document. She rose and headed off to the filing cabinet.

Lawrence watched her go, observing blankly as she reached the cupboard and pulled open a drawer. His eye was caught by the door to the office opening and a man emerging.

The arse with the glasses. Shit. The tosser had seen him and was coming over. *For fuck's sake.*

Williams crossed the floor quickly. Reaching the desk, he planted his palms on the grey surface and regarded Lawrence, the strip-light glinting off his titanium rims. He waited a moment before speaking, trying to make his face impassive.

'Forgive me, but I was under the impression you'd been disqualified from receipt of benefit.'

'No…' sighed Lawrence, staring at the thin sandy hair at the side of Williams' head. He added in a faint voice, 'They allowed my appeal.'

Sandra had come up behind Williams and was trying to get to her seat. He looked round and moved over to one side, glancing back at Lawrence.

'What's the status of this claim?' asked Williams of Sandra quietly, staring all the while at Lawrence.

Sitting down, Sandra sighed and read from the monitor.

'Clear.'

'History?' barked Williams.

Sandra manipulated her mouse. 'One suspension. One disqualification cancelled on appeal.'

For a moment, Williams remained where he was. Then, slowly drawing himself upright, he gave Lawrence one last lingering look, turned and moved off to another desk.

Lawrence watched his back as he went, noticed the wet stains under the armpits of his beige shirt. Seeing these stains, this evidence of his pathetic, frail humanity, it was suddenly hard not to feel sorry for the fucker.

Lawrence let his gaze drift back to the woman behind the desk. She was asking her perennial question.

With a mild, distant smile, he slowly shook his head and, with a perceptible shaking in his hand, reached for the pen.

Lucinda stood with her arms folded, her dark eyes boring fiercely into the claimant's forehead as he pulled the musty brown jumper down over his washed-out nylon shirt, the v-neck covering only one wing of a large faded blue collar.

He glanced up at her, a faint, nervous grin on his face. Pushing the plastered-together glasses back up his nose, he looked down, placed his stodgy hands on his knees, and began hauling himself slowly upright.

As he reached for his jacket, Lucinda spoke, staring furiously at the small flecks of dandruff clinging to the clumps of hair around his ears.

'Excuse me, but can I ask you something before you leave?'

Pulling the jacket around him, the guy turned and squinted at her. She didn't wait for a response.

'Do you remember which desk you went to downstairs?'

The man squinted at the ceiling for a moment.

'Ah … er… that's a question and a half, innit?' He burst into loud laughter.

A new level of ferocity crept into Lucinda's glare. The man was a bloody cretin to boot.

' … sorry, love. I don't … no… a desk is just another desk innit, really … all things told.'

He looked down and began doing up his zip.

'Well, do you remember anything about the person *sitting behind* the desk?'

He screwed his face into another squint and looked at her.

'Well, yeah … actually I do, yeah … best as I can recall, it was some bloke with glasses … bit thin on top - like me in that department, you might say!'

Again he laughed loudly in her face.

However, Lucinda's glower had gone right through the man standing before her, and was now burning a hole in the rear wall.

He looked from her to the door and back again.

'Well … is that all you want to know, is it?'

She refocused on the wretched blob in front of her. 'Yes,' she said, turning from him. 'Yes, it is. Thank you.'

His face fell visibly, and he moved off to the door.

'Righto ... I'll be off, then now...'

She heard a shuffle of feet and the opening and closing of the door.

'Christ!' she spat aloud, whirling round and sitting down heavily on the edge of the bed.

Could that bloody bastard be actually sending them up to her *deliberately*?

She stared at the pedal bin.

It was difficult to see how he could organise it. No, it was impossible. How could he do it without everybody down there knowing what he was up to?

Unless they were *all* in on it.... But that was ridiculous. And yet maybe the sod *had* found some way to do it and cover his tracks.

Then again, maybe this rash of slobs was merely a random event, just coincidence ... but if it was coincidence, how to determine that? Still staring at the bin, she suddenly screwed her face up in fury.

Well, why *bother* determining it? What was the bloody point? So she could *stay* here? Stay in this place? Well, fuck this place.

If he was up to something, then fuck him, and if he wasn't, then *fuck him anyway.*

She could go down there now and cause a scene, find out what -

But no - why not just leave? Now. Without a word to any of them. Just walk out right now. Simply eject the centre from her life this very minute. As Angela had done. After all, she could go with the Mayfair option *tonight* if she wanted to!

She glanced over at the bedside cabinet.

Just *what* exactly was she waiting for? Yes, the hell with it. Lucinda, babe, it's time to bloody-well *jump ship!* Random event or not, this run of horrible slobs was simply the kick up the backside she'd been *needing* -

Her eyes dropped to her knees.

But of course, the idea of walking out this minute was nothing but a glorious bloody fantasy.... She'd have to speak to Jenny, Graham, give in her notice, hang around for another month, expose herself to those *cretins* for another *month....*

Her nostrils flared, and she shot another furious look over at the pedal bin.

A fresh anger broke out across her chest, and at the same time, and without really knowing why, she slowly stood up and began walking, drawn for some reason over to the bin. She stood over it, glaring down at the lid.

But could Roger really have...?

She put her foot on the pedal.

It seemed -

And depressed it.

She found herself staring down at the condom from the last claimant, resting on a whole pile of clouded latex. With a queer horror, she gazed for a moment at the twisting strands of generative material twining round one another suspended in the fluid. There was a sudden pounding in her head, and she let the lid clang shut, an explosion of rage expanding in her breast.

Violently flinging her hair back, she strode to the cabinet and quickly snatched up her things from the drawers, pulling them open and kicking them shut, all except the top drawer, which she merely left hanging open in contempt, after removing the battered copy of Hume from where it had been lying alongside boxes of contraceptives. Then, tying the cord of her robe, she crossed to the door, pausing only for a final glance around the cubicle, her eyes resting on the faint impression of her body on the mattress.

Dismissing the cubicle once and for all, she took her eyes from the hollow in the bed, and stepped out into the corridor. As she closed the door, the numeral, a black 9 came before her eyes. Well. The next door she lay behind would have a bigger number on it than that. How many floors *was* the Hilton?

She turned and strode quickly down the corridor, glancing for the last time at the Modigliani nude and the Robert Mapplethorpe prints on the wall, feeling a sudden thrill of liberation. She was doing it, she was bloody-well *doing* it. Ha HA!

Okay, it may have been kind of safe here for a while. But all she'd done here was tread water. Outside, she at least stood a chance of making some real money. And no dumb beer-gut slob FUCKER would be having her again unless he were seriously paying through the nose for it.

Pushing through the double doors, she turned and entered the empty facilitator suite. She would've liked to have said something to Elaine and Toby, but she wasn't going to hang around until their break. Anyway, she had their numbers and would be in touch. And if Graham and Jenny had a problem with her just walking out, then she'd put in a complaint against Roger. God knew he'd pissed her off enough just with all that skulking around outside the lounge, let alone anything else.

Pushing through a second door, she made her way quickly to her locker.

With a pale hand on the black handrail, Lawrence wearily pulled himself up the last few steps to the second floor, the stem of an erection growing in his trousers despite his almost total dissociation from the coming event.

Stepping finally onto the landing, he let out a heavy breath and stood still for a moment, shaking his head and looking at the floor. Then, with an exaggerated show of pulling himself together, he threw the hair out of his eyes and pushed through the swing doors.

He drifted down the corridor like a wraith, the strip-lights moving back across his head, and again had to throw his head about for a second to keep himself in track with where he was, *who* he was ... *if* he was....

He blinked and squinted over at the passing numerals on the doors.

... right ... here it is, then... Number 9... Let's get it over with....

He sighed once and knocked on the door.

No answer.

He tried again. Still no response. But the woman at the desk had definitely said number 9. Maybe the woman inside was answering but he couldn't hear through the door. Well, what the fuck. Try the handle.

He eased open the door. No one *in* here.

Well, she must've gone to the bog ... or was about to come on shift or something....

He stepped inside, leaving the door slightly ajar, and drifted over to the bed, where he sat down. He could do with a fag, but she'd probably be here any minute, and anyway he didn't want to get thrown out for smoking, or rather he *did* want to get thrown out... He let his head sink between his stooped shoulders, then suddenly jerked it back again with real force and took a deep breath, focusing his eyes on the wall.

'Everythin' aall right for you today?' smiled Harper, drawing the SB40 toward him, his keen eyes taking in the nervous furrow in the brow of the girl sat across the desk.

'Well, I hope so,' began Carla, leaning forward. 'The thing is I - well, I should have come in yesterday, but I forgot. I mean, I got the weeks mixed up. For some stupid reason I thought it was next week.'

'No, that's aall right. Since you've come in promptly, that's aall right. It won't affect anythin'.'

Still smiling, he drew himself up and strolled over to the filing cabinet. As he went, Carla noticed at a desk further down the guy with the glasses cast a quick irritated glance at the Jamaican. The spectacles were then trained for a moment on her, before being switched back to a man at the guy's desk.

Carla frowned in Williams' direction. What's up with *you* today, bloody My Little Hitler *git*. You *know* I'm just a poor sad lady of London come in from the streets to have her hole filled emptily for a few minutes on a cold Wednesday afternoon, so just damn well leave me *alone*.

She took her eyes from Williams and looked up as Harper returned with her file and sat down.

'Aall right. You had any encounter at aall in the last fortnight?' smiled Harper, removing the signing sheet and sliding it across the table.

Carla curled down a corner of her mouth and shook her head, taking up the pen.

Harper ran off a ticket from the dispenser and slid it across the desk. 'Okay. You want to go on up to Number 5, then.'

Lawrence sat in the cubicle, looking down at the palms of his hands. He turned them over, stared for a moment at the network of veins on the back of his right hand, then looked up at the wall.

Well, he ... may as well get undressed. It was an opportunity anyway at least to get undressed in private. He'd never got the hang of all that hateful disrobing in silence in front of the state-issue fuck-worker. Today at least he could avoid that particular piece of nonsense.

He stood slowly and removed his frayed camelhair coat, staring for a moment at the damage to the shoulder, before folding it and placing it on the floor at the foot of the bed. Next, he pulled the black sweater quickly over his head, and likewise folded it, placing it on top of his coat.

The doors to the facilitator suite swung shut behind Lucinda as she stormed out to the landing and headed quickly down the staff staircase, the heels of her flying black boots sending a reverberating clatter up the cold stairwell, each turn in the stairs increasing the hint of a half-smile mixing with her habitual faint sneer. Arriving at the ground floor, she turned left, strode down a short corridor to an auxiliary fire-exit, pushed open the door and burst out onto the pavement, the long mane of her thick black hair immediately lifting on the cold wind as she strutted off down the street.

Carla pushed open the swing doors on the second floor landing and made her way quietly along the cream-painted corridor.

After last night, it was like ... coming *home* to walk down here again. There was even something welcoming in the hospital colour of the walls.

The door to the security guard's office was ajar and she peered in as she passed, catching a glimpse of a burly figure in a brown cap slouched before the television. The low sound of a racing commentary coming from the set filled her with a curious warmth, the horses' names piling up in her mind as she went on down the corridor.

But that was too much. She shouldn't actually be feeling *warm* to be here - that really *was* just sad and sick!

She pushed a strand of hair away from her cheek. Well, here was number 9 like the guy had said. The door was slightly ajar. And she could just make out the guy peering out at her. No need to knock, then.

Lawrence watched the girl enter the cubicle and turn to close the door behind her. Presumably she was late from a break or something. Or was just coming on shift. He looked up at the red bobble on her hat. As she turned again and looked at him, some bizarre, inappropriate sense of etiquette forced him to his feet, despite his nakedness, and he gave her a vague nod of acknowledgement, aware he had his palms idiotically pressed to his hips. And then he knew why he had stood for her the instant she'd turned; she was absolutely fucking beautiful.

Carla returned the guy's nod, and then lowered her eyes, taking two steps toward the chair, where she removed her mittens and took off her coat. From the periphery of her vision, she tried to steal a glimpse of the guy's body, to see if it really was as wiry and hungry as it had seemed from the brief sight she'd already had. Peering out cautiously from her cowl of auburn hair as she unbuttoned her cardigan, she let her eyes roam briefly over a thin pale chest and sinewy leg. As she'd thought, every muscle was perfectly defined, and kind of elegant and ... highly *wrought*, somehow.... She switched her eyes back to her cardigan, a sudden phantasmagoria of thin indie rock stars and consumptive poets flitting through her mind. She concentrated once more on her buttons, aware of the warmth already spreading out below her tummy.

Lawrence stood awkwardly for a moment as the girl undid her cardigan, then he sat down again on the bed. He tried not to watch her. She hadn't been contracted to provide a strip-show for his *entertainment*. She was here merely to facilitate the grim biological discharge.... But it was fucking hard *not* to watch her. He allowed himself glimpses of her, the smooth dome of her forehead, the profile line of her celestial nose and girlish lips just visible through the curtain of her long forward-hanging hair. She placed the cardigan on the chair, and stood again in profile, bringing her hands to the hem of her maroon Lycra top. Something gentle, something vulnerable was expressed in the narrow elbows as she took hold of the sides of the tight garment. His eyes trailed down to the heart-crushing sweep of her jean-clad bottom, taking in the balance it made with her narrow waist and the volume of her hair as she pulled the top up her body. His gaze flashed to a narrow strip of white riding above her jeans - her nylon pants, clinging to smooth, deliciously toned skin. His semi-erect cock lurched from his lap, stabbing the air with an involuntary contraction of the muscle. All right, he was just sitting in a fucking sex dole cubicle, but the sight of this girl was causing wide bright pastures to open up inside him, and as she pulled the top over her head, the fabric sliding up over her small white bra, it was as though his whole fucked existence were being ripped up and overlain with rolling summer grass. He felt another stab from his now solid cock, the sensation filling him with such a shocking surge of unhoped-for joy that he gripped the bed, dazed.

After placing her top on the chair, Carla bent forward to unzip her boots. Well, this might be good, this might be really *good!* The guy had a lovely Christ-like body - but she wanted another look at his face.... She glanced briefly to her left, and through her hair, found herself looking into two dark hunter's eyes, but which were at the same time kind of haunted and nervous, and yet ... really *soulful*, like a sad wolf, or something.... The guy held her glance for only an instant before looking away, but incredibly, this look into his eyes had caused an actual contraction in her knickers, something which at this stage she had never experienced before. Those were the eyes of no football manager, that was for sure! Holly was right after all. There certainly *were* some 'inspiring' specimens to be found here! Though this guy probably wouldn't be Holly's type, but what did *she* know?! Placing her boots next to the chair, she stole another glance at the guy. God, and he had fabulous gaunt cheekbones ... which just looked *great* with his strong, unshaven chin. Wow, and his erection looked so glorious straining up from that dying poet body! But unbelievably, she felt her cheeks immediately flushing at the sight. Quickly averting her eyes, she stood up, turning her back to him to undo her bra - she didn't want him to think she was some idiotic blushing schoolgirl who'd never seen a prick before!

Lawrence had been stunned by the sudden look the girl had given him as she had bent forward to take off her boots. It was like he had never been fucking alive in his life - *ever* - until that moment. Again, this was just a sad session with a sex worker in a sex dole cubicle, but Christ, Christ, there'd been such a fucking heart-stopping *mellowness* in that look! He drank in the curve of her back as she bent over again to place her boots by the chair. Fuck, she was looking round again. Jesus, that shy little glance again, as though she were *interested* in him or - Dear God, she'd just looked at his cock - with that same heart-melting look! What the fucking hell *was* this?

Standing with her back to the guy, Carla reached round and unclasped her bra, trying to will the blush from her cheeks. Why was she *blushing*? She'd never reacted like this before. Well, had she ever seen such a beautiful, pale, slim pelvis before? And the hip bones, the way those delicate hip bones led down to the erection! She bent slightly to place her bra on the chair, the movement revealing to her the wetness between her legs. God, everything in her knickers was just turning to goo! Okay, right, this was just the sex dole and he was just a sex dole guy, but this was going to be by far the best yet, definitely, and we won't be needing Mr. Nick Cave to*day*, thank you very much!

Lawrence watched as the girl placed her bra on the chair and the full length of her naked back came into view, a curtain of shining brown hair fanning out across her shoulder-blades. With a joyous churning in his balls - a sexual effervescence that was *actually fucking united to him*, united to him through *joy* - he looked on, moving his head in disbelief. The gentle, narrow elbows raised themselves slightly as the girl tipped her head forward to unfasten the belt of her trousers. His eyes moved across the rear pockets of her jeans, the exciting swell of her bottom only a few feet in front of his face. The jangle of an opening belt buckle sounded in his ears, followed by the sudden rasp of an opening zip, and he watched, his eyes almost filling up, as the blue denim fell slowly away to reveal the delirious white expanse of the girl's pants, the soft material expressing the heart-twisting contour of her behind in such a way as to reduce to nothing in an instant the entire edifice of his whole depressive, rambling rant of that morning, of *all* his fucked, depressive, rambling rants and ruminations of the past weeks, months, *years*.

Easing down her jeans, Carla lifted her left foot to step out of the leg. Taking down her trousers like this right in front of the guy's face, right in front of this starving poet's face - again, all right, he was a sex dole guy, but who cared, she was here to *play*, wasn't she? - sticking her bum in his face like this felt just so rude it was amazing! And she wasn't embarrassed about the wetness either. In fact she wanted him to see it. Was she crazy? No, no, this was the way it was supposed to *be. Wasn't it?* Wasn't it meant to be fun, just pure *fun? Then let him see it.*

Lawrence sat bewildered, floating halfway up to heaven as the girl bent further forward to pull off the other leg of her jeans, exposing, between the smooth backs of her upper thighs, the soft white almond shape of her crotch and at its centre the dark wet oval of her miraculous and unbelievable enthusiasm for him. A faint scent came to him, a tangy hint of her rear, mixing with the machine-wash aroma of her underwear, unlocking dream fragments and memory smells deep inside him. And without knowing what he was doing, he was suddenly reaching for her, his thin hand no longer projected up on a screen, but there in the real world, in a world that for once was making sense. He spread his fingers, preparing to make the lightest, gentlest, most reverential possible contact. But *would she mind?* Maybe, but he couldn't stop himself, he just couldn't stop himself, he couldn't rein in this fucking *joy*.

His fingertips brushed nylon.

Carla felt the touch as she tugged the trousers from her right foot. It was what they never did. Touch you like *that.* She paused, relishing the tiny feather-light caresses on her bum, the outsides of her thighs. God, it was just fantastic ... who *was* this guy, who - but no, the caresses would end any second and she'd be told to get on with it and get on the bed ... but he was going on ... god, *please*, yes, go on, don't, don't stop -

Lawrence brought his softly circling fingertips gradually down across the girl's nylon-covered bottom, the sleek outline of her hips making the blood thump in his head. It was incredible; instead of just taking his hands away and chucking a condom at him as he might have expected, she was letting him go *on* with this, letting him *play* with her! He felt another strong stab of his eager, rigid cock, and looked down at his groin, almost laughing. All right, then, you mad fucking dog *fuck*head, I need you, I admit it, *I need you* for this undreamed of fucking happiness....

Bending forwards still, Carla picked up her jeans carefully with one hand and quietly placed them on the chair, afraid any sudden movement might disturb the guy; she didn't want to distract him from the wonderful, *wonderful* stroking. And now he was going lower. Oh, no, he'd stopped! Ah ... no, he was just moving his hands. She felt something gentle lightly cup her left buttock - his palm, while - oh, God - there was a tiny delicious spot of pressure right between her legs, so good the accompanying reflex almost knocked her knees together. God, he was doing it, he was *doing it.* The way *she* might. He was making microscopic little spirals through her knickers right on her most sensitive spot, - oh, *God!* The way she'd do it herself, only better, better - round and round ... oh, round and round the garden you go, my thin, starving sex dole baby, but I want to look at you, I want to look at you -

With a blissful pounding in his chest, Lawrence went on cupping the girl's behind with his left palm, as though learning it, as though taking in some sacred new knowledge, while with his right hand he continued to tease the smooth pouch between her legs with the tiniest circles of his gliding, moistening fingertips. He glanced up at the athletic line of her back stretching up and away from the waistband of her briefs, but was shocked to see her peering down over her shoulder at him. Instinctively, he sat back slightly.

Peering down at him, Carla felt the movements of the guy's hands slow. Oh, no, that was it, she'd disturbed him. Suddenly self-conscious about the outrageous way she was holding her bottom, she began to straighten, and in turning her head, her eyes happened to move across the packet of condoms sitting in the open top drawer of the bedside cabinet.

Unsure now what to do with his hands, Lawrence watched the girl as she drew herself up. He caught what he took to be her significant glance from him toward the open drawer of condoms. Well, that was it, she was telling him to get a johnny on now. But that was okay, that was okay, they only had a limited time.... He leaned over and groped for one of the square sachets.

Standing up straight, Carla turned round slowly to face the guy, half-tempted to ask him to go on with what he'd been doing, but well, no, she'd better not push it. It'd just spoil it so much if she forced him to read the rule-book out to her. And now he was leaning over to the drawer anyway. Better get these knickers off, then. But anyway, this was going to be *good!* Running her eyes over his lean, narrow biceps as he reached over to the drawer, she hooked her thumbs under the elastic of her pants and pulled them slowly down her legs, slowly so the feel of the material wouldn't disturb the tingling luxury still spreading through her skin from his touch.

Lawrence brought his body round from the drawer, the sachet in his hand, about to make a tear in it, when he stopped, halted by the sheer visual dream of the girl's delicate hands sliding her panties down her thighs, the material stretching between her knees, her long brown hair hanging before her small, angular shoulders. Jesus, Jesus, *Jesus!* But shit, don't annoy her by fucking about, come on, get this fucking thing on! He looked down at the sachet, forced himself to concentrate, found a crinkled edge and quickly tore off a strip, before glancing up again to see the girl step out of her pants and with a beautiful, seemingly unconscious flourish of her body place them over the back of the chair. And then she was looking down at him again with that incredible, mellow, soul-cushioning look, one side of her face partially obscured by a long S of hanging hair. She pushed it aside with a small, eloquent hand, the action sending through Lawrence an electric thrill uniting his mind and cock in a single burst of barely containable bliss. His mouth hanging open, he looked down again and quickly pulled the condom from the sachet, aware of the girl moving round now and sitting on the bed beside him.

Carla slowly sat down on the bed, imagining what she would do now if this guy were really her lover. She peered at the side of his head as he held the condom over his groin, letting her gaze linger on the sensitive downturn of his eyelashes as he turned the latex over in his fingers. And it was like there was a trace of some ancient pain or something embedded in the tiny lines running along his eyelids. Well, if he were her real lover, then she would lean round and *kiss* those sweet eyelids at this point.... And stroke his cheekbone.... How she would love to stroke that pale cheekbone with the back of her finger! Well, maybe she *could* just stroke his cheek a little. Maybe - was that out of bounds? Probably, well, of *course* - but maybe he'd understand. Maybe he'd *understand* and not get angry.

Pinching the teat of the condom, Lawrence began carefully rolling down the rubber, his dark eyes fixed to the shining purple dome straining up toward him. All right, you fucker, I'm right with you, I'm right behind you, you're right all the way, I need you, you're a piece of me, I needed you all along, I always needed you, you crazy, jerking, spurting piece of shit! You're still a blind, subversive, ugly piece of meat, but you're my *linchpin,* my little connecting peg and for the next twenty heaven-sent minutes you're going to join me to this beautiful life-changing creature of nature, you're going to plug me into the magical fucking *essence* of her, you dirty, veined, beautiful, throbbing extension-of-my-fucking- SOUL-

He felt something on his cheek. Dear God, she was touching his cheek! The contact had almost made him flinch, so long had it been since he'd felt another person touch him there. He wanted to look round, but better concentrate on getting this fucking johnny down - this *fucking foreskin!* - But Jesus this little show of affection - well how could it be affection? - kindness, then or whatever -

Lightly dragging the back of her forefinger across the guy's cheek, Carla stifled a languid whimper; the contact was causing a sensation entirely new to her. Between her legs she could actually feel small involuntary openings and closings, and it was just *amazing!* But didn't that only happen in *animals?* She'd seen it once on a pony in a field as a child, but had never known it was possible in humans! And this was just from feeling the guy's *cheekbone!* She continued the caress, wanting to thank him for not minding. But maybe it *was* annoying him, yes, and he was being polite. So don't push it - because maybe it *is* too personal. She let her hand fall away. Pressing her legs together, and trying not to squirm too much, she trailed her gaze from the guy's cheek up to his charming shaggy hair and down through his line of sight to where he was just rolling the final centimetre of the condom down into place. A storm of butterflies erupted in her tummy at the sight, at the idea that any minute she would be closing herself around that lovely dick – lovely and fearsome – the veins, what thick veins! The top of it was especially lovely, big and very wide and full and curvy and solid as marble - He was turning! She made a quick swallow of anticipation and turned herself, lying back slowly on the bed, wanting to take his hand and pull him down on top of her, but afraid to, afraid that it would be too much. But maybe she *was* romanticising him too much - but no, *no*, she should do what made her *happy,* shouldn't she? While she was here? She reached up, but missed his hand as, in coming toward her, he moved his arm to balance himself.

Struck as though by some divine revelation of truth, Lawrence looked on as the girl lay back her slim body, the mild, tawny complexion of her young nipples detonating fresh bursts of sunlight inside him. But it wasn't just her lovely nakedness, it was also that amazing mellow *something* in her face, which it probably wouldn't pay to look at for too long otherwise you'd never, *ever,* get out of this cubicle - but no, fuck it, en*joy* this, *all* of it, take all you *can* from this. Running his eyes across her forehead - Jesus, just her forehead was enough to soothe a man's fucked spirit - he shifted his weight round and fully onto the bed. Shit, she'd just made some kind of impatient gesture of her arm. Come on, don't upset her, she doesn't want to be just gawped at, for Christ's sake -

Searching the guy's eyes as he moved forward, Carla felt a sudden, coarse wildness race through her spirit, and in a totally unprecedented rush of abandon she took hold of her knees and lifted them right back to her shoulders, at the same time raising and jutting her head from the pillow, staring up at him as he paused open-mouthed to gaze down between the cheeks of her bum. And now he was moving forward again, nearly on top of her. Trying not to gasp aloud, she found her gaze flitting down across the lean, dramatic set of his shoulders and ribcage, down to where he was holding the base of his straight, hard dick. Oh, God, do it, do it, do it - she wanted to call him baby - well she could, in her mind - oh, baby, do it -

Lawrence gazed down, feeling like he could stare for the rest of his life at the way the soft pale egg-shapes of the girl's buttocks cradled the dark oval nest in between. Christ in heaven, he could probably stare for the rest of his life just at the dreamy, tan pigmentation of her little clitoris peeping through the mist of tight, curling hair, and in staring at it, merge with it forever; he wouldn't complain. He wanted to kiss it, but *no way*, it might piss her off, it was against the rules and he sure as hell didn't want to get thrown out now. Moving into position, he looked down at his own body, at his rearing cock, which, he realised with a simple laughing joy, was somehow different; it no longer seemed to have a life of its own, rather it was now merely a blood-filled vessel of his *own* life, a carrier of his own life, his *own* fucking life, his *own essence*. He gripped it by the base, relishing its strength, and bringing it into position, let his other hand descend to where, with the utmost care, and with as much reverence as he could muster, he began gently easing apart the girl's precious, precious little folds. To his joy, her hand came down to help him, the small articulate fingers at the same time holding herself and drawing his cock on. With a final glance down at a well-chewed little fingernail holding open a small groove of tender brown skin, he pushed in, his eyelids falling, as soft warm pressure enclosed him, so good that he pitched forward, letting his weight fall to her, his chest sinking into the backs of her thrown-back thighs -

As the guy pushed in, Carla felt the breath rush out of her, and blinked hard, clenching her teeth, but God, it was sweet, he felt so sweet, *so sweet!!* And then his darling body was coming down on top of her, his lovely, lean chest pressing down on her legs, and his hair, and his face, the smell of his face was in hers - the savoury smell of his skin, it was so - His lips brushed her chin as he moved his head, and she felt a sudden pang because she wanted to kiss him and it wasn't allowed -

An inch from her eyebrows, giddy from the nearness of her soap-scented cheek, Lawrence melted further as a length of the girl's hair brushed his temple, and it was like the whole weight of the fucking *world* were being brushed away. Delaying his hips, simply drowning for a moment in the smell of her and the feel of her around him, he raised his head slightly to gaze down at the urgent face peering up at him from between the hollow backs of her knees, like some little woodland animal. Jesus Christ, the *look* she was giving him, that little look of mellow entreaty, only now it was alternating with a frowning expression of open-mouthed *hunger!* All right then, let's go, babe, let's *go* -

Carla gulped hard, blinking furiously, surprised by the sudden onslaught of thrusting, her breath forced immediately into fast gasps, as though it had been taken from her, as though the rhythm of her breath had been hijacked by his vigorous pounding, and it was like, with her breath, the *whole* of her was being taken up and just carried *away* - and oh, God, *God*, he fit her so well*, so well,* it was as though she were just, just, just ... *dissolving* all around the sweetness of him - yes, yes, go on, my, my, my scruffy hair, my king, my lovely, my lovely, my darling, *darling* scruffy hair *king* - She threw her head back on the pillow - oh, oh, oh, oh -

Lawrence swung in and out of the girl as though fucking for the first time in his life, great waves of pleasure tearing down along his cock and up through the burning sinews of his back to go rolling round his brain, and he rammed on, his mind and balls harmoniously awash with the clear, healing light of shared purpose. Jesus, Jesus, who *was* this girl?! How could she be doing this, how could she be *doing* this to him? She was like some battery of life-affirming positive charge and she was letting him plug in and draw power, bathe in her energy, bathe in*side* her, bathe his fucking dogheaded soul deep inside her - where it was warm, warm, so fucking *warm.* Well, who*ever* she was, God *bless* her, God fucking bless her! Without a break in his rhythm he slipped his arms beneath her body so as to cradle her back protectively in his forearms, her shoulders resting in his palms, and with his fingertips caressing the slopes of her neck, he held her to him like treasure and stepped up his thrusting-

Carla felt herself held like she'd never been held before. The guy was practically cradling her in his arms! It was crazy, crazy, but she'd never felt so secure! And he was tenderly stroking her neck with the fingers of both hands, and it was in total counterpoint to the beautiful violence of his hips and it was just *fantastic!* An image came to her of him tapping his head and rubbing his stomach. She smiled through her panting breath and let go of her legs to reach round his body, closing her eyes as her palms pressed into the bony ribs of his back, the bones feeling like ... little rows of sleeping soldiers beneath her hands or - *God!* She swallowed hard and opened her eyes. Now he was squirming and twisting his dick around inside her, and it was like everything in there was just turning to honey, to flowing honey, flowing around that perfect, *perfect* shape and everything that had ever been missing was here, it was here today in this silly, fabulous cubicle and - shit, he was off again yes, yes, go, go, go on - she held on, the backs of her arms, her calves crawling with pleasure, staring at the lock of dark hair an inch from her eyes, the lived-in contour of the forehead, the creases between the black, stern eyebrows - oh, oh, oh, oh - my god my god my god - oh, *oh*, *OH!* - she was going to come she was going to come she couldn't believe it she was going to - there was a spasm like she'd never - ah, ah, ah, oh *God, GOD! God God* -

His head held an inch above her cheek, Lawrence felt the girl suddenly jerk beneath him, her hands moving crazily around his thrusting back. What, was she coming or something? Surely not. Even in the dim and distant past when he'd actually had the odd girlfriend, when the hell had they ever reacted like *this?* But no, shit, she'd flung her head right back, her eyes clamped shut, her lips stretched out into a wide taut O and she was banging the bed with her fist, and flinging her head from side to side, her hair in her teeth, her eyes, all over the fucking place, and this was the point wasn't it, *this* was the point of his fucking cock, forget the spunk, the genes, the procreation, the point was to fill your fellow creature with this devastating fucking joy, to -

'*AAAAaaaah!!*'

Jesus, she was shouting now! She *must* be coming, look at the state of her! Lawrence gazed in delight at the girl's screwed up eyes, at the lips now pressed tightly together against her crying out - maybe she didn't want the other 'facilitators' to hear her or something, maybe it was something they got embarrassed about - and now she was calming again slightly, her repressed shouts fading to broken murmurs. She was opening her eyes. He slowed his pace right down, almost to a standstill. Christ, her eyes were going right through him, filling him with an almost unbearable light as she tilted her head on one side, swallowing hard and blinking, her shoulders shaking. Should he go on? After all, she'd come quite soon, there was still some time to go, so presumably he was entitled - but *fuck* 'entitled' you rotten bastard! But maybe she expected him to, *wanted* him to. All right, let's just pull back a little, give her a little tenderness and see where we get to -

Carla let her head loll to one side, her mind, her whole body consumed by a sweet drunken ache.... What ... *was* ... this...? To ... come so ... so .... soon....What ... how ... was ... he ... doing ... this ...? And her *vagina* ... was ... just ... *quivering* ... and now ... he was ... *oh, oh, that's nice-*

Keeping his hips absolutely still, Lawrence gazed down at the rich, auburn swirl of the girl's hair spread over the pillow as he delivered a shower of diligent, light caresses to the insides of her thighs, the backs of her knees, the bones of her ankles. Then, watching her trembling closed eyelids, he widened the reach of his touches, bestowing sweetness on her belly, her shoulders, her toes, breasts, elbows and ribs, in an effort to bring to life every little nerve ending in her miraculous little body.

With her eyes closed, relishing the delirium of never knowing where the next caress was going to land, Carla lay suspended in space, as though held immobile on the glowing, warm pole inside her, while the whole surface of her body glittered and sang with sensation under the random, sweeping, circling fingers. She drifted, the caresses floating on the glad warm waves of post-orgasm. And although she had ... just ... come ... it felt like it was just the beginning ... because what he was doing was *doing things* to her ... *oh, god ... it was doing things to her-*

Lawrence felt a sudden contraction around his cock, and then another, a firm ring of possession announcing itself. Christ, what was that? He'd never before - The girl opened her eyes, her clear, light-filled eyes, and it was as though he were being channelled into them through his loins. Another squeeze. And this was what his bloody cock had been on about - the true, answering flesh of another. And now they were both being held, his cock and he, in the unifying grip of these fabulous eyes and this fabulous vagina and he had never known anything like -

Carla went on with her new-found ability. Wow ... oh, *wow!* It was like he ... had somehow made her ... alive down there for the first *time*, *really alive*, and she - it was *moving*, and - she could *control* it ... and give him little squeezes ... as they floated here together, suspended - do you like it, darling ... do you like it? Here's another, baby – *Oh* ... I can see you like it, I can see it in your eyes - and I want you to like it, I want you to like me more than all the others, and so I shall squeeze you, *squeeze you* -

Lawrence had to close his eyes, so incredible were the looks she was giving him with each little grip of her muscle. He had to close his eyes because otherwise he'd never be able to fucking live without her and then he - but God, what she was doing was *so* ... *GOOD* he wanted to moan out loud. Involuntarily, he opened his eyes and despite himself was looking again into hers peering up at him from beneath a now urgent, tense brow. And he wanted to touch the soft corners of her eyelids, but - and it was getting impossible to keep his cock still, maybe she was ready - *he had to come inside this life-saving girl* - and now she was jutting her head forward again, and looking down to where - he felt a jab in each buttock -

Carla dug her heels in, frantically searching the guy's eyes. Do me *more*, do me *more*, *more* ... *please* do me more, it's not time, is it, yet? *Please* do me more - oh....yes.... yes....

Lawrence resumed, at first with gentle collisions of his pelvis into hers, slowly building to a more vigorous swing of his hips. A flash of animal satisfaction ran down his back as the girl once more threw her head back on the pillow-

Carla closed her eyes, her hands pressed to the small of the guy's back, feeling like she was ... on drugs ... or like her vagina was a quivering melting jelly, and when it all melted this time it was going to just flood her.... *flood* her - oh, oh, oh, oh - she let her hands slip down the guy's bobbing backside - his bum was small and solid - bob *away*, little bum, oh, bob, bob away - she wanted - she'd never wanted to with other men but now she wanted to feel *all* of this taut, masculine bum, and yes, feel inside it, deep inside it - she felt a flush in her chest at the thought, but maybe he'd mind, no, he *won't* mind, he *mustn't* mind no, no, he won't mind, ah, ah -

Lawrence felt an outrageous tickle of pleasure - Jesus Christ, she was stroking him right up where the sun doesn't shine! Well, it's shining there, now, all right! Aaah, *Christ* -

Open-mouthed, Carla watched the doleful hunter's eyes close in ecstasy. Yes, yes, let me stroke you there - I'll stroke baby's little bum for baby... there, isn't that nice?... and, and let's see, let's say Mrs. Finger-rabbit, naughty Mrs. Finger-rabbit is, is, walking through your, through your valley and she's looking for a burrow, a nice, warm - are you going to let her in, baby? *Let* her in, here she comes -

Fucking *hell!! What was she* - an image came to him of the girl's well-chewed little fingernail nudging its way inside him and he fell forward, massively increasing the power in his hips -

Her breath forced immediately into stammering gasps by the guy's sudden leap to jackhammer pace, Carla hung on, trying to keep her hand in place, blinking rapidly, startled a second time by the sudden force unleashed between her legs - and then her head was being cradled - gentle thumbs touching her temples - and his head was close, so close as he powered almost alarmingly into her, but not alarmingly because he was holding her face in his hands, as though to tell her that it was all right, that everything was all right, that she was safe, that she was safe with him here in this cubicle. And as if to tell him she understood, she re-doubled the strokes and penetration of his behind. And she wanted so much to kiss him, but no, that might break the spell because it wasn't allowed, that definitely wasn't allowed and he might stop - *no, no*, he mustn't stop, he must never stop - never, never, *never* - ah,ah,ah,ah -

And Lawrence thundered on, glorying in his cock, glorying in this supreme, elevated state the fucker had somehow led him to, as he rocketed in and out of the clutching velvet interior of this incredible girl, this sacred one-in-a-million individual. Biting his lip, he gazed down at the frantic little head bobbing rapidly up and down before his vision. She was watching his hips, then his eyes, and her lips were working madly, grimacing, pouting, folding over each other. And then her finger again. A delirious slice of pleasure ran right up his arse, inspiring his cock to new heights of power. Well, fuck, if she was doing it to *him*, then *she* probably wanted it too - Christ, yes -

With no let up in the furious pumping, Carla felt the hands release her head and go quickly down her body to her bum. She gulped and swallowed as his hands went under and her bottom was quickly hoisted an inch off the bed -

Lawrence pounded on, the soft weight of the girl's buttocks now resting in his hands. And then, his expression almost solemn, he watched the mouth in the madly bobbing head draw back into another wide O as, with firm reverential fingers, he gently eased open her bottom. *Every joy I can give you, I will give you -*

With the room practically flying back and forth around her, Carla let her eyes close in exultation at the sheer animal wildness of the crude outrageous exposure below, and, and it was like ... like... *liberation*, like she was being turned inside out and oh god oh god-

As his hips swung back and forth, Lawrence applied a dab of sweetness to the tiny aperture between his fingertips -

Carla forced her cheek into the pillow, her ear almost chafing on the material, and she was flying, flying, a thousand tiny nerve-endings in her bottom crying with pleasure, crying along with her shaking, screaming vagina -

'*Unnnnh!*'

Lawrence looked down at the blurring head on the pillow as the girl grunted out her happiness, her breath coming almost in ugly snorts so destroyed was she now by what he was doing, and in this state she somehow became so vulnerable and mortal that he just wanted to bundle her up in his arms and always look after her - *fuck, I want to kiss you so much* -

Carla bit hard into the pillow, stopping her mouth against the increasing spasms in her vagina, unable to think, her skin seething and prickling with racing waves of drunken heat -

And Lawrence *was* his cock as he charged furiously up and down inside her, a perfect orchestration of speeding, singing tissue and racing super-charged blood -

Unaware of her audible groans, her eyes shut tight, Carla twisted her bobbing head from side to side, whipped on to new reaches of bliss by the twin onslaught of perfect, charging cock and lashing finger-

'*Uhhhnnnnnn....-*'

Lawrence went into overdrive, releasing the girl's behind and gripping her arms, pinning her to the bed as he drove into her, varying his angle to reach every little nook of her sacred interior, piling into her like he'd piled into no other girl before -

Carla put her finger, her whole hand, in her mouth, then tore it out again, closed her eyes and let out a long tremulous wail, crying with all her lungs as her vagina collapsed into unbearable spasm and a hot flushing wall of honeysweet liquid came flowing down the very core of her -

With her high, wailing cry ringing in his ears, and crashing his pelvis into her so hard he could feel her bones, Lawrence ploughed on like some mad automaton, felt himself become nothing but a soaring, blurring piston and it was pure and it was true and it was right - Oh, Christ it was *right - because she'd put him back together, she'd - this girl had resurrected his - resurrected his fucking soul and was now* - he grimaced, his face distorted by a sudden electric ripple in his racing cock - an excruciating feeling of something rushing into place at the base of it - he was going to come - he took in a sharp searing breath -

Caught in the sweet agony of accelerating orgasm, rocked by tides of sugar-sensation sweeping out to her fingertips and down to her toes, Carla sensed through quivering spasms the change in the spearing presence inside her - *he was going to come* - oh, yes ... *yes* ... *explode* with me ... release ... it in me... release it ... let it *go*, so, so we'll be coming *together* - I never, I never had that, I - And filtering through her drugged senses as she flowed seemingly like a river down her legs, she heard his voice for the first time. First, a small tremulous little boy's gasp and then, as his eyes flashed to hers:

'AaaAAAAAH! -'

Lawrence's furious pounding broke into disarray as he was gripped by the slower, insurmountable rhythm of ejaculation, the semen ripping up through his cock in pulse after hot white pulse. The girl's legs closed around his back. He frantically gripped the bed, the girl's shoulder, as the fourth, fifth, sixth, seventh bolt left his body, almost embarrassing him with a mad sense of incontinence so much of it was there, and still he squirted, an eighth and ninth and final time, and though there was nothing left he crammed into her still, accelerating for a few moments more as though his body were the screaming engine of a motorbike leaving the ground after a collision, its wheels spinning in the air, as though he could go flying on up to heaven, before finally he lost impetus, slowed and shuddered to a writhing, squirming halt.

As gently as he could, he lowered his glowing, heaving chest to the quaking, trembling form below him. Gasping for breath, he let his head rest beside hers, his face in her ear, and listened to her shaking breaths and little choked-off gasps and murmurs, his mind gone, blown, swimming in drowsy warmth.

Carla squirmed, dreaming under the cosy weight of him, his warm breath filling her ear, as the final drawn-out waves of clean uplifting pleasure spread out along her calves and up to her eyelids, bathing her in joy. One arm lay limply hanging off the bed, while the other was draped across his back. A shoulder muscle twitched beneath her fingers. Oh, my baby ... oh my baby ... baby - Another movement; he was lifting his head -

Lawrence wanted ... to speak to her, he *had* to speak to her, but on lifting his head, was fazed by the unreadable look he found in her eyes - he couldn't think, he just couldn't think what to say, and instead began stroking her forehead. God, he wanted to kiss her so badly. But ... it was too late now -

Carla peered up into the dark eyes, the touch of his fingers on her forehead coming to her through the haze. Should she, should she go for the kiss...? Just to make it complete...?

He became aware of his slackening dick. Shit, the condom. No wonder she was looking at him like that! Christ, he'd better deal with it quickly, he didn't want to ruin it all by fucking up on prophylactic etiquette! He lifted his head away.

Just as his head moved off to the side, Carla raised hers from the pillow but his lips had gone. She let her head sink back and looked on, trying not to be disappointed, as the guy simply raised himself up, eased himself out of her, then turned, sat on the edge of the bed and began busying himself with the condom. All right, then.... Okay, so that's it, then, a little stroke on the forehead and that's your *lot,* madam.... She raised herself onto her elbows and watched as the guy went over to the drawer and rummaged for a tissue. Okay ... back to the real world... Playtime's over... Back to the sad routine of the cubicle. She watched him wrap the condom in the paper. He hadn't looked at her *once* since he'd got off the bed. Well, he clearly wanted her out of here. Well, she wouldn't disappoint him! Brushing off her languor, she quickly sat forward, snatched her pants and jeans from the chair and quickly pulled them on.

Crossing to the pedal bin, Lawrence felt dizzy and drunk, so intense had the orgasm been, and for a moment was unaware of the girl pulling on her clothes. Only as he depressed the pedal did he see her pulling her top down over her head. Why was she getting dressed? Well, yeah, she'd been late, so probably hadn't had time to change into her sex worker robe ... probably off now to the changing rooms or whatever.... Shit, don't just go.... He dropped the tissue in the bin, and crossed back to the bed, trying to catch the girl's eye as she pulled on her boot, but she wasn't having it. He sat down groggily and reached round for his underpants. Holding them in his lap, he paused and stared at the girl's back as she loosely threw on her coat. Fucking hell, she could at least *acknowledge* him after what they'd just been through. But then ... why should she? It was just her job. She just happened to be damned good at it, that was all, or else a nymphomaniac or something, which *would help* if you were going to work here, let's face it. Well, whatever, the whole thing had just been another fucking illusion; there had been no connection. Well how *could* there have been, this is just the bonk dole, you pathetic arrogant arsehole - what? - do you think you're so amazing you've broken *through* that, that you made some kind of *connection* with her? Fucking snap out of it.

Carla turned and walked to the door. Right. Great. Out to the corridor for the emptiness, the smack in the face, while I leave you to your *profession*, then...

Lawrence watched the girl go to the door. Watched her hand go to the handle. A sob clutched at his chest. Speak to her.

But all he could utter was, 'Well, bye.'

Turning as she opened the door, and with no let-up in her exit from the room, she gave him a quick, unsmiling look over her shoulder. 'Bye,' she said in a small voice and was gone, the door closing behind her.

Out in the corridor, Carla walked briskly down toward the double doors. "Well, bye." The only two words to come from his lips, his unkissed lips. Well, don't have a cow, that's just the way it *is* here! God, how stupid she'd been, calling him her darling, her baby, he's just a sex worker for God's sake, it's just *sex dole,* you *idiot.* And as for all that 'scruffy hair king' and 'Mrs. Finger-rabbit' rubbish - she cringed. Well, thank God she *hadn't* kissed him, and made an even bigger fool of herself.

She came to the end of the corridor, pushed through the doors and made her way quickly down the stairs.

Lawrence dragged his eyes from the door and picked up his

trousers, choking on the sob threatening to burst from his chest. Fuck, let's just get the *fuck out of here!* He struggled into his jeans, desperately fighting the impulse to cry. He whirled round, snatched up the rest of his clothes and quickly pulled them on. Bending to tie his laces, he stared at his shoes and paused, realising fully for the first time that it had only *been* that sense of *connection* that had 'resurrected his soul'(ha!); it was only that sense of connecting with the girl that had given him such a feeling of ... *integration* ... But it was just fake.

He stood up furiously and reached for his coat. Well, life could never get too good for long, could it? It was in the very *nature* of the fucker. He threw on his coat, and, denying the moisture in his eyes, stormed to the door and left the cubicle.

From where he was standing at the far end of the corridor, Williams watched as the scruffy toerag in the long coat emerged from Lucinda's cubicle and went off toward the stairs. First, the girl, now him. What the hell was going on? He was about to rush forward when he checked himself. Hang on, think for a minute. He had a nasty feeling in his gut. Now, Lucinda's box had been red for well over half an hour. So either the three of them had been having a gang-bang in there, or else she wasn't in there at all, and two claimants had found their way in to the same cubicle and bloody done it with *each other*, and if they'd done it unwittingly then he'd be for the bloody high-jump. Bloody Charter! A good thing he hadn't moved in as soon as he'd seen the girl come out. His instinct had served him well, there.

He waited till the guy was safely on his way down the stairs, and then rushed over to the cubicle.

Right, the bitch wasn't here. Well, it was *her* responsibility for letting this happen, not his. But technically it *was* his responsibility. And if there were an enquiry, heaven forbid, he didn't trust that twerp Henshaw to come down on the right side of the line. He closed the door and made his way downstairs.

But what if she'd twigged something? Jesus, where was she?

Crossing back to his desk, he was hailed by Sandra.

'Roger, Moira said she just saw Lucinda down the bottom of Camden Street. Called to her, but no answer. Just kept going. What's she doing down there?'

'I don't know.'

'Well, her cubicle's still online.'

'I know, I'm about to sort it now.'

'What's she playing at, I wonder?'

'I have no idea.'

He sat down at his desk. What was she *at*? But never mind that for the minute, what about those two claimants? They both appeared to have left the building without starting any bother. And at least it wasn't the girl's usual signing day, so if anything *had* happened, it was unlikely the pair would ever run into each other again. That part of the fiasco at least hopefully wouldn't come out. But bloody hell, what *about* Lucinda? Was she *on to him?* Christ, he should never have started with it. He should ruddy-well never have started with it. Bloody *fool!*

He bowed his head, then quickly raised it again, forcing himself to focus on the monitor before him, unaware of the bright eyes trained on him from the adjacent desk.

Harper removed his glance from Williams and returned his attention to his own monitor.

Her hunched shoulders trembling as the bus ground its way through the traffic-choked junction, Carla watched the tears drip onto the back of her shaking mitten, watched them sink into the faintly grubby white wool of the small circling rabbits. She wiped her nose with the back of her wrist, and thought she could smell him there on her skin. And once again, his hands were coming in, stroking her, cradling her head, cradling her, as she flowed all around him.... She shifted violently in her seat, throwing her tear-blurred vision out at the slow-moving pavement. And his chest, his touch, his *touch,* his face as they had *come* together.... She looked back to her lap, snivelling, her face breaking into open grief. It - it had been the very best thing that had ever *happened* to her. The first true bloody taste of happiness *ever*. She flung her wrist hard against the window - *so why couldn't it have been REAL?*

FORTY-FIVE

As the Monday morning traffic crawled through the damp cold beyond the windows, Williams sat at his desk and stared over at the opposite wall, waiting for the first claimants to arrive, his head swimming with fatigue. It had been nearly a week since he'd had a decent night's sleep, since Lucinda had walked out. The bitch *had* quit, then; that much seemed certain now, at least.... And that probably made two of them, didn't it? After last night he'd be surprised if Briony were still there when he got back.

He took a sip of coffee from his plastic flask-mug, Briony's furious shouting playing back in his mind as the two of them had circled each other till 5a.m in the living room, going round and round and back and forwards over the same, *same*, tired old bloody crap, until, worn out, he'd just given up and stood over his army camp-bed, waiting for her to just leave him and let him sleep. Which she did finally, but not before pushing him, just pushing him from behind, making him graze his ankle on the camp-bed.

What had started it this time? What had bloody started it this time? Oh, yes, his remark about door-slamming championships. Well, why *couldn't* she just *say* what was on her bloody mind instead of knocking the house half-down with all that bloody door-banging!

But what if she'd meant it? What if one day she really did go ahead and leave him? He felt a weakness in his knees, and tried to counter it with the idea that if she *did* go, he might at least be in a position to *get* some again.... He tried to view the strange alternate reality of life without her....

... the old bachelor life again ... the old bachelor life ... but good Christ, not since his undergraduate days had he...-

And suddenly, not only did he feel tired, he felt old too ... old and utterly exhausted. He ran his hand back across his head and let his eyes drift to the plastic seating of the waiting area opposite, torturing himself with a vision of himself sat waiting there.

Elaine came in from the street and headed for the staff staircase, exchanging salutations with Sandra as she passed. Williams watched her go, the sight of the blond facilitator causing his thoughts to switch once again to the vexed question of Lucinda. Right, let's go over it again; the word from upstairs was that Henshaw had started asking questions, and, if Ricky were to be believed, had even dispatched Hopley on a home visit to Lucinda. And then there was Harper. Was he on to something? He'd caught Harper giving him a few funny looks - well, nothing new there, but ... well, even if he *had* cottoned on to something, there was nothing he, Williams, could do about it.... He just had to sit tight.

He drew himself up as the first claimant, a lost-looking guy in combat trousers, approached his desk.

'Hello, is that ... Kentish Town Sex-Benefit centre?.......Hi, my name is Sally Rand, and I'd like to report an abuse of your system.......Yes, I know someone who is claiming fraudulently..... All right....'

Sally sat on the edge of the bed in the penthouse flat and waited, staring down at the plastic wallet of Sacha's SB40 gripped in her shaking hand. She took a furious gulp from the wine glass at her foot and glared at the jacket lying on the floor where she'd thrown it, and over by the door, the tiny silver mobile, still lying where she'd kicked it, and still displaying the text, the text that had sent her reeling out to the bathroom an hour earlier. She shuddered again at the sight of it.

> I LOVE TO FUCK
> U ALL AFTERNOON TOO!
> INGA XXXX'

Who, where, what, was this *'Inga'*? And let's not forget the other one, 'Ulla'! - As if one wasn't *enough* for the fucking rotten shit! As if *two* weren't enough - he had to *claim bloody sex benefit, as well, the bastard! The filthy, dirty, utter-* A voice came on the line. She tried to sound calm.

'Yes, hello. I'd like to report someone claiming fraudulently....' She took another huge gulp of wine. 'My rotten bloody bugger of a boyfriend, that's who.'

A rotund woman with silver hair was just rising from Williams' desk, when the receptionist, Moira, appeared at his side.

'Roger, I've got a woman on the line reporting a fraudulent claim.'

Williams' eyes lit up. He immediately closed down his position and accompanied Moira back to reception.

'Hello, can I help you?' he said into the phone, pressing it into his shoulder as he pulled up a chair and sat down next to Moira, taking the mouse from her, energised by both the break from routine and from his brooding.

'I see,' he said, taking the receiver in his hand. 'Can you give me the name, please? And the reference number on the front of the SB40 ... that's the document you're holding in your hand.' He stared ahead as he listened, but on hearing the name and recognizing the reference number, and despite the misery of his present situation, he had to fight the urge to jump out of his seat. God, *yes*. Oh, God, yes, yes, yes, yes -

'And you found it in his jacket?.............I see.............Two, you say?...' He moved the mouse quickly across the desk, and his fingers went to work on the keyboard '...........Right.............It would help greatly if you could give me the telephone numbers of the two girls............No, I can assure you that we'll be treating this very seriously indeed...............We will, yes.........If it goes to trial, yes, it's technically rape of our staff......... Obtaining sex benefit through deception is equivalent to aggravated sexual assault or even rape............ Good, okay, but we'll need your help................ Well, try to keep hold of any evidence...........That's right, anything like that.........That's great, and you would be prepared .for those to be shown in a court of law?............That's terrific, terrific, okay, now an investigating officer from the fraud unit will get in touch with you very soon, this afternoon sometime hopefully............ Well, if we're going to catch him I wouldn't advise that..........No, I understand that, just don't tell him you've contacted us.........And where is he now?.........Okay, well, as I say, someone will be in touch with you very shortly. Oh, can you give me a contact number for you, please?..........That's it, then, thank you *very* much for your call.... goodbye.'

He put the phone down, somehow resisting the temptation to kiss the receiver. Beautiful, *beautiful!* It was about time the bloody sun came out a bit for a change! God, this deserved celebrating. He smiled unseeingly out at the street.

He'd have an early coffee break. At least relish the sweet taste of this victory without any distractions. Oh, we got you, we got you, now. A girlfriend and two foreign bits on the side! Well, you're going to pay now. You're going to bloody pay for all that now, all right! And all because you went out in the wrong *jacket*, you stupid bugger! That was the best of it, the fact that the clever-arsed bugger had made such a stupid slip-up. Oh, it was the stuff that dreams were made of! Right, give the fraud boys a call, then into the back for a coffee.

He picked up the phone and dialled.

Sandra looked up as Williams entered the staff office and walked briskly over to his tartan flask. She braced herself for a ticking off for taking an early break, but on seeing the bloom on his face, relaxed and picked up her paper again.

'You look cheery, Roger. Won the lottery or something?'

'No, it's better than that, Sandra,' he chuckled, unscrewing the lid of the flask and pouring himself a cup. 'It's much better than that.'

He smiled at her, actually flashing his eyes as he lifted the cup to his thin lips.

FORTY-SIX

Parked inconspicuously between two pools of orange lamplight, the dark-coloured Mazda sat with its lights off, its occupants just discernible when they moved, but who otherwise remained hidden by the gloom and the reflected light from the North London residential street.

'Well, I hope he gets lucky tonight,' sighed a young man in a brown leather jacket in the rear seat, shaking the crumbs out of a packet of crisps into his palm. He spoke to a figure in the front seat cradling a video camera. 'I thought you lot said this bloke was some sort of proper old Casanova or something.'

'Give him a chance. We've only gone out with him one night yet,' replied the man in the front, removing the lens cap from the camera, and rummaging in a black holdall full of equipment.

'He dragged us all *over* the bloody shop last night. And for fuck-all,' complained the man in the leather jacket, licking his fingers.

A large middle-aged figure in the back spoke. 'Look, Terry, he's been having the fucking piss out of them up in Kentish Town for three months. I think we can afford to sit on him for a few nights.'

'Right you are, boss,' said Terry, screwing up the crisp packet.

A hailing message came over a hands-free radio. 'Two-Four, come in over....'

'Roger, Three-One, over,' responded the driver, a man in his thirties with a moustache.

'Just got a call from the girlfriend. He's on his way down from the flat now. Over....'

'Roger, Three-One. Over,' replied the driver.

They watched as a fair-haired young man in a pale blue casual suit emerged from the luxury apartment block and strode energetically down the street to where a sleek red sports car was parked on the other side of the road.

'Hello again, mate,' said Terry, as Sacha unlocked the door of his car.

'All right, Tommo, move us out when he gets about halfway down the road.'

'Righto, chief.'

Terry picked up his hand-held radio. 'Standby, Nick. He's out. Eyeball on target, over....'

The low-slung profile of the sports car emerged from the row of parked vehicles and moved off down the road. A moment later, the dark Mazda, too, crept away from the kerb.

'Tell you what, boss, he knows a few coke-holes, this geezer,' remarked Terry, staring out of the window at the entrance to the Kings Cross club they had been parked outside for an hour. 'Might be worth turning him over for possession.'

'Might be at that. Tom, Pass us a sandwich, will you, mate?

'Righto…' said the driver, opening a Tupperware box. 'What do you want? There's… cheese and Branston pickle, or ham.'

'What about the cheese and tomato? Terry, I told you cheese and tomato.'

'Sorry, chief. I think Tailor's boys got the last of the tomato.'

'Bloody marvellous. Ham, then, Tommo.'

Tommo handed the sandwich to his superior.

'Christ, it's cold in 'ere!' shivered Terry, looking once more out of the window.

'What's the matter with you Terry, you lightweight?' laughed Tommo, as the investigator from the benefit fraud unit in the passenger seat lifted the camera and ran off a few more shots of the red sports car parked at the end of the street.

Terry made a sudden movement. 'All right, boys he's out!' he called in a firm, rising voice; then, 'Oh, fucking hell, he's on his own.'

They watched as Sacha reached his car and climbed inside.

'The night is still young, lads,' said the senior officer calmly, unwrapping his sandwich, and adding as the red car moved off, 'All right, take it away, Tommo.' He leaned back in his seat and took a bite as they crawled away from the kerb.

Terry spoke into the radio, 'Stand by, Nick. Target proceeding on his original, assume eyeball on Caledonian Road, over.... '

'Come on, come on, you scrote, where are you?' Terry's voice hung in the cold air of the car as the four men peered in silence up the road to the entrance of the exclusive private members club.

'Gotta be nearly chucking out time, now,' muttered Tommo from the driver's seat. For a while, the only sound came from the quick rhythm of his chewing-gum.

Terry leaned forward and addressed the officer with the camera. 'You boys do a lot of this, then?'

'Yeah, quite a lot.'

'A wonder you don't go fucking barmy. Or freeze your balls off.'

'Well, it's a long game, sure. You know, you just have to sit with it. Sometimes -'

'There he is,' interrupted Tommo. 'And he's not on his own. Look at that little piece on his arm!'

Terry leaned forward, blowing a quiet whistle.

'Thank Christ for that,' said the senior officer. 'All right, Tommo ... as soon as they pull away.'

'Dirty bastard,' chuckled Terry, watching Sacha and the girl walk down to the red sports car, covered all the while by the video camera trained on them from the passenger seat. He spoke into the radio, 'Okay, Nick, he's loaded. Standby, over.'

'Dirty bastard is right,' agreed the investigator from the fraud unit. 'He's been really having them on, this one.'

A few moments later, the red sports car drew away from the kerb, but pulled immediately into a tight U-turn and sped up the street toward them.

'Shit!' grunted Tommo, putting a full lock on the wheel as the car came past them.

'All right, get after him, Tommo, for fuck's sake!' yelled the senior officer. 'But don't let him clock you! He's in a fast fucking motor, there. If he sees us, we've had it.'

The car wheeled out from the curb and moved off down the road.

The four men stared ahead through the windscreen, the reflected streetlights moving back across their vision as the red car progressed ahead of them, Terry's commentary into the radio punctuating the silence.

'I think we got away with it, chief,' said Tommo.

The car ahead slowed and made a right turn.

'Easy does it, Tommo,' breathed the senior officer.

'Right-right into Woburn Place,' said Terry into the radio. Looks like he's heading for Euston Road, Nick, over....'

'I can't see too clearly, but it looks like the girl might already have her hand on his packet,' said Tommo, 'Are you getting that, mate?'

Terry chuckled. 'Jesus. We'll get him for due care an' all!'

The car ahead continued down to a set of traffic lights and made a left turn into the main thoroughfare crossing the road.

'Nick, he's made a left-left onto Euston Road, you've got the eyeball, over....'

'Roger, Two-Four, over,' came the reply, as the car came down to the lights.

'Can you see them, Tommo?' asked the senior, as they made the left turn.

'Yeah, Nick's up ahead, three cars ahead. Can't see our loving couple, though.'

The radio sounded. 'Two-Four, eyeballed target, proceeding along Euston, over....'

'Roger, Nick, over....'

The car fell silent for a while as the pursuit continued westward.

The radio crackled to life. 'Two-Four, he's making a right-right into Gloucester Place, take the eyeball, over....'

'There he goes, now,' said Tommo, catching sight of a sleek red shape turning right at the far end of the road.

'Roger, Nick, taking up eyeball, over....'

'Come on, Tommo, get your fucking foot down,' said the superior from the back. The car picked up speed, reached the junction and turned right.

'What's he up to, I wonder...?' murmured Terry.

'Looks like he's on his way home,' replied Tommo, 'He's gone a long way round, though.'

'If she *is* giving him a handjob, he probably wants to drag it out a bit,' offered the investigator. 'You know, they get a kick out of it while driving.'

'Why would he head home, though, with that bird still in the front seat?' queried Terry.

'Unless he's going to drop her off somewhere....' suggested Tommo.

'He'd fucking better *not* drop her off somewhere!' growled the senior officer.

'Right-right into Prince Albert Road, Nick, over....'

A minute later, the car ahead slowed and made a left turn.

'Well we're definitely home, then. There's his gaff on the right,' said Terry.

Tommo cautiously nosed the car round into the street.

'Nick, left-left into Wells Rise, over....'

The senior officer leaned forward. 'He's stopping. He's fucking stopping,' he said as the car ahead pulled into the kerb. 'Keep going, Tommo. Go past. Get that camera out of sight, mate.'

'Nick, he's stopped on Wells Rise, take up position at Prince Albert Road entrance, over......... Well, bloody move it along, then, over.' He turned to the senior. 'They're held up at the roundabout.'

'Shit. Right, Tommo, make the next left, wing it round that block up there and come down the top - fucking *quietly* - and get us in on the corner back there somewhere, and we'll just have to hope he's fucking still there when we come back.'

All four looked ahead as they passed the stationary red sports car on the right, and made the left turn.

'Okay, Tommo, get up there fucking sharpish,' yelled the senior officer, as the car swung right and picked up speed.

'Nick, where are you? Over…' said Terry into the radio as they slowed for another right turn, then picked up speed once more. 'Roger, put your foot down, over.'

The car decelerated for the final right turn.

'Okay, easy does it, Tom,' cautioned the superior as they crawled round into the street.

'He's still there,' said Tommo, peering down the road.

'Get in behind this white van!' shouted the senior officer.

Tommo pulled the wheel hard over, and drew up behind the parked van, immediately switching off the engine.

For a moment, they sat in silence, watching the red car parked down the road, looking for any signs of imminent flight.

'I don't reckon he's gonna run, boss,' said Tommo.

Terry added, 'He was probably too busy getting his balls felt to have clocked us, I reckon, chief.'

The senior officer relaxed. 'Thank Christ for that. I don't want to fart around on this bastard any more than we have to.' He addressed the investigator in the front seat, who was busy adjusting the zoom on the camera. 'Is that all right for you, mate?'

'Yeah, ta. I've got a good line on him.'

'Nick, we've got the eyeball. No change, stand by at Prince Albert Road entrance, over....'

'Roger, Two-Four. Coming into position at Albert Road entrance now, over.'

'Roger, Nick,' responded Terry.

Terry leaned forward in his seat. 'Looks like they're just sitting there. Oh, 'ello!'

'Fucking bingo,' said the senior officer in a low voice as Sacha's head disappeared towards the girl's lap. Her head fell back against the headrest.

'Oh, she likes that, look,' remarked Tommo.

'Are you getting that, mate?' asked Terry.

'Yeah... but to really nail him, I'm gonna need shots of him actually on the job. I mean, a good brief would tear this shot to pieces, you know? I mean, *we* know what's going on there, but you can't actually see what he's doing. A good brief would make out he's picking her glove up off the floor or something. Still, I don't reckon we're gonna have long to wait.'

'Why the fuck has he come back *here,* though?' wondered Terry.

'Probably wants to do it right under his girlfriend's nose. Probably gets a kick out of it,' suggested the senior officer.

'Right.... '

Sacha's head reappeared, and he suddenly raised himself in his seat, his hands on the belt of his trousers.

'Oh, here we go, then,' chuckled Terry.

'Give her one from me, mate,' added Tommo, as Sacha's trousers came down across his buttocks. The girl's leg came up over the back of the seat as Sacha bore down on her. There was a moment of inactivity as Sacha's naked rear paused motionless, lit by a shaft of orange streetlight.

'Looks like the boy can't get it in,' said the senior officer from the back. 'Don't tell me after all this he can't fucking get it in!'

'No, there he goes, chief,' said Tommo, as the orange-glowing flesh of Sacha's behind began moving vigorously up and down.

A spontaneous cheer broke from Terry.

'Fucking belt up, Terry!' cautioned the superior.

'Sorry, boss ... but it *is funny*.'

'It is that, I freely grant you. But just keep it down.'

They watched in silence for a few minutes.

'She's a fucking beaut, though,' remarked Terry wistfully.

'Too good for *that* shithouse,' replied Tommo.

Terry leaned round to peer at the LCD monitor of the video camera, 'How's the filming going, mate?'

'Fine. Great. This is the stuff. Any defence brief is gonna have his work cut out with this. I mean, the guy is patently *at it*.'

'Patently....' agreed Terry, nodding at the miniature screen and sitting back.

For a while, the four men watched in silence as the red car continued to bounce on its chassis, Sacha's rear moving back and forth in the orange light. The silence was broken only by the sound of chewing gum coming from the driver's seat.

'He's ready for the Olympics, this boy,' muttered Tommo presently from the front.

'Tommo, do us a favour, mate, and chuck us a Wrigley's,' came the voice of the senior officer.

Tommo passed a stick of gum to the back.

'Cheers.'

'You want one, Terry?' asked Tommo over his shoulder.

'Nah, you're all right, ta.'

'You want one, mate?' enquired Tommo of the investigator.

'No, thanks, pal.'

Tommo put the packet back on the dashboard, and the men lapsed into silence once more, their eyes on the thrusting backside down the street. Twenty minutes passed.

'Christ, I wish he'd get on with it. It's getting fucking tedious, this,' complained Terry.

'I wouldn't mind if we could see more of the bird,' threw in Tommo.

'Look, we're not here to nail the bird, Tommo,' said the senior officer in a weary voice.

'He's going up a gear, now,' said the investigator.

'Hoo-bloody-ray,' shivered Terry.

'Don't reckon we're far off, now....' remarked the investigator, his eyes on the camera monitor.

Terry leaned forward again and peered over the investigator's shoulder, watching the slow pan up Sacha's naked haunches, up through the creases of his shirt to his contorted, straining profile.

'Bet you a fiver he doesn't last more than another ... ooh, two minutes,' said Terry into the investigator's ear.

The other man laughed, 'I'm not taking that bet!'

'Fair enough.'

Down the road, the straining figure framed in the windscreen went suddenly rigid, then underwent a series of jerks.

'There he blows,' said Tommo.

Terry indicated the investigator, 'He knows his stuff, this bloke!'

They continued to watch as Sacha's body shuddered one final time, his orange-lit head thrown back in extremis, before collapsing forward onto the jamb of the passenger door.

'Well, give her a kiss, then, mate,' said Terry. 'Oh, look at that. He's not even going to give her a little thank you kiss.'

'Whatever happened to fucking romance?' said Tommo.

'And now it's *our* turn to fuck you…' Terry glanced round at the senior officer. 'We gonna take him, chief?'

'We are indeed, Terry, but not here. Remember the brief. To fuck him proper, we take him when he signs.'

From her desk, Sandra watched as Williams intoned the question, noting in his manner an extreme impassivity she had never in her life seen in him before. Like the stillness of her cat when watching a bird. Roger's big day. He would have put bunting up in the office, if he could.

'Have you had a sexual encounter at any time in the last two weeks?'

'No,' said the smiling, fair-haired young man in the suit.

Sandra watched as the young man bent forward and signed his name, continued watching as Williams took the signing sheet, stood up and walked over to the filing cabinet, past it and on to the staff office, actually faintly skipping for a step, as he reached the door and went inside, where waited the three plainclothes policemen who had arrived earlier that morning. A movement on the street caught her eye, and she turned to see the roofs of two police cars crawl to a stop before the windows.

Sacha watched as Williams went past the filing cabinet and entered the staff office. Why have you ignored the filing cabinet and why are you now skipping like a little girl into that pokey little hen-coop of a back office, you –

His flow was interrupted by the emergence of three men from the staff office. All three fixed him with their eyes and began walking toward him.

Williams followed the officers, struggling to keep his face straight. God oh God, this was the stuff that dreams were made of, all right. He'd bagged others in the past, many others, but nothing compared to this - perhaps nothing in life anywhere in fact compared to this, to the sensation of finally crushing the flash yobbo underfoot, of grinding the shiny buggering lout into the ground and – but oh yes look at his face, god yes, yes, look at his –

Sacha rose from his seat as the three men reached him. A police warrant badge appeared and filled his vision. 'Sacha Fairfax-Hanbury?'

'Yes?' said Sacha, his racing mind pushing away his shock. The gook? She'd blabbed? But that was –

'All right, sir, we'd like to question you in connection with seven counts of statutory rape,' said the senior officer, as the attention of the whole room fell upon Sacha and the plainclothesmen.

Sacha found his anger. These plod cretins had somewhere down the line got hold of the wrong man.

'What the bloody hell are you talking about? Just whom am I supposed to have raped? And what do you mean, *statutory* rape? That applies to consenting minors, and I've been nowhere near-'

'Not just consenting minors, sir. It also applies to consenting benefit centre facilitators. Such as the seven employees of this office in question, sir.'

For a second, Sacha stared at the scene around him, noted the claimants and their advisors peering at him in silence, saw for the first time the policewoman stationed outside the door and the police cars stopped outside on the street.

'Well, how could I have *raped* them? I was claiming benefit, which they were willingly providing. You do understand that this place is what is known as a Sex Benefit Centre, a place where - ?'

The senior officer removed a photograph from his inside pocket.

'Have you not been in a relationship with this woman for the past nine months, sir?'

Sacha glanced down at the photograph.

Sally.

The day he'd left his jacket....

Scabrous bitch.

And then he knew he was in a fight for his life.

'I'm not having sex with her, if that's what you mean.'

'Have you *ever* had sexual relations with her?'

'Yes, once or twice. But that was over a year ago.'

There was a sudden commotion outside the street door, as a female figure pushed past the policewoman and entered the reception area.

'There you are then, bastard! Getting arrested, are you, bastard? So this is where it all happens, is it, bastard?' shouted Sally, glaring around her in disgust as the policewoman caught up with her and took hold of her arm.

'All right, Miss Rand, we did advise you not to come down here. Leave it to us, please,' cautioned the senior officer.

'No, I want to see this!' cried Sally, trying to tug her arm away from the policewoman. 'You wouldn't bloody be here if it weren't for me. And *he* wouldn't bloody be here if I hadn't gone through ten days of sheer bloody hell pretending to still be his lover, the rotten filthy bastard piece of shit!! Though it'll have been worth it, by God, to see his balls nailed to the wall!!'

Sacha gave Sally a look of ridicule. 'Sally, what *have* you been telling these gentlemen?'

'That you're a lying sack of shit, of course!' She looked from him to the stairs leading up to the second floor. 'That you're a sick, diseased, filthy bloody pervert who pisses on a loving relationship to shag nobodies in a bloody sex dole toilet like some sad -'

'OK, that's enough, Miss Rand,' interrupted the senior officer. 'I understand what you've been through, but please be quiet now or I'll have you removed.' He turned once more to Sacha.

'So you're saying, sir, that you have not slept with this woman for over a year?'

'Yes, that is what I'm saying.'

Sally glared at him with furious hatred, but remained silent.

The officer went on. 'But she lives with you, sir.'

'Yes, I asked her to flat-share. The flat is my property, you understand, but she was lonely, I was lonely, it was a mutually beneficial arrangement. Two friends flat-sharing. Our sexual relations had been prior to this, you see. But although I was interested in resuming a sexual relationship with her, she wanted to keep things platonic. Why do you think I come in *here*, for God's sake? Because I *like* it? Whatever her reasons are now for her lies to you and this unfortunate and hysterical scene we've just witnessed -'

One of the officers brought out a video camera from the satchel he was carrying and handed it to the senior officer, who flipped open the monitor, set the video in motion and held the screen before Sacha's face. 'And is this young lady also keeping things platonic, sir?'

For a moment, Sacha stared at the screen. He flashed the questioning officer a faint smile.

'I must say I'm astonished that our brave boys in blue have so little to do with their time. I had *of course* intended today to declare this encounter to the centre, but -'

'But…?'

'But it slipped my mind. I -'

'Like buggery it did,' threw in Williams, almost laughing. 'I asked you if you'd secured any liaisons in the past fortnight and you emphatically said you had not - and then signed a declaration to the effect! You're *done*, boy! Bang to rights!'

He was waved down by the officer. 'And it slipped your mind to declare all your other encounters, sir? We have two other young women who are prepared to testify in court that you have been engaged in sexual relationships with them during the whole of the period for which you were claiming support.'

'They're lying.'

'A Miss Ulla Bjornstrand, and a Miss Inga Andersen.'

'I never slept with them.'

'They're prepared to swear on oath that you did. As this lady here is prepared to swear on oath that you were having sexual relations with her the whole time you've been signing on here. How do you account for that?'

'For some hysterical reason unknown to me, they have clearly got together and chosen to exploit my vulnerable status as a claimant of sex benefit. I suppose some species of typical female vindictiveness has something to do with it -'

'Sacha -' broke in Sally.

'In fact, yes, now I think about it, that's what ties them together; all three of them have been making requests for substantial loans, all of which I've refused. Sally here for instance has been -'

'I gave them the videos, Sacha,' said Sally with a contemptuous smirk. 'Just give up.'

Sacha fell silent, and stared at her for a long time, his face completely impassive. And then his lips widened slowly, opening out into a stunning dental smile.

He turned slowly to face the police officer, and spoke quietly and deliberately. 'All right. Through a little mild deception I took a few women in a sex benefit centre....' He brought the smile slowly to bear on Williams, raising his eyelids clear of his irises as he drilled into the claimant advisor's expression of smirking triumph. With glittering eyes, he brought the smile down to the paused image of the girl on the camera. 'However ... like Mandy there' - he stared at her - 'like Sally, here -' - he turned slowly, inflicting on her too the full force of his smile - 'like Ulla, like Inga ... the women in this centre are all ... just ... *whores*. Nothing more and nothing less. And I always paid my way. Whether in my *taxes* ... or my *drinks bills*, I always paid my way. I never raped anyone.'

He turned, leaving Sally to gaze into the back of his head as he walked smilingly of his own accord over toward the street door which was being held open for him by two uniformed officers gesturing to the open passenger door of the police car. The three plainclothes officers quickly fell in alongside him, the policewoman a few steps behind, escorting a now-sobbing Sally. Sacha felt a firm hand on his back, as the senior officer's voice once more sounded by his side.

'There's also a small matter of bribery and threatening behaviour involving a Miss Li Naing of Peckham, which we'll go into down the station.'

'I got *you*, boy! That'll teach you to mess with *me*, sunshine!' shouted Williams, his voice pitched queerly, causing Sandra and Harper to glance round at him.

Sacha was bundled outside, all at once looking sick and pallid as he reached for his cigarettes, the smile finally extinguished.

'No smoking in the car, sir,' barked the officer rapidly, shepherding him and an escorting officer into the back of the car and closing the door, before climbing into the front passenger seat as Sacha fumblingly replaced the cigarettes in his jacket.

The car pulled away, the two silhouetted profiles in the rear seat motionless as the vehicle moved off down the road.

As Sally and the last uniformed officers climbed into the second car and disappeared down the street, the reception area fell back into routine once more, with the exception of Williams, who loudly clapped his hands once and rubbed them, before rushing into the staff office, where he took from his coat a rolled-up piece of paper and spread it flat on the table. Next he affixed four balls of Blu-tac to the corners, before tacking it up on the wall. Then he went to the small refrigerator, opened the door and smiled at the large green and gold bottle.

There was a collective jump in the reception area at the loud 'bang' from the staff office. Sandra rose from her desk and went over. On entering the room, she saw Williams sat hunched on a chair, drinking from a plastic cup, while gazing up at a print-off of a Union Jack flag stuck on the wall. He turned to her.

'Champagne, Sandra?' he laughed, springing from his seat and brandishing the bottle. 'I'll get you a cup!

FORTY-SEVEN

With a mug of tea in one hand, a rolled-up copy of *NME* and a half-eaten slice of bread in the other, Carla walked slowly past the lounge, peeking in at Sharona and Ian slumped on the sofa bathed in television glow. She made her way up the stairs, watching the small feet beyond the hem of her dressing gown fall one after the other to the carpet.

A voice sounded below to her left. 'Don't bother making *us* one, then,' said Sharona coming out of the lounge and heading for the kitchen.

Carla stopped, and called after her, 'Sorry ... I didn't want to disturb you ... the kettle's still hot....'

There was no reply, and Carla continued, frowning the rest of the way up to the landing.

Entering her room, she walked over to the table and put down the tea and the magazine, and taking a bite from her bread, began clearing a space, determined finally to get on and write that advert for a guitarist to go in *NME*. It'd already been nearly a month since the last time she'd forced herself to do it, and then the phone had rung. Well, this time, she wouldn't get up until she'd *done* it.

She sat down and eyed the A4 pad sitting on a pile of papers, but reached for her tea instead. She sat for a while, sipping, her eyes moving over the rearranged chaos of magazines and paper on the table.

And then, she was held by something. She stared at the corner of a piece of A4 sticking out from the heap, and cringed with embarrassment. Well, there it was again. Her silly so-called 'portrait' of that sex dole guy. And out of sight, on the rest of the page, would be the poem. It had been weeks since she'd looked at that stupid drawing. Or read the stupid poem. That was a good sign, anyway. And at least she'd stopped gazing all sentimentally at the door to number 9 when she went in now. God, that time when she'd just stood there staring at it so long it had opened, and she'd tried to turn away but that woman had just come straight out and practically collided with her! And then she'd still hung around just long enough to get a glimpse inside of a naked man on a bed, but of course, it wasn't him.

She took another sip of tea and glanced over to her bedside table. She could do with a smoke. But no, she'd done a little too much of that lately.... Either she'd done a little too much of that lately or there really *had* been a miniature horse staring at her from the corner of the room the other night....

But *still* every time she went in a cubicle now, she couldn't quite kill that flutter in her chest in case he was there.

But as Holly had said, it was probably just as well he wasn't. God, that really *would* be a disaster if she started fixating on a sex dole guy! Especially if Holly ended up getting him one time! Which *was* possible - though, as neither of them had encountered him in all this time, it was probably like Holly reckoned; he'd probably been moved to another centre or something, or else had just left for some other reason.

She got up slowly and went over to her CD player.

But *thank God, thank God, Holly had never had him.*

She pressed the play button and made her way back to the table, Tindersticks filling the room.

She pushed her hair from her temple in annoyance. But, no, *let* Holly have him. She was *over* it, she was supposed to be *over* all that nonsense, wasn't she? So why was she still obsessing about it months later?

She flopped down in the chair. But no, she wasn't obsessing about it, she was just thinking about it - because she'd unearthed that silly drawing and that silly poem. Her eyes drifted to where the paper with the crude little biro portrait was sticking out of a heap of music magazines and bank statements.

Suddenly agitated, she jumped up, went over to her night table, brought over her cannabis paraphernalia and began rolling. Lighting the spliff, she pulled over her A4 pad, opened the copy of *NME* and reached for her pen. She flicked through the pad, looking for the page with her previous attempts to write the guitarist wanted ad, and found instead the pleading letter to her father, abandoned mid-sentence. Then came the three attempts to write to her mother.

She blanked them all out, found the right page and began for the tenth time trying to compose her advert. Guitarist wanted for singer-songwriter, blah, blah.... Maybe she'd better think again what to put for her influences.... But whatever you put just made the ad look banal; somehow it always looked like you were admitting you weren't original, that you were just going to be ripping off your heroes. She stared at the paper and sighed. No one was going to bloody answer it anyway! Still, come on, that's not the attitude.

Nevertheless, her attention wandered to a photo in the magazine of some band she'd never heard of, a review of some gig she'd never gone to, and from there, her eyes drifted on to the scrap of paper with the portrait and the poem.

She snatched it out from the pile. Let's just have a *little* look at it to see how bad it is.

Well, the drawing was truly awful. Just shit. And the poem would be even worse, probably. She seemed to remember the first verse was pretty dreadful, really embarrassing. Bracing herself for the flush of shame which always came from reading through her old doggerel, she began:

Slim and unshaven reticent king,
You came to our country to teach us to sing.
An insolent charger you brought to our lanes,
And succulent darkness we pressed to its veins.

Mysterious boy, as you rock on inside me
I look in your eyes for somewhere to hide me.
Something I find there wants me to know you.
Was it the line I wanted to throw you?

Well, I sob like a child and finger your lips
As you come up to speed, accelerate your hips
To the frightening blur of a humming-bird's wing,
And I flow all around you, my shaggy-lock king.

She finished reading, but remained staring at the paper, aware of the tear now rolling off her chin to the table.

She began reading it through again, taking deep drags on the spliff, before slowly reaching for her pen. Then she put a wobbly line through 'As you come up to speed', and replaced it with 'To feel you again,' modifying the tense, so the verse now read:

Well, I'd sob like a child and finger your lips
To feel you again accelerate your hips
To the frightening blur of a humming-bird's wing
How I'd flow once more around you, my shaggy-lock king.

Wiping her face, she moved her eyes intently back and forth across the revisions, frowning, her fingernail between her teeth.

Her eyes went again to the drawing.

No, it was awful, pathetic. It didn't look anything *like* him! She slowly scribbled it out with looping rings of black biro, biting down hard on her nail.

She looked again at the poem, her countenance lightening. The drawing was useless, dreadful, but the *poem*.... If she could just make the last line scan better... then it would be one of the best things she had ever done ... and it was a *love* poem ... and love poems were hard things to write....

She sat staring at it, her head on one side, before sitting back in her chair, her brow creased once more.

Okay, so it wasn't bad, it was good, brilliant; in fact it was the best love poem ever written by man or woman, but....

It was to a sex worker.

She took a breath.

Right. Enough.

Are we going to chase illusions *forever*, Carla, dear?

She let out the breath through flapping lips, and with a determined furrow of her brow, sat forward again and quickly ripped the paper to pieces, got up and threw the scraps in the bin. Retrieving the spliff from the table, she went over to her bed and sat down.

She took a drag, and realised her neck was aching. God, how it was aching.... She put down the spliff, and began trying to self-massage the tendons at the base of her skull, her eyes drifting to the waste-paper basket. She tore them away, forcing herself to look at the carpet as she went on pressing the sinews of her neck.

But it wasn't doing any good....

She flung herself back onto the bed; then sat up just as quickly in a fresh state of agitation, reached for the spliff, inhaled and stared again at the bin, her exhaled smoke irritating her moistening eyes.

And then, dropping the spliff, she launched herself from the bed and rushed over to the bin, knelt down and rummaged inside frantically, before finally drawing herself up, all the scraps of the torn paper held in her palms as she hurried back to the table.

She sat down, her eyes welling up as she fingered the scribbled-over portrait. Sorry, sorry, my lovely! She picked up the scrap and pressed it softly to her lips, held it there for a moment, then put it back on the table and went on stroking it with her fingertip. At least he was under that scribble somewhere, she could imagine him under there - and better than she had drawn him. She lay the pieces out on the table, and then noticed the spliff smouldering on the carpet. God! She jumped up again, picked it up, wiped ineffectually at the black mark on the floor, and returned to her chair. Inhaling from the spliff as she sat down, she began contemplating the scraps laid out before her.

It was like looking down at a torn photograph ... but not of an image - of a memory. A torn photograph of a memory of a kind of happiness.... Or a torn photograph of a memory of the ... *possibility* of the ... *potentiality* of a kind of happiness! She stared glumly at the scraps, watching her chewed ring-finger brushing the black scribble. The crazed black scribble was actually a bit like his hair....

She smiled faintly, and allowed herself to go on stroking the torn scraps for a while.

Pushing her long hair back over her ear, she got up from the table and began looking for the Sellotape.

FORTY-EIGHT

Carlton stood motionless over the filthy kitchen counter and stared down at the hammer. His chin sunk in fat, his small eyes peering out from under a fringe of densely matted unwashed hair, he extended his hand and gripped the shaft of his dead dad's old lump hammer, lifting it slowly, the voices of Kirk and Spock drifting incoherently to him from the lounge. He turned the implement slowly in his fleshy hand. There was a good ... weight on it, like.... He held it for a moment, then let it drop back to the counter, and shuffled out to the sitting room. Picking up his lager, he took a sip and gazed vacantly for a moment at the model starship drifting across the TV screen. He took another sip, spilling some beer on his shirt, which he wiped with the back of his hand, before turning and making his way back into the kitchen, treading over a sliding heap of porn magazines. He stood once more over the counter, gazing down at the hammer. Again, he picked it up, feeling its weight in his palm.

... if they thought he ... he was just gunna fuckin' forget it, like, then they were fuckin' wrong ... how can you forget you want a fuck, like, anyway?... no, they were wrong, like, but the thing was they didn't know *how* wrong ... bastards sittin' behind desks ... bastards sittin' behind fuckin' desks should be made to fuckin' understand... like women should ... like fuckin' women should ... but that bastard with the glasses last week, like ... the way that fuckin' bastard had just sat there readin' to him off the computer that they wouldn't let him back, just readin' out the same shite that was in that fuckin' letter, and all around him all those other bastards were just bein' let up to the women, an' that bastard tellin' him he wasn't allowed an' them goin'up and him bein' told to get out an' them goin' up an' maybe even gettin' his angel -

He felt suddenly dizzy, and stood for a minute shaking his head, as the thin, shivering terrier pushed through his fat legs to begin crunching the stale chocolate biscuit in its bowl.

Using the fridge to steady himself, and narrowly missing putting his foot in a dried-out dog turd, he picked up the hammer and shambled back out to the lounge.

He picked up his coat and slowly pulled on one sleeve, his attention wandering again to the TV screen. Lieutenant Uhura was swinging round in her swivel chair. He looked on dumbly with small eyes and felt again that feeling he'd always felt as a kid, like, a funny feelin' he'd always had whenever he saw Uhura's lovely black tights, but when you were a kid you never wanted to know what was inside 'em, like ... you weren't bothered ... not like now ... not like fuckin' *now*.

His hand drifted down to his groin, but the image of the actress was replaced by a shot of a spaceship. His hand returned to the business of putting on his coat.

... and when you were a kid, you loved the spaceships more than anythin', like ... nearly more than anythin' in the whole fuckin' world....

... not like fuckin' *NOW*.

He put the hammer in his coat pocket and began moving toward the door, but stopped and frowned down at his side. The handle was sticking out of his pocket, like. He put his hand in his pocket, covering the handle with the sleeve of his grimy coat, and left the flat.

Sandra sat in the staff office, finishing her coffee. Glancing at her watch, she began folding her newspaper as Williams entered from the reception area, making for his flask. She peered curiously at him as he passed; he seemed to be getting more haggard by the day.

'Sandra, you remember that flash bugger, don't you?'

'No....' Sandra forced herself to reply.

'A few months back. The false claim. The one in the suit,' prompted Williams, unscrewing his plastic cup.

'Oh ... yes.'

'Went to trial last week. I just heard.'

Sandra nodded blankly and began rising from her seat.

'Anyway,' he continued, struggling to hold Sandra's attention, 'they convicted him. Seven years. Good result, that.' And yet his face failed to register anything to celebrate as he began pouring his coffee, and he added with bitterness, 'Pity we can't put a few more of them away.'

Sandra nodded wearily and picked up her paper. God, he was just getting worse and worse. She left the room.

He was just putting the cup to his lips when Moira the receptionist appeared at the door.

'Roger. Graham would like to see you in his office.'

She headed back out to her desk, leaving Williams to drink his coffee in silence, staring sightlessly at the tartan pattern of his flask.

'Ah, Roger ... sit down.'

Closing the door, Williams crossed the floor and occupied the chair across from Henshaw's desk.

'Roger ...' began Henshaw, regarding Williams, before glancing away as if uncertain how to continue. He sighed and returned his look to Williams, then went on, trying to sound decisive. 'This mess about the termination of Lucinda's contract.... The department have brought it up again, and ... well, the long and the short of it is, she is standing by her allegations, and it looks like there's going to be an enquiry....'

Williams said quietly, 'I see.'

'Now. They wanted to suspend you on full pay pending the outcome, but I managed to get them to spare you that indignity, what with ...' - he looked down at the table - '... the break-up of your marriage and so on....'

Williams sat in silence.

Henshaw regarded him evenly, then cleared his throat and leaned forward.

'I should warn you that ... information has been received, certain potentially corroborating evidence, and ...' he widened his eyes and took in a sharp breath. 'Well, frankly, your situation is not a good one.... However, it is clear you have been under a great deal of stress in recent months, and ... I will endeavour to ensure that any enquiry takes all attenuating circumstances into account....'

'You said you received some information,' replied Williams quietly. 'May I ask what, and from whom?'

'You surely must understand that I am not at ... liberty to tell you that at this stage.'

'Fine. I see,' replied Williams tonelessly.

There was a pause.

Henshaw appeared about to say something, but then reconsidered.

Williams spoke. 'Well ... is that all?'

As though rescued by the question, Henshaw looked Williams in the face and nodded, saying, 'Yes, that will be all, Roger. Thank you.'

Williams rose and headed for the door.

'Roger....'

'Yes?'

'Just ... prepare yourself, that's all.'

Williams gave him a blank look and exited the room.

Arriving once more in the reception area, he made his way straight to the staff office and ran himself a cup of water. He gulped back the contents, standing over the sink. Prepare himself! How do you prepare to lose your bloody job?! And all because of somebody down here, because of some righteous bugger who'd started sniffing about and somehow put two and two together.

He drained the cup and leaned forward, gasping.

The flat tone of Sandra's voice sounded behind him. 'Are you all right, Roger?'

It almost sounded as though the bitch were deliberately taking the ruddy piss!

He whirled round.

'Yes, of course, I'm all right,' he replied, trying to sound calm, wiping a drop of water from his chin, and throwing the cup in the bin. He eyed the woman before him, trying to work out if she were against him, if she were working against him.

'You don't *look* all right.'

Williams stared at her. 'Sandra, you're not being paid to evaluate my welfare. You're being paid to do a job. What are you doing in here now?'

'I was on my way to the loo,' she said with emphasis.

'Well, *go* to the loo, and then get back to your work, please.'

He received a silent look of defiance as Sandra made her way past him to the toilet. He turned and went back out to the signing area, his gaze falling immediately on the back of Harper's head. He approached his own desk, his eyes not leaving the grizzled grey curls framing the Jamaican's temple.

Carlton shifted his weight down Kentish Town Road as quickly as he could, bowling along in a curious waddling motion, his breath turning to snorts as the sex benefit centre came into view past the garage.

... it wasn't right that they could throw you off just for muckin' about with a dab of fuckin' liquid paper. Just for coverin' up a harmless fuckin' rash! Even *they'*d said it was fuckin' harmless, like! Not for life, like, not for fuckin' life!! How could they leave you to rot, like? Just for that, just for fuckin' that?? Fuckin' BASTARDS!! Fuckin'-

A young woman with a push-chair walking ahead looked round at him, terrified, and he realised that he'd shouted the last bit out aloud. Well, if she didn't fuckin' like it, like, then she should let him FUCK her, then he might calm DOWN!

'Then I might calm DOWWWN!!' He shouted aloud, looking her in the eye as he overtook her, not knowing whether he'd shouted accidentally again or on purpose.

...but he'd better fuckin' cool it a bit, like, save it for when he was inside with them. Otherwise it'd be like in Camden fuckin' market, when the fuckin' police had come and pushed him into the car and driven him home and all those fuckin' cows had just stared at him like he was a fuckin' monster... like that woman just had with that fuckin' push-chair -

He stopped and turned round, tightening the grip on the wooden shaft of the hammer in his pocket, causing the woman behind him to stumble to a petrified stop, her hands tensed on the handle of the push-chair. A cloud of her white, terrified breath drifted into Carlton's furious snorted exhalations as they stood facing each other. The toddler in the push-chair peered up at Carlton with wide eyes.

The face-off lasted only a couple of seconds before Carlton took his wild glare from the woman's young blue eyes and turned. He continued toward the drab concrete building ahead, while the woman remained where she was, debating with herself whether even to continue in her original direction.

Reaching the entrance door of the centre, Carlton forced himself to calm down. He didn't want to get thrown out by the security bastard before he'd even fuckin' started, like.

He slowly pushed open the door and stepped inside, keeping his head low and his eyes on the carpet, imagining this would somehow make him less conspicuous. Crossing to the ticket dispenser, he tore off a white V-shaped ticket, the sight of which caused a pang of grief to break out across his chest, and he wanted to take the hammer out there and then and start breaking up the dispenser. But no, he shouldn't do that, like, cos then he'd throw away any chance he might still have of makin' the bastards understand and gettin' them to let him back on. He had to just try to keep playin' it cool, like....

With his right hand still thrust in his pocket, and holding the ticket in his left, he shuffled over to the waiting area. Only when he had sat down did he dare raise his eyes to the signing desks. The black bloke was in, like. And the bastard with the glasses. The old bag with the grey hair. And some bloke. If only he could get the black bloke. He was all right, him. He'd smile and see you all right, like, that bloke....

But hang about ... he was fuckin' dreamin', fuckin' dreamin' again, like he'd been dreamin' in the pub when he'd bought that cow them Pringles ... cos this place was about rules, wan't it, like, not fuckin' smiles! An' if he got that black bloke, he'd just still be told to fuck off but nicely like, an' then like it wouldn't be that bloke's fault, an' then it'd be wrong to hit him, like, an' someone in here needed fuckin' hittin' if they weren't gunna fuckin' understand an' let him back on. And of course the fuckin' bastards weren't gunna let him back on, it was all written down in their fuckin' computers, an' in their fuckin' cupboards an' in their fuckin' eyes that they weren't gunna let him back on, so let's have that bloke with the fuckin' glasses, then, cos if anyone's gunna get it, like, best it's him, like.

Williams watched the claimant before him, a well-presented, double chinned man in a smart beige raincoat, as he leaned forward to sign his name. As he wrote, Williams caught sight of a large unkempt figure waiting over on the plastic seating. It was that stupid fat bugger again! Some of these fools just would not be told, would they!

The man with the double chin pushed forward the signing sheet and handed back the pen as Williams handed him his ticket and SB40. 'Number 2, then.'

'Thank you,' replied the claimant, beaming effusively as he rose from his seat.

Williams was filled with a sudden outright disgust for the man, and made no response other than to drop his eyes and cue on the next claimant.

Carlton looked on as the LED counter finally flicked over to the number on his ticket. His small eyes sought out the free desk. Yeah ... yeah, sound, fuckin' sound, the fucker in the glasses....

He stood up and shuffled over, his heart racing. Right, then, fucker, you four-eyed bastard, are you gunna tell me what I want to hear, like, you fuckin', fuckin' bastard, or are you ready for a fuckin' hammer, like? A fuckin' hammer in the fuckin' head?

As he approached Williams' desk, Carlton was watched intently by Harper. The Jamaican continued to observe as the great shambling figure sat down, then switched his glance to Williams' pinched, bitter profile, before returning his attention to his own claimant.

Williams took in the lumpish figure sat before him, the stains on the shirt, the filthy matted hair. Christ, look at the state of him. And there was a smell. Bloody hell, there was a smell coming from him.

'And what can we do for you today?' said Williams with open sarcasm.

Harper heard Williams' tone, and looked round for a moment as his own claimant signed his claim sheet. He watched as Carlton answered.

'I want another chance, like ... I -'

'I told you before. It's quite useless you coming in like this.'

Harper was alarmed by the clear smirk on Williams' face.

Carlton tightened his grip on the hammer, felt himself about to pull it out, but some instinct reminded him that would be the end and - better to keep tryin', like - 'Look, you don't ... you don't understand, like.... It was just ... like, it was just a fuckin' mistake, like ... that form.... I never meant to, I never -'

'Do I have to read it all out to you again?'

'No, no, I know what it says, like!' said Carlton loudly, his agitation increasing. Several heads turned.

'Listen to me,' said Williams sharply. 'You-'

'I -'

'Listen to me!' snapped Williams with closed eyes, and waving down Carlton's protests. 'You have been caught tampering with a medical form which means you automatically forfeit all rights to claim. The decision is final and binding. That's it. Finito. How can I make it any clearer for you?'

Carlton slammed the desk with his left hand, and lurched in his seat, his face twisting with a final agonised appeal.

'But I'll fuckin' never get another fuck in my LIFE without this!'

Harper looked on, appalled, as Williams, with a now naked contempt, replied evenly and deliberately:

'Well ... you've already had more than nature intended. Now get out of my sex benefit centre.'

There followed a moment of confusion as both Harper and Williams watched Carlton struggling to pull something from his pocket, an odd look almost of panic on his face. And then the hammer was out, and Carlton was on his feet, screaming.

Williams caught a brief flash of dirty black metal swinging in toward his face, instinctively pulled his head back as the hammer whipped past and down, landing smack on the back of his right hand. He howled with pain and jumped out of his chair, as Carlton brought the hammer down a second time on the keyboard, snorting and roaring half-formed, slurred obscenities.

Harper, too was on his feet; all the claimant advisors were now up, retreating from their desks, as Carlton landed another blow on Williams' monitor, cracking the casing. The claimants were also up, some moving back toward the walls, as the security guard limbered over, his arms spread in an effort to contain the wildly flailing figure.

Williams had drawn back to the door of the staff office, wincing and holding his hand, while Harper and another junior advisor had stepped forward again, their arms outstretched, entreating Carlton to put the hammer down. Sandra had retreated to the reception desk, where she instructed Moira to call the police.

Snarling, Carlton dealt another shattering blow to the monitor and pointed at Williams. 'Fuckin' come out here, y'fuckin' bastaAAAGHD!!'

Williams made no move.

'All right, mate, just put it down, put it down -' ordered the guard, looking for his chance to move in. He made a sudden feint, eliciting from Carlton a clumsy parry.

Distracted from Williams by the guard, Carlton edged back toward the window, and stood swinging the hammer through the air, but increasingly now without any apparent object, his head and shoulders twitching violently as though in the grip of a fit. After each spasm, his face appeared somehow more and more abstracted, though he continued to swing the hammer vigorously from side to side.

Seeing his opportunity, the guard lunged forward, but Carlton, coming back to himself, made a lucky, low swing of the hammer and caught his assailant a powerful, winding blow to the stomach, sending him in agony to his knees. Carlton stumbled back against the window, and bellowing incoherently, turned and put the hammer through it, showering the pavement with glass. A girl cowering near the reception desk screamed.

Still brandishing the hammer, Carlton looked round and saw the security guard attempting to get to his feet. Hefting his weight around, Carlton quickly bustled himself out of the door, knocking over a revolving stand of leaflets as he went. The guard made an attempt to follow, but sank to his knees again at the door and crumpled forward, holding his stomach. Harper and a man with a beard rushed over to help the injured guard, Harper yelling at Moira to call for an ambulance.

A siren was now sounding in the distance, and staff and public alike moved over to the windows to watch. Carlton could be seen outside shambling about in panic and then falling into the side of a stationary vehicle stopped at lights.

'What's he doing?' asked Williams, who was still standing at the back of the room.

'He's screaming at the woman in that car,' replied Sandra.

There was a sound of breaking glass, and a cry of 'Jesus Christ!' from someone at the window.

'He's broken the window on her car!'

'The police are at the other end of the street -'

'He's getting in-'

'What the hell's he doing?'

'She's got out of the car -'

'He's nicking her car, he's bloody nicking her car -'

Williams cautiously approached the window, still holding his hand and wincing with pain.

Outside, the car lurched forward, stopped, then kangarooed across the junction, hitting a van coming in the opposite direction, before mounting the kerb for several yards and then once more returning to the road and continuing down the street. The van meanwhile, spun round once and came to a sideways stop, blocking the junction.

For a few moments, people continued to stare out of the window, though now there was little to see until the police arrived, other than the woman whose car had been taken speaking frantically with the stunned driver of the van, and the driver of another car, who had stepped out to help.

Williams took his eyes from the scene outside and glanced round at the broken glass, the smashed equipment, the dazed-looking crowd of claimants and advisors. His eyes fell on Harper and the group helping the injured guard, and he realised jealously that no one had helped him with his hand or even bloody asked him how it was.

And he actually muttered - almost spat - under his breath, 'Well, don't anybody bother to ask about my hand.'

Sandra seemed to hear, giving him a look, but he couldn't be sure. Anyway, she made no move toward him. He gazed around again at the wreckage, feeling suddenly sick. He had to ... sort this out. Had to ... get the place together.

He wiped his forehead and set about re-establishing order, trying not to gasp with pain as he spoke.

'All right, let's ... come away from this glass.' A few people stepped back, but the majority remained where they were, watching the scene outside. Williams looked at Harper. 'Alex, can you pick that stand up, please -'

Harper, still kneeling by the guard, fixed Williams with his bright eyes, his expression severe. Ignoring the stand, he got to his feet and took a step toward Williams. He regarded him for a moment with eyes of liquid indignation, and then spoke.

'I aalways knew you were messed up, man. Now I know how much.' His eyes flashed, and he made a wild gesture of his arm. 'You caused this! You! You caused it aall by taalkin' to the guy the way you did. Well, I'm tellin' Henshaw the whole thing, everythin' you said -'

'And you'll enjoy that, won't you?'

'What? You're crazy, man, completely crazy!'

'I know very well you've gone upstairs behind my back.'

A defensive look came into Harper's eyes, but only for a moment.

'It was my duty. You were messin' with the procedures. I don't know why you were doin' it, but I knew someone should tell Henshaw. Like someone should tell him this. So I'm goin' up the stairs again - and not behind your back!'

He turned, but was immediately arrested by Williams gripping his pullover sleeve with his good hand.

Harper looked round, his eyes blazing. 'Let go, Roger.'

'Don't....' said Williams, his voice pitched strangely, 'don't tell him what I said.'

'I'm tellin' him! Everythin'!' He tried to pull himself away, but Williams' hand remained on his pullover, the material stretching absurdly between them.

'Alex, don't.'

'Let go, maan!' cried Harper before the amazed onlookers as he tried again to pull himself away, the polyester jumper stretching a ludicrous distance.

Williams heard female voices calling his name, became aware of Sandra and Moira at his side, saw their hands prising his fingers from the fabric of Harper's jumper; he watched, detached, almost amused, as first one, then two, three fingers were pulled away, and Harper was free, making his way to the staff staircase.

And then the women stepped quickly away from him, regarding him with different eyes as they moved off to take charge of the situation, and he was left alone with the killing throbs from his broken hand. Suddenly, all he could think of was the pain.

He felt like throwing up, and guessed he was probably in shock. Water, he needed water. No, sit down. He needed to sit down, but he felt disoriented; it was as though the whole room had changed. Christ, the pain! He drifted through a clutch of bewildered claimants and collapsed into a seat. Glancing down, he saw that one of the ridge bones of his right hand appeared to have been mashed into a different shape. Oh, Christ! Christ! But presumably, hopefully, the ambulance would be here soon. The sight of his hand was too awful, and he looked up and stared over at the stains running up the opposite wall from the heating units, trying to shut out the pain, but everything seemed to be coming to him somehow in reverse. His gaze drifted down the far wall, and, refocusing his blurring vision, he realised with a shock that he was sitting across the room, directly opposite his own desk.

He was sat on the plastic seating of the waiting area.

He was on the other side.

He'd better ... better stand up. But he felt too weak to move.

Instead, he put his forehead in his left hand, stared unseeingly at the carpet, and, wincing, listened gratefully to the approaching ambulance siren.

After running out into the street, Carlton had smashed the passenger window of the car in the continuation of his blind rage rather than from any logical plan of escape, but on hearing the police siren, had found himself pulling open the door and climbing inside, bellowing at the terrified woman driver to move off.

Seeing the little cubes of glass all over her knees and her skirt, and a man with a hammer climbing in next to her, the woman made a quick calculation to just get out of the car, and did so, in her panic leaving the engine running.

'Fuckin' get back in!' shouted Carlton, who had only had two driving lessons in his life, as the woman began crying to passersby for help.

The siren grew louder, and Carlton's eyes flitted to the steering wheel, and next thing he knew he was lifting himself with difficulty over the gearbox and into the driving seat. Gripping the wheel with his huge hands, he frantically pumped different combinations of clutch and accelerator, until the car began lurching forward, the over-revved engine whining painfully, until the engine engaged and he shot out into the box junction, clipping the fender of the white van, and careering over to the kerb where the left-hand wheel bounced up onto the pavement. The steering wheel was wrenched from his control as the right-side tyre ground along the kerb. He struggled to hold on until the car finally dropped down back into the road.

And although he was there trying to keep control of the car, he was also back in the centre, back there swingin' the hammer at that fucker's face, but he'd fuckin' missed ... but he *had* got his hand, he'd got his hand, like - but it wasn't enough, but he'd got that guard bastard, he'd got him good, like, yeah, that'd bin sound ... but 'ang on, there was somethin' somethin' wrong there, the bloke hadn't really ... hadn't really deserved it like, he was just a bloke, a bloke doin' his fuckin' job -

The car bounced again into the kerb, the jolt unlocking his tears.

- he'd had it now, he'd fuckin' had it now, he'd done that bloke in, and he shouldn't've, he fuckin' shouldn't've, because that bloke, like, he wasn't, wasn't, wasn't ... the enemy, like - not even, not even the fucker in the glasses was, really -

He caught sight of a pretty girl in a short skirt and red tights walking along the pavement.

- no, it was them.

Fuckin' them!!

He should've done that woman with the fuckin' pram, not that guard, like - like he should do her, there -

He swung his head round at the girl as he drove past, the sight of her beautiful hair lifting on the wind making him sob with rage.

Grunting and blinking away his tears, he returned his wet-eyed vision to the road. On the pavement ahead in the far distance on the left were three more girls, their backs to him as they headed down to Camden, dressed in long black or rainbow-coloured cardigans, slinky black tights and platform boots. And everything about them, their laughter, their thin, sexy legs, the smooth skin of their pretty faces, seemed to be telling him not just to fuck off, but to fuck off and die. Their black hair in the sun made it clear he was as good as dead, that he'd always been as good as dead. And, though he could never have articulated it, he intuited, as he stared madly at the gentle rotation of their young pelvises, that there in that heavenly cradling motion, was located somewhere the authority, the ultimate authority rubber-stamping his exemption from life.

And then he was screaming, his heart exploding with a mad incandescent hatred, as his fat hands pulled the wheel to the left, and he was on the pavement again, putting his right foot to the floor.

- well, YOU'RE fuckin' dead an' ALL -

The girls grew larger through the windscreen, as the adrenalin pounded in his neck.

- bye, then, Camden girls, fuckin' BYE-BYE!!

The girl on the left started to look round over her shoulder.

And everything seemed to slow down.

Over the girl's petrified face there seemed to pulse a brief image of a tower block balcony in sunlight, a small child, himself, playing with his toys, his Thunderbird Three.... And then he was simply looking again at the girl's turning, terrified face, but it became the face of his mother the day she'd told him for his own good not to have any more crushes on girls at school, the day she'd told him to 'adjust' and 'learn his place'.... Again the face became the girl's, breaking into a scream as she broke away to her left. Carlton remained on course for the other two, who only now began to turn their heads. With tears streaming down his face, he ground the pedal into the floor.

And now he was zooming into their horrified eyes, their slim waists perfectly in line with the leading edge of the bonnet of the car -

A friendly female voice filled his head.

... HEY, SOLDIER.....

And the smiling face of the angel was there, floating before the windscreen, her golden hair spread out on the pillow, as she called to him from the bed once more, reaching out to him again....

His cry shifted pitch to a sob of remorse, as at the last instant he pulled the wheel hard over to the right, missing the girls, and smashing to a dead stop as the engine of the car forked itself around a thick iron bollard, the impact breaking his neck, killing him instantly.

FORTY-NINE

Lawrence opened the patio door and stepped outside. Remaining by the door, he took out his cigarettes and tried to get a sense of the day, looking out over the overgrown garden. It wasn't exactly warm, a notch above fucking freezing, but there did seem to be a faint perfume on the air. He delayed lighting his cigarette for a moment, smelling the breeze. Yes, a mild scent was definitely being emitted from some piece of foliage somewhere. Still, this vague essence of 'spring awakening' seemed to be about the only sign of the bastard. He lit up, obliterating the delicate aroma, and scanned the blank canopy of cloud. There was a sort of fragile, rheumy streak of blue off to the right of the tower block.

He turned and peered back into the flat, hearing the toilet flush. A mild expression of distaste crossed his face and he looked out once more over the tangled garden, his glance following the broken stone path down to the work shed at the bottom. He leaned on the door-frame and inhaled, as heavy footfalls sounded behind him from the living room.

'Ah, I needed that.... Sorry! It's a long drive down from my neck of the woods.'

Lawrence turned and sent out a weak, dutiful smile to the tanned middle-aged man coming up beside him. Better offer him something. 'Er ... do you want a cup of tea or anything, first..? Coffee?'

'Er, no ... I think not. I think not. Thank you, though, Lawrence. Actually, I'm in a bit of a rush. Jill's motor's in for a service, so I've got to drive halfway out to bloody Esher this afternoon and pick her up from the clinic. In for a bit of a service herself, you might say!'

'Oh, yes?' said Lawrence without interest, beginning to lead the way down to the shed.

'Yes. Bit of lipo. Bit of a reshaping job. Her idea, of course,' said the man, addressing the grass, as they approached the shed.

An image came to Lawrence of a blueprint showing the preferred geometry of a female curve, the finishing touches to the plan being applied by whatever repulsive presence lay dormant inside the guy's trousers.

'Tell you what, Lawrence. Next time, I'll just hand her over to you, eh? You can trim a bit off with one of your sculpting tools!'

'Yeah ...why not...' replied Lawrence from under a thunderous brow, without looking round.

'No, I'm joking, of course. Anyway, she'd probably throw a fit just at the sight of the shed! Jill likes her little comforts, these days. Acquired a bit of a taste for the good things in life. As have I, of course. Which is why I'm here, of course!'

Lawrence made no response other than to keep the hostility from his face as he drew out his keys and unlocked the shed door, only speaking again when they were inside the damp-smelling workshop.

'So, er ... which one was it you were interested in again? There were three I had cast.'

'It was a crouching female figure.... I'll know it when I see it.'

Lawrence bent down to open a small cupboard, but was stopped by an exclamation from the visitor.

'Crikey! What've you got under that sheet? It's bloody enormous!'

Lawrence followed the man's gaze to the shrouded dog-loined sculpture. 'I'll show you if you like.'

'Go on, let's have a look.'

Lawrence stood up, went over to the dark, rearing mass, and began unwrapping the black plastic sheeting, until the figure stood as though half undressed, the black plastic having being pulled down to a point halfway down the thighs, between which, fused to the sinews of the groin, continued to snarl the ferocious skinned head of the dog, its ears drawn back, brow alive with fury as the jaws continued their relentless grip on the figure's right hand, the black pits of the eyes still locked into their crazed blind stare.

'God, that's a bit weird!'

Lawrence said nothing.

The buyer continued to regard the piece, his hands on his hips. 'Not exactly subtle, is it?'

'No. It isn't,' replied Lawrence with a stern look.

'Almost a comedy piece!'

Lawrence shrugged. 'Maybe it is, at that.'

'Amazing, though.... What are you going to do with it, then?'

'I haven't the faintest idea. Probably let it stand *there* for twenty years.'

'Actually, it would look quite good in the corner of our mezzanine. We need something big to go there. But I don't think Jill would appreciate it though!' He burst into loud laughter.

'Well, exactly,' murmured Lawrence.

'No, she'd prefer something more Roman. From a garden centre, of course. No taste, that's her problem.'

Lawrence nodded blankly.

The buyer turned away and glanced back down at the small cupboard, rubbing his hands. 'So where's this cast of mine, then?'

Lawrence once more bent down to the cupboard, opened it, and carefully brought out three small bronze figures, which he lifted to the dusty work-table. However, the buyer's attention had been caught by something else.

'Cor! This is incredible, this is!'

Lawrence turned to see the buyer bent over a smooth wooden carving standing at the end of the table.

'Thanks ...' said Lawrence quietly, returning his attention to the figures before him. 'Right ... I've found the casts. I think this must have been the one you were interested in last time.'

The buyer glanced round, then back down at the carving before him, a finely-worked female nude. The figure was prone, the legs drawn up to the chest, with the hands clasping them behind the knees, the head craning forward. 'How much do you want for this?'

Lawrence smiled faintly. 'Actually, that one's not for sale. Er ... I've got the other one out you were interested in ...'

'No, no, this is the one I'm interested in,' said the buyer abruptly, returning his eyes to the figure.

'Well ... the thing is, you see, the thing *is* ... she's the mate of this character over here with the canine knob. His chosen mate. And they're destined to live happily ever after together. Here, in this filthy shed.'

The buyer continued to scrutinise the piece in silence. To Lawrence's intense annoyance, he began testing the surface contour with his fingers.

'No, I'm taking this one,' he said finally, without looking up.

Lawrence paused, watching as the buyer unsmilingly pulled out his chequebook and turned to him.

'Come on, Lawrence. How much do you want for it?'

'Er ... look, I've just told you it's not for sale,' replied Lawrence with an uncomprehending look.

The buyer laughed, and immediately bent down to write out the cheque. 'All right, we'll call it two grand. That's twice as much as you'd get from a gallery sale, isn't it?'

'Well, the price is all right, but I told you it's not on the market. This is pointless.'

'Not for sale at any price, eh? I don't think so. I don't think so, Lawrence. Look, I'll bump you up to two and a half. Can't say fairer than that! Now, do you have something to wrap it in -'

'Look, you're not *fucking having it*! Okay?' shouted Lawrence, his eyes suddenly wild.

The buyer, still bent over his chequebook, paused, staring at the paper, then quickly drew himself up, closed the chequebook, and put away his pen. He gave Lawrence a quick, cold smile. 'Actually, I think I'll leave now without buying anything at all. How's that?'

'Yeah, fine, whatever,' said Lawrence to the floor, slightly ashamed.

The buyer brushed past him to the door. 'I'll find my own fucking way out. I didn't sit for two bloody hours on the M25 to be spoken to like *that*.'

From behind him, Lawrence heard the shed door slam shut.

He glanced at the carving, then out of the window at the figure hurrying back up to the house. He knew he should get up there and apologise, try to smooth things over with the tosser, but instead remained where he was, looking at the floor.

'Fucking hell!' he spat into the dust, before finally turning and dragging himself out of the shed and back up the path, nevertheless half-hoping he'd already left it too late.

He walked through the lounge at an even pace, and entered the hall to find the front door hanging open. He closed it with a quiet sigh.

Noticing two items of post, he stooped to pick them up and carried them through to the kitchen. Hovering over the table, he examined the envelopes. The first one was a bank statement. Yeah, well, that was going to be looking a little lighter in the future ... without the good custom of Simon Morris Esquire, property developing fuck of highest repute. He let the envelope drop to the table. The second letter was from the sex dole. He eyed it grimly for a moment before letting it drop too. Going over to the fridge, he poured himself a glass of orange juice, returned and sat down, lighting a cigarette. He drew across the sex dole envelope and opened it with a vague feeling of dread.

But it was okay. It was just a general leaflet announcing some new legislation shit, the introduction of some crappy new scheme or other. Not an actual summons to an interview or some other such hell.

Anyway ... he'd decided he was definitely going to sign off next time they tried to sit him down in front of any more of their fucking marker boards and TV trolleys. But then, he'd been just as determined to get the hell off after the session with *her*, the mysterious little nymphomaniac - who had now so tragically captivated the heart and cock of Mr. Morris.

He rocked back in his chair and exhaled.

For three whole days after that infuriating, tantalising illusion, he'd been determined not to go back, afraid of getting her again, afraid of … afraid of the sheer fucking embarrassment of such an encounter for one thing, and also of course because she'd made it feel almost *right,* while it should *never* feel right, and that had made it even worse than ever. But there'd also been something else … something else that had disturbed him, but which he couldn't quite fathom ... a feeling of ... he hadn't ... well, he was fucked if he'd ever be able to put his finger on it exactly....

He rocked forward again and reached for his orange juice.

Anyway, the upshot of the whole thing was that he'd decided to stop, but of course, here he was, months later, still going down.

Maybe he was still going actually *because* of some forlorn unconscious hope of having her again. Well, it hadn't happened.… … (although he *had* encountered one or two of the others more than once now). But he knew that wasn't it. He knew he didn't really want that torture again. No, the simple bitter truth was that he was caught in the stupefying grip of benefit-dependence, pathetically unable to do without that dreary once-a-fortnight shag.

But so the fuck what?... fuck it...

He drew in a long, slow breath.

... that was just the way it would have to be... until something else came along...

He twisted his head in irritation. 'Until something else comes along...' How fucking lame was that?

He wearily stubbed out the cigarette and leaned forward onto the table, letting his head rest on his forearm.

Drifting through his mind came fragments of half-conversations with the occasional vaguely friendly girl in the pub; eyes of female friends-of-friends vainly encountered at birthday drinks; the faces of friendly but indifferent girls from the two dead-end parties he'd so far been to this year, the girl who'd drifted in and out of his washout gallery show opening, his number in her pocket on the way out, a number he'd insisted on furnishing her with, a number never dialled...

He smiled wearily. Well, after all ... maybe he'd been looking at it all wrong ... maybe the fucking sex dole was actually the way forward ... might even be the next step up for all of humanity, for all he knew.

He lifted his head slowly from his arm and reached lazily for another cigarette, grimacing sourly, suddenly disgusted by the increasingly dull sarcasm, the almost feeble-minded self-pity that seemed to cloud his thinking all the time now. He pushed himself slowly up from the table, and gloomily headed back out through the flat to the garden.

Entering the shed once more, he approached the three bronze casts with the intention of putting them away, but was instead drawn by the carving standing at the far end of the table.

Thank Christ he hadn't sold it to that cheesy git.

Walking down to the carving, he had to check a sudden wild impulse to sob. He'd rather starve than lose this piece of wood. He ran the back of his finger gently across the smooth dome of the forehead.

As a likeness it was pretty rough ... as far as he could remember...
... still, it was enough -

But what and who the fuck *was* she beyond the crazy, tight-lipped, incontinently orgasmic little dynamo he'd encountered in that damned cubicle?

He let his finger slide slowly down the leading edge of the cowl of long hair. Are we going to get on with some work, or are we going to go over it all again?

We're going to go over it all again.

As he'd suspected before, maybe there was a clue in the question itself: if she could work *there*, taking all that redundant cock day after day, week after week, doing all that noble work, and *still* be so sexually excitable - and over *him*, for Christ's sake! - then perhaps that indicated some aberration somewhere, maybe even some kind of personality disorder, something beyond the idea of her merely being 'good at her job'. Maybe she was even in treatment or something, as he'd previously speculated. Perhaps she attended a clinic near here. Again, the more he thought about it, the more it seemed to him that her enormous enthusiasm had bordered on the unhinged; the *looks* she had given him, the caress on his cheek, the way she had dug her heels into his backside - her finger, for God's sake! And who knows, maybe through some twisted psychological process, this ... over-enthusiasm was all the result of being abused as a kid or some such nightmare. Bloody hell, that just didn't bear thinking about.

Afraid suddenly, he glanced down at the ring finger on the figure's left hand, where he had even carved the detail of the chewed back fingernail. He covered it with the tip of his own finger.

But he knew he was extrapolating wildly now. How in fuck could he possibly guess anything at all about her?

He raised his finger once more to where the head jutted forward from between the drawn-back legs, placed his finger on the roughly creased brow.

How old had she been? Twenty-three? Twenty-four? What did that tell him? Not a lot. Only that she was younger than the others he'd encountered.

He stared down at the small carved breasts, feeling like some voodoo witch doctor standing over his wooden fetish. Again he stroked the wooden cowl of hair, lightly touched the carefully chiselled, slightly off-centre little snub-nose.

What had he felt since that afternoon? Nothing but the same irritated antagonism to the whole question of penis and vagina as he had felt *before* that brief fake moment of bliss, and yet mercifully the mental pain of the preceding weeks, the psychotic sense of the loss of himself, had in fact relented to a degree, had been reduced to something approaching a bearable, dull ache. Was that down to her? Had those twenty minutes in some way 'saved' him after all? But saved him for what? This tedious, ongoing shit? This bearable, but numb, white-out fucking limbo?

The whiteness was suddenly filled by a brief flash of her squirming body beneath him -

Christ.

The joy ... the joy had been a hallucination, but by Christ it had the power to prick him!

And for a moment, he surrendered to it....

... how she ... how she had wailed when she had come, how she *had grunted and cried - and how he had gloried in the sound of it....*

And then he was sobbing openly, holding on to the workbench for support.

Christ ... what ... the fuck *was* this?!...

FOR FUCK'S SAKE!

Stop it, come on, *stop it now, arsehole!*

He straightened himself, wiped his nose and forced himself to cease, only to be shaken by a fresh bout of sobs.

From his position on the dusty floor of the shed, he gazed through wet, narrowed eyes up at the carving on the edge of the worktop, leaning his head back on the flaking wall. He remained like this for several minutes, until finally he gave vent to low, faintly hysterical laughter. Shaking his head, he leaned forward and lit a cigarette. On the first inhalation, his face became fixed once more, his dark eyes locked on the wooden form above him. Further down, the three bronzes remained on the bench, waiting to be put away.

He hadn't cried over this shit for nearly a month.

Maybe this was the other thing he'd been afraid of, the thing that had been bugging him, but which he couldn't quite bring out of the shadows: the fact that she'd fucking-well *sown* something in him or something. It was beginning to look like that!

This ... government-issue sex worker, God love her, had gotten under his fucking *skin.* Why else had he shouted at Morris and thrown away two and a half thousand quid to keep hold of this fucking carving? Why had he carved it in the first place? It wasn't the 'valuable anatomical exercise' he'd told himself it was, nor was it the mere 'souvenir of an interesting afternoon' - *bullshit!*

He drew on the cigarette and again squinted up at the figure.

She'd given him something, she'd given him something, all right, but the trouble was he couldn't work out what and how much. What was it exactly he was supposed to have taken away with him that day from that insane fucking cubicle?

Maybe he should ... maybe the thing to do ... would *be* to hope to get her again one time, and see if ... see if....

... and what if he were wrong, and she were forced simply to set him straight, could he bear to see that face adopt the cold, vaguely reproving smile worn by just about every other fucker in the place? Could he fucking bear *that*?

A cloud of exhaled smoke was accompanied by low, grim laughter.

Jesus....

He thought again of her chewed-off fingernail, and had to shut his eyes tightly.

Opening them again, he blinked quickly and put the cigarette to his lips.

And why had she been late? What had that been all *about?*

Had it been her lunch-break? Had she ... been delayed ... at the bank or something? Or had she been coming on shift, as he'd first guessed?

Well, had any of the others been late? Previously, the answer to that had been no, but now it was yes. Once. The older blond woman two weeks back ... but she *had* been wearing a *robe....*

Yeah, the lack of a robe - the other probably totally inconsequential detail that he'd built up into the great mysterious anomaly! If it *was* important, he couldn't see how; if she'd been late - and she *had* been late - then naturally she might have skipped the palaver of getting changed. The other woman simply hadn't been so late, that was all....

But again, was there anything else he could deduce about her from her clothes...?

Again, there didn't seem to be anything beyond what he'd already gone over: the jeans and the top were pretty commonplace; the boots, black, though plain, perhaps exhibited a certain self-confidence, while the crimson Afghan coat... Well, as he'd thought before, these days you tended to see coats like that more often on little girls or adolescents aspiring to be grown up rather than on grown women themselves.... Then there was the bobble-hat, a bit too cute, perhaps... and that button-up cardigan - was there a certain reserve to be detected in the choice of that cardigan? That would be - but look, what the hell did *he* know about why women wore what and when, for Christ's sake!

He glanced out of the window opposite.

It was just a waste of time, going over all this shit again. He'd sat here half the afternoon already.

He let out a long sigh, crushed his cigarette into the dust, and began slowly picking himself up.

Keeping his eyes away from the carving, he went over to the three bronzes, picked them up and wearily locked them away in the small cupboard, before kicking open the shed door and making his way back up to the flat.

Coffee ... he'd have a coffee, then try and get on with something....

Entering the kitchen, he flicked on the kettle and leaned back on the counter. Noticing the unopened bank statement, he picked it up, opened it, glanced at it, then dropped it back on the table, fixing his eyes once more on the kettle, his arms folded.

The only time ... the only time she had appeared *distant* was when she had left - this was the other '*riddle*' he'd been making so much of. Well, again, what could that possibly mean other than that the moment had been over, and she had to go - after all, if she enjoyed her work so much, perhaps she would have to force herself to underline the boundary between herself and the punters, and that distant look had been her way of doing that...

He shifted himself from the counter, slung a spoonful of coffee into a mug, and lifted the boiling kettle.

But shit, the way she had walked over to the door, her amazing face as she had looked at him that final time, peering round that long S of hanging brown hair, that mitten on the door handle -

He froze, the steam from the kettle searing his face.

He hadn't remembered the mitten before.

He slammed the kettle down on the counter.

Well, what in God's name had she been WEARING MITTENS FOR?!

He stared down at the kettle, not daring to breathe.

Why had she gone to the bother of putting her fucking mittens back on if she was only going down the corridor? Her *coat* may*be* - you'd possibly wear it rather than carry it - but together with the mittens it was -

She'd been going out to the street.

He experienced a slight buckling of the knees.

And who goes out to the street? Who goes out to the fucking street after a session in a shag dole cubicle?

Jesus *Chriiist!* Shit.

SHIT!

Fuck.

She must've been a punter.

A FUCKING PUNTER!

He felt himself turning in space.

... and everything, *everything* fit if you looked at it from that perspective, it fit like a fucking glove, and not only that it made a lot more *sense* that way, and - holy shit, she must've *gone* for him, she must've really -

There must've been a cock-up or something - somewhere down the line they must've fucked it up downstairs or something -

He launched himself from the counter, and began walking erratically around the kitchen, as the meaning of the girl in the cubicle became gloriously inverted and twisted inside out, bathed in wondrous light.

Finally, falteringly, he took out a cigarette, and with shaking hands tried to light it.

If he were right - and he had to be right, he *had* to be! - then, then that restored the miracle, didn't it?

He kept flicking the lighter, but he really was shaking too much. He flung the lighter at the table, laughed, and continued to take sudden strides from one cupboard to the next, the unlit cigarette hanging from his mouth, his heart thumping in his chest.

It had been real.

And then he stopped again in his tracks. Because it didn't stop there. If it had been real and it had flowed both ways then...

...perhaps...

... oh, shit, then perhaps ...

... perhaps he could have it all ...

Perhaps he could find her.

But how the fuck ... and what if he was wrong? Yeah, you silly wazzock and what if you're *right*?

He retrieved the lighter and redoubled his efforts to light the cigarette, finally succeeding. He sat down at the table, but sprang up again immediately, unable to contain the pounding energy in his chest, the blood rushing around his face.

But how the Christ could he find her? If she even wanted - but no, he'd cross that bridge when he came to it. After all, this was the best lead he'd had in his life. To chat up a strange girl - but one whom you'd already shagged! Presumably you had the right to talk to them in such a case! It was wild, wild -

But where do you begin to hunt someone down in this godforsaken city, where do you fucking -

Well, shit.

That was fucking *obvious*, wasn't it!

But then he'd have to -

And almost three months had passed.

So there's no time to lose, then, is there? Start now ... but it was crazy ... it would mean - in order to be sure -

Come on, tosspot, this is what you've been waiting for, life could be *fucking beckoning*.

He turned his head and stared out in the direction of the hall, his chest heaving, his face flushed. He stuffed the cigarette in his mouth and bolted, half skipped, into the hall, snatching his coat off the hook and flinging it on as he went out of the door.

After the exhilaration of the walk down and the accompanying romantic uplift that came with the resolve to take this sudden chance to break out and smash the glass wall, he was surprised to feel a momentary deflation in his spirits as he rounded the corner into Kentish Town Road and the benefit centre came into sight. Suddenly, this proposed decisive action of his appeared less heroic than somehow deranged.

But this doubt was washed away by a fresh soaring of his soul as his eyes found the entrance door and he imagined how she had looked going in and out that day, and what may have been going on in her beautiful head.

And with this view of the building, he already felt as though he had recovered something of her.

Crossing the road, he noticed the boarding across one of the windows. Some joker must've put a brick through it or something. And no wonder.

He cast his eyes across the posters, hit by a wild, insane certainty that he, at least, would never be setting foot in the place again.

Nevertheless, he walked slowly along the facade feeling faintly ridiculous. Finally, just beyond the entrance, he came to a stop and looked about him.

All right, then, here we are. So which of these filthy fucking concrete pillars looks the most comfortable?

He walked along to the furthest column, gave it the once-over with a slightly pained face, turned, and let his shoulders fall back against the concrete. And waited.

For the first two days, he stood against the pillar, watching the snarled-up traffic and passersby, his collar turned up against the increasingly cold spring weather.

On the first day, he had smoked only occasionally, bitterly regretting that he hadn't restocked on cigarettes on the walk down. For the whole afternoon, he had jealously eyed the newsagent's down the road, but hadn't abandoned his post, reasoning that if he were serious about this business then it had to be done properly. He had remained at his station, surveying the street, shivering occasionally, observing the flow of pedestrians, now and then meeting the eyes of claimants going in and out of the centre.

By the second day, he had taken to making a game of trying to guess in advance which individuals were going to break off from the stream of people and be sucked through the double doors alongside him. He usually guessed wrong, but was surprised by the regularity with which the break-offs would occur, and indeed began to notice a rhythm, the slow pulse of the centre working like a valve or an organ to massage the need of a people. The passersby would be blind to it, but he could almost see it beating: a dull throb measuring out the low beat of a society's agitated, frustrated desire.

Occasionally, he would glance in through the window behind him, recognising most of the staff, though by the end of the second afternoon, he realised that he hadn't seen the guy with the glasses once, and surmised that he was possibly on holiday, and considered that, after all, the guy had always looked in dire need of one.

From these glances through the window, he followed the slow circulation of the frustrated through the interior of the building itself, keeping track of this one or that one as they came in off the street, took their seats, went up to the desk, then up the stairs, before, some time later, finally coming back outside to the pavement. He watched the exits from the building with particular interest, noting that eyes were usually fixed somewhere on the ground, or on the wheel-arch of a passing bus, or else way up in the sky. Sometimes, the eyes would meet his, defensively, or even at times, fiercely.

Toward the end of the second afternoon, he had begun struggling to keep hold of his conviction that the girl had been an ordinary member of the public; he almost pulled to pieces the case for her being so. And yet, the next morning he returned again to his spot bristling with a messianic confidence, once more born aloft by the golden evidence of the mittens. And his happiness that morning increased still further with the knowledge that this was the second day he had seen her fail to arrive with the facilitators. He stood on, doggedly refusing to be depressed by the possibility that she may simply have been moved to another centre, or that even if she *had* been a claimant, then she may have stopped signing. On this third day, he was further buoyed by the fact that he had brought sandwiches with him, not wishing to repeat the mistake of the agonising hunger he had endured on the second.

It was when he came to eat this small repast, during the afternoon of the third day, that he finally sank to a crouching position on the pavement, leaning back against one of the grimy blue panels of the facade, and this position he maintained for the rest of that day, as he sat on, his back complaining, the dreary rhythm of the traffic lulling his mind.

It was shortly before closing time that the older woman with the silver bob from behind the desks came out and looked down at him for a moment and told him to move on. He realised that she took him for a beggar, and it amused him to think that in sitting there on the pavement his purpose was for once in fact the exact opposite. Still, he picked himself up, taking his plastic carrier bag with him, and loitered a few yards down the road until the woman had gone inside, whereon he returned to his spot, though keeping his head below the windows. Sitting back, he was relieved to feel the building at his back once more, noticing nothing odd in the idea that he could actually receive comfort from physical contact with a piece of mouldering sixties architecture - simply because it was his only link to *her*.

Later that afternoon, after drifting again into a prolonged reverie about the girl, he became aware of a ruckus going on inside the building. First there was a man shouting, 'What are you doing here?' Then came a female voice screaming back in response, 'What are *you* fuckin' doing here?' After a commotion of indistinct raised voices, the two antagonists, a man and woman in early middle-age, finally spilled out into the street, kicking and slapping each other as they disappeared down the road.

Toward the end of that third afternoon, there came along the street and up to the doors of the centre for the first time a person known to him.

Lawrence cursed silently and shrank slightly into the wall as the biker from the flat above approached. The heavy-set, leather-clad figure slowed his pace on recognising Lawrence, but, making the decision to ignore the somewhat destitute-looking character crouching on the floor clutching his carrier bag, switched his eyes to the traffic as he went up to the entrance, pushing the door wide open with a single hard shove. Lawrence watched him go in, happy enough at being ignored.

Shortly afterwards came another, just as a steady patter of rain began to fall. Lawrence had just placed the carrier bag on his head, and was sheltering underneath it, when an older, bearded man in a green anorak detached himself from the flow of people to put his hand on the entrance door of the centre, his head down. Lawrence watched him enter then pause just inside the door, fumbling for a moment in his pocket, his face sunk in the grey fuzz of his beard, before bringing out a handkerchief and proceeding to wipe the rain from his glasses. Lawrence knew he'd seen him before somewhere but couldn't place him, guessing that perhaps he'd stood behind him once in a supermarket queue.

As the man disappeared inside, Lawrence imagined him taking his place alongside the biker. He felt a curious brotherliness toward both men, curious because he suspected he would not have felt it if he had been sitting inside, waiting to go up to the desks. At that point he realised the idea of ever being inside there again was becoming more and more remote to him; the traffic, the rain, the pavement, the damp shoulders of the passersby, the mothers with prams, all seemed to be telling him that she was on her way, and he continued looking up and down the street with a strange equanimity, the plastic carrier bag pressed to his head, rain dripping from the growth on his chin to the darkening patches on his soaking jeans.

As this third afternoon became evening, he was questioned and moved on by two community police officers, but, keeping the centre constantly in view, he waited up by the newsagent's until they were out of sight, then once more returned to his spot and crouched down. A pair of brand-emblazoned trainers approaching from his left caught his attention and he raised his glance to meet a quizzically sneering yet familiar face peering down at him, that of the blond red-cheeked youth in the baseball cap from the "workshop". Lawrence winked at him, provoking an expression of disgust from the youth as he went past and pushed open the swing door.

The fourth morning also brought no indication that the girl was working at the centre, increasing Lawrence's excitement as he laid out his provisions for the day, placing a can of lager at his side and unwrapping a fresh packet of cigarettes.

He had just lit up and was shifting his weight to ease his aching backside, when he became aware of an approaching pair of heels, and looked up as a slim, elegant woman of about fifty came past. He felt only faint surprise to see her leave the flow of pedestrians and place her hand on the door of the centre. He just had time to see, passing above him, the profile of what appeared to be a living copy of the Nefertiti head from the Cairo museum. He was struck not only by the woman's astonishing profile, but also her odd air of calm assurance.

The woman was soon followed by a puffy, washed-out middle-aged woman, immediately behind whom came tramping along a miserable-looking shapeless girl with a ponytail and trainers, both of whom gave Lawrence brief, wary glances.

As they, too, went inside, and were followed through the day by others, middle-aged women, youths, old gents, and labourers - and these coming after days of smart-looking city-workers, red-faced boozers, professional women in their thirties, dark-eyed young men like himself, Japanese wearing headphones, athletic women in cycling shorts, decorators in overalls, plump girls in high heels, slim girls, thin lads, fat lads, rappers, hippie women in their sixties, Rastafarians, punks, Goths, grey-eyed men in London Transport uniforms, men and women of every ethnic type, small and large men in overcoats, bomber jackets, tracksuits, hoodies and business suits - Lawrence felt as though he were watching some bizarre and tragic parade of the carnally displaced; but it was more than that, it was overwhelming: a panoramic sweep of the clanking sexual dysfunction of a society, a huge, melancholic pageant of lonely flesh, untouched and unshared - the isolated, uncaressed flesh of a city, flesh of a myriad different textures, consistencies, shades, colours and ages. Of course, it was a pageant which he had been part of - but, he realised once again with a racing heart, it was one he was now breaking away from, because she was coming. For him it was all over, he was on his way out, because she was *coming*. Because she had *come* with him, and she was going to come with him again.

He took a sip of beer, and peered up and down the street for a while until his eyes were finally dragged into the lazy flow of the traffic.

On the fifth day towards the middle of the afternoon, after a further altercation with the woman with the grey bob, who had come out a second time to move him on and after which he had decamped for half an hour to a point several yards down the road before once more coming back, he sat with the carrier bag over his head against a faint drizzle, debating with himself whether or not to eat his sandwich. He found himself unwrapping it anyway, watching his slow spidery fingers, bemused because he was still perfectly undecided whether he wanted it or not. It was then that he felt a curious tingle at the side of his head.

He turned and looked up, but found himself smiling not into the eyes of the girl but rather the aggressive stare of a shaven-headed, bull-necked man with a red cross of St. George tattooed in the middle of his forehead.

Lawrence recognised him immediately as the disruptive bigot who had threatened him at the workshop, but nevertheless he kept the smile on his face and took a bite of his sandwich, some of the filling falling on his chin. He felt the scrap of food clinging to his stubble but made no effort to wipe it away.

The man stood over him for a moment, then began moving slowly around him, peering down at Lawrence all the while with a vicious look, the red cross on his forehead contorting with hatred. 'Well, well. Someone's let their dog shit on the pavement.... Small world, innit, mate? Remember me, do you?'

Lawrence chewed on his mouthful and made an affirmative

movement of his eyebrows.

'You were well out of fackin' order as I recall that day up in Tafnell Park. Well out of order.' He lifted his leg and with the tip of his boot flicked the carrier-bag from Lawrence's head. 'A bit of rain will do you good, *twat*. You could do with a fackin' *bath*!'

Lawrence merely peered up at him mildly through the light rain.

The boot came to rest lightly on Lawrence's shoulder.

'Yes, wanker. You're beginning to give off a bit of a *smell*, I reckon.' The boot rocked back and forth beside Lawrence's head. 'Anyway, FACKIN' DOGSHIT wants kickin' into the FACKIN' GUTTER!'

He lifted the boot away and gave Lawrence a single, hard kick to the ribs. Lawrence choked and held his side, as the man drew back his boot a second time. But the kick failed to materialise as the man for the first time became aware that they were not alone on the bustling street, appeared to debate something with himself, then turned quickly, punched aside the swing doors of the building and headed inside. But no sooner than he had disappeared within than he came straight back out. 'I'm late right now and I've got to go inside, but I tell you what, you fackin' barstard, next time I see ya, I'm gonna *fackin' belt ya proper*. Orwight?'

Still holding his side, Lawrence managed to give him a polite nod of acquiescence, though continuing once more to chew on his mouthful.

The man peered down at him for a moment more, staring in disgust at the piece of pickle still clinging to Lawrence's chin, before finally disappearing inside.

Lawrence watched him go in, finally wiping the pickle from his chin, but carelessly so that it fell onto the collar of his coat, and then turned his face back to the pavement to see two black ladies' boots slowing and coming to a stop before him.

FIFTY

As he slowly raised his eyes, and the fur trim of the burgundy Afghan coat came down across his vision, Lawrence was almost sick with a cocktail of joy, disbelief and mad panic, the reality of her arrival making him realise that in fact he had never in the most fundamental part of himself really believed she would come at all, and that his long watch had instead merely been some weird act of nihilism. This idea crossed his mind in the time it took for his gaze to rise to the two mittens flanking her hips, the sight bursting his heart, the detail of the chains of rabbits filling him with such apocalyptic delight that it bordered bizarrely on outright nervous terror. And then his eyes were racing up the soft fleece trim to the first glad lengths of her long auburn hair as a quiet, slightly embarrassed 'Hi' broke over him and he was bathing in her face once more.

'Er, hello,' he replied in a voice made barely audible through days of non-use. He smiled, coughed and repeated, 'Hello,' finally placing the sandwich on the plastic carrier bag at his side, though in his shock completely neglecting to stand up.

She continued to peer down at him from behind a long S of hanging hair, her brow furrowed slightly in confusion. The furrow grew as she began inclining her head quizzically to one side, her eyes flitting to the sandwich and the carrier-bag, before once more centering heart-stoppingly on his own.

'What are you doing out *here*?' she asked suddenly, laughing.

Lawrence forced himself out of the sheer shock of seeing her again, quickly deciding to proceed with what he had been rehearsing in his head for the last five days.

'Ah, yes ... what am I doing out here…? As opposed to in *there….*' he laughed, looking from side to side, before falling silent and smiling up at her.

He raised an eyebrow, let his face become serious, then reached into his pocket and brought out a slim plastic-sheathed document. He waved the SB40 slowly back and forth between them.

Carla regarded it blankly for a second, before screwing her eyes up in total confusion, then opening them wide, her mouth following suit.

'My ... GO-D!' The last word was brought out with a burst of disbelieving laughter, a mitten flying up to her mouth. Lawrence saw one heel rise and stamp the ground.

'Well, precisely,' laughed Lawrence with a charming mock-frown as he looked down the street then back up into her eyes, his heart leaping with hope.

She looked about her. 'I- I don't be*lieve* it!' She looked back at him. 'So you weren't ...'

He shook his head, mouthing a silent 'no', peering up at her from under a devilish brow.

They stared at each other for a second, then burst out laughing together, Carla putting her hand over her mouth, closing her eyes tightly, swallowing, then laughing again, and shaking her head. Lawrence watched her, delighted, nodding and frowning ironically as though confirming some great calamity.

She stopped laughing first, then appeared suddenly to have difficulty in meeting his eyes, her glance flitting repeatedly to the shop windows down the street. Lawrence was convinced she was about to issue him with a 'well, anyway...' and move on, when she threw a strand of hair away from her face and fixed him with a steady look. She swallowed hard, keeping her eyes on him.

At this look, Lawrence simply merged with her irises, his expression made fierce by the pounding in his chest and the blissful excruciating silence between them.

Christ, he was going to make it.

Do it.

He indicated the SB40, consciously contorting his face into what he hoped was a look of devastating charm.

'Er ... you have one of these, too, I take it?'

'...Yep!' she replied biting her lip, and jutting her head forward, laughing again.

'Aha ...' nodded Lawrence. 'Let's have a look at it, then,' he continued, though cringing inwardly at the possible over-forwardness of this.

Apparently happy to oblige, she merely shrugged and reached into her bag. She drew out the document and handed it down, peering intently at him.

He took it graciously, murmuring his thanks in a low breath. She had given it to him face down. He slowly turned it around in his hand, reverential wonder coming into his eyes as the box containing the name revolved into sight. His breath caught slightly at the beauty of it:

CARLA MOORE.

He heard her speak. 'Can I see yours?'

'Sure.'

Still not thinking to get up, he handed up his SB40, his glance roving across the heart-twisting curve of her cheek. He watched her as she took the document and read, her lips parting slightly, before her eyes crept back to his, her expression once again falling to something serious, almost tremulous.

She glanced again at the half-eaten sandwich and the carrier bag.

'Oh,' he said, slightly thrown. 'You're probably wondering what I'm doing here on the pavement.'

She nodded, her eyes now fixed for some reason he couldn't understand to the collar of his coat.

But go on, do it. All the way.

'Well,' he began, 'if you give us that back, I'll show you.'

She handed back his SB40, her eyes once more intently on his.

He took the two signing documents, placed them carefully one over the other, lining up the edges until they were perfectly flush.

He looked deep into her eyes, forcing himself to hold the look longer than was decent or comfortable. But she returned it steadily. And then, still holding her irises, he began tearing the documents in two.

'Hey, what are you -?!' cried Carla as he flung the pieces with real ferocity into the gutter.

She peered down at the scraps floating on a grey stream of rainwater, then looked back into his eyes, her expression suddenly unreadable.

Trying to give her his most confident, commanding look, he slowly raised his hand toward her and smiled softly. 'Well ... are you going to give me a hand up?'

She made no move, merely regarded him impassively.

Lawrence panicked. He squinted down the street, avoiding her eyes. 'Er, right. I shouldn't have done that. I'm sorry... It was reckless, impulsive, presumptuous, not to mention arrogant, and certainly totally disrespectful toward you as a person - *but for once in my fucking life, I thought I -*'

Warm mitten wool closed around his hand as Carla reached down and pulled him to his feet.

Sat on the edge of her bed, Carla struggled to place her tea on the floor with her free hand as his tongue went on with its first delectable exploration of her mouth, an endless, luxurious probing, increasing to an almost unbearable pitch the deep, sweet pain between her legs, which had been present virtually from the moment she'd seen him on the pavement. Drunkenly, vaguely, she realised that five, ten minutes must have passed before she had even *thought* to put her tea down.

His mouth went on brushing and pressing hers, her own tongue playing its part in the prolonged dizzying silence of this first longed-for kiss. Fleeting images from the afternoon they had spent together emerged behind her closed eyes: his charming little boy laughter as they'd nervously chatted on the walk down from the sex dole to the pub; the funny ironic faces he made at her from the bar while waiting to be served; the adorable sour expression that came into his face when they'd sat swapping sex dole anecdotes; his soft smile just now as his eyes had moved over the illustrations in the Beatrix Potter she'd caught him with when she'd come back from the loo (had any guy else shown the slightest interest in them?); the way when after she'd decided what the hell, she'd show him the poem, he'd actually had *to fight a tear as he'd read it!*; the look she'd found in those beautiful, haunted eyes when he'd peered up from the last line and said in that quiet voice 'fucking hell' - she hadn't known you could get so much ... *poignancy* into that phrase! The poignancy of it was still ringing in her ears. Ringing in her ears, reverberating in her heart… flowering in her knickers! And it was almost as though the reality of him was even more like the fantasy she'd projected on him in the cubicle than the projection itself, or something - and it was - she put her finger to his cheekbone - and oh god, he was here, he was *here* - and -

But her ability to think slipped away from her as his hands came up to cradle her head, and his lips enlarged to enclose her whole mouth in the most voracious kiss she had ever known.

With auburn hair falling around his fingers, his thumbs nestling gently under the soft lobes of her ears, Lawrence plunged his tongue deep under her palate and felt her suck on it like a baby, as everything inside him once again knew that holy sense of integration, that sacred fucking joy she'd blessed him with in the cubicle, and if his cock was killing him now, it was only because of its current uncomfortable position in his underwear. He almost wanted to tell her this thought; it might give her a laugh - he couldn't wait to hear her laughter again! - Christ how she'd laughed at his shit in the pub! And how she'd made *him* laugh with her suggestion they sue the benefit centre for the mix-up! She had wit on top of everything else! She had sense, and imagination - he suddenly thought of the poem being composed in the small, fragile space between his fingers, and he increased still further the urgency of his kiss. It occurred to him, but hazily, through a wave of intoxication brought on by the deep draughts of exhaled breath he was taking from her finely sculpted nostrils, that if he'd finally, *finally* got the thorny question of knobbing sorted out ... then maybe he, *they*, could go on to the next level, the next thorny human aspiration, the next stage - what was it called again? 'Love' or some such - but that was a whole other fucking story, a -

He lost the thought as a hand crept under his shirt, her small warm fingers causing him to moan involuntarily into her mouth. And then her lips detached from his as her head pulled back to begin moving down toward his chest, a look of such languor on her face she appeared almost in suffering. He let his own swimming head drift down through her long hair, let it drift, kissing, across her shoulder, down to where the sleek form of the side of her ribcage was being expressed by her clinging top. Their bodies continued to move sideways across and down each other, Lawrence aware of her cheek, her mouth brushing his shirt as she passed his midriff, though neglecting to open his shirt buttons. As her hands came out from his shirt and went to his belt he realised with a scorching ecstasy that she wanted his trousers open first. The waistband of her own jeans was coming slowly into view as she pulled her legs onto the bed, so as to lie alongside him, her pelvis presented to his face. He heard the soft jangle of his slowly unbuckling belt, his face pounding as he heard and felt his zip coming down. He moved his fingers toward the descending curve of her own zip, shuddering as his pants were slowly, carefully exposed by small, gentle hands. And then, as he took hold of her zip fastener, at the same time bringing his head in range of her heart-bursting trouser smell, he felt through his cotton underwear the first gentle overtures of her precious, nurturing, life-giving lips. He felt the thing lurch in response, only to be caught by her mouth and held. He froze in a silent gasp, and, his mouth hanging open, began the incremental opening of her jeans, the parting teeth of the zip revealing a thin line of white. With reverent fingers he slowly pushed aside the denim until there before him lay the soft, white triangle. And though its power was as inscrutable as ever, he was happy now to lose himself for good in its impenetrable mystery. He let his head descend. And as the whiteness grew, filling his vision with its soft, mesmerising contour, he finally closed his eyes and opened his mouth to meet it.

ABOUT THE AUTHOR

Steven C. Harvey was born in Stafford, UK in 1967, and now lives in Athens, Greece. As well as an author he is an internationally critically acclaimed visual artist, whose work has been collected by European museums of modern art and published by global premier art publisher, Phaidon Press.

Printed in Great Britain
by Amazon